Sam and the O'Malley Brothers

by

John M. Sloke

Sam and the O'Malley Brothers
by John M. Sloke

Copyright 2013. John M. Sloke. All rights reserved.

No part of this book may be used or reproduced in any manner whatsoever without written permission from the author.

ISBN-13: # 978-0615808642
ISBN-10: # 0615808646

Dedication

This novel is dedicated to the memory of
Father Vincent Robert Capodanno
and all the other Veterans who gave
their lives in the defense of our country.

Foreword

I hope that you will enjoy reading *Sam and the O'Malley Brothers*. This book is a work of fiction. New Dublin, Jefferson City, Springfield located on the Cherokee River cannot be found on any map. However, there are segments of this novel that are based on true facts. Historical events are accurate. However, Marine Corps Sergeant Joseph Flynn is a fictional character and the story he relates in this novel is also fictional. His rendition is based on actual events. Father Vincent Capodanno is an American hero. His actions on September 4, 1967 were above and beyond the call of duty. He was posthumously awarded the Congressional Medal of Honor on January 7, 1969. The narrative in the chapter is only a small sampling of the courage he displayed while in Vietnam. In the course of writing this novel, I came across a documentary on the Eternal Word Television Network (EWTN) regarding the *Grunt Padre*. At the time, I had not heard of Father Vincent Capodanno. After watching the program, I felt a sense of comradeship. He and I were serving in Vietnam at the same time although I never personally met him. He was assigned to the Marine Corps and I was a crew chief/door gunner on a "Huey" helicopter in the Army. I can visualize the firefight, the sounds, the smells, the wounded, and the dead.

Father Capodanno's story was a perfect fit for this novel. He has been designated as a "Servant of God" which means that the Catholic Church is investigating his life and works for possible canonization. I felt that it was appropriate to dedicate this book in his memory and the memory of all those other veterans who made the ultimate sacrifice. You can learn more about Father Vincent Capodanno by visiting the website for the Archdiocese for the Military Services, USA www.milarch.org (click on "Offices"). I would also like to thank Father Daniel L Mode, a U. S. Navy Chaplain, who graciously allowed me to use his book, *The Grunt Padre,* as a guideline to write the chapter regarding Father Vincent Capodanno. A portion of the proceeds from the sale of this book is being donated to Archdiocese for the Military Services, USA to benefit the Father Capodanno cause.

The second segment that is based on fact is more humorous in nature. It pertains to the Army convoy that makes a stop in New Dublin. Sam, Theresa and Johnny sell sodas to the soldiers who were unable to leave the trucks. My father was a career soldier. I was born at Ft. Benning, GA and we lived in adjoining Columbus. Our home backed up to Victory Highway which was a major thoroughfare. About 1956, when I was nine years old, a convoy stopped on the shoulder behind our house. Seeing military vehicles and helicopters flying overhead were not out of the ordinary As I walked past the convoy, one of the soldiers said that he would give me a quarter if I went and bought him a soda. It was like a domino effect. Everyone wanted one. I was running back and forth from a nearby local juke joint called "The Chatter Box". Woodrow, an extremely short black man, worked there. He was my friend. He would have the drinks sitting on the counter awaiting my return. Time was ticking. When the convoy finally pulled away, I squared away with Woodrow. I had a pocket full of change. Like Sam, Theresa and Johnny, I thought I was rich.

The original idea for *Sam and the O'Malley Brothers* came in part by two films of the 1940's; Bing Crosby who portrayed Father O'Malley in *The Bells of St. Mary's* and *Going My Way,* hence the title of this novel. These movies portrayed Catholic Priests in a positive manner. The theme morphed into a century long storyline that emphasizes, God, Country, Family, Friendship and Community.

Chapter 1

The Early Years (Circa 1880 – 1899)

Alice O'Malley was standing on her front porch when Edward O'Neal stopped at the front gate. "Alice, I was at the dock. The mail bag arrived from Jefferson City. This letter was addressed to you. It is from the U.S. Army. I thought it might be important."

"Thank you Mr. O'Neal."

Alice opened the envelope. The letter read:

Dear Mrs. O'Malley,

I regret to inform you that your husband, Private Connor O'Malley was killed in action during the Battle of San Juan Hill on July 5, 1898. I was extremely fond of Connor. He often spoke of you and your three sons. He had a sense of humor that seemed to lighten the load in the most difficult of times. Connor was God fearing and a true American patriot. His heroic actions saved my life and the lives of three of his fellow "Rough Riders". He will always be in my thoughts and prayers until I breathe my last breath.

Connor will be interred at the Arlington National Cemetery in Arlington County, Virginia.

Again, Mrs. O'Malley, I extend my heartfelt condolences to you and your family.

With Sincerest Regards,

Charles H. Taylor
Captain
Troop F, 1st U. S. Calvary
Santiago, Cuba

Enclosed with the letter was an informational sheet setting out other burial options that included costs which had to be borne by the family. It also included procedures for Alice O'Malley to file for her widow's pension. A sense of guilt came over Alice. She felt that she was dishonoring her husband by not having him buried in New Dublin but she had no other option. There was no extra money. A soldier's salary was minimal at best and the thought of a window's pension was helpful but it would not be sufficient for her and her family to survive. Alice did find solace in the fact that Connor would receive a proper funeral.

Jimmy came up and saw his mother. He asked, "Mama, what's wrong? Why are you crying?"

She didn't answer him but said, "Go and get your brothers."

Jimmy was the oldest. Pop and Billy, who were twins, were ten years old. They soon returned. Alice and the boys joined hands. Alice explained to them in simple terms that their father would not be coming home. He had gone to be with God in heaven. The twins did not fully comprehend death but Jimmy was deeply crushed. He was close to his father. Alice then told them, "You boys run along." She summoned Jimmy back to her. He stood in front of her. Alice took both of her hands and caressed his face. She took her thumbs and wiped away his tears. Jimmy was mature for a twelve years old. Alice said, "Jimmy, everything will be all right. You are now the man of the family. I need your help in watching out for your two brothers."

"Mama, you have a lot of worries but one thing that you don't have to worry about is us O'Malley brothers. We are close and we will be close forever." Jimmy then leaned over and hugged his mother, "I love you."

"I love you too. Now, you run along."

Jimmy ran off and caught up with his brothers. They were with their two best friends, Albert Swartz and Sean Ryan. Jimmy told them about his father. They immediately ran home to tell their mothers. It was not long before Rachel Swartz and Molly Ryan were seated beside Alice consoling her. These three ladies were childhood friends back in Dublin, Ireland. They along with their husbands immigrated to America in 1880. They first settled in Jefferson City but there were so many immigrants that the prospect of finding work was discouraging. Twenty families of Irish descent banded together in 1886. They acquired land grant acreage on the Cherokee River about fifty miles north of Jefferson City. Alice was pregnant with Jimmy at the time New Dublin was founded. The community began to thrive. More Irish families arrived. Connor O'Malley was a master carpenter. When he didn't get paid for his services, he would barter for food. Life was comfortable for the O'Malley clan. This changed on February 15, 1898 when the USS Maine was sunk in Havana harbor resulting in the death of 266 sailors. Spain was blamed for the sinking. Although the sinking of the USS Maine was not the total cause for the Spanish American War, it was the catalyst. "Remember the Maine" became the call to arms for all Americans. Connor O'Malley felt that it was his duty to serve his country. The 1st U. S. Calvary was looking for volunteers. Connor was qualified. He was an expert shot and there was no horse that he couldn't ride. He was immediately mustered into service and sent to Tampa, Florida where the "Rough Riders" were mobilizing for an invasion of Cuba. Alice was in full agreement with Connor's decision. She knew that death was a possibility but she was an eternal optimist. Connor would do his duty; come back home and life would return to normal. However, life was never predictable.

Everything was swirling in Alice's head about the future of her and her boys.

Rachel asked, "What do you plan to do?"

"I don't know. I do know that I have to earn money. The salary that Connor got from the military was barely enough to make ends meet." Alice then showed Rachel the informational sheet. "It says here that I'm eligible for a widow's pension. It doesn't say how much that would be but it has to be less than Connor's pay. I'm thinking that I should move back to Jefferson City and find a job."

Molly was adamant. "You aren't going anywhere. You have a house here and no one in this community is going to let you or your boys starve."

"You're right but I have more pride than to sit around waiting for hand outs." Alice continued, "It's a decision that I don't have to make today. I still have to come to terms with Connor's death."

Rachel and Molly stayed with Alice the rest of the afternoon but Alice wanted to be alone. She insisted that her friends go home. It was time for them to prepare dinner. She assured them that she was fine. Alice was a strong woman but inside, she was grieving. She and Connor had a good marriage. She began missing him as soon as the paddle boat pulled away from the dock heading south to Jefferson City. Little did she know that it would be the last time she saw him. The thought of Connor never returning home was almost unbearable.

Jimmy entered through the screen door. He was alone. His mother hugged him and with endearment asked, "How are you feeling?"

"I feel sad. It hurts to think that I won't ever see Daddy again."

"I know. I feel the same way but your father wouldn't want us to sit around feeling sorry for ourselves. As long as we stick together as a family, life will slowly get better." Alice pulled out the letter from Captain Taylor and read it to Jimmy. "You should be proud of your father. He died a hero saving the lives of four other soldiers. Make sure your brothers understand this when they are older. Speaking of your brothers, have they said anything to you?"

"Billy asked as to when Daddy was coming home after he visits with God. I just told him that it may be awhile."

"Go get your brothers. You boys must be getting hungry."

Early the next morning, Rachel and Molly were at Alice's house. They sat down beside Alice who was sitting in a rocking chair on the front porch. Molly asked, "Have you decided what you are going to do?"

Alice responded. "I didn't get much sleep last night. I mulled over all my options...which weren't very many. The only answer that I came up with was for me to find a job and the jobs are in Jefferson City. I am going to take the paddle boat tomorrow. I will find something. I will be gone for several days. Can the two of you feed my boys while I am gone? They can stay in the house by themselves."

"Before you do that, listen to what Rachel and I came up with." Molly said with enthusiasm. "You are a smart person...a lot smarter than me. You are constantly reading books. I would say that you are the most educated person in town. Your boys can read and write which is a rarity in New Dublin. Your new job is going to be our first teacher."

Rachel was in complete agreement. "There is no way you can say no. You are going to be the new schoolmarm."

Alice perked up. The thought of being a teacher was pleasing. Also, it was a solution to her problem. "I like that idea but we don't have a schoolhouse. I need textbooks, paper, pencils, pens and books to create a small library."

Rachel was reassuring. "We have the will and we'll find the way. If we set our minds to it, you can be teaching school in a matter of weeks."

"What about students?"

Rachel responded, "Albert will be your first."

Molly chimed in, "Sean will be your second. Add in your three boys, you are now up to five students. I assure you that there will be plenty more." Molly continued, "Father Maher will be here tomorrow. You can ask him if you can speak to the congregation after Mass this Sunday."

Friday morning came. Alice responded to a knock at the front door. It was Father Maher. He was wearing his cassock and biretta.

Alice pushed open the screen door. "Good morning, Father. Would you like to come inside? I still have some coffee on the stove."

"No thank you. Let's sit out here on the porch. It's a beautiful morning."

The two of them sat down in the rocking chairs. Father Maher said, "I wanted to come by and pay my respects. Connor was my friend. He always had a smile on his face. Some of his corny jokes were actually funny. I always looked forward to seeing him when I came to town. I will miss him. We will offer this Sunday's Mass in his memory."

"That will be nice. He was very fond of you too." Alice changed the subject. She explained to Father Maher of her intentions about opening a school. She asked him if she could speak to the congregation after Mass.

Father Maher was agreeable. He offered her encouragement. "The superintendent of the Jefferson City School District is a friend of mine. I am sure that I can get you some older textbooks and other school supplies. Also, I have shelves of books. I can pick out some good classics. It may be awhile before any of your students will be able to read them but you will have them available when the time comes."

"Bless you, Father. It would be nice if I could find a set of encyclopedias."

"You're in luck. I have a set in my office." Father Maher jokingly continued. "I have no use for them. I know everything there is to know about everything. So, I will donate them to you."

"Bless you again, Father. Are you sure you don't want a cup of coffee?"

"No thank you. I have to get onto the church. I have two baptisms this afternoon and a wedding tomorrow. I will see you Sunday."

St. Patrick Mission Church was under the auspices of St. Ignatius Parish in Jefferson City. There were two other mission churches within the parish. Father Maher rotated every week among the three churches.

Sunday came and as Mass ended, Father Maher approached the pulpit. He told the congregation, "Please sit down. Alice O'Malley would like to speak to you on a very important matter."

Alice began, "First of all, I want to thank all of you for your words of kindness in regard to Connor. His sons are proud of their father. He died a hero savings the lives of four other soldiers. That was typical Connor. May God bless his soul. Secondly, New Dublin needs a school and I want to be the teacher. Father Maher has agreed to help in getting us textbooks and other supplies." Addressing her comments to the gentlemen of the congregation, she continued. "All I need now is for you to build us a schoolhouse."

Ronald Ryan was the first to stand. "A school is exactly what we need. If Father Maher is agreeable, we can build the school right here next to the church."

Father Maher answered, "I think that it would be a perfect location but since you own the land, the decision is yours."

Out of modesty, Ronald Ryan did not directly respond but he was willing to donate the land for the new school. "I will see that all the building materials are here this week. On Saturday, we can have a good ole barn raising. If we have enough volunteers, we should be able to build the school in one day.

Alice spoke up, "So, I can count on you to be responsible for getting the school built?"

"Yes, but with one condition. You ladies prepare us a fine lunch."

Rachel Swartz stood, "I will get with the other ladies to find out what dishes they plan to bring. We'll have a feast."

Alice continued, "I see the schoolhouse in having a large room with tables and benches to accommodate about twenty students. There should be large windows to allow the sun to shine in. We need a pot belly stove for the cold days and on the warm days, we can open the windows. We also need shelves built along the walls. As a personal request, I would like to have a bell on the outside and an American flag displayed on the inside."

Ronald Ryan, who was still standing, told Alice, "We can build the schoolhouse exactly as you described." Mr. Ryan continued, "I would like to see a show of hands as to who will be here on Saturday morning." Everyone in the church raised their hands with the exception of Father Maher.

Father Maher joked, "I feel bad that I will not be available to be here. It's not that I would look forward to doing manual labor but I'm going to miss all that good food." Everyone laughed.

Alice felt uncomfortable. She had to talk about money. "I am a widow. I have three boys to raise. I thought about moving back to Jefferson City to find a job, but I want to stay here. This is where my friends are. Many of you came here on the same day that Connor and I did. Through our labor, all of us have built a community that we are proud to call home. I want my boys to grow up here in New Dublin. In order for me to do this, I have to make a living wage. So, we will have to charge tuition. There is no set amount. You pay whatever you can afford. If you can't pay in cash then you can pay in goods and services. Regardless of your financial condition, no child will be turned away. Those of you who wish to enroll your child, please see me after Mass. Thank you."

Alice was inundated with parents. She had a list of twenty five students and there probably would be more before the first day of school. Alice was in a panic. She searched the crowd standing around in front of the church until she found Mr. Ryan. "Ronald, I have a problem. I told you that we needed a school for twenty students. I under estimated. We need to double that."

Ronald replied with confidence, "That's easy to fix. We just build the schoolhouse twice as big."

Alice was shortly relieved. The thought of teaching so many children at one time caused her self confidence to wane. She reconciled with herself. There was nothing that could be done to change the fact so she would take it one day at a time.

Later in the week, a horse drawn wagon stopped in front of Alice's house. She stepped out onto the porch.

The driver said, "Mrs. O'Malley I have two large wooden crates for you. Where do you want to put them?"

Alice knew the crates were from Father Maher. She thought before she spoke. "Let's take them up to the church. Give me a second. I need to get a hammer and a pry bar." Alice briefly disappeared back into the house. She came out and jumped on the back of the wagon along with three gentlemen. Apparently the crates were heavy. They unloaded the wooden boxes inside the vestibule of the church. Alice was excited. She immediately removed the tops. The textbooks were used but were in remarkably good shape. She was extremely pleased with the reading primers. There was an assortment of supplies. She plowed through the second box. It contained the set of encyclopedias along with a variety of novels. Alice said out loud, "Thank you God and please bless Father Maher." Alice spent the rest of the day sorting through both crates. Mentally she formulated her first day of school.

Alice has put on a happy face while in front of her boys or out in public but she cried herself to sleep every night since she received the letter regarding Connor's death. She mourned in silence. The next morning she had breakfast on the table when the boys got up. She was also busy baking a cake, making potato salad and cooking a pot of snap beans for the lunch at the school. Alice, along with her sons, walked toward the church. She was surprised to how much progress had already been made. The schoolhouse was framed and the roof had been shingled. The volunteers were actively working on the tables and benches while others were applying the siding and making the windows. Alice had her doubts that the schoolhouse could be completed in one day but it appeared to be a possibility. Regardless, the construction would definitely be finished by Monday morning, the first day of school. At exactly noon, Alice went over to her newly installed bell. She rang it loud and long. It was lunchtime. This is what made New Dublin a great place to live. The community had come to together to tackle a task that benefited all the children. To watch the fellowship as everyone gathered to enjoy a bounty of food was why Alice didn't want to move away.

There was no scheduled Mass on Sunday. Rachel and Molly came to Alice's house. Their husbands were already at the school making final touches. The three of them walked to the school. The schoolhouse was ready for occupancy. Alice and her two helpers stood and admired the new building. "It's beautiful," commented Alice. There was a pleasant aroma of freshly cut pine. The three of them began to unpack the crates. They placed many of the books neatly on the shelves. Alice sorted through everything and pulled out all the materials that she needed for the opening day of school. Rachel, Molly and Alice were having fun.

There was a lot of laughter. They were just plain silly, but at times, that's what good friends do. The O'Malley brothers, Albert and Sean came running. They went inside and marveled at their new schoolhouse.

Jimmy asked his mother, "Which one is my seat?"

"I will decide that tomorrow but I know one thing, none of you boys will be sitting next to other." This was a smart decision on Alice's part. When these five boys were together, mischief was abound.

Alice was satisfied. Everything that could be done was done. Alice and her three sons returned to their house where Alice prepared dinner.

This night was a milestone for Alice. She fell asleep without shedding a tear. The healing process had begun.

Mrs. O'Malley was at the schoolhouse early. The school day was to be from 8:00 A.M. to 2:00 P.M. At 7:50 A. M., she rang the school bell. Most of the students walked while others came on horseback. One group arrived by a mule driven wagon. They began to file into their new classroom. Mrs. O'Malley advised each child as where to sit. She counted all the students present. There were thirty two ranging in ages from seven to sixteen. She instructed all her students to stand. They said the "Lord's Prayer." Mrs. O'Malley then told the class that they were now going to say the "Pledge of Allegiance." She explained, "Place your right hand over your heart and repeat after me."

Mrs. O'Malley began, "I pledge allegiance to my flag..."

The class responded, "I pledge allegiance to my flag..."

"...and the Republic for which it stands..."

"...and the Republic for which it stands..."

Mrs. O'Malley finished, "...one nation indivisible with liberty and justice for all."

The class responded in kind.

Mrs. O'Malley continued, "This is how we will start out each school day." She inquired of the class as to who could read and write. Only the O'Malley brothers raised their hands. From a teacher's point of view, this was good. Regardless of age, all the students were educationally equal which wouldn't require numerous lesson plans.

Mrs. O'Malley didn't expect to accomplish much this day. She introduced the class to their textbooks and other materials. She went through the alphabet and had the kids count from one to ten. It was lunch time. The children brought something to eat, either in metal buckets or paper bags. They all went outside to eat. Plenty of fresh water was available from the well behind the church. There was a privy just inside the tree line.

Mrs. O'Malley asked Albert to stay. She said, "Albert, I know that you are Jewish. If you don't feel comfortable in reciting the Lord's Prayer, then you don't have to. I feel that you should stand with the others out of respect for their religion."

Albert answered, "I don't have a problem in saying the Lord's Prayer. Jews and Christians both believe in the God of Abraham. I don't think God would be offended if I praised him with a Catholic prayer."

Mrs. O'Malley was somewhat taken aback by his answer. "Albert, you are very wise for such a young man."

Albert was anxious to get outside with the others. "Thank you, Mrs. O'Malley. Can I go now?"

"Yes...go."

Mrs. O'Malley stood at the window watching all the children playing in the school yard. She let them stay outside longer only because this was their first day of school. When she thought that it was time to get back to the class, she ordered them back inside. After everyone was seated, she had the class repeat the numbers one to ten, five more times. She could see that her sons were going to be an asset. They took it upon themselves to help the younger kids to count one to ten on their fingers.

Mrs. O'Malley told her class, "I have a book here that was sent to me by Father Maher. It is *Twenty Thousand Leagues under the Sea.* It is written by Jules Verne. It is science fiction. Fiction means that it is not true. It's just a story. Use your imagination to picture what it would be like if it were true. I think all of you will like it." Mrs. O'Malley began to read. It was not long before the students were enthralled. They were hanging on to everything she said. With the exception of the O'Malley brothers, they were amazed that words were actually coming out of the book. No one had ever read them anything in their young lives. Mrs. O'Malley read for about an hour. She looked at Connor's pocket watch that she kept on the desk. It was about thirty minutes before dismissal. She closed the book and said, "That's all for today." This did not sit well with the class. They begged her to read some more. Mrs. O'Malley assured them that she would read more tomorrow. She had the class again repeat the numbers. She then asked Kevin, the youngest in the class who was seated next to Jimmy, "Kevin, do you think that you can count from one to ten?"

Kevin said with pride, "Yes ma'am." He stood up. He took his right index finger and began to count the fingers on his left hand. He then took his left index finger and finished counting his fingers on his right hand. He stood there with a huge smile on his face.

"Kevin, that was very good. Does anyone else want to try?" Hands went up throughout the room. Mrs. O'Malley picked several more and they too were able to count from one to ten. Mrs. O'Malley was pleased. She had a bright class. Mrs.

O'Malley said, "It is time for dismissal. I will see all of you in the morning." Like a flash, the room was empty with the exception of Sally.

She walked up to Mrs. O'Malley's desk and asked, "May I see the book?"

Mrs. O'Malley pushed the book to the edge of her desk. Sally opened it and all she saw were printed words. "The story you told us came out of this book?"

"Yes. Someday, you will be able to read a book just like this."

Sally was fascinated. It was almost like magic. "How long will it take me to learn to read?"

"You are a smart girl. It won't take you long."

This seemed to satisfy Sally. She turned and raced out the door.

Mrs. O'Malley was happy with herself and how the day went. She thought, "Today is the beginning of a new era for New Dublin."

Several weeks passed. It was Friday. Father Maher was scheduled to be in town. Mrs. O'Malley was anxious to see him. Late in the morning, Father Maher knocked on the opened door. Mrs. O'Malley motioned for him to come in. She said, "Class please stand up and say good morning to Father Maher."

The class recited, "Good morning, Father."

"Good morning boys and girls. Please sit down. I wanted to come by to see your new schoolhouse. It's the nicest schoolhouse that I have ever seen." He looked around the class until he found Kevin. "Kevin, the word around town is that you are the smartest kid in the class."

Kevin stood up. He responded as only a seven year old could. "Yes Father. I am the smartest." The rest of the class snickered.

Father Maher leaned over and whispered to Mrs. O'Malley. "I ran into his mother on the way over here. She is one that told me that he was the smartest one in the class."

Mrs. O'Malley smiled as she whispered back. "It's called mother's pride." She continued by saying to the class. "Father Maher is the one who gave us *Twenty Thousand Leagues under the Sea.*"

Father Maher asked, "Did you like it?"

Everyone tried to answer at the same time. It was obvious that the book made an impression on them.

Father Maher asked another question. "Who was your favorite character?"

Without hesitation, the class answered, "Captain Nemo."

"He was mine too. I will try and find some other books that Mrs. O'Malley can read to you." Father Maher continued, "I just wanted to stop by and say hello. I need to leave so you can get back to your studies." He headed for the door and Mrs. O'Malley followed. They stepped outside.

Mrs. O'Malley said, "Father, I want to personally thank you for sending all the books and supplies. You cannot imagine how they have made my job so much easier."

"It was my pleasure, Alice." Father Maher, who was concerned about her well being asked, "How are you doing?"

"It's been difficult but every day it gets a bit easier."

"That's good to hear. I have been keeping you in my prayers."

"Thank you." Alice had a question. "Father, do you think that you could get in touch with your superintendent friend? I need a chalk board in the worse way. The community has been generous and I have some extra money in the coffers. If they don't have a spare, at least they could tell you where I can purchase one."

"I will let you know."

"Also, I will need chalk."

Father Maher with his sarcastic wit responded. "One thing that I have noticed over the years is that a chalk board is of no use unless you have chalk."

Alice, with her own gibe response, "Very funny, Father."

Both of them smiled at each other as they parted ways.

****

After school, Jimmy told his mother that he, his brothers, Sean and Albert were going fishing. She didn't have any objections. She said, "If you catch a mess, clean them and we will have fish for dinner." The five of them headed down to the river joking with each other as kids of that age would normally do. They sat there on the river bank talking about how neat it would be if they had their own *Nautilus*. They could travel the entire Cherokee River all the way down to the Atlantic Ocean. They got tired of fishing. Including the fish caught by Sean and Albert, the O'Malley brothers had enough for dinner. They sat around in a circle. Albert came up with the idea that they should build a raft and name it the *Nautilus*. They could sail it down to Jefferson City. All were in agreement and they decided that they were going to do it during the summer break. It was getting late. They did their normal ritual. They grabbed each other's hands in the middle of the circle. They recited together, "Friends forever".

****

Saturday morning came. Father Maher scrounged around until he found a can of red paint and a brush. He took the two crates that were still in the vestibule. He stacked them on top of each other in front of the entrance to the schoolhouse. Father Maher had an artistic ability. He meticulously painted across the front *Connor O'Malley School.*

The next morning before Mass, Molly was standing out front eagerly awaiting for Alice to arrive. As they walked up, Molly grabbed Alice and led her next door. Alice looked up and saw the name of the school. Her boys gave her a group hug. She began to cry. They were tears of gratitude that someone had taken the time to honor the memory of her husband. She entered the church and went straight to the sacristy. She found Father Maher and gave him a big embrace and said, "You are a kind and decent man."

Father Maher blushed. He was not good at accepting compliments. "I did it for both of us. Don't forget, Connor was my friend."

Father Maher returned to Jefferson City the next day. Before the week was out, three men in a horse drawn wagon pulled to a stop at the school. They had two packages. One was a chalkboard. The delivery men brought some tools along with them. It was not their responsibility but they installed it immediately. Mrs. O'Malley opened the other crate and laughed. It contained more novels along with a lifetime supply of chalk. Mrs. O'Malley said a prayer. "Thanks again God. Please continue to bless Father Maher."

****

Benjamin T. Putnam was a long time employee of the Jefferson City Paddleboat Company. He would have been terminated years ago but his sister was married to the owner. He was a bitter man who lacked any semblance of a pleasant personality. He was promoted to dock master and transferred to New Dublin mainly to get him out of the home office. Mr. Putnam was a portly man of middle age. He wore a white shirt every day with his tie hanging loosely against his rotund belly. His head was covered with a straw Panama hat and he was seldom seen without a lit cigar. Loud and boisterous would be a good description of his demeanor.

Jimmy entered the small wood frame office located at the end of the boardwalk. He walked up to the only person in the office. He asked, "Are you the man in charge?"

"Yes, I am. How can I help you?"

He stuck out his hand in confidence. "My name is James O'Malley but my friends call me Jimmy."

"My name is Benjamin T. Putnam but since I don't have any friends, I am only known as Mr. Putnam but you can call me Mr. Ben."

"Mr. Ben, I need a job. Looking around here, I think you can use some help."

"You do, huh?"

"Yes sir. I have a good eye for these things."

"You do, huh?"

"Yes sir. I am the man of the house and I need to make money to help support my family."

Benjamin T. Putnam's was impressed by the young man. He asked, "Jimmy, how old are you?"

"Twelve."

"Twelve, huh, and you are the man of the house?"

"My father was killed at the Battle of San Juan Hill in Cuba. He died a hero. My mother is always telling me that I am the man of the house. Mr. Ben, this is why I need a job."

Jimmy must have touched a well hidden sensitive spot with Mr. Putnam. He was somewhat compassionate. "I am sorry to hear about your dad. I know what it is like to grow up without a father. My dad was killed at the Battle of Gettysburg. You must be proud of him."

"Yes sir, I am."

Mr. Putnam asked, "Do you go to school?"

"Yes sir, my mother is the schoolmarm."

"I don't need any help around here but I like you kid," Benjamin T. Putnam said. In reality he didn't like anyone but he saw something in Jimmy that he thought would make his job easier. "You can start tomorrow after you get out of school. I quit at six o'clock...not a minute before...and not a minute after. We work on Saturdays from seven in the morning until three in the afternoon. You can be my errand boy. How does that sound to you?"

"That sounds good to me. Jimmy turned and headed for the door."

Mr. Ben yelled out to Jimmy. He stopped in his tracks. "Don't you want to know what you will be paid?"

Jimmy totally forgot about his pay. "Yes sir, I need to know that."

"I will pay you fifty cents a day and a dollar and a quarter for Saturday. Does that meet with your satisfaction?"

'Oh, yes sir. That is real good. I will see you tomorrow."

The next day Jimmy's mother asked him to stay while the others went outside to eat lunch. She asked, "Do we have enough wood cut at the house?"

"Yes ma'am."

"When you get home start a fire in the stove so it will be hot when I get there."

"I can't Mom. I have to go to work."

"What do you mean? You have to go to work."

"I am going to be the errand boy for Mr. Benjamin T. Putnam down at the dock."

Alice was silent. She needed a minute to digest the unexpected news. She was proud that Jimmy had taken the initiative to find employment but at the same time she felt inadequate as a parent simply on the fact that Jimmy thought that it was necessary to find a job. She said, "Jimmy, we will be fine without you working."

"I know Mama but this is what I want to do."

Reluctantly, Alice agreed. "I have told you that you are the man of the house. This is your decision but if it interferes with your studies you will have to quit."

"Don't worry, I can do both."

"What time do you get off?"

"Six o'clock."

"I will have dinner on the table when you get home."

Jimmy liked his job. He was slowly getting adjusted to Mr. Benjamin T. Putnam. Jimmy realized that Mr. Ben was more bark than bite. Whenever Mr. Ben went into one of his tirades, Jimmy did not take it personally. He would just let Mr. Ben vent. Afterwards Jimmy would calmly ask, "Do you feel better now?" Mr. Ben would smile and say "Yes." It became a relationship of common interest. Benjamin T. Putnam needed Jimmy as much as Jimmy needed the job.

A lady stepped inside the office. "Sir, do you have someone who can help me with my trunk. It's not heavy. It's too awkward to handle it by myself."

Mr. Ben with his seldom seen politeness, said "Yes ma'am. Please have a seat. I will get my errand boy." Mr. Ben went outside and with a voice that echoed throughout the dock area, "JIMMY!" It was so loud that it actually startled the lady inside. Mr. Ben was impatient. He yelled again, "JIMMY GET YOUR BUTT HERE NOW!" Jimmy had already dropped his broom and was running toward the entrance to the office. Mr. Ben lit into him. He accused Jimmy of sleeping on the job. Mr. Ben, back with his polite demeanor, reentered the office accompanied by Jimmy. With courtesy, he spoke to the lady, "My errand boy here will be more than happy to assist you."

Jimmy recognized the lady. "Hello, Mrs. Stacey."

"Hello, Jimmy. How long have you been working here?"

"About two weeks."

"That's good. You are a fine young man. Do you think you can help me load my trunk?"

"Yes ma'am."

Before they walked out the door, Mrs. Stacey turned to Mr. Ben. "What is your name?"

He answered, "Benjamin T. Putnam."

With no uncertain terms she replied, "Mr. Benjamin T. Putnam, if I hear of you talking that way again to young Jimmy, I will have my three sons come here and have a little chat with you."

Jimmy and Mrs. Stacey loaded the trunk onto the paddleboat. Mrs. Stacey attempted to give Jimmy a tip but he adamantly refused. She said, "You are like your father. He too would have helped me without expecting anything in return."

"Thank you, Mrs. Stacey."

Jimmy entered the office and Mr. Ben started in on him. Jimmy felt comfortable enough to confront Mr. Ben. Jimmy shook his index finger back and forth at the same time he was saying, "No. No. No. You heard what Mrs. Stacey said. She has three sons...three big boys...really big boys. They are also dumb...really dumb. When she says they will come and chat with you, there will be very little talk and a whole lot of pain."

"So if I understand it correctly, my well being rests in the hands of a twelve year old."

"Exactly."

Mr. Ben smirked. He realized that he had met his match. "I like you kid. I guess that I will have to be nice to you from now on."

Jimmy felt a sense of superior leverage. "You can yell at me all you want but don't do it when someone else is around."

From that day forward, Mr. Ben never raised his voice again to Jimmy. The thought of the three Stacey boys weighed heavily on his mind, but at the same time, he realized that Jimmy had the savvy to be an asset in running the office...something that he needed to keep management happy back at the home office. This is not to be misconstrued. There was no epiphany. Mr. Ben was still an obnoxious individual which he exhibited regularly with the stevedores. He had a reputation to maintain.

Chapter 2

The O'Malley Family Goes to Washington
(Circa 1899)

It has been over a year since Connor O'Malley had been killed in action. The school had a successful first year. Alice received enough compensation to frugally support her family. She put her widow's pension into savings to finance a trip to Arlington National Cemetery. This trip was not only for Alice but also for her three sons. It was Alice's way of making a final tribute to her husband. School was out of session for a short summer break. Alice packed three small suitcases with enough clothing to cover their four days of travel. The four of them with their luggage in hand headed for the dock. Alice bought tickets from Benjamin T. Putnam. He was in his polite mood but he wasn't pleased with the fact that Jimmy was going to be gone. Jimmy had to threaten to quit before Mr. Putnam acquiesced in granting time off...without pay of course. Benjamin T. Putnam had many faults and laziness was one of them. Jimmy no longer was the errand boy. He actually performed most of the duties that Benjamin T. Putnam would normally do in accordance with his employment contract. But with Jimmy gone, Mr. Putnam would have to earn his salary.

The paddle boat pulled away from the dock. They were underway heading north to Springfield. The O'Malley brothers were excited. This was the first time they had ever been outside of New Dublin. They were in awe when Springfield came into view. They had never seen so many buildings. The paddle boat docked and Alice asked for directions to the train depot. The boys wanted to stop and peer into every storefront but Alice had to push them along. She didn't want to miss the train. Four tickets were purchased for Washington D.C. They had an hour wait. They walked around the downtown area not to venture too far from the train depot. They were back in plenty of time and were standing on the loading platform when the train pulled into the station with black smoke billowing from the stack. The boys were amazed at the enormity of the locomotive. Alice gave her tickets to the conductor and boarded. They found their seats which faced each other. It was not long before there was a jolt. The train began to move forward. It would be a long ride. They would not arrive in Washington D.C. until early the next morning. The boys were glued to the window taking in every sight and sound. The sun was setting. Alice and her sons went to the dining car. Alice browsed the menu and decided on the dinner special for all of them. Surprisingly, it was quite good. With their appetite satisfied, they returned to their seats. There was not much to do. It was too dark to see any of the scenery. One by one they feel asleep only to be awakened when the train came to a stop at another train depot. Once the train restarted, sleep bestowed them again. They did not arouse again until the sun peered through the window. They took turns in going to the lavatory. It would not be long before they reached their destination. The boys were impressed with the size of Springfield but as they pulled into the B & O Train Depot, it was beyond their imagination. There was no comparison between the two. Alice claimed their baggage that had been placed on the loading platform. She found a brochure inside the depot that gave directions to all of the major governmental buildings. Alice's goal for the day was to see the Executive Manson, the Capitol, the Supreme Court and if they had enough time, the Smithsonian Institution. They would visit the cemetery tomorrow morning. They set out following the map in the brochure. Pennsylvania Avenue was only two blocks away. They strolled down the sidewalk until they reached the Executive Mansion. There was a gentleman on the front lawn playing fetch with a Cocker Spaniel. Alice recognized him from newspaper clippings. It was President William McKinley.

Alice proceeded up to him and introduced herself. "Mr. President, my name is Alice O'Malley. These are my three sons." Alice began to introduce them. This is Larry. His nickname is Pop. This is his twin brother Billy and this is Jimmy, my oldest."

President McKinley was cordial. He shook the hands of each of the boys. He asked, "I see that you have suitcases. Where is your home?"

"We are from a little community called New Dublin. It is about fifty miles north of Jefferson City."

"I know it well. Before I was President, I used to travel the Cherokee River on a regular basis and New Dublin was a port of call."

"Yes sir. You have a good memory."

President McKinley continued with another question. "What brings you to our fair city?"

"My husband, Connor, was killed at the Battle of San Juan Hill. We came to visit his grave site. We plan to walk there tomorrow morning. We will begin our trip home later in the afternoon."

President McKinley felt personal remorse for the death of Connor O'Malley for it was he as Commander in Chief, took the United States to war against Spain. He compassionately said, "I am truly sorry for your loss." He inquired, "Have you found a place to stay?"

"No sir. Today I wanted my boys to see the Executive Mansion, the Capitol and the Supreme Court. I am sure that I can find a hotel between here and the Capitol."

"There is the Hotel Baltimore. It is past the train station on the left hand side. It is on the way to the Capitol. Stop by there and ask for Walter Cox. He is the manager. Tell him I sent you and ask him for the 'brother-in-law special'. He will give you a good rate. Also, I will have one of my carriages there at eight o'clock tomorrow morning to take you to Arlington National Cemetery. It is too far to walk and stay on your schedule."

Alice graciously tried to decline the offer. "That is kind of you Mr. President, but it is not necessary."

President McKinley said, "It is the least I can do for the family of a fallen soldier."

Alice accepted the gesture. She again thanked the President for his thoughtfulness. She started to leave but the President had another question. "Have you eaten today?"

"No sir."

"I was about to go inside for lunch. Would you care to join me?"

Alice responded, "No sir but I thank you for your offer."

President McKinley was not going to take no for an answer. "I insist. I hate to eat by myself. It is nothing formal. Verona is the best cook in all of Washington. To turn down one her of meals, is next to sacrilege."

The O'Malley brothers wanted desperately for their mother to change her mind. They looked at her and Jimmy spoke up, "Please Mama."

President McKinley did not give Alice a chance to respond. "It's settled. Follow me."

The five of them along with the Cocker Spaniel entered the residence through the side kitchen door. The President announced, "Verona will you please put out four more settings. I brought some guests with me."

"Yes sir, Mr. President."

As Verona put silverware and glasses of ice water on the worn wooden table that sat in a dining area adjacent to the large kitchen. President McKinley exhibited good political skills. He remembered everyone's name as he introduced them to Verona. They all sat down in bow back wooden matching chairs. President McKinley preferred the kitchen especially when he was eating alone. Verona prepared each plate separately. She placed the first one in front of the President. After everyone had been served, President McKinley led his guests in saying grace. The President was correct. Verona was a good cook. The meal was not fancy. It was home style cooking. They had roast beef, rice with gravy, green beans, black eyed peas and cornbread. Pop, Billy and Jimmy devoured their meals.

President McKinley asked, "Do you boys want seconds?"

All three of them answered, "Yes sir."

Alice interrupted, "Boys, where are your manners? I don't want the President to think that I have raised a bunch of heathens."

Verona voiced her opinion. "President McKinley may run the country but I run the kitchen. It is not rude to ask for seconds, in fact, I take it as a compliment. I have three boys about the age of your sons. They are bottomless pits and I want your boys to be full when they leave here."

Alice, smiling, responded as she handed her plate to Verona, "I would hate to offend you. I will also take another helping."

Both President McKinley and Verona laughed.

President McKinley asked Alice, "What do you do back in New Dublin?"

"I am the schoolmarm. I have thirty two students. We just completed our first year. It is a bright class."

"My sister was a teacher. Is there anything I can do to help you?"

Alice was hesitant to respond especially in view of the fact that she just admonished her sons for bad manners. "Mr. President I am reluctant to answer you but I feel I should ask on behalf of my students. Do you have any books on American history, the Presidents or Civics? Also, I could use a copy of the Declaration of Independence and the Constitution. I don't mean any documents that are of historical significance just extra copies that you may have."

"Mrs. O'Malley, it will be my pleasure to search through our library. We have many duplicate copies of the same book. I will have my aide put a package together and send it to you." The President stood up. "I have thoroughly enjoyed our visit but I must leave. I have a meeting scheduled with the French Ambassador. Take your time and finish eating. Verona will show you the way out."

Alice and her sons stood. "Mr. President, I along with Pop, Billy and Jimmy want to thank you for everything."

"You're welcomed."

Alice again complimented Verona for an excellent meal as they said good-bye at the gate to Pennsylvania Avenue. The four of them walked back down the street. They passed the train depot and found the Hotel Baltimore. It was plush. It even had electric lights. They proceeded to the counter inside and asked for Walter Cox.

"I am Mr. Cox. May I help you?"

Alice responded, "Yes sir. President McKinley sent us down here and told us to ask for you. He said that you would give us the 'brother-in-law special'."

"We do have a 'brother-in-law special' only for the personal friends of the President. How much did you expect to pay for a room?"

"I thought that a dollar would be appropriate."

"What a coincidence. That is exactly the cost. How many nights do you plan to stay?"

Alice answered, "One night."

Mr. Cox had Alice sign in on the guest register while he retrieved the key to room 317. "Your room is on the third floor. You can take the elevator or use the stairs."

They stepped away from the counter. Jimmy asked, "Mama, what is an elevator?"

"I don't know. I have never seen one." They looked around the lobby and they saw a small room with a sliding door. People were seen going in and the door closing behind them. They concluded that that must be the elevator but they were leery. Alice said, "Let's take the stairs." The boys were in complete agreement. They found their room and went inside. Alice immediately realized that this was not a dollar a night room. Billy found the light switch. He kept turning it off and on. He was mesmerized until his mother told him to stop. Jimmy yelled to his mother. "Mama, come here and look at the lavatory. It has a toilet and a tub." Pop turned on the faucets on the sink. "They even have hot water." After the newness wore off, Alice gathered up her sons and set out for the Capitol. They climbed the stairs and entered the Rotunda. It was magnificent. They found the Senate Chamber and the House of Representatives. Congress was not in session and the entire building was relatively quiet. They also found the Supreme Court. They took their time and took in all the historical aspects of the Capitol. They returned outside and sat down on the steps. Alice used this time as a learning moment.

"There are three equal branches of government: the Executive Branch, the Legislative Branch and the Judicial Branch. No Branch is more powerful than the other. Our founding fathers set it up this way as a means of checks and balances. Congress creates laws. They send the law to the President at the Executive Mansion. He can agree with the law with his signature. If he doesn't agree, he can veto the bill and send it back to Congress. Congress can override the veto with seventy five percent of the Senate and the House of Representatives voting in favor. If by chance the law passes the Congress and the President signs the bill into law, then it can be challenged by the people. It will then proceed through the court system until it reaches the Supreme Court. The Justices will rule as to whether or not the law is constitutional. If they decide that the law is constitutional, then it becomes the law of the land. Should they rule the other way, then the law is sent back to Congress to be rewritten or the law is simply discarded. One thing that I want you to remember is that the States formed the Federal Government and not vice versa. The Federal Government is intended to be a weak central government uniting all the States under one flag. It is not intended to dominate the States or the people."

Alice and her three sons took their time in returning to the hotel. They paused to admire the window displays of the many shops along Pennsylvania Avenue. They finally made it back to their room. Alice was getting irritated with Billy. He continued to play with the light switch. He didn't stop until Alice threatened to spank him.

All afternoon, Alice had thoughts of taking a long relaxing hot bath. She told her boys, "I am going in the lavatory and I don't want to be disturbed."

Jimmy answered, "We are going down to the lobby."

"That's fine but all of you stay together."

"Yes ma'am."

They went out into the hallway. Pop suggested, "Why don't we take the elevator."

"Yea let's do it," said Billy.

Jimmy was more reluctant. "We don't know how to operate an elevator."

Pop said, "We wait here and when someone gets off, we get them to show us."

The three of them stood patiently in front of the elevator. They could hear the elevator working but it passed their floor. When they were about to give up, the door opened and an older couple got off. Jimmy asked, "Excuse me sir, can you show us how to use the elevator? We have never ridden one before."

"I would be happy to do so, young man. It's easy. You step inside and pulled this metal scissor gate close. The outside door will also close. Then you push the button with the number one. It will take you down to the first floor. That's it."

"Thank you, sir. That sounds easy enough."

The three boys went inside and closed the gate. They were apprehensive. The outside door closed. It had the number three written on it. Jimmy punched the number one button. The elevator jolted. All three of them jumped. The elevator began to move downward. It came to an abrupt stop. They pulled the gate back and stepped outside. They were proud of themselves. They began to meander about the lobby checking out everything of interest. They eventually sat down on a davenport. There were periodicals on the table in front of them. Jimmy picked up a copy of *Harper's Weekly* and began to thumb through the pages. Pop had the morning edition of the *Washington Post*. He showed the front page to his brothers. It had a picture of President William McKinley. Their interest in the printed word was short lived. They headed back upstairs. Billy pushed the button for the eighth floor. They rode up and then back down to the third floor. The elevator was fun. Alice was finished with her bath. Pop, Billy, and Jimmy began to argue as to who was next. "Rock, paper, scissors" was their way of settling disputes. Billy was eliminated on the first round and Pop beat Jimmy. After the three finished their bathes, they turned in for the night. Jimmy and Pop were in one full size bed and Billy and his mother were in the other.

Alice was already awake when the sun came up. She rousted the boys out of bed. She pulled out some fresh clothing from the suitcases. They dressed and went down to the lobby. There were muffins and hot beverages. The boys could not convince their mother to take the elevator. Alice kept an eye on the clock. It was almost time for the carriage to arrive. She returned the key to the front desk. Alice saw a street vendor selling flowers. She purchased four long stemmed roses. As they were standing on the sidewalk near the street, the doorman ushered the four to the side. He stood in front of them as to prevent them from blocking the entrance. He informed them, "The President's carriage is arriving. It is here to pick up some important people."

Jimmy didn't say anything but he felt insulted.

The driver got down and approached Alice, "Are you Mrs. O'Malley?"

She answered. "Yes."

"I am Jake. I am going to be your escort today." He went and held open the door on the carriage to allow Alice and her sons to climb aboard.

The doorman realized that he had made a mistake but he didn't apologize. He turned to Jimmy. "Sir, may I help you with your suitcase?"

Jimmy was polite but he got his point across. "No sir. We unimportant people can manage our own baggage."

Jimmy put his suitcase in the carriage. He then asked the driver, "Mr. Jake can I ride up front with you?"

He replied, "Sure."

They rode the streets of Washington. People were curious when the carriage passed. They looked to see if it was President McKinley or a dignitary that they recognized. Jake led the two horses across the Potomac River and entered Arlington National Cemetery. Jake knew his way around. He had been there on many occasions. He found the area in which the "Rough Riders" were buried. He climbed down and opened the carriage door and addressed Alice. "Mrs. O'Malley I don't know which one is your husband's grave but it will be in this area. Take your time. I will be here waiting for you."

"Thank you Jake." Alice gave each of her boys one of the roses. They fanned out checking the names on all of the headstones. Billy found it. "Mama, here it is."

Alice and the O'Malley brothers gathered at the foot of the grave. Alice became emotional but she restrained herself. She wanted this visit to be a celebration for the father of her sons and not an occasion filled with sorrow and remorse. They placed the roses at the base of the headstone. Alice told stories about their father. She wanted Jimmy, Pop, and Billy to know that he loved his boys. Alice had contemplated saving enough money to have her husband reinterred in New Dublin but she changed her mind. Connor was buried in a place of honor with the men he fought and died with. This is where Connor would want to be. The O'Malley family joined hands and Alice led them in prayer.

They returned to the carriage where Jake was standing with the door opened. Jake informed Alice. "The President wanted me to take you and your boys to one of his favorite eating places."

Alice tried to decline. "I don't think that we are appropriately dressed."

"Mrs. O'Malley you are fine."

Alice pulled out her purse to check to see how much money she had left.

"Don't worry about paying. President McKinley gave me the money to buy your lunch. But he did tell me that he would fire me if he found out that your boys did not get enough to eat."

Alice smiled. "He is such a nice man."

"Yes he is...Mrs. O'Malley...yes he is."

Pop and Billy began to argue as to who was going to ride up front with Mr. Jake. "Rock, paper, scissors" would settle the matter. Billy lost. Pop laughed at his brother. "You are a born loser." This made Billy mad. He started to hit Pop but Alice grabbed him by the collar and yanked him back. "Get up in the carriage and don't say a word."

They crossed back over the Potomac River and Jake turned onto a side street at the foot of the bridge. He was heading for one of the many city parks. He stopped in front of a cart with a huge umbrella with "Frankfurter" written on it. He said to Alice, "This is it. The President and I stop here every time we are on this side of town."

Alice laughed. "I think we might be over dressed."

Jake smiled. He then ordered a frankfurter for himself and the others along with lemonades. They sat down at a table situated under a large live oak tree. The boys went back for two more each. As they were taking their last bites, Jake asked Alice, "Where does all that food go?"

"I don't know. They eat like that at home. They are so skinny. You would think that I was starving them to death."

He then asked the boys. "Are you full?"

They answered together, "Yes sir, Mr. Jake."

Jake opened the carriage door. He said to Billy, "It's your turn to ride with me."

Billy looked at Pop and snidely said, "Who's the loser now?"

Pop wasn't happy. He leaped forward to punch his brother. Alice snatched him back. "You boys are going to be the death of me."

Alice made a request to Jake. "Can you take us to the Smithsonian Institution? We have enough time before we have to catch our train. There is no need for you to stay. We can walk to the depot."

"Yes ma'am."

Jake stopped at his destination. He climbed down and aided Mrs. O'Malley with the suitcases. He told her, "I enjoyed escorting you and your sons today. It is nice helping home folk. I have to hold my tongue when I am around some of those snooty diplomats."

"Thank you, Jake. Please tell the President that his hospitality was greatly appreciated."

"I will. Have a safe trip back. Good bye boys."

"Good bye, Mr. Jake."

Alice and her boys enjoyed the Smithsonian Institution. They boarded the train at dusk for the long ride back to Springfield. Jimmy, Pop, and Billy were exhausted. It was not long before they were asleep. Alice did not disturb them. She went to the club car where she obtained an ink pen and stationery. Alice sat there and wrote a thank you note to President McKinley. She finished and sealed it in an envelope. Alice returned to her seat.

She had to move Billy. He had stretched out taking up the entire seat. Alice got as comfortable as possible. She too dozed off.

The next morning, Alice and her sons went to the dining car and had a hearty breakfast. They took their time in eating. It was still another three hours to Springfield. They returned to their seats. Alice entertained her boys by playing a game to see who could be first in finding a horse, a cow or whatever. It kept the boys occupied until the train pulled into the station. Alice wasn't sure of the departure time of the paddle boat. They went straight to the dock except for a short stop at the post office where Alice mailed her letter to the President.

The dock master advised that the paddle boat should arrive in thirty minutes. The trip down river was faster. They were flowing with the current. Benjamin T. Putnam was there to greet them as they disembarked. He had but one thing on his mind. Was Jimmy returning to work the next day? Jimmy assured him that he would be on the job at his regular time. Benjamin T. Putnam was pleased.

The boys raced ahead of their mother. They went into the house and changed out of their dress clothes. In a flash, they were heading back out the front door as Alice was stepping up on the front porch. Jimmy said to her, "We're going to find Albert and Sean. They are never going to believe that we had lunch with the President of the United States."

****

Three weeks passed. Benjamin T. Putnam came into the office. He was surprised. "Jimmy, there is a crate out here addressed to your mother. It is from President McKinley."

"I told you that we went to the Executive Mansion. Now do you believe me?"

He would never admit it but he did have his doubts. "Of course, I believed you."

Jimmy made arrangements with one of the farmers to carry the package to the school. Alice was still there. She got her hammer and pry bar and opened the wooden crate. There was an envelope on top of the books addressed to Mrs. Alice O'Malley. It was a note from President McKinley:

Dear Mrs. O'Malley,

I received your letter. Thank you for your kind words.

I am hopeful that the books and documents that I have sent you meet with your satisfaction.

With fondest regards,

William McKinley

Alice went through the entire box. Not only did it meet with her satisfaction, it exceeded her expectation. Over the following days, Mrs. O'Malley helped her students draft a letter to the President. It was her students' words. Mrs. O'Malley only offered guidance. When the letter, which consisted of ten sentences, was agreed upon by the class, Mrs. O'Malley assigned the task of writing the letter to Sally. She had the best penmanship. Each student signed his or her name. Mrs. O'Malley mailed the letter.

It was Father Maher's weekend at New Dublin. He arrived on the morning paddle boat from Jefferson City. He proceeded toward the church. But first he made a visit next door at the schoolhouse. When he walked inside, all the students stood and greeted him. "Good morning, Father." He returned the greeting, "Good Morning." Father Maher was smiling. He had good news. "Mrs. O'Malley, you and your class are famous." Father

Maher pulled out the Jefferson City Gazette which he had tucked under his arm. He opened the newspaper. He held it up so all could see. On the front page was a picture of President McKinley. The captioned underneath the photograph said: *President McKinley recently shipped some American history books to Mrs. O'Malley's class in nearby New Dublin. The students wrote a letter to the President thanking him for his generosity. He was so moved by the letter that he had it framed. The President is seen here hanging it on the wall in his office at the Executive Mansion.*

"I have brought enough copies of the newspaper so each of you can have one to take home. They were too heavy for me to carry from the boat." He then made a request of Jimmy, "When you go to work today can you take a wagon with you and bring the newspapers back? They are sitting inside the office."

Mrs. O'Malley interjected. "Jimmy, go now and get the newspapers."

"Yes ma'am."

Father Maher congratulated the class and then he excused himself. After he left, the entire class gathered around Mrs. O'Malley's desk and each took turns looking at the picture. Jimmy came back and handed out a newspaper to all of his fellow students.

Chapter 3

The New Millennium (Circa 1900 – 1915)

It was the beginning of a new century. The school was doing well. There were two new students, both seven years old. One older boy had to drop out. His father died at an early age and he had to assume the responsibility of running the family farm. Today, two were absent. Pop and Billy were home sick. Mid morning, Mrs. O'Malley asked Jimmy to run home and check on his brothers. He went to the house and the twins were nowhere to be found. Jimmy immediately headed for the river. He found Pop and Billy scrounging around trying to find fish bait. "You guys are in big trouble. Let's get back to the house."

They picked up their fishing poles and followed Jimmy. Jimmy asked, "Did you catch anything?"

Pop, who was mad, said, "No! Your stupid brother forgot to bring the worms."

Billy didn't like Pop's attitude. "Who are you calling stupid?"

"I am calling you stupid because you are stupid."

"I'm not stupid. You're the stupid one."

The two of them tangled up. They were wrestling. Neither one got the upper hand. Jimmy wanted to let them fight but he broke them apart. He had to get back to school or his mother would be asking too many questions.

As they walked back toward the house, Billy asked, "Are you going to tell Mama?"

"I don't know yet."

When they got back to the house Jimmy ordered both of them to get into bed. "I am going out on the front porch and when I come back in, I will ask you guys if you are feeling better and you will answer yes. Do you understand?"

Jimmy went outside. He then returned inside and went straight to his brothers' bedroom. He asked them, "Are you guys feeling better?"

Both of them answered, "Yes."

"Now when Mama asks me how you two were doing, I will say to her that I went to the house and they were in the bed. I asked them if they were feeling better and they said yes. This way I am not lying to Mama."

However, Jimmy wasn't going to let this incident go to waste. He had leverage. The twins would be agreeable to anything to keep their mother from finding out that they had been playing hooky. But since they were his brothers, he went easy on them. "The next time we need to chop wood, both of you will do my share. Do you agree?"

Pop and Billy had no other option. "Agreed."

"If I were you, I would be in bed when Mama gets home."

Jimmy returned to the schoolhouse. His mother asked exactly what he had anticipated. He did not lie. Alice was satisfied.

****

Father Maher was the bearer of bad news. He brought with him a copy of the Jefferson City Gazette. He waited until school was out for the day and walked next door when he knew Alice was alone. He showed her the front page. The headline read,

President McKinley Dies. The article said in part:

> *"President William McKinley died September 14, 1901 from wounds he received from an assassin's bullet on September 6, 1901. He was visiting the Temple of Music at the Pan-American Exposition in Buffalo, N.Y. President McKinley was in a reception line shaking hands when Leon Czolgosz, a self- proclaimed anarchist, fired two shots at the President. One shot grazed the President while the other hit him directly in the abdomen. Prognosis for recovery was favorable until he developed gangrene to which he succumbed..."*

Alice was emotionally moved. "This is so sad. President McKinley was a good man. This is a great loss for our country."

Father Maher agreed. "We will offer this Sunday's Mass in his memory."

****

The twins had recently celebrated their fourteenth birthday. They had a business idea but they needed some financial help. They went to the dock to see Jimmy. They entered the office. Jimmy was busy handling paperwork and issuing tickets to passengers. Benjamin T. Putnam, with his feet propped up on the desk, was sound asleep. Jimmy, the errand boy, was doing a fantastic job in running the entire operation.

Pop said to Billy in front of Jimmy, "Jimmy is the best brother anyone could have."

Billy responded, "You're right. He would do anything for his two little brothers."

Jimmy wasn't buying it. "Cut out the bull malarkey. What do you guys want?"

Pop said, "We want to know if you will loan us twenty five dollars? We have talked to a lot of the neighbors and they told us they would be willing to buy a variety of foodstuffs from us. We can buy the groceries from Jefferson City and then resell them here. What do you think?"

"My little brothers want to be businessmen. I like it."

Billy then asked, "Does that mean that you will loan us the money?"

"That's a dumb question. Of course, I will. You are my brothers." Jimmy continued, "The man you need to see is Mr. Blakely. He owns the American Mercantile Company which wholesales all sorts of commodities. He comes here every week to buy produce to take back to Jefferson City. Hang around. The boat is running late today. It should be arriving shortly."

The twins sat down inside the office. Jimmy went back to his paperwork. Billy started laughing. He leaned over to Pop and said, "Mr. Putnam sounds like a pig with constipation." Jimmy overheard his brother. The odd sounds emanating from his boss didn't bother him. He was used to it. But for the sake of his brothers, Jimmy walked over and tapped Mr. Ben on the sole of his shoe. He cracked opened one eye and tried to focus. Jimmy said, "You're snoring again." Benjamin T. Putnam was silent as he moistened his mouth and went back to napping.

It was not long before the captain blew the whistle as the paddle boat neared the dock. Jimmy went and shook his boss. "Wake up Mr. Ben. The boat is here." Benjamin T. Putnam got up and splashed some water in his face. He adjusted his Panama hat and then lit another cigar. He went dockside and started yelling at the stevedores; instructing them on how to tie off the paddle boat as if they didn't know.

Mr. Blakely was the first to disembark. He proceeded to the office and greeted Jimmy. Jimmy said, "I have two new customers for you." He then introduced his brothers. Pop explained what he and his brother had in mind.

Mr. Blakely, an honest and hard working man, was impressed with their entrepreneurship. He also had a lot of experience in the retail business. "I know what products will sell. Coffee, tea, sugar, and bars of soap are always in demand. When you buy coffee from me, it comes in a twenty five pound bag. I charge you eighteen cents a pound because it is in bulk. You price it at twenty five cents a pound. When you sell the entire bag, you have made one dollar and seventy five cents profit. You need a scale to weigh out a pound. I have one in my office that I don't use any more. I will give it to you. Soap is a hot item and it is a good profit maker. You buy it from me at three cents a bar and then you sell it for a nickel." Mr. Blakely then asked, "Can you read and write as well as you brother?"

Pop answered, "Yes sir. No only can we read and write better than he can but we are a lot better at arithmetic."

Jimmy was not going to let that snide remark pass without comment. "Don't forget who is financing your business venture."

Billy was more conciliatory, "Jimmy is smarter than both of us."

Mr. Blakely laughed. "Billy, at least you are smart enough not to look a gift horse in the mouth." He continued, "I don't see any reason why you two aren't a success. I will put an order together of items that I think will easily sell. I will also tell you what I think is a good selling price. If your customers want to make a special order for maple syrup, yeast, gum or whatever, I will do my best in filling that order. I'll will see the two of you right here one week from today."

Pop and Billy thanked Mr. Blakely and said good bye to Jimmy. They headed out to the house. They were excited. They now had a home delivery grocery business.

The next week moved at a snail's pace for Pop and Billy. They spent their week in making contacts with potential customers. They had a long list of special orders. When school was dismissed, they headed for the docks pulling two wagons. The paddle boat had already arrived and was being unloaded. They searched the dock area until they found Mr. Blakely. He was happy to see the O'Malley twins. Their enthusiasm was obvious. Mr. Blakely teased them, "Hello boys. I am sorry to tell you that I couldn't get your order finished. It will be next week."

Pop and Billy's excitement quickly turned to disappointment.

"I am just kidding. Your order is sitting on the side of the office."

Pop and Billy lit up. Pop said, "Mr. Blakely you shouldn't joke like that. We are too young to die from a heart attack."

Mr. Blakely amusingly answered, "I wouldn't want that to happen. You haven't paid me yet."

Pop and Billy laughed as they handed Mr. Blakely their special order list.

Mr. Blakely scanned over it and said, "I don't see a problem in filling this order." He presented the O'Malley boys with an invoice, to which, they immediately paid. The shear size of their order was larger than they had anticipated. It required two trips to the house. They sat on the front porch portioning out a pound of coffee and then pouring it into a small paper bag. They did the same thing with the sugar, flour, and corn meal. Word traveled fast. Nearby neighbors were steadily coming by and making purchases. Pop and Billy prepared for the next day by loading the two wagons with a sampling of everything they had ordered.

After school the next day, they started out going door to door. They were met by happy customers and happy customers will continue to buy week after week. At the end of the day, Pop and Billy were confident that their business was going to be prosperous...and it was. Over the next several years, the business steadily grew. They paid Jimmy back with interest. The mode of transportation was upgraded by the purchase of a horse and wagon.

The O'Malley brothers were doing well. Then, metaphorically, disaster struck. There was a new student in their class. Her name was Sarah Murphy. She and her family had recently moved to New Dublin from Jefferson City. Her father and two older brothers were going to till the soil...something that her father did prior to coming to America. She was a cute sixteen years old with beautiful red hair. The O'Malley brothers along with Albert and Sean were acting like bumbling buffoons. They were falling all over each other in an effort to garner her attention. Their heightened friendly rivalry was in full force. Mrs. O'Malley noticed the interest the boys had in Sarah the moment she entered the classroom. She assigned Sarah a seat in the back as far away as physically possible from the love struck boys. Sarah was a smart girl who had been in the tenth grade in the Jefferson City School District. Mrs. O'Malley quietly had a sense of self satisfaction. Her students at the same grade level were far more advanced. Mrs. O'Malley would remedy that with some special attention.

Over the next several weeks, the boys made Sarah the center of attention. Sarah was enjoying all the doting but she never gave any indication that she favored any one boy. Pop soon realized that winning the heart of Sarah was a lost cause. He decided that he had enough. He was not going to make a fool of himself anymore. He would let the others battle for her affection. But little did he know that Sarah had made a decision. It was Pop from the very first day. Pop had isolated himself from the others. For the next several days, he ate his lunch with some of the younger kids while his brothers, Sean and Albert ate their lunch with Sarah. She didn't like the fact that Pop was ignoring her. One day at lunch and without saying a word, Sarah got up and went over and sat down next to Pop. This was the beginning...the beginning of a life long love affair. Billy, Jimmy, Sean, and Albert all looked at each other with astonishment. The game was over and Pop had won.

From that day forward Pop and Sarah were inseparable. Every day she rode with Pop and Billy as they made their rounds selling their groceries. Pop established his route so that his last stop was at Sarah's house.

The school year was coming to an end. The make up of the class will change. Jimmy, Billy, and Pop will graduate. Even though there were two years different in their ages, they were all educationally equal. Their mother felt that she could teach them no more. They needed exposure to advanced studies. Billy and Jimmy traveled to Jefferson City and made application to Independence University. They excelled on the entrance exam. The admission office found a scholarship program set aside for the children of veterans of the Spanish American war. It was not a full scholarship but along with the money Billy and Jimmy had saved, they could financially afford to go to college full time without the worry of finding a part time job. They received notification from Independence University whereby both were accepted for the fall semester. Pop decided that he would stay in New Dublin and manage the ever growing grocery business. He was of the belief that the business could support him and Sarah should they ever decide to get married.

Jimmy continued to work throughout the summer. He kept telling Benjamin T. Putnam that he was quitting in August to attend college but Mr. Putnam was in a state of denial. He thought, through a stroke of luck, that Jimmy would change his mind. Mr. Putnam even offered Jimmy more money in hopes that it would convince him to stay. When this failed, Benjamin T. Putnam was in a pickle. He knew that without Jimmy, he was doomed. Jimmy asked Sean if he wanted to replace him at the docks. Sean eagerly accepted the offer but after two weeks on the job, he quit. He told Jimmy, "The man is impossible. I don't how you worked for him for over eight years." Jimmy then offered the position to Albert. Albert didn't even give it consideration. "If Sean can't get along with Benjamin T. Putnam, I wouldn't last one day." Poor Mr. Putnam...his future was bleak.

It was the day that Jimmy and Billy were departing for college. Their mother, Pop, Sarah, Sean, and Albert were all there on the dock to see them off. Benjamin T. Putnam looked tired. Apparently he had not been getting his afternoon naps since Jimmy left. Jimmy and Billy boarded; each carried a suitcase. As the boat pulled away from the dock, they waved good-bye. Alice stayed until the paddle boat disappeared. It brought back memories. It was on this dock...in the very same spot that she last saw her husband. She felt an inner peace to know that her boys were going off to school and not off to war.

Jimmy and Billy found their dormitory room. Billy was still fascinated with electricity. He flipped the light switch off and on until Jimmy threatened to break his finger if he didn't stop. Fortunately for Jimmy, Billy's obsession was short lived. Electric lights in Jefferson City were commonplace. Billy read an article in the *Gazette* regarding the United Gas and Electric Company. The company set out an aggressive expansion plan. They had budgeted funds to expand their electric transmission lines northward into the rural areas but due to the high cost, they would only be able to expand at a pace of ten miles a year. Billy thought this was good news but it would still be five years before they reached New Dublin.

Jimmy and Billy quickly adapted into college life. Academics came first but they soon mastered the art of revelry. The O'Malley brothers were good looking young men. Jefferson City had an abundance of attractive young women. It was a combination that Jimmy and Billy took advantage of, especially on the weekends. But no matter how many wild oats were sowed the night before, they were both in church on Sunday morning.

By the end of their sophomore year, their revelry had turned into reverence. They were now attending daily Mass. They befriended Father Matthews. He was the Associate Pastor at St. Theresa's which was located several blocks from the University. He was young, outgoing, and friendly. They were impressed as to how he interacted with the parishioners. He always had a smile on his face. He was a cornucopia of corny jokes.

Occasionally, Jimmy and Billy would join Father Matthews for breakfast at the Rectory. One morning, Jimmy asked, "Father, how did you know that you wanted to become a Priest?"

"That's an interesting question. Apparently, you have been toying with the idea."

"Billy and I have talked about it."

"But to answer your question...it's a process." With humor, he continued, "You don't wake up one morning and ask yourself, what am I going to do today? Oh I know. I will become a Priest. It is a whole lot more complicated than that. God will guide you. Obviously, He has started you on the path. You need to pray for guidance. You have years of schooling to finish before you have to make that final decision. By that time, you will know."

Billy had another question. "What about celibacy? Jimmy and I still like the ladies."

Father Matthews couldn't let this moment pass without kidding his young friends. He looked around the kitchen as if to make sure no one could overhear them even though they were the only ones in the room. He motioned for Jimmy and Billy to lean toward the middle of the table. Father Matthews also leaned it. Jimmy and Billy were anticipating that Father Matthews was about to reveal some centuries old priestly secret. Father Matthews whispered, "I like the ladies too." He leaned back in his chair and laughed out loud. In his normal voice, he said, "Of course, I like the ladies. I may be a Priest but I am still a man. If you guys didn't have an attraction to members of the opposite sex, then I would think there was something wrong with you." Father Matthews continued seriously. "Celibacy is a sacrifice. You fight temptation through prayer and mental discipline. It is a lot easier than one might think."

"That is good to hear," responded Billy.

Father Matthews continued, "I suggest that when you go home you should talk with your father and asked for his advice."

Jimmy said, "Our father died in the Spanish American War."

"I am sorry. Bless his soul."

"Thank you."

"Is there another father figure in your life?"

Billy answered, "Yes there is. It is Father Maher. Our father was his friend."

"I know him well. He is perfect. Excuse the pun but he can give you some good "fatherly" advice."

Jimmy responded, "That was bad."

"I know but both of you are smiling. If there is one thing that you learn from me is this...I have dedicated my life to Jesus Christ. That doesn't mean that I can't have fun and be religious too. Sometimes a good laugh and a smile can work miracles."

Billy answered, "That is good advice." Billy along with Jimmy stood. "We've got to go or we'll be late for class."

"Give my regards to Father Maher."

"We will Father. See you later."

****

The spring semester was over. Jimmy and Billy packed their suitcases and set out on the three mile walk to the dock. Father Maher was there. Apparently this was his weekend to go to New Dublin.

Father Maher was happy to see them. "Well, if it's not the O'Malley brothers."

Both of them replied, "Hello, Father."

The three of them boarded. They decided to sit out on the deck. It was a beautiful Friday morning. Their conversation was general in nature until Jimmy brought up the subject of the priesthood. Father Maher was pleased to hear that both Billy and Jimmy were contemplating a life of service to Christ. They discussed all the aspects of being a priest.

Father Maher had a caveat. "I must forewarn you. St. Joseph Seminary is isolated. It is about one hundred miles from New Dublin. You can't get there by boat or train. You have to travel by foot, horseback, or carriage. The Seminary is self-sustaining. You will be a student but you will also be assigned chores. You may be a farmer, cattleman, carpenter, or whatever. With that said, do you want me to talk to the Bishop?"

Billy answered, "Yes, Father, we definitely want to go to the Seminary. Like Father Matthews said, we have years of schooling before we have to make that final decision." As an after thought, Jimmy continued, "Oh, Father Matthews sends his regards."

"Father Matthews is an excellent young priest. He is one of my favorites."

The Captain blew the whistle as they neared the dock. Father Maher and the O'Malley brothers gathered at the rail. Father Maher said, "I see a welcoming party. I don't think they are here for me." He was right. It was Alice, Pop, Sarah, Sean, and Albert. It had been months since Billy and Jimmy had been home. Homecoming was always special for the O'Malley family and friends. Everyone piled onto Pop's horse drawn wagon. Pop called out, "Hop on Father. I will give you a ride to the church." He jumped on the back between Sean and Ryan. Their legs were dangling off the end of the wagon.

That evening, Alice had prepared a feast. It had been awhile since her whole family had sat down for a meal. It met with everyone's satisfaction. When supper was ended, Pop had an announcement to make. "Sarah and I wanted to wait until Jimmy and Billy got home. We have decided to get married. We have to schedule the wedding with Father Maher but we plan to get married next month."

Alice was ecstatic. She got up and hugged Sarah and Pop. "You two have made me so happy."

Jimmy requested, "Mama, you may want to sit back down. Billy and I have more good news."

Alice sat back down with a questionable look on her face.

"Billy and I have decided to enroll in St. Joseph's Seminary. Father Maher is working out the details."

The tears began to flow. "This has got to be the greatest day of my life. I wish your father could be here. He would be beaming with pride."

****

It was a simple wedding. It was well attended as are all weddings in New Dublin. It was a festive occasion. After the reception, the couple boarded the paddle boat for a three day honeymoon to Jefferson City. Family and friends congregated on the dock to see them off. Pop and Sarah could not be gone too long because they had a business to run. They planned to stay with Alice temporarily until they saved up enough money to build their own house. If Alice had her way, the young couple could stay there forever.

Father Maher brought a signed letter from the Bishop on his next visit to New Dublin. It was a letter of acceptance for Jimmy and Billy to attend St. Joseph's Seminary. The letter gave a date to which the boys had to be present for the beginning of classes. It was only a week away. Over the years, Alice had been diligent in saving her widow's pension. It was her nest egg fund to be used for rainy days or for her children. Alice bought a horse and covered carriage for Jimmy and Billy to travel to and from the seminary. There was enough money remaining to help Pop and Sarah in building their new house.

It was Sunday morning. Pop had provided enough provisions for the three day trip. Alice furnished some cooking utensils. The carriage was almost loaded. They brought along their father's double barreled shotgun. It was needed for protection or for the killing of wild game should their food supply run low. Jimmy and Billy walked out of the house carrying their suitcases and bedrolls. They proceeded to the church for morning Mass. Father Maher asked the congregation to pray for Jimmy and Billy to have a safe journey. When church was over, everyone stood by awaiting their departure. Jimmy and Billy kissed their mother good-bye. Sarah and Pop consoled her. This would be the last time she would see them for at least six months. The O'Malley brothers climbed into the carriage. Father Maher offered a blessing. "May almighty God bless you in the name of the Father, the Son and the Holy Ghost." Billy snapped the reins and they were on their way. Father Maher had informed them that they would be traveling through the wilderness. There were no towns between New Dublin and St. Joseph's Seminary. He said let the wagon trail be your guide. It would lead them directly to the edge of the Seminary. Jimmy and Billy were excited about their trip. It would be an adventure.

Since the first day they acquired the carriage, Jimmy and Billy had tried to come up with an appropriate name for their horse. Shortly into their trip, Jimmy said, "I have the perfect name! I have been staring at this horse's butt for the last two hours. It reminds me of my former illustrious boss. Henceforth our horse shall be called *Putnam*." They both laughed but the name stuck.

They bedded down the first night in a field next to a small stream. This would allow Putnam to have food and water. As night fell, they built a small fire and prepared their bedding underneath the carriage. Morning came quickly. They stoked the fire until there were hot coals. Pop had given them plenty of ground coffee. The iron skillet was used to fry some eggs and heat pieces of smoked ham. It was delicious...so delicious that they would have the same breakfast the next morning. They cleaned the coffee pot and skillet in the stream. They hitched up the carriage to Putnam and were back on their way. On many stretches of the trail, the trees had overgrown to form a natural canopy. It was like riding through a tunnel. Deer and other critters were abundant...even a black bear. It stepped out onto the trail and stopped. He turned his head and stared at the oncoming carriage. Putnam spooked. He reared up onto his hind legs but Billy was able to keep him under control. Jimmy reached back and grabbed the shotgun. It was a short standoff but finally the bear ambled off into the forest. They waited a few minutes. Billy then said, "Giddy-up Putnam." They passed the spot where the bear was last seen and Putnam remained calm. They were out of danger.

After breakfast the next morning, the O'Malley brothers continued their journey. They didn't have a clue as to where they were or how far they had come but they were confident that they were getting close. Mid afternoon they knew they had arrived. It was beautiful...picturesque would be a better description. The church dominated the small hill that overlooked a large lake that had been formed by damming up the creek that flowed across the property. There were four out buildings that Jimmy and Billy presumed to be for housing and classrooms. There was a large barn painted bright red. Crops were growing in the field and livestock grazed in the wide open pasture. Billy guided Putnam across the wooden bridge and entered the grounds of St. Joseph Seminary. Father Slovka, the son of Polish immigrants, was the headmaster. He greeted them.

Father Slovka was not fat but he was somewhat over weight. This pleased Jimmy...at least there would not be a lot of fasting. Billy and Jimmy introduced themselves and gave him a packet of documents that included the Bishop's letter and a copy of their transcripts from Independence University. Father Slovka glanced through them. "I see you two are from New Dublin. I go through there to catch the boat down to Jefferson City. This seminary is in the Diocese of Jefferson City and I have to make an annual pilgrimage to pay homage to the Bishop Almighty."

Billy asked, "Do I note a hint of hostility?"

"The Bishop is a burr under my saddle. He is always giving me suggestions and recommendations as to how to run this seminary but he has never step foot on these grounds. He is a city boy. I personally think that he may be intimidated about sleeping on the ground. He is a good man and I know that he means well but I find his attitude downright arrogant when it comes to this school."

Billy continued the conversation. "Father Maher had warned us about you. He said that you didn't mince words and that you did not hesitate in speaking your mind."

"Now, that Father Maher is a real priest. I would say that he is the best priest in the whole diocese. I admit that I may have a slight bias. I am the one who taught him everything he knows."

By this time, all the other seminarians, priests and brothers had circled the carriage. Father Slovka took his time and introduced everyone to Billy and Jimmy.

Jimmy said to Father Slovka, "You and I have crossed paths before. I worked at the docks in New Dublin for about eight years."

He studied Jimmy's face. "I remember you but you have grown up."

Billy interjected, "He has grown physically but mentally he is still a child."

Father Slovka laughed. "I see you boys will fit in just fine around here." He then instructed Brother Lambert to get them settled in.

****

Over the next several years, the grocery business continued to grow. More customers were actually coming to the house versus buying from the horse driven wagon. It was time to make plans to move out of Alice's house. Pop and Sarah had already stayed a year longer than they had originally planned.

Sean had become a successful businessman. He opened a hardware store. Almost immediately, he was making a profit. He never looked back. He foresaw that Main St. was going to be the center of commerce for New Dublin. He bought every piece of property that came available. He teamed up with his friend, Albert, who at that time, had a fledging construction company.

Sean was the developer. Albert took the plans and completed the project to Sean's specifications. Their friendship never faltered as many do when money is involved.

Pop and Sarah dropped by the hardware store. They discussed with Sean that they wanted to build a grocery store with living quarters on the second floor. They wanted indoor plumbing and the building wired for electricity even though the United Gas and Electric Co. would not reach New Dublin for another six months. Pop wanted a deep well drilled in the back of the store so that there could be running water with the use of an electric water pump. Sean had the perfect piece of property. It was on the corner of Main St. and First Ave. Pop and Sarah paid cash. Alice tried to give them money from her savings but they refused. They preferred that she use that money to upgrade her house.

Pop needed a sign to go in front of the store. He knew of only one person that had the talent to perform the task at hand. It was Father Maher but would he agree to do it? Pop wasn't taking any chances. On Friday morning, Pop was at the dock with his horse drawn wagon. He was standing there when Father Maher walked across the plank. "Good morning, Father. Do you need a ride to the church?"

"Good morning, Pop. Sure...it beats walking."

Pop reached down and took Father Maher's bag. Father Maher was becoming skeptical. Pop was up to something. "OK, what do you want?"

"Father, I am offended. You are the nicest Priest that I have ever known. Can't someone offer a good gesture without you thinking of an ulterior motive?"

"First, if I am not mistaking, I am the only Priest that you know. So, I could also be the meanest Priest you have ever known. Both would be truthful. You have O'Malley blood flowing through those veins and I know the bloodline well. I am going to ask you again, what do you want?"

Pop took Father Maher's bag and threw it in the back. The two of them climbed into the seat. Pop answered, "I want to know if you would be so kind as to paint a sign to go in front of my store?"

Father Maher humorously answered, "Of course I will but as a renowned artist, I must charge a mere pittance. To do otherwise would be an insult to all the artists who have gone before me."

"This doesn't sound good."

"My son, my son, do not forsake me. All I ask for is a pound of coffee, a pound of tea and a pound of sugar. I am just a humble man."

"Yeah...a devious humble man. I have no other choice than to accept your demands."

Father Maher in more serious tone said, "I will need some supplies."

Pop pointed to the back of the wagon. "I am way ahead of you. I have a board, paint and brushes. I would like it to be red with white lettering on both sides. It should read *Pop's Grocery*." Pop joked, "I thought of that all by myself."

"Your mother must be so proud. I will try and work on the sign tomorrow if I don't get too busy in church work."

"Thanks, Father."

After Sunday Mass, Father Maher asked Pop and Sarah to stay until everyone had left. He took them around to the back of the church and showed them the sign. It was professionally done and everything Pop had expected. "Father, you do have the talent."

"Thanks, I hope you like it."

"We do," said Sarah.

Father Maher and Pop carried the sign out to the wagon. They laid it down on a blanket so that it wouldn't get marred. Pop pulled out a bag. It was his end of the bargain. "I think I got the better end of this deal."

"I don't know about that. Every time I walk into your store, I will look up and admire my handy work."

The next day Albert was steadily finishing up the store. He was working on the counter and shelves. Pop coaxed him into helping him in hanging the sign. They hung it underneath the wooden awning that protruded out over the sidewalk. The name could be read from both directions. Albert and Pop stood back and looked at the sign. Albert said, "It won't be long before *Pop's Grocery* will be open for business. You can start stocking the shelves. You won't be in my way."

Pop headed back to the house. He and Sarah began to load the wagon from their storeroom which doubled as the living room. Alice never said anything but she would be happy when all the groceries were gone. They made two trips. They thought that they had a lot of inventory but after they stocked the shelves with what they had, they realized that the majority of the shelves were empty. They would have to start doubling up the orders with Mr. Blakely.

The front screen door opened. It was Mrs. Shanahan. She was a widow. She and her daughter lived in a small house on the edge of town. She picked up a few items and took them to the counter.

Sarah waited on her. "Congratulations, Mrs. Shanahan. You are our first customer in our new store."

"I feel honored. You and Pop have a lovely place here."

"Over time we will fill these shelves with a wide variety of groceries."

"Are you going to sell any pies?"

"We don't plan to at this time."

"I make apple, peach and blueberry pies. I am always getting compliments as to how good they are. If I make a pie, can you buy it from me for fifty cents? You can sell it at whatever price you want."

"Mrs. Shanahan that is an excellent idea. I normally don't like dealing with perishable goods because of spoilage but if I can sell your pie in a day or two then I will keep buying from you. Can you bring me a pie tomorrow morning? We will see how well it sells."

"That's fair enough, Sarah."

At exactly 6:45 the next morning, Mrs. Shanahan entered Pop's Grocery. She was carrying two pies. She told Sarah, "You can pay me for one pie now. You don't owe me anything on the other pie unless it sells. I will check back with you later this evening."

Sarah reached under the counter and pulled out a wooden box. It contained cash and coins. She took out fifty cents and paid Mrs. Shanahan. "If these pies taste as good as they look, we won't have a problem in selling them."

Later that morning, a man entered the store. Pop knew everyone in town and he had never seen this stranger before. He was a tall, well over six feet. His cowboy hat had been well worn. He was well tanned in the face, typical of a man who works outdoors. Pop asked, "May I help you?"

"Yes sir. My name is George Campbell. I am with the electric company crew. We are working down the road a piece. I came to town to pick up a few supplies."

"My wife and I just built this store. We had electric wires installed awaiting your arrival. How much longer will it be?"

"We have been averaging about a mile a month and we're about two miles south of here."

"It's going to be the longest two months. I can't wait to walk in here and switch on these lights." Pop had made enough small talk. "Let's get your order filled."

George starting clearing the shelves. A "few supplies" turned out to be the largest single sale Pop had ever made. George saw the two pies, "Are these for sale?"

Sarah joined into the conversation. "Yes sir. The whole pie is seventy five cents or ten cents a slice."

"How about giving me a slice." George asked, "Are they any good?"

Sarah answered, "I don't know. I have never tasted one. A local widow lady made them and asked us to sell them for her. Pop and I will join you."

The three of them stood at the counter and ate their slices. George commented. "That was fantastic. Both of you should strongly consider putting this lady on the payroll. I will take that whole pie." George then asked for a pencil and some paper. He started making a list of supplies he would need next week. It was twice as large as what he bought today. "I will need the same supplies every week along with three pies. My men are going to like these."

Pop explained to George, "My wholesaler will be here today with my regular order. I will give him your list and your supplies will be here next Tuesday but it won't be ready for you to pick up until Wednesday."

"That will work for me."

Pop joked, "Forget about what I said earlier. If you are going to buy this many groceries every week, I want you to take your time in getting here."

George thought that was funny. "I will see what I can do. A little more good news for you. When we get to town, we expect to be here for months hooking up customers who want electricity."

"My friend Albert who wired this store is loaded down with work. He went through classes at your company in Jefferson City to learn how to be an electrician."

"That's good to know. People don't realize how dangerous electricity can be. If you don't know what you are doing, it can kill you."

Sarah wrote up the bill. George scanned it. "You forgot the slice of pie."

Sarah said, "After what you bought here today, it's on the house."

"Thank you ma'am." George then inquired, "Do you know where I can buy a shovel and an axe?"

"There is a hardware store two blocks down on the left side. Sean Ryan is the owner. He can help you."

Sarah and Pop stood at the window and watched George ride off. When they felt confident that they wouldn't be seen, they hugged each other and started dancing all around the store. They stopped when they heard the whistle blast from the paddle boat. Pop told Sarah, "I've got to go and meet Mr. Blakely."

Pop pulled his wagon to a stop at the foot of the dock. He tied the horse to the hitching post. Mr. Blakely was busy with several farmers in buying their produce. He saw Pop. "I'll be with you in a few minutes."

"Take your time. I will go ahead and load my order."

Pop had a big grin on his face when Mr. Blakely met up with him. He said, "Pop, you look like the fox that finally made it into the hen house."

"Even better, Mr. Blakely." Pop handed him his special order.

Mr. Blakely looked at it and replied, "This is your biggest order yet."

"I know. This is going to be my special order every week for the next four or five months. It is for the crew from United Gas and Electric Company. They are the ones stringing the power lines to New Dublin."

"I am happy for you and Sarah."

"I know you are. I want you to come and see our new store. We opened yesterday."

The two of them boarded the wagon and headed for Main St. Mr. Blakely was impressed with the exterior. He added, "I like your sign."

"Father Maher did that for me."

"He did a good job."

They entered through the screen door. Sarah greeted them. Sarah acted as tour guide and showed him the downstairs and the upstairs. Mr. Blakely was glad for both Pop and Sarah, the same as he would have been if they had been his own children. But he was critical. "This place is bare, bare, bare." The three of them sat down. Mr. Blakely began by giving them some sound business advice. "Both of you have said that you didn't want credit but there are times when credit is a good thing. You need to fill these shelves now. I know exactly what you need. I have many customers that have grocery stores just like yours. Next week, be prepared to spend days in putting up stock. You can pay me back a little bit at a time. If by chance your business fails, you don't owe me a thing. That is how much confidence I have in you two."

Pop and Sarah sat there absorbing everything that Mr. Blakely was saying. He offered them assurance that he would do exactly what he said he would do. "Pop, since the time you and Billy started this business, have I ever lied to you or cheated you in any way?"

"No sir. In fact you have always given us the benefit of your experience that has kept us from making stupid mistakes."

"With that said, I want you to trust me. This is the best way for your business."

The three of them stood. Pop shook Mr. Blakely's hand. Sarah gave him a hug. "Thank you, Mr. Blakely."

Pop then said, "Let me give you a ride back to the dock."

"No. I'd rather walk. It's a beautiful day."

They stood at the window until Mr. Blakely was out of sight. With the exception of their wedding, this had to be the best day of their young lives. They danced some more.

It was near closing time when Mrs. Shanahan, accompanied by her daughter Shannon, returned. She asked Sarah, "Did the pies sell today?"

"Yes ma'am. Pop and I had a slice. It was delicious. Two pies a day will be fine but I have two special orders. On Tuesday morning, I will need a total of three pies. On Wednesday, I will need five. Can you make five pies in one day?"

Mrs. Shanahan was happy to hear that her pies were so well received. She answered Sarah, "Yes I can make five pies but that is the most I can do in one day."

Sarah pulled out her wooden change box. She paid Mrs. Shanahan the fifty cents she owed her. "Have a good evening. I will see you in the morning."

Business was steady all week and there was hardly any inventory left by Tuesday morning. Sarah and Pop were glad that their order would be in today. They were filled with anticipation wondering as to what Mr. Blakely had decided to send. The paddle boat whistle was heard. Sarah placed a sign in the window to let their customers know that they would be gone for an hour. Sarah and Pop rode down to the dock. They were met by Sarah's two brothers, who had agreed to help.

Mr. Blakely presented Pop with an invoice. It was for $ 1207.47. Pop was somewhat shocked but he trusted Mr. Blakely. Mr. Blakely explained that he had added interest and that every week there would be an extra charge on each invoice of $ 8.00 a week for the next three years until the debt was paid off. Sarah and Pop agreed to the conditions of the loan.

Sarah presented a pie to Mr. Blakely. "There is no charge. This is our way of saying thank you."

The wagon was filled to capacity three times. Massive amounts of physical labor were expended in loading and unloading, but the entire order was finally sitting on the floor in the store. There was little room left to move about without stepping on something. Pop and Sarah immediately went to work. Pop began getting George Campbell's order ready for tomorrow morning. Sarah took one box at a time and emptied the contents onto the shelves. They brought out several kerosene lanterns so that they could keep working well after sunset. They toiled late into the night. They went home and managed to get several hours of sleep before they were back at the store. They opened the store just before Mrs. Shanahan arrived at 6:45 a.m. with her five pies. Sarah paid her and went straight back to stocking shelves.

Pop had George Campbell's order ready. Pop was relieved when he saw George ride up. There was always that possibility that Mr. Campbell would not come back. He walked through the door and looked around. "This is a whole lot different than when I was here last week. I can see that you two have been busy."

Sarah responded, "You're right. It's been non stop." Sarah got up and went to the counter. "I have your bill here but I haven't totaled it up yet. Is there anything else that you are going to buy?"

"No. This is it."

Pop said, "I will help you load this up."

****

Jimmy and Billy hitched Putnam to a wagon. They were not using the carriage because they were carrying a small kitchen table with chairs that Jimmy had built in the carpentry shop. In the short time he spent with his father, Jimmy learned some of the basics in building furniture. Brother Lambert, also a master carpenter, continued in being a great teacher. They had the shotgun, suitcases and provisions. Billy snapped the reins. "Giddy-up Putnam." They were underway for the long trek back to New Dublin.

Three days on the road was uneventful. This was the first time they had been home in six months. It was impossible to write letters so they were unfamiliar with the events that had happened during this time period. Billy turned Putnam onto Main St. heading toward their mother's house. They noticed several new buildings and they were surprised to see one with a sign that said "Pop's Grocery."

Jimmy said to Billy, "Well look here. Our brother has made it to the big time."

Billy pulled up on Putnam in front of the store. He tied off to one of the columns. They went inside. Pop was sitting behind the counter. He was happy to see his brothers. As he walked around the counter, he yelled to Sarah, "We have company." The three of them hugged. Sarah came out and hugged them too.

Jimmy said as he peered around the store, "This is real nice. Pop, it is obvious that you made the right decision in dumping Billy as a partner. He was just holding you back."

Billy responded. "You don't understand Jimmy. He would not have done as well as he has if I had not taught him everything he knows."

Pop put his arm around Sarah. "You're both wrong. Sarah is the brains behind this operation."

Jimmy said, "Now that makes sense."

Sarah was getting real good as being a tour guide. She showed Jimmy and Billy around the store and then they went upstairs. Sarah and Pop were living there but the furnishings were sparse. When they got to the kitchen, Jimmy asked "What is this?"

Sarah, with a sense of humor said, "That is our dinner table and chairs. Your brother built it all by himself. Aren't you proud of him?" Sarah was referring to a large empty crate box turned upside down. This was the dinner table. There were two smaller wooden crates that substituted for chairs.

Jimmy said, "Let's get this out of here. Billy and I have brought you a house warming gift." The four of them carried the empty crates downstairs and out the back door. They walked back through the store to the wagon out front. They unloaded the table and four chairs and took them upstairs. Pop and Sarah were pleased. The quality of the craftsmanship guaranteed that the table and chairs would some day become a family heirloom.

Sarah said, "Thanks to the both of you. This is beautiful."

Billy responded, "Don't thank me. Jimmy made it with his own two hands. Pop and I are twins and we are alike in many ways. I couldn't have done any better than Pop's creation."

"This calls for a celebration," Sarah said as she looked at Pop. "Go downstairs and get us a peach pie."

It was time for Alice to be home from school. According to Sarah, Alice had been antsy all week anticipating her boys' homecoming. Jimmy and Billy were about to leave heading for the house. Sarah insisted that Pop accompany them. She would stay and be along after closing time.

Alice was ecstatic when her three sons entered through the front door. After a tearful reunion, she did what most mothers do...cook. She instructed the boys to get some firewood for the stove. She glanced out the window and smiled. Pop, Billy, and Jimmy were grown men but the kid in them came out from time to time. They were playing "rock, paper, scissors" to determine who was going to chop wood. As always, Billy lost.

****

George Campbell entered Pop's Grocery along with two members of his crew. Pop was concerned. "You're here early. I don't have you order ready."

George smiled. "You need not worry. We are here to hook up your electricity. Your life will be better in about an hour."

Pop had developed a friendly relationship with George. "What are you waiting for...get started."

George and his crew were busy outside. When they finished, George reentered the store. George was standing by the light switch next to the front door. "Sarah, you have the honor."

Sarah walked over and turned the knob to the "on" position. The overhead lights lit up. She and Pop rejoiced. George then said "Let's go into the storage room and check to see if the pump is properly wired. Sarah turned the switch beside the sink. The sound of the water pump could be heard kicking on out back. Sarah cut the water on. It spit and sputtered but gradually a steady flow of water began to fill the sink. The three of them checked all the lights and the water supply upstairs. Everything was working properly. George left to move onto the next building.

Sarah then rushed upstairs. Pop asked, "Where are you going?"

She answered, "I can't wait to use indoor plumbing for the first time in my life."

Jimmy and Billy came to visit. They immediately noticed the electric lights. Billy began turning the light switch off and on. Jimmy was annoyed. He said, "What is this fascination you have with light switches?"

Billy tried to explain. "God gave us brains to solve complex problems. Men like Alva Edison used their minds to discover ways to harness electricity. It is so amazing to me. This is the greatest invention of the nineteenth century. Think about it.

There is a power plant in Jefferson City generating electricity. They take that electricity and send it fifty miles over wires right to this light switch and I can turn that electricity off or on just by turning this little knob."

Sarcastically Jimmy replied, "I now understand but I have one word for you...STOP!"

For no other reason than to irritate his brother, Billy turned the switch off and on one more time.

Within the next two weeks George Campbell and his crew connected all the houses and business that were ready for electricity. This included Alice's house. George stopped by Pop's Grocery to say good-bye to his new found friends. "We have reached the end of the line. We are heading back to Jefferson City but we will be back from time to time to hook up new customers and to service the existing lines."

Sarah said, "Be sure to come by. There is always a piece of pie waiting for you."

"That alone may be worth the trip."

Pop shook hands with George. "Be safe on the trip back."

"Thanks,"

George Campbell was not the only one making a trip. With Putnam leading the way, the two O'Malley brothers set out on the first leg of their final trek to and from the Seminary. This will be their last year.

****

Pop and Sarah began carrying the Jefferson City Gazette but some of the newspapers were a week behind. This didn't seem to matter. More and more of the locals were learning how to read. All thanks to Alice. Pop looked at the front page of the most current edition. The headline was highlighting the sinking of the RMS Titanic on April 15, 1912. This news hit close to home. Sean had been telling everyone about his cousin Michael who was immigrating to America to take a job with Sean. He was to travel from Dublin down to Queenstown where the RMS Titanic would make a port of call prior to the voyage across the Atlantic Ocean. Michael had chosen the RMS Titanic because it was the most modern ship sailing to America and the steerage accommodations were the best of any ocean liner.

Pop showed the article to Sarah and after she read it, he left to go to the hardware store. Sean was behind the counter waiting on a customer. Pop stood to the side until they finished.

Sean was always glad to see his friend. "Well, if its not my favorite O'Malley brother."

Pop didn't want to joke back because of the nature of his visit. "Is your cousin still coming to America?"

"Yes. I expect him to be here around the first of the month. Why do you ask?"

Pop didn't answer. He just handed the paper to Sean. Sean said as he began to read the article, "This is terrible." Sean read further and tried to be optimistic. "It says here that there are 705 survivors. Maybe he made it. I guess I won't know for sure unless he shows up here. If he didn't survive, I will get a letter from his parents. Let's hope for the best."

Pop was sympathetic. "I am sorry that I had to be the bearer of bad news."

"You need not apologize. I prefer hearing the news from you than any one else. Thanks for coming by."

The following week, Sean went to the dock every time the paddle boat was scheduled to arrive. Twice, he stood there and watched every passenger disembark but Michael was not one of them. If Michael is not on the next boat to arrive on Tuesday, then Michael is not one of the survivors. Tuesday morning came. Pop was at the dock waiting to pick up his order. He was standing next to Sean when the gang plank was lowered. They stood there in great anticipation. There was a rush of passengers at first. Then they trickled off. Sean was becoming discouraged. A young man appeared on the deck. He was dressed in a worn, snug fitting suit. He was wearing a brown fedora and carrying a large brown paper bag.

Pop leaned over to Sean. "Do you think that might be him?"

"It could be. He looks to be the right age. The clothes he's wearing sure looks that of an immigrant."

Sean approached the man. "Are you Michael Ryan?"

"I am and you must be Sean."

Sean hugged him. "I was beginning to think you were dead."

"You aren't the only one." Michael who spoke in a strong Irish brogue said in a humorous manner, "How do you like my duds? I got them from Catholic Charities in New York City." He pointed to the paper bag. "This is my suitcase. Everything I own is in this bag or I am wearing."

"All that can be replaced. I thank God that you're safe." Sean then introduced Pop.

Pop shook hands with Michael. He said, "If you two guys will give me a hand in loading my supplies, I will give you a ride to the hardware store."

When they finished, the three of them climbed up into the seat on the wagon. Both Pop and Sean desperately wanted to know the details of the sinking of the Titanic. Sean was the first to ask.

Michael began, "It was late at night. I couldn't sleep so I was walking the deck when we hit the iceberg. It knock me to the floor. Just from the sound and force, I knew it was bad. The crew was yelling for all the passengers to prepare to abandoned ship. I helped to load three lifeboats. I believe in that old motto, 'women and children first'. My three lifeboats were full to capacity. I say this because I later learned that many of the lifeboats were only half full or less. From what I could see, all the lifeboats had been cast over the side. I felt that I was a dead man walking. The ship started listing severely. I jumped. The water was freezing. I found a piece of debris and started swimming to the sound of voices. Fortunately, I found one of those lifeboats that was only half full. I was pulled aboard. I had to get out of my wet clothes. Some of the passengers gave up some of their clothing from under their jackets. We were in the water for several hours when we were rescued by the ship *Carpathia*. We were taken to New York City and here I am."

Pop said as he pulled to a stop in front of the hardware store, "The man upstairs was sure with you that night."

Michael responded, "He sure was." He then said, "Thanks for the ride."

****

Jimmy and Billy graduated from the Seminary. They were ready to move on to the next chapter in their lives. But they were also sentimental about leaving. The Seminary had been their home for the past four years. They had developed lasting friendships with their fellow seminarians and the staff. Also, there was the fact that each person residing within the boundaries of the Seminary relied on each other for all the basic needs of life. There was always that sense of responsibility when you were tilling the soil, tending to the livestock or hunting for wild game. You were your brother's keeper. Thanks to Brother Lambert, Jimmy developed artistic skills in crafting furniture. Jimmy graciously accepted a set of wood chisels from Brother Lambert. He knew that Jimmy would continue to build fine pieces of furniture. Father Slovka prepared diplomas and bestowed them upon Billy and Jimmy in a simple ceremony. They were the only two graduating.

Billy and Jimmy hitched Putnam up to the carriage. They were ready to leave. They went around and shook everyone's hand and said their final good-byes. They climbed aboard. Billy snapped the reins, "Giddy-up Putnam". They crossed the wooden bridge and turned east on the wagon trail. They looked back at everyone standing in the courtyard and made their last wave. Upon returning to New Dublin, Jimmy and Billy had no further need for Putnam and the carriage. They were given to Pop. He in turn sold the carriage and gave the proceeds to his mother. Pop put his horse out to pasture and kept Putnam. Putnam was a younger, stronger horse that was able to pull the wooden wagon with little effort.

Jimmy and Billy were ordained at the Cathedral in Jefferson City. Their family was present along with many of their friends who could afford the trip. It was a beautiful ceremony. Billy and Jimmy were assigned as Associate Pastors in two different Parishes within the city limits of Jefferson City.

****

Pop opened the store and after several hours, Sarah still had not come down stairs. He went to check on her. She was in the bed crying. Pop sat down on the bed next to her and asked, "Are you feeling ok?"

"No. I think there is something seriously wrong with me. We have been married for over four years and I haven't been able to get pregnant."

Pop consoled her. "Don't worry about that. It will come in due time."

"There's more. I have these knots in my breasts. I don't know the reason why my mother died so young but maybe it is heredity. I may have what killed her. I am so tired and I keep loosing weight."

"Why haven't you told me this before now?"

"I kept thinking that I would get better. Besides, I didn't want you to worry."

"Get up and get dressed. If we hurry, we can catch the boat to Jefferson City. You are going to the doctor. I will pack a suitcase. We will have to stay three nights and catch the boat back on Friday."

Sarah began dressing. Pop packed the suitcase. He went downstairs and wrote a sign to put on the door. "Gone to Jefferson City on business. We will be open on Friday morning."

They arrived in Jefferson City. They had no clue as to what doctor to go and see. Pop didn't want to contact his brothers or Father Maher. Sarah and Pop boarded a horse driven jitney and went to the city hospital. Pop spoke to the nurse at the reception desk and explained the symptoms that Sarah was encountering and asked if she could recommend a doctor.

The nurse answered. "Doctor Walker is the person you need to see. He is on staff here at the hospital. You won't find a better doctor within five hundred miles." The nurse directed them down the hall.

Sarah checked in with the receptionist. They sat down in the waiting area. Shortly, Sarah was led back to an examination room. The nurse assisted Sarah in putting on a gown. Doctor Walker was an older gentleman. He was cordial and put Sarah at ease. He completed his examination and instructed Sarah to get dressed. Afterwards, the nurse brought Sarah and Pop to the doctor's office. They sat down in the two leather chairs in front of his desk.

Doctor Walker has been practicing medicine for many years. It has never gotten easier to inform a patient of bad news. He exhibited as much compassion as possible from one human being to another but there is no easy way to inform someone of a fatal illness. "Mrs. O'Malley, it is with deep regret but I must tell you of bad news. You have cancer. It has spread throughout your body. The prognosis is not good."

Sarah began to cry.

Pop was numb. He asked, "When you say that the prognosis is not good, what does that mean?"

"It means that there is nothing that can be done to cure the cancer and your wife may have less than six months to live."

Pop questioned the doctor. "Are you sure?"

"I can give you the names of several other doctors. You can get a second opinion."

Sarah interjected, "That won't be necessary. You have only confirmed what I already knew."

Doctor Walker summoned his nurse. "Will you take Mrs. O'Malley to get freshened up?"

When Sarah had left the office, Doctor Walker informed Pop as what to expect. "Mr. O'Malley, I am so sorry. Cancer is a terrible disease. Maybe some day we will be able to treat it more aggressively. Your wife's health will steadily deteriorate. She is going to be experiencing pain. I know that you live up in New Dublin and there is no doctor there. Do you think that you can administer morphine with a hypodermic needle?"

"If I have to...yes."

"Your wife will be experiencing pain. I want you to give her a shot whenever she thinks that she needs it. Morphine is highly addictive. She will want more as the time goes on. I will give you enough doses to last for awhile but you will have to come back here if your supply gets low. I have to order more vials. I need to show you how to use a hypodermic needle." Doctor Walker demonstrated the technique and the proper dosages. He finished prior to Sarah returning to the office.

Sarah and Pop checked into a hotel. They spent the next two days visiting the many tourist attractions that Jefferson City offered. Evening walks were cherished. The two of them enjoyed their short stay in the big city. When they returned home, Sarah asked Pop to inform her father and her brothers of her condition. She didn't have the heart to tell them.

Sarah's stamina declined day by day until she was totally bedridden. Pop dedicated every waking hour in taking care of his wife. He catered to her every need. It was his desire to make her remaining days as peaceful as possible. But Pop was also a casualty. A piece of his heart died every day she suffered. The love of his life was slowly slipping away.

The inevitable time had arrived. Family members had gathered at Sarah's bedside. Billy administered the Sacrament of Extreme Unction. Pop sat in a chair next to the bed holding Sarah's hand. She squeezed as hard as she could but then her grip went limp. It was over.

St. Patrick Mission Church was full with family and friends for the funeral Mass. The pallbearers carried the casket and placed it in the back of Pop's horse drawn wooden wagon. The three

O'Malley brothers noticed a difference in Putnam's behavior. He held his head high and strutted as he pulled the wagon to the cemetery as if he was paying his respects to Sarah.

****

Four years later, there was a change at St. Ignatius Parish. The elderly Pastor was in poor health and he decided that it was time to step down. The Bishop promoted Father Maher to Pastor however, this created a vacancy for a priest to oversee the three mission churches. The Bishop and Father Maher had a friendly relationship. The Bishop trusted Father Maher's counsel. It was agreed that St. Patrick Parish would be established at New Dublin. It was also agreed that Father James O'Malley and Father William O'Malley would be reassigned to St. Ignatius Parish.

Jimmy and Billy, with their personal belongings in hand, arrived together at the Rectory. Father Maher was there to greet them. "Hello boys. It's good to see both of you. You can put your bags in the bedroom down the hall. You'll have to share a bedroom. It has twin beds."

Billy said, "That's good. I swore as a kid that when I grew up, I would never again share a bed with my brothers. Jimmy was the worse. He would roll over several times a night and every time he did, he would elbow me in the head. I remember one time I woke up with a bloody nose."

Jimmy added, "That wasn't done by accident."

Jimmy and Billy put their things away and returned to the parlor. Father Maher told the O'Malley brothers to sit down and make themselves comfortable. He told them, "One of you will go to New Dublin to establish a new parish and the other one will spend his time between the other two mission churches. Which one of you two wants to go to New Dublin?"

Both of the O'Malley brothers pleaded his case as to why they should be selected. Father Maher said, "I have no problem in either one of you going. I know that both of you would do a good job. I will make my decision by a flip of a coin."

Jimmy said, "We don't need a coin. We have our own way to settle disagreements. Both of them stood up facing each other. After three attempts, there was a winner. Jimmy had "rock" and Billy had "paper". Billy raised both arms in the air and started dancing around his brother chanting, "I win. I win. I win."

Father Maher watching the demonstration said, "There has to be more to this story."

Billy said with pride. "There sure is! We have played 'rock, paper, scissors' all of our lives. I never win and I want to put the emphasis on "never". This is why my loving older brother didn't want to flip a coin. He thought that it would be like money in the bank..." Billy rubbed it in some more when he glared at Jimmy, "...but he was wrong!"

Jimmy responded, "I want a do over...you cheated."

"I can't believe that you called a Catholic Priest a cheater."

"It's not a sin when a Catholic Priest calls his brother, who is also a Catholic Priest, a cheater. Isn't that right Father Maher?"

Father Maher who was thoroughly enjoying this exchange said, "Don't ask me. I am not going to get in the middle of this fray." He continued, "It looks like I made a wise decision in splitting you two up."

Jimmy said, "We O'Malley brothers may at times have differences of opinions but we do agree on food. We are getting hungry."

Father Maher responded. "I'm hungry too. There is a restaurant down the street. They serve good home cooking. I'm buying."

Billy answered, "Not referring to my brother...but that sounds like a winner."

Chapter 4

The New St. Patrick Parish (Circa 1916 – 1937)

Father O'Malley moved into his mother's house. He started saying daily Mass at the Mission Church. Father Maher had been celebrating two Masses on Sunday before he became Pastor. Father O'Malley added an additional Mass in an effort to alleviate the overcrowding. Father O'Malley was charged with what seemed to be an impossible task; Build a church, school, and convent and then celebrate the first Mass on the feast of St. Patrick, March 17, 1918. That was sixteen months away. As Father O'Malley contemplated the massive undertaking, he wondered if he had actually "won" when he beat his brother at "rock, paper, scissors".

Father O'Malley became a force to be reckoned with. The Diocese provided some seed money to get started but it was nowhere near enough to complete the project. The first thing Father O'Malley had to do was to acquire land. He knew the perfect person to talk to.

Sean greeted Father O'Malley. "Top of the morning to you Billy. Why am I honored to have the presence of your Excellency on such a beautiful day?"

"I just came by to visit my lifelong friend."

Sean was skeptical. "You want something."

Father O'Malley was patronizing. "I can't fool you. You are too smart."

"You're right but what do you want?"

"I want a 'shamrock deal' on the five acres across the street."

Sean was now even more skeptical. "Define 'shamrock deal' to me."

"A 'shamrock deal' to me is where you sell that land to me for one dollar."

Sean ranted, "That is prime commercial property!"

"OK! OK! Calm down. I will go to five dollars but not a penny more."

Sean really didn't want to sell the land to the church. He expected to make a substantial profit on the property. Sean caved, because if he didn't, Billy would put him on a major guilt trip. "I will sell it to you for what I paid for it and *that* is a 'shamrock deal'. Does that make you happy?"

"Look at me Sean. This is a happy face. There is a special place in heaven reserved for Sean Ryan."

Sean barbed his friend. "There is also a special place reserved for you but it won't be in heaven."

Father O'Malley smiled as he left the hardware store. Mentally he scratched off item number one on his long 'to do' list.

****

The development of New Dublin met a new milestone. President Woodrow Wilson's signed the Federal Road Act of 1916 that brought a new breath of optimism. New Dublin was fortunate to be in the path of one of the first federal highways. What had been an old pig trail became a modern roadway that dissected the middle of town. The automobile was taking hold throughout the country. People were beginning to travel and they needed rest areas whereby they could find restaurants, gas stations and nice accommodations for overnight stay. New Dublin was in a perfect location to meet those needs. It was nestled about half way between Jefferson City and Springfield. Main Street continued to develop. A new and upcoming company called Texaco built a gas station. Their sign, a big red star with a green "T" in the middle, stood out prominently for all the motorists to see. Sean built a new hotel next to the hardware store. For those who couldn't afford to pay for a hotel room, an impromptu campground was established on the edge of town whereby travelers could sleep in their cars or pitch a tent. Many enterprising residents realized that poor folks were like anyone else; they had to eat. Meals or sandwiches were prepared in their home kitchens and sold at the campground for a reasonable price. With the advent of the automobile and trucks, the Jefferson City Paddle Boat Co. could foresee that their business was in jeopardy. Slowly over the following years, revenues declined to the point that it was no longer feasible to stay in business.

****

World War I was raging in Europe. America was still neutral but it was only a matter of time before war would be declared against Germany. America was mobilizing. Throughout the country, there was a steady stream of volunteers lining up at the recruiting offices. Five young men from New Dublin answered the call to duty. Father O'Malley asked them to come by and see him at the church. He knew each one of them. He knew their parents, their brothers and their sisters. Not only did their family want them to return safely but it was the same sentiment of the entire community of New Dublin. They sat down in the front pew of the small mission church. Father O'Malley gave them words of encouragement and led them in prayer. He gave each one a St. Christopher medal. They placed the medals around their necks. Father O'Malley made them promise not to take them off. He spoke. "Boys be as careful as you can and go to Mass whenever possible. I will keep you in my thoughts and prayers until you come home."

They responded, "Thanks, Father."

****

Father O'Malley was on a mission in regard to the building of the church, school and convent. What he lacked in funds, he made up in determination and fortitude. He mustered together every able body in the Parish. Man, woman or child; it didn't matter. If one could hammer a nail, lay brick, cut wood, prepare meals or carry water for the workers to stay hydrated, they were pressed into service. He even co-opted his older brother, Jimmy to put his master craftsman skills to work. He built all the cabinets in the sacristy. The pulpit was a work of art. Saturdays became a social event in New Dublin. Entire families participated. Father and sons worked on the construction while the mothers and daughters prepared lunch. It was community spirit at its best.

Father O'Malley overcame all the obstacles and he reached his goal. St. Patrick Church was dedicated on schedule. There was standing room only when Father O'Malley celebrated his first Mass in his new church. His homily was not your typical sermon. It was more words of appreciation to the entire town of New Dublin. He spread accolades to many of those present but he saved a special thank you to his friend Albert and the entire Swartz family. All of which were seated in the front pew. They were still the only Jewish family residing in New Dublin but Albert Swartz was the most ardent volunteer. He was at the church working every spare moment of every day even on the Jewish Sabbath. He justified his indiscretion by saying, "When you are doing God's work…God will forgive." Besides, he temporarily moved his Sabbath to Sunday. Father O'Malley had at one time asked him why a Jewish man was so dedicated to the building of a Catholic church and school. His answer was simple. "It was the right thing to do." When he finished his homily, Father O'Malley asked his fellow parishioners to pray with him for the safety of New Dublin's finest who were now serving in France. After Mass, the congregation proceeded outside where a feast had been prepared that even St. Patrick himself would have been pleased.

****

Father O'Malley offered his mother a teaching position at the school. She declined. Alice wanted to take life a bit easier. This didn't mean that she would not be involved in school activities. There would always be the need for a substitute teacher. Besides, she along with Molly and Ronald Ryan and Abe and Rachel Swartz planned an extended trip to Dublin to rekindle their childhood memories. They wanted to make this pilgrimage back home before they got too old. But these plans were on hold because of the war in Europe.

****

Father O'Malley's work was not done. The school was nearly finished but the volunteers had just begun on the construction of the convent. There was sufficient time to have everything completed by the opening of school on the day after Labor Day. Father O'Malley had become accustomed to problems that had arisen since the cornerstone had been laid on the church. Most of which were resolved with a minimum of effort but he was about to meet the problem or all problems. A black sedan pulled to the curb in front of the Church followed by a delivery truck. Thirteen nuns from the Sisters of Mercy slowly emerged from the automobile and the back of the delivery truck. They all stood on the sidewalk. Sister Monica went toward the school and asked as to the whereabouts of Father O'Malley. He soon appeared. Father O'Malley greeted Sister Monica and they exchanged some pleasantries. Sister Monica, who also was the Mother Superior, explained that the other twelve nuns where to be the new teachers and how it had been miserable trip. All she wanted to do is to get settled. She and Father O'Malley could discuss their responsibilities tomorrow.

Sister Monica asked, "Father, if you would be so kind, can you direct us to the convent?"

Father O'Malley pointed toward the back of the school.

"I'm sorry Father but I don't see a convent."

"You see that wooden frame. That is your convent."

This is where the sparks began to fly. Sister Monica, with her Irish accent, lit into him. She was told that a brand new convent had been built awaiting their arrival. She was waving her finger in his face as she went into a tirade that Father O'Malley had never witnessed before. He didn't say a word. This was wise. When she finished, she stomped her foot and said, "Jingles".

"Jingles?" Father O'Malley questioned. "Is that the Christian way of saying an expletive?"

"You're DAMN right it is."

Father O'Malley looked directly at Sister Monica eye to eye. He cocked his head backward in disbelief. He smiled. He was not offended. In fact, he was delighted. This woman had spunk and spunk is exactly what he needed in running the school. Sister

Monica was taken back herself. She used her hand to cover her mouth to hide her smile.

"Well Sister, obviously there has been a break down in communications. You were not to be here for another three months. Be that as it may, I have to find you a place to stay. I can't have you camping out on my front lawn."

Father O'Malley walked across the street to meet with Sean who was standing on the sidewalk in front of his hardware store.

Sean saw Father O'Malley coming and greeted him at the door. "Good morning, Billy. I see that our new faculty has arrived."

"Yes, but I have a problem."

Father O'Malley explained the situation and Sean was willing to help. There were sufficient rooms available to accommodate the nuns on a temporary basis. However, Billy didn't know this and Sean wasn't going to make it easy for Billy.

"Sean, if you do this, there will be a special place in heaven for you."

"You need to explain something to me. When I gave you the 'shamrock deal' on the land, you told me then that I would have a special place in heaven. When I installed the blackboards, you said that I would have a special place in heaven. Now, if I help you, I will have a special place in heaven. How many special places are there in heaven?"

Not to be outdone by Sean, Billy responded with an analogy. "Heaven is like a movie theater. Your first special place was in the balcony. Your second special place put you down on the ground floor. Your third special place will put you right on the front row."

"I am happy with the ground floor seat. Therefore, I don't think that I will be able to help you this time."

"That's fine. I completely understand. You have done more than your fair share. I will have Mother Superior come here and speak with you. I forewarn you that this is one tough lady. I speak with experience. You tell her that there is no room at the inn and that they can stay in the stable in the back as long as they don't touch the manger."

Sarcastic but effective thought Sean. "Billy, you are wearing our friendship a little thin. Send the nuns over and I will take care of them."

Billy put his hand on Sean's shoulder. "Thanks. I had no doubt that you would help in my time of need. I remember when the five of us took the oath to be friends forever."

"You got what you wanted. You can stop trying to butter me up."

Sister Monica gathered up her flock and proceeded across the street. The nuns were in a line one behind the other; each carrying a small suitcase. It was like the ducklings following the mother duck. However with the nuns' habits and white starched wimples, they looked more like penguins.

The next morning at the 7 O'clock Mass, Sister Monica and the other nuns were seated in the front two pews. Father O'Malley was pleased. With the nuns present, it was just another step closer in fulfilling the master plan. But he knew the master plan had a long way to go to be completed. The nuns may be the new teachers but in the short run, they were thirteen new volunteers. Sister Monica was in a much better mood. She tried to apologize but Father O'Malley stopped her in mid sentence. "You can't apologize unless you've offended someone and I am not offended." This little gesture would go a long way with Sister Monica. After Mass, Father O'Malley gave them a tour of the church and school. He gave them the time schedule he had in place to have all of the construction completed. He also asked Sister Monica if it was against their religious order for the nuns to change into more suitable clothing for doing manual labor. Sister Monica said that the only requirements are that we are modestly dressed and that our heads are covered. However, the nuns had to pack light and they did not bring any work clothes. Father O'Malley assured her that he had a solution.

Father O'Malley went to his office and took some money out of his desk drawer. He walked down to the Texaco station. He met with the manager, Bryan Boyle. "Good morning, Brian."

"Good morning, Billy. How are you?"

"Fine. It's a beautiful day the Lord has made."

"That it is, my friend. What brings you down this way?"

"I need thirteen pairs of overalls and thirteen hats just like you got on."

"Thirteen pairs? Did I hear you right…thirteen pairs?"

"Yes…thirteen pairs. I know you have heard that the nuns have arrived and I am going to put them to work painting. They have to dress modestly and their heads need to be covered. You can't get any more modest when you're wearing men's overalls."

Bryan was somewhat embarrassed. "Billy, I would like to donate this to the church but….."

"No. No. No. I know that your salary isn't that much. That is why I brought cash we me. Besides, there is always Sean. He has plenty of money."

"So you have Sean in your hip pocket."

"Yes I do. There is a special place in heaven for Sean just as long as he doesn't go broke." Both of them laughed.

Bryan went to the storage room and returned with the overalls and hats.

Father O'Malley did ask a favor of Bryan. "Would you be so kind to give me a ride in your truck? I can't carry all these boxes in one trip."

"Sure."

Father O'Malley put all the boxes on the front desk at the hotel. He took a piece of paper and wrote, "Here are your modest work clothes. Please meet me in front of the Church after lunch". He underlined the word "modest". He folded it over and wrote "Sister Monica" on the front and gave it to the desk clerk who would see that it and the overalls were delivered.

Father O'Malley and Pop were standing on the front steps with big smiles when Sister Monica emerged from the hotel followed by her merry band. They marched in single file up to the Church.

Father O'Malley greeted them. "My Texaco girls look so cute in their new uniforms. I believe you ladies may be making a fashion statement."

With the exception of Sister Monica, they all giggled just like little school girls. They were young…younger that Father O'Malley who was thirty. Sister Monica was the oldest, maybe in her late thirties.

Father O'Malley addressed the nuns. "I want to introduce my twin brother, Pop. He owns the grocery store down the street. Please feel free to make any purchases that you need. Pop will put it on account. I will see that the bill gets paid. I would also like to take this opportunity to formally welcome you to St. Patrick Parish. Pop and I grew up here and this is a great place to live. You will never find nicer people anywhere. This is going to be our home for many years to come. Most of you will probably retire here. I know I will because I have no other place to go. We have all dedicated our lives to Jesus Christ but that doesn't mean that we can't have fun and be religious at the same time. A good laugh and a smile can sometimes work miracles. I want all of you to feel that you are a part of this community. I promise you that many of you will develop life long friends. Now, I want to establish a pecking order. If any of you have a problem with me, you are to go to Sister Monica. She, in turn, will come to me and vice versa. I am asking your forgiveness in advance. It will take me some time before I learn all of your names. 'Sister' will have to suffice for awhile. I asked Pop to come over because he is our volunteer paint foreman. You Texaco girls need to be aware because he is a real tough boss. (Pop shook his head in disagreement). He will get you the paint and supplies that you may need. Again welcome. Hopefully you will find this a happy place."

St. Patrick Church became the focal point of the community. It was the equivalent of a town square. It was commonplace for people to be sitting on the small brick wall that line the front sidewalk. There were benches throughout the church yard. The most popular benches were the ones situated under the shade trees that dotted the property. A large bulletin board had been erected. It was full of notices regarding items for sale or trade. Newspapers articles were displayed especially about the war. Street vendors would set up small stands selling vegetables grown in home gardens. St. Patrick's was always a beehive of activity.

****

The five New Dublin doughboys enlisted together, they served together and they returned home together. Through the grace of God, none were wounded. A large crowd of family and friends waving small American flags congregated in front of St. Patrick Church waiting for the bus to arrive. Cheers went up as the bus pulled to a stop and the door swung open. Off stepped the five still in their uniforms. Hugs and kisses flowed from all the family members. Father O'Malley moved forward and shook their hands. All five of them pulled out their St. Christopher medals and proudly displayed them to Father O'Malley. One remarked, "A promise made is a promise kept." A young boy in the crowd had a drum. He started tapping out a marching beat. A spontaneous parade began. As they walked, the sound of the drum brought neighbors out of their houses and to the curb. They were waving and clapping as the parade passed. Many joined in. Patriotism was a hallmark of New Dublin.

****

Weeks turned into months; months turned into years. The stock market crash of 1929 and the following Great Depression affected every region of the country. The larger cities seemed to suffer the most. New Dublin faired well because of its agricultural history. A new Rectory had been built. All of the original nuns were still there which is testament in itself.
The Texaco girls were still wearing their old uniforms when they were working in the garden or doing household chores. They were tattered and still had paint stains from 11 years prior. Father O'Malley wrote a note to himself, "Buy new Texaco uniforms". This would be a good gift to give the nuns at Christmas. St. Patrick's Day had become one of the most celebrated days of the year. The entire community shut down. Main Street was blocked off. Huge banners were strung high above the street. After Mass, Father O'Malley, accompanied by altar boys led the parade that began at the church. He was followed by gentlemen of Irish decent. They were dressed in green hats and jackets. The Sisters of Mercy were next. Behind them was the rest of the community. They marched down Main Street and meandered around town until they ended back in front of the Church. Afterwards, the parade disbanded. The street was filled with booths and games for the kids. It was one of those events that made New Dublin a great place to live.

****

The following five years was a sad period for the O'Malley brothers, Sean, and Albert. Their parents were now in the presence of God. They were so thankful that they all had made the trip to Ireland to visit family and renew old friendships. None of the founders were still alive. The future of New Dublin now rested with the next generation and they were doing a good job.

****

Jacob Swartz was one of the first graduates from St. Patrick School. He pursued his secondary education at Independence University, School of Medicine, in Jefferson City. While he was in his sophomore year, he married a nursing student named Ruth. She gave birth to their first born son, Isaac, in 1930. After Jacob received his medical degree in 1935, the young family moved back to New Dublin where they opened a clinic on Main Street. One of the examination rooms doubled as an operating room where minor surgery was performed. Many of Dr. Swartz's patients would pay for their medical treatment by giving food or providing personal services. Dr. Swartz was always cordial to those patients who where unfamiliar with the Jewish dietary laws. He would graciously accept the hams, bacon and chops. He in turn would give the pork to Father O'Malley who proclaimed that he was one gentile that had a fond affection for the pig.

****

Father James O'Malley was replaced as the missionary priest for St. Ignatius Parish. Over the years he became the pastor at two different parishes in Jefferson City. In 1937, the Bishop died at the age of 76. Father James O'Malley was named as his replacement. This met with overwhelming approval of all his fellow priests in the Diocese. The late Bishop liked both of the O'Malley brothers. This is the reason why Father William O'Malley was able to remain at St. Patrick's Parish for so many years. Now that his brother Jimmy was the new Bishop, it was guaranteed that he would never be transferred.

Chapter 5

World War II (Circa 1938 – 1941)

There had been no change in the ranks of the nuns. Father O'Malley felt that he had been blessed when the Sisters of Mercy arrived over 20 years ago. Sister Monica had done a fantastic job as principal. Father O'Malley assisted in teaching religion classes but he had very little to do with the day to day operation of the school. If he did get involved, it usually pertained to some type of financial matter whether it was the purchase of new books or supplies for the playground. St. Patrick's Day Festival had grown exponentially over the years. The nuns took over the total operation of the festival. They used it as a fund raiser for the school.

While New Dublin enjoyed a peaceful existence, the rest of the world was at war. Adolf Hitler and his Nazi regime were on course for world domination. Countries were falling one by one. France at this time was occupied by Germany. Hitler had turned his attention to Britain. They were being bombed on a regular basis. The United States was neutral but like in World War I, it was just a matter of time before the young men of America would be on the front lines. In anticipation, President Franklin D. Roosevelt had issued a variety of contracts to build tanks, weapons, ships, airplanes and anything else that was needed to create a massive war machine. New Dublin was the recipient of one of those contracts. An aircraft manufacturing plant was being constructed at the edge of town. New Dublin had been one of many communities being considered for the new facility. Phillip Nelson, the owner, related to Father O'Malley that the reason why New Dublin was selected was primarily due to the people. They were God fearing, friendly, patriotic, possessed a good work ethic and were well educated. Father O'Malley appreciated the compliment especially the reference to "well educated" because the Sisters of Mercy at St. Patrick School were responsible for the quality education of the majority of their new work force. Father O'Malley proudly passed the compliment onto Sister Monica. The aircraft manufacturing plant brought new challenges. This was the biggest boon for New Dublin since the federal highway was built. The school, as it existed, could not accommodate the influx of new residents to the community. Father O'Malley began immediately to make plans to build a separate high school. He requested that Sister Monica contact her motherhouse to see whether or not four more nuns were available for transfer to St. Patrick's. That created another problem. The convent would have to have a new addition. The ribbon cutting ceremony for the new aircraft plant was well attended by all the politicians, even the Governor was present. Newspaper and magazine reporters took pictures. There was an up and coming illustrator for the *Saturday Evening Post* there capturing the entire event on canvas. The next day the assembly line began. Soon there were planes being completed on a daily basis. The sight and sound of aircraft flying overhead became commonplace in New Dublin. Sean Ryan was the quintessential entrepreneur. He was steadily building new housing. They were shotgun type houses that had all the essentials for daily living for one or two people. Sean, under contract with three separate customers, built a movie theater called the "Rialto"; The Bank of New Dublin and the "Apothecary" drug store. According to Father O'Malley, Sean's greatest business venture was the "Leprechaun Pub and Grill". Father O'Malley became a regular Saturday night visitor for a pint of beer (maybe two or three) and a plate of corned beef and cabbage. Sean, Albert and Pop would join him. It became a weekly ritual. Father O'Malley was proud of what Sean had accomplished. The plant was operating at partial capacity and New Dublin was able to absorb the arrival of all the new workers. However, this would soon change not only for New Dublin but the entire country.

"Yesterday, December 7, 1941 – a date which will live in infamy -the United State of America was suddenly and deliberately attacked by naval and air forces of the Empire of Japan." These were the opening remarks that President Roosevelt said in his speech to the joint session of Congress. The United States of America along with Britain declared war on Japan. Three days later, Germany declared war on the United States. It was official. America was now at war on two fronts, the Pacific theater and the European theater. Literally overnight, the aircraft manufacturing plant began operating twenty four hours a day, seven days a week. This created a shortage of workers at the plant. It was only exacerbated by the fact that many of the young men quit their jobs to volunteer for active duty, even though they were offered waivers from the military. With the shortage of manpower, the plant turned to women to fill the positions. This was unheard of before. Women just didn't work in manufacturing jobs but these were desperate times. As it turned out, the women were quite good. Sean Ryan was building houses as fast as he could but there were more workers than his housing project could accommodate. Sean's houses soon became known as the "Barracks". They were all the same, built side by side in long rows. Sixty had been built and twenty more were under construction. The community opened their homes and rented out spare bedrooms. Father O'Malley was thankful that he had the foresight to build a new high school and add the addition to the convent. It was complete but again, the classrooms were full. Sister Monica managed to overcome the adversities to fulfill the educational needs of all the students. The arrival of the four new nuns was a God send.

Chapter 6

Sam Meets Pop (Circa 1942)

It has been almost six months since the bombing of Pearl Harbor. The screen door to Pop's Grocery opened and in walked a young boy dressed in a white t-shirt and blue jeans which were rolled up at the bottom exposing his black and white Converse basketball shoes. He moved toward Pop who was standing behind the cash register.

"I am looking for the owner."

"I am the owner can I help you?"

He stuck his hand out with confidence. "My name is Samuel Jenkins but my friends call me Sam."

Pop shook his hand. "My name is Pop and my friends call me Pop. What can I do for you, Sam?"

"I need a job. Looking around here, I think you could use some help."

"You do, huh!"

"Yes sir. I have a good eye for these things."

"You do, huh!"

"Yes sir. I am the man of the house and I need a job to help pay the bills."

Pop was impressed with the young man. He asked, "Sam, how old are you?"

"Twelve."

"Twelve, huh! You are the man of the house?"

"Yes sir. My father was a pilot on a B-17. He got shot down over France. He died a hero. My mother is always telling me that I am the man of the house now. Pop, that is why I need a job."

"I am sorry to hear about your dad. I know how hard it is to grow up without a father. My dad died in the Spanish American War. He too was a hero. You must be really proud of him."

"Yes sir, I am."

"Sam I have never seen you in here before. Are you new to town?

"Yes sir. My mother has a job at the airplane plant. We live in the Barracks."

"I guess she is Rosie the Riveter."

"Oh no, her name is Alice."

Pop did everything he could to keep from laughing. It was obviously Sam was serious in everything he was saying. "Alice is such a pretty name. My mother's name was also Alice."

"Yes sir. Alice is a pretty name."

"Where do you go to school?"

"Sir, I go to St. Patrick's and I am in the sixth grade."

"Have you met Father O'Malley?"

"Yes sir."

"Have you met his paddle?"

"No sir but I have heard stories."

"You need to be good in school because he is one mean old man. I heard where he paddled a boy so hard that he couldn't sit down for three days."

Sam's eyes bugged out. He had heard stories but nothing like that. "Yes sir, I intend on being good."

Sam was tugging hard at Pop's heartstrings. "I'll tell you what I'll do. When you get out of school, you come straight here. I need some help in sweeping up around here and stocking the shelves. Also, I may get you to deliver some groceries. How does that sound to you?"

Sam was excited. "Yes sir, that sounds great." Sam turned and started running for the screen door.

Pop yelled out to him and Sam stopped in his tracks. "Don't you want to know what you are going to get paid?"

Sam totally forgot about his pay. "Yes sir, I need to know that."

"Yes you do. I will give you seventy five cents a day and two dollars for Saturday. Is that satisfactory with you?"

"Yes sir, yes sir. That is real good. I will see you tomorrow."

The next morning, an attractive young woman came in the store. She was wearing overalls and a red bandana on her heard. Pop couldn't help but to think about when he and his brother Billy met the Texaco girls in front of the church. Billy had said they were making a fashion statement with the uniforms and hats. Little did he know at the time, but he was right. However, it took over twenty years to catch on.

The young lady introduced herself to Pop. "My name is Alice Jenkins. I am Sam's mom."

"I am very happy to meet you. You have a fine son."

"Thank you. He is a good kid…all boy. But I promise you he is no angel."

"He did strike me that he may have a little mischief in him and in my book…that is a good thing."

"I want to thank you for hiring Sam but I look around your store and it doesn't look as if you need a stock boy. I know he told you that he was the man of the house and he needed to get a job to help pay the bills. I make enough money for the two of us to live just fine. It is not necessary for him to have a job."

"I figured as much but it is not just for Sam but for me too. My wife died years ago. We were never able to have children. My twin brother is Father O'Malley at St. Patrick's and our other brother is the Bishop. So, obviously I don't have any nieces or nephews. If you don't mind I can be his substitute grandpa."

"Grandpa is good. My husband and I were both raised in an orphanage. I met him when I was five and he was six. He was like a big brother and watched over me. Orphanages can be cruel, not from the nuns but from the other children. At times they can be mean and hateful." Alice was having difficulty in telling the story. Her eyes were watering. She continued. "Somewhere along the line the brother/sister relationship changed. He was my best friend and my soul mate. Life was good. Our future was planned. We were going to have three children and have a house with a white picket fence. Then the war…it changed everything. I hate this war. I miss my husband so much. I am so thankful that I have Sam because without him I believe that I would pray to God to take me early so that I could be with my husband."

Pop did not respond. Alice was in pain and there was nothing he could say to make the pain go away. Pop just changed the subject. "Sam says that his dad was a hero. Is that true or is that his image of his father?"

"No, his father was a hero. His co-pilot wrote me a letter to inform me in regard to the circumstances surrounding my husband's death. He was the pilot. They were on a bombing run and they took heavy anti-aircraft fire. The B-17 took a direct hit on the right wing. The plane was shaking violently. He ordered the crew to bail out while he fought the controls to keep the plane level. The co-pilot said that he was at the door ready to jump when the right wing broke off. The plane started in a tail spin and my husband was unable to make it to the door to bail out. The co-pilot said that he watched the plane crash and he never saw a parachute. The way he saw it, it cost my husband his life to save him and the rest of the crew."

Pop and Alice talked briefly. She had to leave to get to work on time. She said, "Thank you for hiring Sam. It will be good for him."

"Maybe I can put some of those untapped grandpa skills to use."

"I hope so."

School was out and Sam showed up on time. He was eager to start to work. Pop took a new apron and with an ink pen wrote "Sam" on the front. It was a man's size. It was way too large for Sam but it would have to do. Sam put it on. The bottom of the apron touched the laces on his basketball shoes. Sam looked down and exclaimed, "Perfect fit."

Pop said, "Your mom came by to see me this morning. She is very pretty."

"Thank you. She's the best."

Pop wanted to boost Sam's self esteem. "She told me that you are the man of the house and the extra money you make here will be helpful in paying the bills."

"A man has gotta do what a man has gotta do."

Pop instructed Sam to get the broom from the storage room and start sweeping from the back of the store. He was busy when Theresa Kelly and Johnny Jernigan came in. They were Sam's classmates. The three of them were instant best friends from the first day Sam enrolled at St. Patrick's. Sam, being polite, tried to introduce them to Pop but Pop explained that he already knew Theresa, Johnny and everyone else in town. They all have come through the front doors at one time or another. Pop pulled the lid off of the large class jar that sat on the counter. As he customarily did, Pop let each of them to reach in and get a piece of hard candy. Johnny and Theresa thanked Pop and said good bye to Sam as they left the store. After Sam finished sweeping, Pop gave him a cloth and told him to dust off all the groceries on the shelves. Sam was through right at closing time. Pop motioned for Sam to follow him into the storage room. He closed the door and hammered a nail into the back of the door. He told Sam to take off his apron and hang it on the nail. Pop removed his apron and hung it on the nail beside Sam's. Pop followed Sam out to the front so that he could lock the door. "I will see you tomorrow. You did a good job today."

"Thanks Pop." Sam went straight home. He was tired. It had been a hard day at work.

Sam took his job seriously. He was punctual and had a strong work ethic especially for such a young man. He learned the prices of everything in the store and where each item was located. He would assist customers with their purchases. Home delivery became more popular. It was not unusual to see Sam, using Pop's little red wagon with wooden slatted sides, pulling a load of groceries.

Chapter 7

Tragedy in Sam's Life (Circa 1943)

It was almost a year since Sam went to work at Pop's Grocery. Pop turned out be good at the grandpa skills. He and Sam grew closer every day. This is exactly what Alice desired. She felt that Sam needed a man in his life and Pop was the ideal role model. Sometimes when life is good, bad things happen.

Sister Monica answered the phone in the Principal's office. "Oh, my God! Hold on. I will find him." She was in a panic when she turned to the secretary, "Where is Father O'Malley?"

The secretary responded, "I believe that he is in the third grade class, teaching religion."

Without responding, Sister Monica bolted out of the office. She grabbed her habit and pulled it up so she wouldn't trip. She ran as fast as she could. She summoned Father O'Malley from the class. "I have a telephone call from the plant. Sam's mother has been seriously hurt."

The two of them ran back to the office. He picked up the receiver, "This is Father O'Malley."

"Father, this is Howard, Alice Jenkins has been hurt real bad in a freak accident here at the plant. All she keeps saying is that she needs to speak with you and Pop."

"Where is she now?"

"She is being taken to the clinic."

"Thanks, Bye." Father O'Malley turned to Sister Monica, "Please call Pop and tell him that Sam's mother has been in an accident and have him meet me at the clinic. Tell him to hurry."

Pop met up with Father O'Malley outside of the examination room. Dr. Swartz finished assessing Alice's injuries and he had made a prognosis. He brought the two inside.

Alice grasped both their hands, "I am so thankful that you made it. I think my time is near."

Pop said, "Don't say that. You'll be ok."

Pop and Father O'Malley glanced up at Dr. Swartz who was standing on the other side of the gurney and out of view of Alice. He shook his head. Death was imminent.

Alice continued by speaking to Pop, "Sam loves you very much."

"The feeling is mutual."

"I know. That is why I am asking you to raise Sam. I don't want him to go to an orphanage. I can't bear the thought of him growing up like me and his father did. Promise me."

"I promise. Besides, he will have two uncles who will help in his upbringing. Don't worry, the O'Malley brothers will do the best we can."

Alice squeezed their hands, "That pleases me very much." Her grip slipped away. Peacefulness came over her face.

Pop said to his brother, "In a strange way, this may have been God's plan. He healed a broken heart and brought new life to us."

Father O'Malley was puzzled as he prepared to administer the last rites.

Pop said, "I'll explain it to you later."

A full day had passed before the funeral. The casket sat at the foot of the altar. The plant manager along with several employees who had befriended Alice were present. A few parishioners who had become acquainted with Alice were also present. Sister Monica was there. In the front pew sat Johnny, Theresa, Sam, and Pop. After the funeral Mass, Father O'Malley led the procession out of the Church to the nearby cemetery. Theresa held hands with Johnny and Sam as they followed the casket. It was a moving sight. Pop followed the three.

After the interment, Theresa was still holding hands with Johnny and Sam. The three of them walked down to the river. They sat down on the bank. Sam, who had not shed a tear since first learning of his mother's death, broke down and began to sob uncontrollably. Both Theresa and Johnny began to cry. They consoled each other. Sam's lost was their lost.

Bishop O'Malley contacted Catholic Charities in regard to Sam's adoption. Within a few months, Lawrence "Pop" O'Malley officially became the adopted father of Samuel A. Jenkins. There was no surname change. Pop was adamant about this. Sam had two loving parents. To change Sam's last name to O'Malley would only tarnish Sam's memory of his mother and father.

Chapter 8

Sam's First Christmas (Circa 1943)

Pop put a sign in the window saying that he would return in two hours. He locked the door and walked to the Rectory. Father O'Malley was waiting. They went to the Western Auto at the north end of town.

They were greeted by the manager. "What can I do for the O'Malley boys this morning?"

Father O'Malley responded. "Andrew, we're here on our first annual Christmas shopping extravaganza."

Pop knew exactly what he wanted, a new bicycle with an extra large basket on the front. Sam could use the bike to carry groceries instead of using the red wagon. Father O'Malley wasn't quite sure as to what he wanted to buy but he would know the right gift when he saw it. The three went up and down each aisle. Andrew made suggestions but nothing met Father O'Malley's fancy. They came upon a shelf with model airplanes.

Father O'Malley asked Pop, "What kind of plane did Sam's father fly?"

Pop answered, "B-17."

Andrew pulled one of the larger boxes from the shelf with a picture of a B-17 on the front. "We just got these in. It is made out of balsa wood. The paint, glue and decals are already in the box."

"This is perfect," said Father O'Malley.

Andrew inquired, "Do you want me to have it gift wrapped?"

"No. I will do it myself."

Pop sarcastically chimed in, "This should be real interesting."

"I'll have you know little brother that I have skills that you aren't even aware of. When we were in school I made an A+ in gift wrapping."

"How come I don't remember it?"

"You were absent that day."

Pop and Father O'Malley examined the Christmas trees leaning up against the front of the store. They were in mutual agreement for a tree at Pop's apartment and one for the Church. They were set aside to be picked up later. At Pop's request, Andrew agreed to mount the basket on the bike and hold it until Christmas Eve. Pop wanted it to be a surprise but he didn't have any place to hide it without Sam accidentally finding it.

As Pop and Father O'Malley walked back to the Rectory, Pop asked, "What's our big brother going to get Sam for Christmas?"

"He has already done his Christmas shopping. He bought Sam a Gilbert Erector Set."

"That's good. Sam will like that." Pop continued, "Do you think Jimmy can come over Friday night? We can decorate the tree just like we did as kids. I will fix us some sandwiches for dinner. Jimmy can stay overnight with you and then go back on Saturday."

"I have to meet with him tomorrow on Church business. Unless he has a conflict, I am sure he'll be here."

Pop returned to the grocery store and Father O'Malley went back to the Rectory. He was preparing for the meeting with the Bishop.

Sister Monica was at the office door. "Am I interrupting anything?"

"No. Please come in."

"I was sorting through some of the photographs we took at the St. Patrick's Day Festival and look what I found." She handed Father O'Malley a picture. It was a photograph of Sam and his mother.

"This is simply overwhelming. This is probably the only photograph of Sam's mother. Do you have the negative?"

"Yes."

"Tomorrow, I will drop it off at the drug store in Jefferson City and have it blown up to an eight by ten. Jimmy can pick it up and bring it with him."

"Do you think we should give it to Sam for Christmas? This is his first Christmas without his mom and dad."

"Without question, yes."

"I wasn't sure but I will go with the woman's intuition." Father O'Malley then asked, "Can you do me a favor?"

"Sure."

He handed her the model airplane box. "Can you wrap this for me? Don't tell anyone. Pop thinks I am going to wrap it."

"No problem. When you get the picture back, I'll wrap that too."

"I know you are commonly known as 'Sister Witch with a switch' but to me you're an angel." Both laughed. It was obvious that these two had a close friendship that dated back to the early Texaco girls.

It was Friday evening. Sam and the O'Malley brothers were seated at Pop's kitchen table. He had made some roast beef sandwiches and a pot of vegetable soup. Sam was selected to say grace. Afterwards, all said together, "Amen". Pop used his wife's favorite ladle. It had been a wedding gift. He scooped the soup from the pot. As he filled each bowl, he would hand it to Sam who then placed it on the table. Sam said, "Here you go Bishop."

Bishop O'Malley told Sam, "You are now a member of the O'Malley family. We will never replace your mom and dad but you will never find three men who could love you more. From here on out, I am Uncle Jimmy. Father O'Malley is Uncle Billy and Pop is Pop."

"Yes sir." But Sam had a question, "How did Pop get the nickname 'Pop'?"

Uncle Jimmy motioned to the other brothers, "I'll take this one because I remember it clearly. First of all, his given name is Lawrence and we called him Larry. When we were young boys, our father had a jack-in-the-box. The ones today are made out of metal; back then they were made out of wood. He would put us one at a time on his knee. He would turn the crank which only played the tune. He would sing the song."

The O'Malley brothers sang the song for Sam. They knew it by heart:

> *All around the mulberry bush*
> *The monkey chased the weasel*
> *The monkey stopped to tie his shoe*
> *POP! Goes the weasel*

Sam responded, "You guys are pretty good."

"It's just one of our many talents, my son." Uncle Jimmy continued, "When it was Larry's turn, Dad would sing the song. The clown would pop out and Larry would laugh and laugh. It was a contagious laugh. It got to the point that Dad would just say "Pop!" and Larry would start laughing. Even to this day, if I say the word "Pop!" he starts laughing." Pop, playing along, let out a big barrel laugh. Sam thought this was funny. "Pop stuck as a nickname and that is what we have called him ever since. After hearing that story, you may be having second thoughts about joining up with such a goofy family."

"Nope. This is where my Mama wanted me to be and I had a smart Mama."

"Well said young man…well said."

They finished dinner and cleaned up. They then gathered around the Christmas tree. Pop strung the lights and gave Sam the honor of plugging them in. They all lit up. All four of them shared in the decoration. Sibling teasing was commonplace. Sam was the brunt of much of the joking. He was unable to reciprocate out of respect to his elders but Sam thoroughly enjoyed the attention. It was fun for all. The garland was wrapped around the tree. After the last ornament was placed on the tree, the four of them stood back and admired their accomplishment.

Not a word was said until Uncle Jimmy spoke, "We did a good job. What do you think, Sam?"

As honest and sincere as a thirteen year old boy could say, "I think it is the prettiest Christmas tree I've ever seen."

Again there was a long pause with each gazing at the tree.

"You know, Sam, I think you're right," responded Uncle Jimmy.

Pop said, "I have one of Mrs. Shanahan's apple pies. Who wants a slice?"

Everyone answered without hesitation, "I do."

From the very first day that Sarah bought the first pie over thirty years ago, Mrs. Shanahan had gained the undisputed honor of being the best pie maker in all of New Dublin. She made five pies a days, six days a week. Pop bought all of them. There was never a day that all the pies were not sold. They were so popular that the community had a saying, "When you eat a slice of Mrs. Shanahan pie you are eating a little piece of heaven."

It had been an enjoyable evening but it was getting late. Uncle Jimmy and Uncle Billy bid good night. They walked back toward the Rectory.

Uncle Jimmy said, "That Sam is a fine young man."

"Agreed but have you noticed how much happier Pop seems to be since Sam has been around?"

"Yea, I noticed it too. I can remember him saying that when he got married, he wanted a house full of kids. It was sad that Sarah could never bear children but I have never once heard him complain."

"Me either. He also never talked about why they didn't adopt any children but I always presumed that it was because of Sarah's condition."

"You know, Billy, you and I made a conscious decision to take a vow of celibacy when we became Priests. Pop never had an inclination toward the priesthood. The sacrament of marriage was his calling. Do you think this is one of God's mysterious ways especially how the series of events occurred that brought Sam to live with Pop."

"The same thought has crossed my mind. I know one thing, Pop will make a great father and his two brothers will be the two best uncles a boy can have."

Jimmy continued, "I don't know about you but this is the most excited I have been about Christmas since we were kids."

"So you are able to be here Christmas morning."

"Yes. This is my plan. You have to celebrate midnight Mass here at St. Patrick's. I have to celebrate midnight Mass at the Cathedral. When you finish, go to bed and don't wait up for me. Just leave the door unlocked. When I finish midnight Mass, I am going to drive up. I will slip in and go to bed. Make sure that I am awake because I won't get but a couple hours of sleep. You and I will celebrate Christmas day Mass together."

"Sounds like a plan to me."

The next week went by fast for the O'Malley brothers. It was business as usual. But for Sam it went as slow as cold molasses being poured from a Mason jar. Pop was giving Sam mixed signals; one day he would tell Sam not to expect much for Christmas and blamed it on the war; other days, he would tell Sam that he may be pleasantly surprised on Christmas morning. Sam was thoroughly confused as what to expect. Also the fact that there were no presents under the tree didn't help matters either.

Finally, Christmas morning had arrived. The sun was far below the eastern horizon, when Billy knocked on Jimmy's door. "Are you up?"

Jimmy mumbled something that Billy didn't understand but he took it as a "Yes".

Jimmy and Billy loaded the gifts into the basket on the bicycle. They pushed the bike. Jimmy wanted to ride the bike but Billy discouraged it. He didn't think Jimmy could make it the four blocks without falling off. It would be too difficult to explain to Sam as to how his bike was all dented up. Pop was out on the sidewalk in front of the grocery store watching the two come toward him.

"Merry Christmas," Pop greeted his brothers. They responded in kind.

They quietly went upstairs to the apartment. Sam was still asleep. The pine scent of the Christmas tree was strong but it didn't overpower the aroma of the fresh brewing coffee. Coffee was what the O'Malley brothers needed especially Jimmy and Billy. They would need mass quantities to make it through the day after only a few hours of sleep. They reminisced about Christmases past.

Billy ribbed Jimmy by telling Pop that Jimmy was so excited about this Christmas that he was about to wet his pants. This was in reference to one Christmas when Jimmy got up Christmas morning but didn't go to the privy like both of his brothers did. As he was opening presents he couldn't hold it any longer.

Jimmy replied, "You guys are never going to let me forget that…"

Pop interrupted, "No. Funny is funny and that was funny."

"…but I will tell you that I did have that warm all over feeling."

The O'Malley brothers were getting anxious. Sam was still asleep and the sun was already up. They began to talk louder. Pop banged a few pots in the sink. Finally they heard Sam moving around and going to the bathroom.

When Jimmy heard this, he said, "Smart kid."

Sam stumbled into the living room. His eyes lit up when he saw the bicycle. The look on his face was worth Billy and Jimmy's loss of sleep. Pop could not have been happier.

"Is this mine?" Sam said in disbelief.

"Yep. It's all yours," replied Pop. "There are some more gifts under the tree."

Sam unwrapped the model plane kit. "Wow." He held it up to show the others. "This is the plane that my Dad flew."

Billy answered, "I know. Do you like it?"

"It's fantastic." Sam ripped open the next gift. "Wow, an erector set. This is what I have always wanted."

Jimmy said, "Maybe we can play with it later."

Pop then said, "Sam, there is one more gift. It is in the back of the tree."

Sam, on all fours, crawled and retrieved the nicely wrapped gift. He was still on his knees and then he sat back on his heels. He was somewhat puzzled. The tag read, "To: Sam / From: Mom." He tore open the wrapping paper exposing the picture of him and his mother. He didn't say a word. He just stared at the picture. Sam took his finger and touched his mother's face. Still silent, he got up and went to his bedroom and closed the door behind him. He put the photograph on the nightstand next to the picture of his father in his Army uniform. Sam sat on the edge of the bed and spoke out loud but in a low voice as he admired the pictures of his Mom and Dad. "I love both of you very much. There is not a day that I don't miss you. Don't worry about me. The O'Malley brothers are doing a good job in taking care of me. Merry Christmas."

Meanwhile, the O'Malley brothers were having second thoughts about giving Sam the picture as a Christmas gift. This was soon proved wrong when Sam reappeared.

Sam hugged Pop. "Thank you for the bike."

Sam hugged Uncle Billy. "Thank you for the model airplane."

Sam hugged Uncle Jimmy. "Thank you for the erector set."

Sam stood before the O'Malley brothers and addressed all three of them together. "Thank you for the picture of me and my Mom. It was the best gift of all."

It was somewhat suspicious but all three of the O'Malley brothers had to clear their throats at the same time.

Sam turned to Pop. "Can I go out? I want to show Johnny and Theresa my new bike."

Pop answered. "Don't be gone long. You have to get ready for church. You and Johnny are altar boys this morning and Theresa is scheduled to ring the bell."

"Thanks. I'll be back in plenty of time. I love you guys."

Jimmy and Billy headed back to the Rectory to get ready to celebrate Mass. Pop straightened up around the apartment.

After Mass, Johnny and Sam quickly got out of their surplices and cassocks. They went and found Pop and got permission to go ride the bike for awhile. Pop said it was ok but be back at the Rectory in less than an hour because Sam had to help set the table for Christmas dinner. Johnny and Sam then sped off and met Theresa at the bike parked in front of the church. Johnny got on the crossbar and Theresa got on the handlebars with her feet dangling in the basket. The three of them were heading off toward the river.

Sam was back as promised. He helped Pop and his uncles set the table and they all sat down. Sam was the one who said the blessing but there was a problem; there was no food on the table. The door to the Rectory opened and in marched Sister Monica and her merry band of angels. Each was carrying a separate dish. They were singing Jingle Bells and each laid her dish on the table. They proceeded around the table in single file and then disappeared through the door they entered. It was truly a feast; much more than Father O'Malley had expected. Even Sam was impressed.

Jimmy turned to Billy, "These are the times that I miss being a parish priest."

Chapter 9

Playing Hooky (Circa 1944)

Father O'Malley telephoned his brother. "Is Sam home sick today?"

"No. He should be in school."

"Well, he's not and neither is Johnny nor Theresa."

Pop told Father O'Malley to hold on while he went and checked on something. He came back to the phone. "The fishing poles are gone. I know exactly where they are. As soon as I can close the store, I will be over there. You can meet me outside."

Pop pulled out one of many signs that he used to place on the front door whenever he had to leave. This one said, "Be back in an hour."

Pop and Father O'Malley walked the five blocks to the old wooded dock where the paddle boat used to tie off. They left the roadway and followed a well-traveled path that led down to the waters edge. As they neared, they could hear the three of them talking, laughing and apparently having a good time. They moved closer where they could see and not be seen. All three were ok. In fact, they were actually catching fish. Pop moved forward to go and apprehend the three desperados.

Father O'Malley grabbed him on the back of the shirt and pulled him back. "Let's let them be for awhile. They are having such a good time. These kids are living through some tough times. They are kids just being kids. I will come back later this afternoon and round them up."

"I think we should get them now and make them get back to class."

"O Ye of little memory. You and I did almost the exact same thing when we were kids but Jimmy caught us in less than an hour. Besides, we didn't catch any fish because you forgot the worms."

"You're still blaming me for that!"

"Yes! ...because you are the one that *forgot the worms.*"

Pop reluctantly agreed but inside he thought it was a good idea. They both walked back toward the Rectory. Pop returned to the store and Father O'Malley went to Johnny's house to speak with his mother. They didn't have a telephone. Mrs. Jernigan was alarmed to see Father O'Malley at her front door. Her fears were soon relieved when he began to tell her about Johnny and that he was going to administer punishment when he brought them back to the school this afternoon. Father O'Malley had to reassure her that skipping school was not going to lead to a life of crime. Mrs. Jernigan was thankful that her husband was overseas because had he been at home, Johnny would have felt his father's wrath over and above Father O'Malley's paddle.

Father O'Malley sat down at his desk and pulled out a telephone directory of St. Patrick's parishioners. He thumbed through it until he found Jack and Judy Kelly. He dialed the number. Jack answered.

"Jack, this is Father O'Malley. What are you doing home?"

"My departure was delayed. I will ship out tomorrow."

"Are you wearing your St. Christopher medal?"

Without ill will, Jack was irritated. This was the third time Father O'Malley had asked him the same question. "Yes Father. As promised, I have it around my neck next to my dog tags. The least you could have done was to give me a smaller medal. This thing is huge."

Father O'Malley responded in his usual dry humor. "What are you complaining about…it was free. Besides it was the only size I had. Just make an old man happy and keep wearing it. I guarantee, it will protect you."

Jack knew that Father O'Malley was truly concerned about him. He was the one that baptized him, paddled him in school, was the celebrant in his marriage, and baptized Theresa. He just didn't want Father O'Malley to preside over his funeral.

"Father, I know that there is another reason for your call."

"Well Jack, we have a little problem with your daughter. She, along with Johnny and Sam, are playing hooky today. They are down at the river fishing. I will take care of the situation later this afternoon."

"Are they going to get the paddle?"

"Of course, at least the boys will. I leave the discipline for the girls up to Sister Monica."

"Do they still call her, 'Sister Witch with a switch'?"

"Yes, a reputation that is greatly over exaggerated. She is really just a little harmless kitten."

"Since I am no longer subject to your paddle, I am here to tell you that you are really the harmless kitten. My father's spankings make you look like a sissy. I remember both times you paddled me."

"Let's keep that secret among friends. The fear of the paddle is far more powerful than the paddling itself. Also, the fact that you recall both paddlings means that they had their intended effect."

"I guess you're right."

"Of course I am right. I am always right. Father O'Malley joked. He continued, "I don't want you punishing Theresa when she gets home. You are leaving tomorrow and it may be a long time before you see her again. You don't want to leave her with any bad memories of you. Now, give me your word."

"Yes, Father."

"Theresa, Johnny, and Sam are good kids. They are the reason why you are going off to war. I personally know Theresa's dad and he too wasn't a perfect kid and he turned out just fine. May God be with you and WEAR THAT ST. CHRISTOPHER MEDAL!"

"I will and thanks Father."

Father O'Malley went back to doing the normal business of the day. He finished and neatly stacked the papers on the desk. He glanced up at the clock. It was 1 o'clock. It was time. He walked down the street and turned onto the path. As he approached the three, he changed his demeanor and spoke with a low authoritative voice. He wanted to give the impression that he was mad.

"So this is where you have been. We have been looking for you all day. You three are in trouble."

Theresa, Johnny, and Sam got up without saying a word. They *knew* that they were in trouble. When Sam pulled the stringer of fish from the water, Father O'Malley was quite impressed but he dared not acknowledge the fact. Father O'Malley directed them to go to Pop's Grocery. Sam pulled open the front screen door and the four of them entered.

Father O'Malley spoke, "You three had Pop worried sick. He thought something terrible had happened to you. Father O'Malley directed his next words to Sam, "Give Pop those fish to clean. He can fry them up for dinner tonight. It's a sin to waste food."

Pop took the hint from Father O'Malley. He also wanted to eat the fish for dinner. It was a nice stringer but he too could not let the three know of his approval. "Father, I will fry these up tonight. It is like you said, 'it's a sin to waste food.' However, Sam may have to stand up to eat." Pop looked at Sam, "Remember the first day you came here. I told you how Father O'Malley paddled one boy so hard that he could not sit down for three days." Sam swallowed hard but he remained silent. Pop continued, "I'm glad that I'm not in your shoes."

Father O'Malley instructed Theresa, Johnny, and Sam to head for the school. The three knew that judgment day was only minutes away. They were determined to take their punishment like men (and woman). They stood straight with their chests out and their heads held high. In single file, they marched in stride with their arms swinging in unison. Their eyes never deflected from straight away. When they passed the playground, all the children ran up to the fence to watch. But Theresa, Johnny, and Sam were defiant. They continued to stare straight ahead with no outward signs of fear.

Father O'Malley instructed the three to sit down in the chairs in front of the principal's office. He went inside. He reappeared a few minutes later. "Johnny, you're first." Johnny rose. As he moved in front of Theresa, she briefly grasped his hand in a sign of solidarity. The sound of the paddle was clearly audible to both Theresa and Sam. Each time the "Pow" sound was heard, Sam flinched. After five whacks, it was over for Johnny. He came out and sat down. He was proud of himself. He had survived Father O'Malley's paddle.

Sam was quick in asking, "Did it hurt?"

Johnny answered, "No." But he would have never admitted it even if it did.

Theresa said, "I have a plan!"

Sam wanted to know her plan but she refused. "I will tell you if it works."

Sister Monica summoned Theresa. She got up and followed her inside. Johnny and Sam could hear Theresa talking from the time the office door closed but they could not distinguish what she was saying. It was a short time before the door opened and Theresa came out and sat down.

Sam was anxious to hear the plan because he was next in line. "What was the plan?"

"I started repeating out loud over and over again, 'Sweet Baby Jesus, don't let this woman kill me.' I figured that there was not a nun on the face of this earth that could resist a kid pleading for mercy."

Johnny wanted to know if it worked.

"I guess it did because it was a piece of cake."

Sam was disheartened with Theresa's plan. He doubted that Father O'Malley would fall for such theatrics.

It was Sam's turn. Theresa grabbed his hand and said, "It'll be all right."

Johnny and Theresa sat there in silence as they counted five "pows".

Sam strutted out of the principal's office with a big smile on his face. He placed both of his hands on the wooden arms of the chair and slowly lowered himself. He let out a sign of relief. He was worried that he was not going to be able to sit down for three days.

Johnny said, "I told you we were going to get caught."

Sam responded, "I know but I must say that this has got to be the best day of my life."

Johnny questioned, "So you think it was worth it?"

Theresa answered the question with pride, "DAMN right it was!"

Johnny and Sam looked at Theresa with shock and surprise. They couldn't believe that she had said the word "damn". Sam told her she had spunk. Theresa made her hand into a fist and extended it in front of her. Sam did the same thing and placed his fist above hers. Johnny placed his fist on top. Together they swore their oath, "Friends Forever".

Father O'Malley came out of the office and stood in front of the three. He was still in character. He was shaking his finger. "I hope that the three of you have learned your lesson. Johnny and Theresa, I want both of you to go straight home. Sam, you have to go to work. Tell Pop that I will be there about six o'clock for that fish dinner. Now, the three of you get out of here before I change my mind and give you detention."

In an instant, they were on their feet. Theresa draped her arms on the shoulders of Johnny and Sam. Father O'Malley watched them as they headed toward the front entrance of the school. They were silhouetted against the bright sunshine outside. He smiled and thought to himself, "Even in troubled times, life CAN be good."

Chapter 10

The Messenger of Death (Circa 1944)

An olive drab Chevrolet sedan with a big white star painted on the side entered the community of New Dublin from the south. It proceeded up Main St. at a slow pace because of the traffic and the numerous stop signs. Pedestrians walking along the sidewalk stopped and stared at the passing car. Many made the sign of the cross. The staff car was recognizable to all. The military official was in town to notify the next of kin. Someone in town had been killed in action. Those who had loved ones serving overseas immediately returned home in the event they were the one who would be the recipient of the bad news.

Corporal Brown parked the sedan in front of St. Patrick Church. He got out, lit a cigarette and stood waiting by the car. Captain Stephen Stewart straightened his uniform and put on his hat. He walked to the Rectory and was greeted by Father O'Malley who was seated at his desk.

Captain Stewart sat down. "Father, I appreciate your assistance in this matter. It makes it a little easier for me."

"I know that you have a tough job."

"This detail lasts for eighteen months and during this time, you can't even submit a request for transfer. After that, it is still uncertain whether or not a transfer would be approved."

"I know that this may be hard for you to believe but you are doing the Lord's work. I have seen the way you interrelate with the family members. You have heart. You have compassion. God's plan is to have you doing what you are doing at this point in time."

"Thank you, Father. That helps a bit. Captain Stewart continued. "I love your town. My father was in the Foreign Service and we have lived all over the world but there is no particular place that I would call 'home'. My parents are now retired and living in Florida. I have a sister in California and a brother in Texas. When I get mustered out of the service, I am going to make New Dublin my new hometown."

Father O'Malley said, "The welcome mat is always out for you. Maybe you can get a job at the plant."

"I am an accountant by trade. I will open a business."

"That would be good. We don't have any independent accountants here." Father O'Malley continued but he didn't want to ask the question. "Captain, who are we going to see?"

"Mrs. Ann Kelty."

Father O'Malley didn't immediately respond. He lowered his head and said a silent prayer. He regained his composure and looked at Captain Stewart. "Robert was one of my favorites."

"Father, I don't mean to be rude but the last two times that I have been here you said that they were one of your favorites."

"Captain, they're all my favorites, however, Robert was very high on my list. I know his grandparents. I married his father and mother. I baptized him and his older sister. I married Robert and Ann. They went through school here at St. Patrick's. I can remember when they first started dating in high school. It is almost impossible not to build a life long relationship with all of my parishioners."

Father O'Malley and Captain Stewart got into the sedan. Father O'Malley gave directions to the Kelty residence. As they turned onto one of the residential streets, neighbors were out front on the sidewalk or standing on their porches. It was bittersweet for the neighbors. They were happy that Captain Stewart wasn't stopping at their front door. They were sad that one of their neighbors would not be so fortunate.

Father O'Malley motioned to Corporal Brown to the third house on the right where a young woman in a blue dress was standing. Corporal Brown pulled to the curb. Ann Kelty took a couple of steps backwards and sat down on the steps. She buried her face in her hands and began to sob and gasping for air. Father O'Malley sat down beside her and he put his arm around her. Ann still crying, turned and hugged Father O'Malley. He tried to restrain himself but he too cried along with her.

After a few minutes, Father O'Malley said, "Ann, this gentleman needs to speak with you."

"Mrs. Kelty my name is Captain Stewart. I regret to inform you of the death of your husband on February 9, 1944 at Anzio, Italy. I cannot give you details of how he was killed in action. That information is being held in abeyance until the details are investigated and confirmed. I am authorized to tell you that you that your husband is being considered for the Congressional Medal of Honor. You will be notified of the decision of the Commission as soon as the facts are received and reviewed. Again, Mrs. Kelty, I want to extend my sincerest condolences. Father had many kind words to say about you and your husband."

Ann's mother had heard the news and she was running up the street to be with her daughter. Robert's parents had also arrived. Father O'Malley thought it best to let family console family. He and Captain Stewart returned to the sedan and headed back to the Rectory. Captain Stewart again thanked Father O'Malley for his assistance.

Corporal Brown drove away. He said, "Captain, it doesn't get easier, does it?"

Captain Stewart full of grief himself responded, "No Corporal, it doesn't."

Chapter 11

Albert Swartz's Synagogue (Circa 1944)

Father O'Malley stood at the pulpit and spoke to his parishioners. "I am going to give you a break today. I am going to forego my homily. That should make most of you happy except for those of you who normally sleep through my sermons. First of all, I want to recognize our guests on this beautiful Sunday morning: Albert and Naomi Swartz; Dr. Jacob and Beth Swartz, along with their son Isaac. When we built this church, school, and convent, Albert was one of the hardest working volunteers. Glance around, Albert's personal touch can be seen in everything you see from the altar, the stained glassed windows, the pews and even the plaster on the walls. He worked tirelessly. I remember asking him why a Jewish man wanted to help to build a Catholic Church and school. He simply answered, 'It was the right thing to do.' But it was more than that. We all realized at that point in time that we had an obligation to the next generation to provide a quality education. Jacob was one of the first recipients of that quality education. I would like to think that St. Patrick School was partially responsible for him excelling in medical school."

Father O'Malley pointed to the nuns. He continued, "Young Isaac is also receiving a good education thanks to these ladies sitting right here in the front row." The entire congregation applauded in agreement.

Father O'Malley said, "I had heard through the grapevine that Albert was considering building a synagogue because the Jewish community had grown to twenty families mainly due to the growth of new workers at the aircraft plant. He was hesitant in asking for our help because he thought it was begging. I had to set him straight. It is not begging...it is neighbor helping neighbor. The same as he did years ago."

While Father O'Malley was speaking, Sister Monica leaned over and spoke to her fellow sisters. They were smiling and nodded their heads in agreement. Sister Monica stood up, "Excuse me Father."

Father O'Malley acknowledge her, "Yes, Sister."

"I just had a brief conference with my colleagues and we have decided to bring the Texaco Girls out of retirement for an encore performance. We aren't as spry as we use to be but we can still swing a mean paint brush." This brought laughter and applause from the entire congregation.

Father O'Malley turned to Albert, "Now you have your first volunteers. You have your paint crew. These ladies are not only good teachers but they are good painters." Father O'Malley continued, "…and Sean has agreed to make a sizable donation."

Sean stood up and said with disgust, "Billy O'Malley, you know that you shouldn't fabricate such stories. You're a priest and priests should tell the truth. This is the first that I have heard about Albert's plan to build a synagogue so how could I have said that I was going to make a sizable donation."

"I prayed to the Holy Spirit to come to you in a dream. Obviously you didn't get the message."

"No, I didn't." He made eye contact with his friend. "Albert come by the hardware store and I will give you a good deal on your lumber and other supplies."

Father O'Malley smiling, "Sean, there is a special place in heaven for you."

"Billy, can't you come up with a better line than that? The next thing that you will tell me is that I am going to be St. Peter's right hand man."

"Sean, just keep up your good deeds and I'll see what I can do."

Sean, smiling, shook his head in disgust and sat back down. Father O'Malley enjoyed ribbing Sean. It was tradition. Other members of the church began to raise their hands to volunteer. Father O'Malley told those who wanted to help Albert to sign the tablet in the vestibule after Mass.

Father O'Malley began an informal introduction. "Albert is a decent and honorable man. He is a good father. He is also a scholar on the Old Testament. If any of you are students of the Bible, Albert can teach you a whole different perspective on the Old Testament. He explains the passages in historical context which makes it more understandable. I know he has taught me a lot. Albert wanted to briefly speak to you so I am going to turn the pulpit over to him."

"Thank you, Father. On behalf of myself, my family and the New Dublin Jewish community, I want to thank each of you for the out pouring of your generosity. It is truly heartfelt. For the last several years, I have had this dream of building a synagogue but I didn't know if the time was right. We are at war. Should I wait for a more peaceful time? I have prayed for divine direction but I am still at a loss. If any of you feel that it is inappropriate to begin construction at this time. Please tell me now. The plans can be put on hold."

Mrs. Kelty stood up. "Albert, you knew my son. He died a hero fighting for freedom. I miss him. His father misses him and his wife misses him. I don't want to think that his death was in vain. If he were here today, he would tell you without hesitation, build your synagogue! And as a side note…I'm going to help."

"Thank you, Mrs. Kelty, for your words of encouragement. I believe that God has just spoken through you. He has answered my prayers for guidance. I now know without a doubt which way to proceed. I have always been of the belief that we should never…never…never drastically change our American way of life because if we do, we lose and they win. My goal is not to build an elaborate synagogue. I want it to be basic, whereby over time, we can make additions as the need arises. I will be working on obtaining all the necessary building materials. I will then contact each of you who have signed up as volunteers and together we can formulate a construction schedule. I don't want to waste anyone's time. However, I do have one personal request. One of my fondest memories when we built St. Patrick's was the lunches we had on the church grounds. It was a family affair. I am hopeful that we will be able to do that again. I would also like to add what Father O'Malley said that I may have enlightened him on the Old Testament but he has taught me a lot about the New Testament."

Albert wanted to express feelings that touched every American. "As I speak to you today, many of New Dublin's young men are in Europe fighting for freedom. Mrs. Kelty, my heart goes out to you and your family. Your son made the ultimate sacrifice. We should always keep these soldiers and their families in our thoughts and prayers. Hitler must be stopped. The Nazis are taking entire Jewish families and executing them or sending them to concentration camps; not because they are the enemy but simply because they are Jewish. When all the Jews are gone, they will come for the mentally ill and the infirmed. Next will be the religious including the Catholic Priests. When they are all gone, then they will come for you. The Third Reich is the devil incarnate. We all are doing our part; no matter how trivial. Those of you who work at the plant are just as important as our soldiers on the front lines. It is not as dangerous but it is just as important. We will never win the war without airplanes. My son Jacob made me very proud. He wanted to enlist in the Army but fortunately I was able to convince him otherwise. Our military needs good doctors but it can also be his patriotic duty to stay right here. He is the only doctor in fifty miles. I would venture to say that most of you at one time or another have been patients at his clinic. It is his job to keep us all well so that we can build more airplanes. We had some very wise forefathers as to how they addressed freedom of religion. I am humbled today to see how we as a people can accept each other's religious beliefs. In an obscure way, building this synagogue is our way of showing the world that America will never be defeated. May God bless the United States of America, may God bless the town of New Dublin and may God bless each and every one of you. Thank you.

The entire congregation stood and applauded as Albert left the sanctuary.

Father O'Malley returned to the pulpit. "Thank you, Albert. That was inspiring. I also have some more good news. I talked with your friend, the Bishop. He wanted me to offer his congratulations on your new synagogue and that he was starting today to build you a pulpit."

When Mass was over a line formed to sign up as volunteers; even Johnny, Theresa and Sam agreed to be "helpers". Father O'Malley took the tablet and handed it to Albert. Albert responded, "Thanks for everything, Billy. It's amazing how goodness can thrive when there is so much evil in the world."

****

Albert and a small crew were busy during the week. Building supplies were delivered. Foundation piers were put into place. Early Saturday morning came and the volunteers began to arrive. It did not take long before there were sounds of heavy construction. Several men were cutting wood to specifications while others were hammering the boards into place. Framing of the side walls was being nailed together on the ground and then being lifted and put into place. In the late morning, the women showed up bearing a bounty of food. Tables were set up on the lawn. The weather wasn't a problem. It was a beautiful sunny day. All work stopped. Everyone gather around the tables filled with a variety of food dishes. Albert made a few comments as to how it warmed his heart at the outpouring of his fellow neighbors. He said the blessing and lunch was served. It was everything that Albert had envisioned; just like the original days at St. Patrick's.

Albert was diplomatic in his efforts to get everyone back to work. He was fighting full stomachs and the desires to snooze under the shade trees. Slowly but surely, construction resumed. Before dusk, real progress had been done. The entire building was framed and the roof with slate shingles was in place. Work ceased for the day.

Construction continued for the next two Saturdays. The synagogue was finished with the exception of cosmetic work. The Texaco Girls armed with their paint brushes began the task at hand. The more agile nuns climbed the ladders and painted the ceiling and then downward to where the others could paint up to shoulder high. There were two crews; one on the interior and the other on the exterior. They made the work fun. Chit chat was commonplace which was only interrupted when they sang their favorite hymns. With seventeen enthusiastic women, the painting would be completed before the day was done.

A pick up truck pulled up in front of the synagogue. Out stepped Bishop O'Malley. He summoned help from three men. The four of them carried the pulpit inside and placed it where Albert had instructed them. All the volunteers, including the Texaco Girls, stood and admired Bishop O'Malley's handy work. It was a masterpiece; better than the one he crafted for St. Patrick's.

Albert said to the Bishop, "Jimmy, this is beautiful. Thank you very much."

Jimmy responded, "You're welcome. It was a labor of love. This is a house warming gift from the Diocese of Jefferson City."

The next morning, the Jewish Community gathered in front of St. Patrick Church waiting for Mass to end. They carried a large banner with the word "Shalom". They greeted all the parishioners with a handshake and "Thank You" as they departed the church.

Father O'Malley said to Albert, "This is a nice gesture."

"It is our way of showing our gratitude. Besides, it is my Irish heritage. I think my mother, your mother and Sean's mother brought seeds from ole Ireland and planted them right here in New Dublin."

"You're right, Billy, and the fruits of those seeds are constantly blooming every day. God has truly blessed us all."

Chapter 12

Robbery at Pop's Grocery (Circa 1944)

Pop was at the cash register tending to a customer when the telephone rang, "Sam can you get that?"

"Yes sir." He answered the phone. "Pop's Grocery. Sam speaking."

"Sam, this is Mrs. Kennedy. I need a few items. Can you deliver them?"

"Yes ma'am. Let me get my pencil and pad." Sam cocked the phone receiver between his ear and shoulder. "Go ahead."

"Give me a quart of milk and a loaf of bread. Get Pop to cut me four pork chops about ½ inches thick and a pound of sliced bacon. What kind of dry beans do you have?"

Sam was knowledgeable of everything in the store. He answered without hesitation, "We have large lima beans, northern beans and pinto beans."

"Give me a bag of large lima beans. Do you have any fresh eggs?"

"Yes ma'am. We got some in this morning."

"Good. Give me a dozen. That is all I need today."

Sam was a good salesman. He pitched a few more items. "Mr. Jones brought in some of his home grown vegetables this morning. We have corn and tomatoes."

"No, not today."

Sam was not going to give up. "We have several of Mrs. Shanahan's pies still left."

"Now that does sound good. Give me one of her apple pies."

"Yes ma'am. I will get this order together and deliver it to you in about thirty minutes."

"Tell Pop to put it on my account."

"Yes ma'am."

Sam turned to Pop, he didn't ask but more or less instructed Pop, "Cut me up four ½ inch thick pork chops and a pound of sliced bacon."

Pop was impressed with how Sam had taken to running the store. He was all business. Pop did what he was told to do while Sam rushed around and filled the rest of the order. Sam rang up the sale and logged the amount into Mrs. Kennedy's account. He bagged up everything. He took off his apron and hung it up on the nail on the back of the storage room door. As he walked out the door with the groceries he yelled to Pop, "I'll be back shortly." He loaded his groceries in the basket on his bicycle and headed off. He was careful not to jar the groceries as he traveled down the sidewalk. He went to Mrs. Kennedy's front door carrying two bags of groceries. He took his foot and tapped on the door.

Mrs. Kennedy greeted Sam. "Come on in, you can put the bags on the kitchen table."

Sam walked in and headed back toward the kitchen. He had been there many times before and he knew the way.

Mrs. Kennedy pulled out a small black change purse. She pulled out a quarter and gave it to Sam. "Thanks. You're a fine young man."

"Thank you." Sam then left and headed back toward the grocery. He was pleased with the quarter. It was a good tip.

Meanwhile back at the grocery store, Pop was confronted by an intruder who flashed a hand gun and demanded, "Give me all your money." Pop tried to talk his way out of the situation but the robber was not listening. He was nervous. Pop wasn't going to give this guy one red cent without a fight. Pop picked up a baseball bat that he kept by the cash register. He swung it hitting the intruder in the head. Blood spurted all over the counter. The gun fired. The bullet hit Pop in the abdomen. Pop fell to the floor. The robber moved around to the back of the counter and emptied the cash register. He stuffed the money in his pockets and ran for the awaiting car.

Sam put down the kick stand on his bike and started to enter the store. The robber came running out. He had a gun in one hand and his other hand was on a big gash in his forehead. He knocked Sam to the ground as he made his escape. Sam got up and ran inside. Pop was lying behind the counter clutching his stomach.

Sam was scared and crying. "Please Pop. Don't die. I can't lose you. I just can't."

He told Sam, "I am going to be ok. Go get some help." Sam bolted and ran down the street to the hardware store. Sean Ryan was there. Sam screamed, "Mr. Ryan, Pop has been shot." Sean, along with three male customers followed Sam back to the grocery store. Sean talked with Pop and assured him that he would be all right. He told Sam to go upstairs and bring him several blankets. After Sam had done this, Sean told him to go to the clinic and tell Dr. Swartz that we are on our way. Then run and get your Uncle Billy. Sean raced out of the store; climbed on his bike and headed for the clinic. He told Dr. Swartz that Pop had been shot and Mr. Ryan would be there in a few minutes. Dr. Swartz prepared his examination room for Pop's arrival. Sam went to the Rectory and found Uncle Billy. When he heard the news, his face went pale. Billy pulled up his cassock and ran as fast as he could to the clinic. Sean laid Pop on the blanket and each of the four men grabbed a corner and lifted Pop. They exited the store and headed toward the clinic. Other gentlemen on the street offered assistance until there were eight men grasping the blanket. Sean and Billy arrived at the same time. Billy grabbed his brother's hand. It was covered in blood. Billy told Pop, "Hang in there brother. You'll be fine." Dr. Swartz directed them into the examination room. He told everyone except Billy to stay outside. Dr. Swartz cut open Pop's shirt and observed the wound. It was serious. Dr. Swartz cleaned the wound and was able to stop the bleeding but he was concerned that Pop may be bleeding internally. He needed surgery immediately. They had to get him to the hospital in Jefferson City. Billy suggested calling for an ambulance. Dr Swartz said that that would take too much time. They had to get him transported now. Billy went outside of the examination room and asked Sean to go and get his panel truck. It was needed to travel to Jefferson City. Sean sprinted out and in a few minutes he was parked in front of the clinic. Dr. Swartz removed the cushions from the gurney and laid them on the floor of the panel truck. They gently maneuvered Pop inside. Sean drove. Sam was in the front seat. Billy and Dr. Swartz were in the back with Pop. The nurse called the hospital in Jefferson City and alerted them to have the operating room prepared for surgery. She also notified the Sheriff's office about the robbery and aftermath. She then called the Cathedral and got word to Bishop O'Malley. Sean sped out of New Dublin. Several miles down the road, the Sheriff came up behind them with his emergency light flashing and the siren blaring. He pulled along side Sean and motioned for him to follow. They now had an escort to the emergency room. This would save precious time. Sam was praying as hard as any young man could. He got up on his knees and turned backwards on the front seat looking over at Pop who was floating in and out of consciousness. Pop reached up and grabbed Sam's hand. "Don't worry, Sam. I am not going to leave you." Uncle Billy also reassured Sam even though he himself was extremely worried.

The Sheriff pulled into the emergency room portico followed by Sean. Bishop O'Malley was standing outside with the orderlies awaiting their arrival. The orderlies opened the back door of the panel truck and assisted Dr. Swartz and Billy in getting Pop onto a gurney. Bishop O'Malley greeted his brother as they were wheeling him inside. "There are excellent doctors here and they will take good care of you." When the gurney was stopped, Sam and the O'Malley brothers along with Sean joined hands and Jimmy said a short prayer for a successful operation. Sam hugged Pop. Pop then placed his hand on Sam's shoulder, "Like I said earlier, I am not going to leave you." Sam stood teary eyed as he watched them wheel the gurney toward the operating room." Dr. Swartz had received permission from the surgeon to observe the operation. He was at the entrance to the operating room as Pop passed. He told him that he was in good hands and that he was going to be with him throughout the entire operation. Pop responded, "Thanks Jacob."

Sean, Jimmy, Billy, Sam, and the Sheriff sat down in the waiting room. The Sheriff needed to speak with Sam to find out what happened to Pop. Sam explained, "I was returning from delivering a grocery order to Mrs. Kennedy. I got back to the store and this man came running out. He knocked me down. He had a gun in one hand and he had his other hand on his head right here." Sam pointed to the left side of his forehead. "He was bleeding. He jumped in the passenger door and they drove off."

"So there were two of them?" questioned the Sheriff.

"...at least two. I don't know if there was anyone else in the car."

"Do you know what kind of car?"

"Yes sir. It was a 1937 Black Ford Coupe."

"Are you sure?"

"Yes sir. That is one of my favorite cars."

"Did you see the license plate?"

"No sir."

"How old do you think he was?"

"He was a lot younger than Pop but he wasn't a teenager either."

"What color hair?"

"Black."

"How tall?"

"He was about as tall as you are."

"What was he wearing?"

"He had on dark britches and a white shirt."

"Do you know what caused this man to be bleeding?"

"No sir. Pop did keep a baseball bat behind the counter. Maybe he hit the man with the bat."

The Sheriff glanced up to the admission desk. There was man there that fit the description provided by Sam. He had a blood soaked towel up against the side of his head. The way in which Sam was sitting he could not see the individual. Sheriff calmly told Sam. "I want you to sit back in your chair. Don't say a word. I am going to ask you a question and I want you to just say yes or no. Do you understand?"

Sam was confused but he did as the Sheriff asked.

"OK Sam, I want you to look at that man over there. Do you recognize him?"

Sam got excited, "Yes sir. That's him. That's the man that shot Pop."

The Sheriff patted Sam on the leg. "Just sit here and don't say a word." The Sheriff leaned over to Billy who had been listening to the conversation and said, "All of you get up quietly and go outside through that door over there."

Billy rose from his seat along with Sam. He whispered to the others to follow him. After they were safely outside, the Sheriff pulled his revolver and moved toward the man. He positioned himself in such a fashion that if he had to shoot the robber he wouldn't put the nurses behind the counter in jeopardy. He eased up behind the robber and told him, "If you want to live put both of your hands on the counter. The robber did exactly as told. The Sheriff told the nurses to leave. He continued with the robber, "Lay your head on the counter and put your hands behind your back." Again the robber complied. The Sheriff put handcuffs on the robber and stood him up. The gash on the robber's forehead was wide enough to expose the skull. It was steadily bleeding. The Sheriff said, "Pop hit a homerun on your head."

The robber answered, "Who is Pop?"

"Pop is the man you shot. You better hope that he doesn't die."

"I didn't mean to shoot him. When he hit me with the bat, the gun went off."

The Sheriff didn't want to hear excuses. However, he did want more information. "If you don't want to bleed to death, you're going to tell me where your partner in crime is?"

The robber readily gave up his accomplice. He was in the car in the parking lot. The Sheriff got his name and description. He called the local police department and gave them the details. They dispatched several police cars. The officers scoured the parking lot until they found a 1937 Black Ford Coupe. They made the arrest without incident. In the interim, the nurses had the doctor on duty sew up the robber's head. The Sheriff apologized for all the blood on the counter and the floor. It was not long until an orderly had the whole area cleaned up. The police officers came inside with the accomplice in handcuffs. The Sheriff took custody of him.

Sam and the others returned to the waiting room. They all congratulated the Sheriff for a job well done. It was not long before the Sheriff left with his two prisoners. The excitement was over. It was now back to waiting. Sam was emotionally exhausted. He laid his head in Jimmy's lap and went sound to sleep. One hour passed and no word. Two hours passed and still no word. Dr. Swartz then appeared. He informed everyone that Pop was doing well in the surgery. They had removed the bullet that had lodged on the back side of the ribcage. He had been bleeding internally and the surgeon was slowly but surely clamping off each source of blood flow. It would still be several more hours before the surgery was finished. This was encouraging news. Dr. Swartz returned to the operating room.

Sam was awake. Uncle Jimmy suggested that they all go down the hall to the hospital cafeteria and get something to eat. He wasn't worried about himself but he thought that Sam was probably hungry. He told the nurse behind the counter where they were going. She agreed to come and get them if anything happened. Uncle Jimmy was right. Sam was hungry. He inhaled his meal. Uncle Jimmy could not believe that a fourteen year old boy could eat that much food. Sean tried to pay for the meal but Billy refused to let him. Under different circumstances, Billy would have let Sean pay in more ways than one. Tonight was different. It was not a time for fun and games.

They all returned to the waiting room. It has now been over five hours. The length of time only fostered thoughts of the unthinkable. Finally, Dr. Swartz and the surgeon entered the waiting room. The surgeon who looked tired began, "Barring infection, I do not see why Mr. O'Malley will not make a full recovery. That bullet did a lot of damage but none of the vital organs were permanently impaired. He is now in the recovery room. I want to keep him here in the hospital for several weeks so that we can monitor his progress. After that, he can convalesce at home. Is there someone at home who can take care of him?"

Sam spoke up with confidence. "I will take care of him."

Billy did not want Sam to think that he was incapable of watching Pop. He added, "Sam will do a good job in caring for Pop and we will have others helping him out." The surgeon understood Father O'Malley's answer.

Bishop O'Malley asked if they could visit him. The surgeon recommended against it at this time. He was still under anesthesia and rest was important to his recovery. "Tomorrow would be better." The surgeon also stated, "I understand that the Sheriff arrested the shooter right here in the emergency room."

Uncle Jimmy somewhat proud said, "Yes sir. It was all because of Sam here. He was the only witness and he positively identified the man as the robber. He is our hero."

The surgeon reached out and shook Sam's hand. "Good job."

"Thanks sir."

Uncle Jimmy went back to the Cathedral Rectory. Sean, Sam, Billy and Dr. Swartz rode back to New Dublin. Sean dropped everyone off in front of the church. Father O'Malley said to Dr. Swartz before they parted ways, "Jacob, what you and the surgeon did tonight definitely saved Pop's life. I am forever grateful."

Sam piped in, "That goes for me too Dr. Swartz."

Jacob modestly responded, "I grew up going in and out of Pop's grocery. He is a good man. I didn't want him to die either." Dr. Swartz turned and walked toward his residence which was several blocks past the clinic.

Uncle Billy picked up a change of clothes at the Rectory and he and Sam went to Pop's. He was going to stay with Sam at the apartment above the store. Without saying a word, Sam went to the storage room and got a bucket of hot water along with a bottle of pine scented cleaner. He grabbed a couple of rags as he walked through the door. Sam and Uncle Billy wiped up all the blood. Even after the area was cleaned to perfection, there was still a stain in the hard wood floor. Uncle Billy said, "As soon as the floor gets good and dry, we can put a rug over the stain." Sam agreed. Uncle Billy continued, "Throw that water out on the grass in the back. Rinse the bucket out and put the rags in the trash."

"Yes sir."

After Sam had finished, the two of them went upstairs to the apartment. Uncle Billy grabbed a couple of sheets and a blanket from the closet and made his bed on the couch. Sam went to his room and sat on the edge of the bed. He looked at the pictures on his night stand, "Mom and Dad you don't have to worry. Everything is going to be all right."

The next morning at six o'clock Sam arose from bed. It was still dark outside. He went to the bathroom and took a quick bath. He put on some clean clothes, brushed his teeth and combed his hair. He went downstairs as quietly as possible so as to not awaken Uncle Billy. He turned on the lights and opened the front doors. He donned his apron and put the money that he got from the Sheriff back into the cash register. He grabbed the broom and started sweeping. It wasn't long before the local vendors started arriving. Mrs. Shanahan was the first. She had her five pies. Sam made out a receipt and paid her cash from the money in the till. She inquired about Pop's condition and Sam assured her that he would be ok. Mrs. Shanahan said, "Tell Pop that he is in our thoughts and prayers."

"Yes ma'am."

Robert Baker brought fresh vegetables and eggs; David Regan arrived with several slabs of meat and even the milk man who was from Jefferson City had heard about the robbery. They were all anxious to hear about Pop. Sam was cordial and repeated the story to each of them as if it was the first time. Uncle Billy stood at the top of the stairs watching Sam. He was concerned that the store would have to temporarily shut down until Pop recovered from his injuries. Those concerns quickly faded as he watched Sam deal with the vendors. Pop's Grocery was in good hands. Uncle Billy thought to himself. "Sam at times is a fourteen year old boy going on thirty. He is very mature. While at other times, he is still that fourteen year old kid."

Uncle Billy told Sam, "It looks like you have everything under control. I am heading over to the Rectory. Why don't you close up around four o'clock. We'll go and see Pop.

"Yes sir."

Sam handled all the business of the store as if he had been the manager for years. He took several orders over the phone that required deliveries. Sam put his own sign in the window, "Gone to make a delivery. I'll be back in 30 minutes." It was a steady flow of customers through out the day. Each one asked about the well being of Pop. Sam was courteous and answered everyone's questions but he had to admit to himself that it was getting mundane. Four o'clock came quickly. He posted a sign in the window, "Closed for the day. Gone to see Pop." Sam washed up and put on a clean dress shirt but he kept on his blue jeans and basketball shoes. He headed over to the Rectory where Uncle Billy was waiting.

Uncle Billy asked, "How was your day?"

"We were busy and everyone asked about Pop."

"Everyone that I met today asked me about Pop too. It gets old doesn't it?"

"Yes sir, but I was nice to everyone who asked."

"I was too but it still gets old."

Sam smiled at his Uncle Billy. "Yes sir, it does get old." He continued, "Do we need to take something to Pop?"

"Yes, you're right." Uncle Billy looked in his desk and pulled out a pair of scissors and handed them to Sam. "I got a vase around here somewhere. While I am looking for it, you go around the yard and cut us a bunch of flowers. Pop will like that." Sam was back shortly with a handful of flowers. They put them in the vase and added a little bit of water but not so much that would spill out on their trip to Jefferson City.

Sam and Uncle Billy arrived at the hospital and inquired at the front desk for the room number for Lawrence O'Malley. They walked down a long hall. The smell of a hospital was distinct. They found Pop's room. A note was posted on the door which said "Family Members Only." They entered. Uncle Jimmy was sitting in a chair beside the bed. He said, "Look Pop, we've got company." Pop was alert and in good spirits. It was obvious that he was happy to see Sam. Sam put his flowers on the nightstand and gave Pop a hug. Pop put his finger under Sam's chin and lifted his head until they were looking at each other eye to eye. He said sternly, "I told you I wasn't going to leave you."

Sam said, "I know but I have already lost my mom and dad. I was so scared that you were going to die. I thought that maybe I was bad luck."

"No...No. You're never bad luck. You are good luck to me and your two uncles here. I can't explain why God took your mom and dad. You have two Priests here and they have a difficult time in explaining God's will. Now you are unlucky because you have to put up with three cranky old men."

"Oh no. You guys are the greatest."

"I may be the greatest but I have my doubts about your uncles."

Sam laughed.

Uncle Billy said to Pop, "Sam brought you some flowers."

Pop rolled his head over and looked at the vase on the nightstand. "Those are the prettiest flowers that I have ever seen. Thank you Sam."

"Uncle Billy helped."

Pop turned back to look at his brother and sarcastically said, "Thank you too Uncle Billy."

Uncle Billy joked back, "You were always Mama's favorite. She used to tell me how you were her flower child."

Pop glanced back to Sam. "Uncle Billy thinks he is funny." Pop continued speaking with Sam, "How was business today?"

"We were busy. Everyone asked about you. They all said that you were in their thoughts and prayers."

"That's nice. You didn't have any problems? Did you get all the vendors paid?"

"No problems. I paid everyone. Mrs. Shanahan was there bright and early."

"I know. You can set your watch by Mrs. Shanahan arrival each morning. She is there at 6:45 a.m. every morning except Sunday. It sounds like you have everything under control. I am real proud of you but I don't want you cutting any meat. You could lose a finger."

Sam was sure of his abilities. "I cut meat this morning and I did just fine." He held up both hands and wiggled his fingers. "How many do you see?"

Uncle Jimmy said with a smile, "I see nine and one stub."

"Oh Uncle Jimmy, you are so silly." Sam enjoyed the way Pop and his uncles joked with him.

Pop added, "Just be careful."

"I will."

"Did you eat today?"

"Yes sir. I made a sandwich and had some milk. After we leave here, Uncle Jimmy, Uncle Billy and I are going to a diner down the street. Don't worry about me. I am not going to starve to death. Don't forget I live in a grocery store."

"Good point, Sam. I promise you, I will not worry. I remember when you first came into the store. You said that you were the man of the house. Now you really are the man of the house."

The doctors were impressed with Pop's progress in the last 24 hours. There were no signs of infection. The prognosis was good. This is not to say that Pop was able to get out of bed and do an Irish jig. He had a long way to go before he would be back to his normal self but time will heal his wounds.

Uncle Jimmy, Uncle Billy, and Sam entered the diner and sat down in a booth. The waitress dressed in a white dress with a red apron came over, "Hello, Bishop O'Malley. I see that you have some guests tonight."

"Yes, Florence, this is my brother Billy and my nephew, Sam."

"It's nice to meet you. Two priests in one family, that is fantastic."

"Our mother was a saint."

"I guess that you were over seeing your other brother. I hope that he is doing fine."

"He is. Thanks for asking.

Sam and Uncle Billy looked at each other and smiled.

After Florence had left to get water and silverware, Uncle Jimmy asked, "What is so funny?"

"Sam and I were talking earlier about all the people who have asked about Pop and how it was getting old telling the same story over and over."

Uncle Jimmy laughed too. "I know. I also had the same problem. I think what we need to do is to write a short status report and whenever someone asks us about Pop, we just hand them a copy. What do you think about that, Sam?"

"I like that idea."

The three of them scanned the menu before Florence returned. "Do you know what you want?"

"Yes", said Sam. "I want a hamburger with everything on it; an order of home fries and a root beer."

"…And you, Bishop?"

"Give me the special and coffee."

"…And you, Father?"

"I'll take the special and a Coca Cola."

After they had finished eating, Uncle Billy said to his brother, "The dinner was good. Do you come here often?"

"I get by here once or twice a week. I usually come on Tuesday. Tuesday's special is meat loaf and it is out of this world. It is almost as good as Mama's."

They paid the check. Uncle Jimmy headed back to the Cathedral Rectory. Uncle Billy and Sam walked back to the hospital to get the car. Before they were out of town, Sam was sound asleep and he slept all the way back to New Dublin. Uncle Billy parked in front of the grocery store. "Wake up Sam. We're home." Sam was groggy as he got the keys out of his pocket and unlocked the front door. He didn't waste any time in climbing the stairs and going straight to bed.

The surgeon had been adamant. He wanted Pop to stay in the hospital for two weeks for observation and he did not deviate from that time frame. Pop was to be discharged this morning. Bishop O'Malley said that he would pick up Pop and bring him to New Dublin. Sam was anxious. He was constantly peering out the front window watching for Uncle Jimmy. Finally, they arrived. Sam yelled to Uncle Billy, "They're here! They're Here! Pop is back!"

Uncle Billy got up from the stool behind the counter and walked to the sidewalk. Sam opened the car door. He and Uncle Billy assisted Pop.

Billy said, "Welcome home brother."

Pop responded, "Thanks. This place looks like heaven compared to the hospital."

Billy and Jimmy supported Pop under each arm. They moved toward the biggest obstacle…the stairs. Billy was concerned, "Pop do you think you can make it?"

"If I hold on to the rail and take it one step at a time, I should be ok."

Pop maneuvered each step and paused. Billy and Jimmy were behind him just in case he might fall. The whole procedure was time consuming but Pop made it to the top. It was painful but tolerable. He entered the apartment and gently lowered himself into his favorite chair. Sam brought over the foot stool. Pop lifted his legs and made a sigh of relief. "This is much better." Someone rang the counter bell. Sam ran downstairs to assist the customer. Pop told his two brothers that they needed to get back to work. He assured them that he was going to be fine but he knew that he had to get well before Sam went back to school in the fall. After his brothers left, Pop took a long snooze. He had expended a lot of energy.

Sam periodically went upstairs and checked on Pop. He did not disturb him. Several hours later, Pop awoke. Sam was standing over him. "Hello, Nurse Sam."

Sam laughed.

"Are you also Chef Sam?"

"…if you want me to be."

"I got a hankering for some good vegetable beef soup. The hospital food was terrible. If I give you the ingredients, do you think you can make us a big pot?"

"Sure."

Sam followed Pop's instructions precisely. It wasn't long before the aroma filled the entire kitchen.

Sam set the table. He put out a loaf of bread for dipping. They had tea to drink. He took several bowls from the cabinet and filled both of them to the brim. He gingerly walked over to the kitchen table so as not to spill any of the soup. "Supper is ready." Sam went over to the chair and helped Pop to his feet. He walked slowly to the kitchen table and sat down.
They both bowed their heads as Sam said the blessing.

Sam tasted a spoonful of soup, "Mmmmm, I done good."

"You done real good. This is delicious."

Pop's health improved each day. However, it was several weeks before he ventured downstairs. He helped Sam as much as he physically could but by the early afternoon he would have to go back upstairs to rest. Pop was relentless. Every day he tried to stay longer.

Early one morning, Johnny and Theresa came into the store. "Sam, come with us. There is a whole convoy of Army trucks down at the old campground. They are working on one of the trucks that broke down. It will be fun to go and look at them."

Sam wanted dearly to go. Sam was in conflict with "Sam the Man" and "Sam the Kid". "No. I need to stay here with Pop. You guys go and then come back and tell me about it."

Pop interjected. "Sam you can go. I will be fine. Go and have a good time."

This was music to Sam's ears. "Are you sure?" This was Sam's way of giving Pop a second chance to change his mind.

"I'm sure. Go."

Sam took off his apron and hung it on the nail on the storage room door. The three of them went flying out of the store. Johnny got on the crossbar and Theresa got on the handlebars.

Off they went to the campground. The convoy was a big thing for a little town like New Dublin. The trucks were filled with soldiers who were in the back under the hot canvas canopies. Sam parked his bicycle and he, Johnny, and Theresa began walking down beside the trucks.

One of the soldiers yelled out, "Hey kid. I'll give you a quarter if you go and get me a soda. Another soldier said, "I'll give you a quarter too. Most of the soldiers wanted sodas. Sam said, "I'll be right back." He hopped on his bicycle and headed back to the store. He ran into the store. Pop wanted to know why he was back. Sam explained that he needed every cold soda in the store. The soldiers are thirsty. He loaded as many as he could in his basket. He grabbed a bottle opener on his way out the front screen door. Johnny and Theresa unloaded the drinks and began selling them as fast as they could. Sam raced back to the store to get another load. He repeated this three times until all the cold sodas were gone. The convoy began to move out. Sam, Johnny, and Theresa stood at attention and saluted until the final truck passed. The salute was returned by everyone who witnessed the young patriots.

Sam, Johnny, and Theresa went over to a near by shade tree and sat down. They emptied their pockets of all the change. They counted out $ 12.50.

Theresa said, "We're rich!"

Sam responded, "We have to pay Pop first. We owe him $ 3.00. That leaves us $ 9.50."

Theresa exclaimed, "We're still rich!"

Johnny suggested, "Tomorrow is Saturday. They have a new Hop-a-long Cassidy movie at the Rialto. It's the *Forty Thieves*. It starts at nine o'clock. We can meet there in the morning. What do you think?"

Theresa answered, "I think it is a good idea."

"Count me in," said Sam.

They split up their booty. They then piled on Sam's bicycle and headed back to the grocery store. They squared up with Pop. Pop was happy for them that they made such good money. He was in agreement with the three overly excited kids about going to the movie. He assured Sam that he was able to run the store in the morning. The three of them then went upstairs to Sam's bedroom. They hung around lying on the bed and on the floor talking about things that fourteen year olds talk about. After several hours, Theresa and Johnny left. Sam went back downstairs and put on his apron. Pop decided to go upstairs and rest.

Chapter 13

Huckleberry Finn Revisited (Circa 1945)

Johnny, Theresa, and Sam were in the drug store gorging themselves on vanilla milk shakes. Johnny said, "Let's do something different this summer."

Sam responded, "Yea, that's a good idea but what are we going to do?"

Johnny answered, "I don't know. What do you want to do?"

Theresa replied, "Do you guys remember that book we had to read last year? It was the *Adventures of Huckleberry Finn.*

Sam said, "Yea, that was a good book."

Theresa continued, "The whole time I was reading that book, I was thinking how neat it would be to take a raft down the river to Jefferson City. We could build a raft out of logs that are always drifting down the river. We know they float. It will be fun. What do you think?"

"I think that is a fantastic idea." Sam stated.

Johnny added with excitement, "Let's do it."

Theresa ordered, "You two will be my deckhands."

Johnny joked back, "Who put you in charge?"

Theresa snapped back, "I did. Do you have a problem with that?"

Johnny and Sam humbly answered, "No ma'am."

Johnny asked, "What about our parents? You know that they will never give us permission."

Theresa answered, "We don't tell them. It will be a lot easier to get forgiveness than it will be to get permission. We can leave them a letter just before we leave."

Johnny, somewhat concerned, said, "We need to be careful. I don't want to die."

Theresa empathically stated, "You aren't going to die. We are fifteen years old. We can do this safely. I am ready to get started."

The three were enthusiastically in agreement. But first they needed about 150' of rope and a hand saw. They went to the hardware store and bought the rope and Johnny got a hand saw from his father's workshop.

The next morning the three of them met down at the river. Their enthusiasm was still at high levels. They walked the river bank until they found a small cove. This is where they would build their raft.

Theresa spotted the first log floating in the river. "There's one. Let's get it."

Johnny, the best swimmer, took the end of the rope and swam out to the log. He tied off to one end and swam back to the shore. The three of them started to pull on the rope using an oak tree as leverage. The log began to swing around downstream. They kept pulling until finally the log was in the cove. They all celebrated. They had the first of ten logs they would need to build the base of the raft. They all hopped down into the shallow water of the cove and secured the log. They took turns using the hand saw in cutting off the root ball. This was no easy task. Once the root ball was removed, they pushed it out into the river and it floated away. They decided to walk the river's edge. They found several more logs on the bank. They cut off the root balls first and Johnny rode the logs downstream to the cove. Sam threw the rope out to him. It took several attempts but Johnny was able to grab the rope. He tied it off at the end and swam back. They pulled the second log back to shore. Again they celebrated; two down and eight to go. Before the day was over they had a total of five logs. There were no more celebrations. They were too tired. It had been a hard day's work.

The next day they repeated the same procedures until they had their ten logs. Johnny had brought a hatchet. He cut notches in three places on each log. They used the rope to lash the logs together. The purpose of the notches was to allow the rope to sit down below the top of the log so that they could build a floor without the rope being in the way. After they had finished, they all jumped around on the raft. It was sturdy and the raft handled their weight without any problem. The raft was secured to a stump. They cut a bunch of tree limbs and covered the raft to camouflage it so that it would not be accidentally found by others traveling the river.

Now they needed lumber. There was a collapsed barn up the river about a mile away. They should be able to scrap enough pieces together to make the flooring and the side rails. Theresa, Johnny, and Sam were at the barn early the next morning culling through the good and bad boards. By noon, they had made a pile sufficient enough to complete the raft. A long 4" X 4" board was also found. A wooden fin would be affixed to the end. This will become their steering rudder. The problem now was getting the lumber to the cove. It took three trips tramping through the high brush but the mission was accomplished.

Johnny raided his father's workshop again. He got a hammer and a coffee can full of nails. The three cut the boards and nailed them in place. A rail was built to help prevent them from falling overboard. By the end of the day they finished the raft and the steering rudder. The raft was ready to sail. Theresa said, "We have to give her a name." She looked straight at Sam. "Johnny and I thought that if it was ok with you, we would name the raft *Miss Alice* after your Mama."

Sam was deeply moved by the gesture. "Thanks guys. That would be nice."

Theresa brought out a small can of black paint and a brush. She did a nice job of inscribing the name on the front rail. The three of them stood back and admired the raft. Johnny said, "We did a good job." The other two agreed.

Theresa said, "Now that we have the raft finished, we need to work on supplies. We need another 150 feet of rope. Sam, will you get that for us?"

"I will but Mr. Ryan may get suspicious."

Theresa responded, "Just tell him that we are building a swing down by the river."

"But that would be a lie."

Theresa somewhat frustrated, sarcastically said, "If you have to tell him that then we will make a swing and you can use it to dive into the water. Afterwards, we can take it down. That way you aren't lying. Heaven forbid. I don't want to have a guilty conscience when you are damned into the eternal fires of hell for telling a little white lie."

Sam was pleased. "That will work for me."

The three of them made a grocery list for Sam:

> 8 Cans of soup
> Jar of mustard
> Corn meal
> Lard
> Smoked ham
> 2 loaves of bread
> Candy bars
> Matches

Sam was also to get his fishing poles, a can opener and a pocket knife.

Theresa was bringing a steel skillet for frying fish, a pot, eating utensils and her pocket knife. She was also bringing an inner tube that they will use as a life preserver. In addition, she dug up some bait in the worm bed in her back yard.

Johnny was in charge of getting water. He was to go by the drug store where there were empty Coca-Cola syrup bottles out back. They would be perfect for water containers. He was also bringing a hunter's knife.

Theresa said, "Do we have everything we need? Think hard. I don't want to get down the river and realize that we forgot something." They thought through the entire voyage and they believed that they had enough supplies for the three day trip. Theresa said, "Let's go get everything except the food. Sam you can get that in the morning before you leave. We don't need the critters eating our food tonight."

Off they went to complete the task at hand. Sam jumped around between Theresa and Johnny so they could use his bicycle to help carry the supplies. They put everything on the raft except for the rope. Sam took the rope and climbed a nearby tree and tied it off to an overhanging limb. He stripped down to his shorts and swung out over the river and dove in.

Theresa turned to Johnny, "Obviously he told a fib to Mr. Ryan."

"Obviously", repeated Johnny.

Sam climbed out of the water and began untying the rope. Theresa said to him, "Did you make it right with God?"

"Yes but when I was talking with God, He said that he was concerned about you. He said that you are a facilitator of sin."

"Facilitator of sin? I like that. Johnny do you think that I am a facilitator of sin?"

"Oh yes...definitely."

They all laughed.

Theresa taking charge said, "We sail at daybreak!"

Sam and Johnny saluted as they responded, "Aye, aye, Captain."

None of the three slept well that night. They were about to embark on the greatest adventure of their young lives. Sam was up early. He slipped down stairs and gathered up the groceries. He figured up what was owed and he placed it in the cash register along with a note that he had written to Pop. He loaded his bicycle and headed toward the river. He was the first to arrive but it wasn't long before the other two showed up. The sun was slowly peaking through the trees. There was a fog mist rising from the glass like river. It was a beautiful morning. Sam hid his bicycle in a thicket. They climbed aboard and shoved off. The raft floated out into the river and began drifting downstream. They were underway.

Pop got up. He checked on Sam but he was gone. The bed was made. Pop had told Sam that he didn't have to work for several weeks. He wanted Sam to enjoy a portion of his summer but Sam leaving the house before sun up had Pop concerned. He was going to have a talk with Sam today to find out what he, Johnny, and Theresa were up to. Sam had been secretive in regards to what they were doing. It was 6:45 a.m. precisely. "Good morning, Mrs. Shanahan."

"Good morning, Pop."

Pop opened the register and took out enough cash to pay Mrs. Shanahan. He saw the note. He pulled it out and laid it on the counter. Pop counted out the money to Mrs. Shanahan and said, "Have a good day."

"You too, Pop."

Pop opened the note. He now knew why Sam had left so early. He hung his apron on the nail beside Sam's. He scribbled out his own note informing the other vendors to leave their wares and he would pay them tomorrow or that they could wait for several hours until he got back. He taped it to the window. He didn't lock the door. It was a chance he had to take. He headed straight for the Rectory. Billy was having a bowl of cereal. Pop handed him the note, "Read this."

Billy read the note and smiled. "Well good for them."

Pop wasn't amused. "What do you mean…well good for them?"

"Don't you remember when we were kids? We planned to do the same thing but for some reason, we never did. I have always regretted it."

"Me too. We are now adults and we see the dangers that you don't see as kids."

"You are truly becoming a mother hen."

"Let's go and check the river. We might be able to stop them."

"Can I finish my cereal?"

"No!"

Billy reluctantly got up. He was in no hurry either. The two of then went to the river and started walking the river bank. They found Sam's bicycle but there was no raft.

Pop was distressed. "If we hurry, we might be able to catch them at the bridge."

Billy ribbed his brother. "We can take your car."

"You know that I don't have a car. You are just being a smart aleck. Remember, I have whipped your butt on more than one occasion and I am not too old to do it again."

Billy's smile turned into wide grin. He said, "Cluck, cluck, cluck", mimicking the sound of a mother hen.

Billy slowly drove the three miles and stopped midway on the bridge. They were too late. They could see the raft downstream of the bridge. They were out of earshot range. Inside, Billy was happy but he felt that he had teased his brother a little more than normal. He said in a compassionate voice, "Don't worry Pop. They will be fine. These are three smart kids. I am sure they thought this thing through thoroughly." There wasn't much Pop could do but wait and pray that they would be safe.

It was midday and everything was going smoothly. They made sandwiches; smoked ham and mustard between two pieces of bread. It didn't sound appetizing but to them, they were delicious. Theresa was still at the rudder. Johnny and Sam were stretched out on the deck. Sam saw something out of the corner of his eye. He jumped up. It was a water moccasin swimming straight for the raft. Theresa went berserk. She began screaming at the top of her lungs. Johnny couldn't take the shrill. He yelled, "Shut up, Theresa!" This had little effect. Sam grabbed one of their poles and poked it in front of the snake. The water moccasin wrapped itself around the end of the pole. Sam slung the snake high in the air. It spun around several times before it hit the water well away from the boat. The snake was last seen swimming toward the opposite bank. Theresa was still screaming until Johnny convinced her that the water moccasin was gone.

Johnny said to Theresa, "You scream like a girl!"

"...but I am a girl."

"Sometimes I forget."

Sam added, "I thought you were our fearless captain."

"I am...except when it comes to snakes."

Johnny reached down and shook the rope and yelled "Snake."

Theresa jumped back and screamed. When she realized it was only the rope she yelled back, "Stop it!"

Johnny and Sam laughed uncontrollably. Afterwards, Johnny turned to Sam, "We now know how to keep her in line."

"If you two are through having your fun, how about getting the fishing poles out and catch us some supper."

Johnny and Sam baited their hooks and threw the lines over the side. It wasn't too long when Sam's cork started bobbing. "I'm getting a bite." He picked up the cane pole and waited for the cork to go completely under the water. He set the hook. The fish fought hard but Sam was able to get it on board. It was a two pound channel cat.

Theresa said, "Fantastic. Now we need two more just like it."

Johnny used his hunter's knife and filleted the catfish. Sam baited his hook again and threw the line over the side. Within thirty minutes they had a meal. Sam pointed to an upcoming sandbar. "Let's spend the night there."

Theresa steered the raft toward the sandbar. Johnny jumped off and tied the raft off to a tree. The other two got off and began to stretch. Theresa and Johnny wasted no time in gathering enough driftwood to keep a fire going all night. Sam prepared the meal. He opened several cans of vegetable soup and poured them in the pot. Water and ham were added. He melted some lard in the skillet and coated the fish filets with corn meal. The coals were hot. The grease was ready. Sam dropped the fish into the skillet. The fillets sizzled until they turned a light brown. The three of them sat around the campfire and gorged themselves on the soup and fish. The Cherokee River posed many perils for Sam, Johnny, and Theresa but one peril that was non-existent was starvation.

Early the next morning, Theresa, Johnny and Sam boarded the raft and shoved off. They took turns steering the rudder. Theresa pointed out a ten point buck drinking water at the river's edge. The farther south they traveled, the more farm houses were seen. Kids would come out and wave at them. In the heat of midday, Johnny took the inner tube and tied the rope to it. He stepped inside and jumped overboard. He floated downstream behind the raft for about an hour. He pulled himself back to the raft and Sam took his turn. It wasn't long before Sam was back on board. Theresa climbed in the inner tube and slowly drifted behind the raft.

Sam and Johnny were full of mischief. They started yelling "Snake! Snake!" and pointed as if there was a snake. Theresa, at lightning speed, reeled herself back to the raft, screaming the entire way. Once she was on board, she realized that Sam and Johnny were joking.

Theresa cold cocked Johnny in the shoulder, knocking him to his knees. He grabbed his shoulder and responded, "That hurt big time! You may scream like a girl but you hit like a man." Theresa then went after Sam but he bobbed and weaved all around the raft. Theresa could never get a clear shot at him. She said, "I will get you when you least expect it." She then ordered, "You two go up front and get away from me." They did as told.

They sat down with their feet hanging in the water with their arms and heads resting on the rail. Sam asked, "Do you think it's ok to hit a girl?"

Johnny thought for a second. "For most girls I would say no; however Theresa is a different story but I wouldn't advise it. It would only make her madder. I pity the guy who marries her." Johnny continued with a strong sense of assurance, "You know she is going to get you."

"Yep. Just like she said...when I least expect it."

The raft was drifting toward a sharp bend in the river. Johnny could see a barge being pushed by a tug boat coming around the bend in the middle of the river. He yelled to Theresa, "Head for the bank! Head for the bank!"

Theresa pushed the rudder arm to the left as far as she could. The raft turned but the speed was slow and constant. The tug boat and barge were closing. The tug boat captain saw the raft and pulled back on the throttle. His forward momentum continued but it was enough to allow the raft to get out of harm's way. However, the raft rode the first wave ok but the second wave lifted the raft and threw the right front end of the raft high up on the bank. The force knocked Johnny off. He landed in a thicket but only suffered minor scratches. The tug boat captain stuck his arm out the pilot house window and gave a thumb-up and then a thumb-down. He was trying to find out if everyone was all right. Theresa, Sam, and Johnny all gave thumbs-ups. The captain waved. He throttled up and steadily moved upstream.

"That was close." Theresa said as she made the sign of the cross.

Sam agreed. "Let's get this raft back in the water."

Sam, Theresa, and Johnny lifted and shoved on the raft but it didn't move. They sat down on the edge of the raft. Johnny asked, "What do we do now?"

Theresa replied, "We have three options. First; we wait until another tug boat comes by and when the wake hits the raft, we push it off the bank. We could be waiting an hour or five days. Second; we could wait until the spring thaw and when the river rises, we can float the raft out of here. But that's nine months away. Third; we can dig it out. The third option was the only reasonable solution. Theresa told Johnny to get the hatchet and go cut a tree about four inches in diameter and cut the end into a point. She told Sam to start digging with his hands around the bottom of the raft. Theresa, using the soup pot, kept pouring water on where Sam was digging. This was making mud which made it easier to remove the dirt. Johnny returned with the pole that he made from a freshly cut tree. The three of them jammed the pole down into the mud as far as they could. Johnny was the strongest. He shoved upward on the pole. The raft showed signs of movement. Sam and Theresa got on the raft and moved to the opposite corner. They began to jump up and down to help free the raft. Their counter weight along with Johnny's efforts, were enough. *Miss Alice* was afloat again. Everyone cheered. Johnny pushed the raft back out into the river and jumped aboard. They were again underway.

It was getting later in the afternoon. Johnny and Sam started fishing and caught enough for supper. They looked around to make camp for the night. They came upon a cleared pasture. It was decided it was an ideal spot. Theresa steered the raft to the shoreline. Johnny hopped off and tied off the raft. It was the same scenario as the night before, including the same meal. It was good yesterday and it would be good today.

Theresa found her opportunity. She made a fist and swung as hard as she could. She hit Sam squarely on his shoulder. It hurt but Sam wasn't letting on. "Is that the best you've got?" This was a mistake. Theresa came around with her left hand and nailed Sam in the same spot. It hurt so bad that it brought tears to his eyes. Theresa, wagging her finger, sternly told Sam and Johnny. "Now we're even. Do you understand?"

Both answered, "Yes ma'am."

The next morning, Theresa stoked up the fire and added more logs. Sam got the frying pan out and began heating up slices of ham. As each piece got hot they would reach in and grab a slice. The three of them were startled when a man appeared wearing a hunting cap and vest. He had a shotgun cradled in his arms. "Good Morning," he said.

Sam responded, "Good morning, sir."

"Are you all traveling the river?

"Yes sir," answered Theresa. We're riding the river from New Dublin down to Jefferson City.

"Well that sounds like fun,"

Johnny said, "Yes sir. It's been a lot of fun."

Theresa asked, "Do you live around here?"

"I live just over the hill. I have been out hunting for squirrels this morning. This is my land."

Sam was concerned. "We aren't trespassing ...are we?"

"You can't trespass if the owner gives you permission to be on his land...and I give you permission to stay as long as you want."

Theresa responded, "Thank you sir. That is nice of you."

"I was a kid once. I spent many a day on this river."

Theresa offered, "Would you like a piece of hot smoked ham?"

"I don't mind if I do." He reached down and picked up a slice. "Hmmm. That's good." He ate several more pieces.

Johnny asked, "Can you tell us where we are?"

"Right now you are about ten miles up river from Jefferson City. You're almost there."

Sam asked, "Do you have a phone at your house?"

"Yes, I do."

"Can you do me a favor and call my father. He worries a lot. His name is Pop O'Malley. He owns the grocery store in New Dublin."

"I know Pop. I used to sell him eggs years ago. He's a good man. I will be happy to give him a call."

"Thank you, sir."

He bid the three farewell and told them to be safe. He left toward the wooded area. Johnny, Theresa, and Sam gathered up everything and climbed aboard the raft. They estimated that they would be in Jefferson around noon.

As they rounded a bend in the river, they could see the top of the First National Bank of Jefferson City. It was the tallest building. They knew that they were getting close to the end of a journey of a lifetime. They approached the downtown area and began looking for a place to dock. There was a riverside park. Theresa steered toward the bank. There were two young boys fishing. Johnny jumped off and tied off to a tree.

Sam asked the two boys, "Doing any good?"

"Yea, we've been catching a few. The boy continued, "That is a mighty fine raft you got there."

"Thanks, we built it ourselves. We rode it down the river from New Dublin. There is no way that we can get it back there. Do you want it?"

"Are you kidding?"

Sam answered, "Nope. It's all yours, if you want it."

Both boys enthusiastically answered, "Yes."

"There is the rest of a smoke ham, some mustard and bread. Do you want that too?"

"Sure. What about the inner tube?"

"You can have that too." Sam cautioned, "The raft goes where the river takes it. So you have to be careful not to end up miles downstream."

"There is a creek about a mile from here. We will ride it down there and then pole our way up the creek. Thanks again."

All of the cooking and eating utensils were loaded in the back pack. Theresa helped in putting the pack on Johnny's shoulders. Sam picked up the cane poles.

Theresa asked, "Does anyone know where we are going?"

Sam responded, "I've been to Jefferson City more than a few times but I am not sure as to how to get around. I know the Cathedral is right in the middle of town and we should be able to find it without any problem."

Theresa draped her arms around Johnny and Sam. The three of them headed off for the downtown area. The streets were full of men in uniforms. Whenever they passed a soldier, they saluted out of respect. Not once was the gesture not returned. As they walked, they came upon a popular hamburger joint. Sam was insistent that they stop and get something to eat. He explained that these burgers were nothing like the ones at the drug store. They were small and delicious. It didn't take too much to convince the others. They pooled their money; a total of $ 3.28. It was enough. Sam left the cane poles outside. They went inside the long and narrow restaurant. They sat down on stools at the counter. Sam put the back pack down at his feet. They ordered four burgers each and a root beer that came in a frosted mug. When they finished, they left a quarter tip and paid the cashier. They asked for directions to the Cathedral. It was five blocks down and three blocks up. Off they went heading for the Cathedral. When they arrived, they left their gear outside and entered the church office.

Sam greeted the secretary. "Good afternoon Ms. Jane. Is Uncle Jimmy in?"

"Yes along with your Uncle Billy and Pop."

"That's not a good sign," Sam said somewhat concerned.

"Go on in. They have been expecting you."

Johnny, Sam, and Theresa straightened their clothes and used their fingers to comb their hair. The three bonded their fists together in a sign of friendship and unity. They stood up straight and entered. They were greeted by Uncle Jimmy. "Well look here. The wayward travelers have returned."

Uncle Billy rose and walked around the three of them as they stood at attention in front of Uncle Jimmy's desk. He inspected all three carefully and concluded, "Except for a few scratches, they appear to be unharmed."

Pop spoke calmly, "Sam, you disappoint me."

Sam thought to himself. "Oh no...not the guilt trip. I hate the guilt trip. Why can't he just paddle me and get this over with." He answered simply "I'm sorry."

"Why didn't you come and ask me if you could go?"

"Would you have said yes?" Pop hesitated in his response so Sam continued, "You know as well as I do that you would have said no. So, as Theresa said when we first thought about the trip that it would be a lot easier to get forgiveness than to get permission."

Uncle Jimmy and Billy held back their smiles when Sam said this. Their sentiments about the entire situation were totally opposite from Pop's position.

Pop never really answered Sam. He went on to say, "Your vacation days are over. Tomorrow morning you will be back working in the store."

Pop and Uncle Billy turned and left. Uncle Jimmy motioned the three to move closer to his desk. He leaned forward and spoke in a low voice. "Sam, don't worry about Pop. He won't stay mad for long. But I want to know one thing. Did you guys have a good time?"

Their faces lit up. "Oh yes sir, it was fantastic."

"You're safe and you had fun. That's all that matters."

"Thanks, Uncle Jimmy. See ya later."

During the ride back to New Dublin, Uncle Billy wanted to know all the details about the trip. Johnny, Theresa, and Sam talked over each other as they excitedly related the entire trip from beginning to end. Pop remained silent so as not to outwardly endorse their actions but inside he was pleased.

The next morning Sam had a delivery to make. He stopped by Theresa's house. They sat on the front steps and talked a few minutes. Sam asked Theresa how her mother had reacted. Theresa told him that she could not leave the yard for the next two weeks except to go to church or to the hospital because if she in fact did leave the yard, she would end up in the hospital. Sam proceeded over to Johnny's house. He was out cutting the grass. Sam stayed on his bike and Johnny walked up to him.

Sam asked, "Well how did it go?"

"I am on restriction until I am 21 years old."

"How long do think that will last?"

"Maybe a week."

"That's not too bad. I've got to get going. Pop will be wondering where I have been if I stay gone too long."

Chapter 14

Jack Kelly Returns Home (Circa 1945)

It was Sunday morning. The bells had been rung ten minutes earlier. The church was about full. Father O'Malley was at the pulpit marking the day's Gospel. He looked up and his face was beaming. One of his "boys" was home. In the back stood Jack Kelly, flanked by his wife, Judy, and Theresa. Jack was dressed in his uniform. He was on crutches. He had his right leg suspended so as not to put weight on it. They started walking down the center aisle. Judy reached up and snatched off Jack's hat. Father O'Malley motioned for the congregation to rise. He began to clap. The rest of the congregation joined in. They clapped until Jack and his family were seated. Father O'Malley returned to the sacristy where the altar boys were waiting to process into the church proper. Afterwards, Father O'Malley was preparing to do his opening blessing; he looked straight at Jack and said "Welcome Home." He then addressed the entire congregation, "Let us offer this Mass for Jack and all of the other New Dublin young men currently serving overseas."

When Mass was over, Father O'Malley proceeded out to the front of the Church where he greeted the parishioners as they departed. After everyone had left, Judy came up to Father O'Malley and told him that Jack was still in the Church and he wanted to speak with him. Father O'Malley returned inside and sat down close enough where he could put his arm around Jack and give him a hug.

Father O'Malley said, "It's good to have you home."

"It's good to be home." Jack continued, "Father, I have a story that I want to tell you. I know you have heard the saying, 'War is Hell'. Well, it's true. If ever there is a place that's hell on earth, it is Iwo Jima. I have seen things that no man should ever see. I have done things that no man should ever do. Whenever I was scared, I would grasp my St. Christopher medal and pray as hard as I could and every time I did this, I thought of you. Being scared is not unmanly…we were all scared. Overcoming that fear and continuing to do what was required is called bravery and I am here to tell you that these United States is the 'home of the brave'. The Japanese were dug in on the side of the mountain and they had the strategic advantage over us. They had our entire platoon pinned down. I was ordered to take my squad up the hill and take out the machine gun nest. We were half way up the hill and were moving in small increments, literally feet at a time. I stood up to have my squad to move forward and I was hit in the chest. It was a sharp stinging pain. I was knocked backwards and I landed flat on my back. I look down at my chest, fully expecting to see blood gushing but there was nothing. I motioned for the rest of the squad to hold their position. I couldn't figure out what happened. I reached inside my shirt and pulled out my St. Christopher medal."

At the same time, Jack pulled out his St. Christopher medal to show Father O'Malley.

Father O'Malley said "Oh my God" as he made the sign of the cross. He could not believe his eyes; a bullet was fused into the St. Christopher medal.

"Father, I give you credit for saving my life. I wasn't going to wear the medal because it was so big but you made me promise that I would keep it around my neck and I can't make a promise to a Priest and not keep it."

Father O'Malley who was astounded responded, "It was not me who saved your life. It was St. Christopher interceding on your behalf. I am a man just like you. I don't possess any heavenly powers. The last time I tried walking on water, I sank straight to the bottom."

Jack thought this was amusing, he laughed. "Say what you want to say but I will be forever grateful." Jack continued on to finish his story. "My squad slowly made it up the hill. We were receiving heavy fire. I had two men work their way up above the machine gun nest. One was on the left flank and the other on the right flank. The rest of us gave them cover by firing on the entrenched Japanese. I ordered a cease fire because both Marines were close to being in position above the small opening. I gave them the signal. They pulled the pins on their grenades and simultaneously chunked them inside. There was a loud explosion and the machine gun went silent. I lost two good men that day. I was the only one who got wounded. I was shot in the leg. After the firefight, I got evacuated to a field hospital. At first, they wanted to amputate my leg above the knee, however, the head surgeon said, "Let's wait. There is the possibility that it could heal. If needed, we can amputate it later." Thankfully, they decided to wait. The doctors now say that I should fully recover. There is the possibility that I may walk with a limp but only time will tell. I have been reassigned to Camp Le Jeune. They have a good physical therapy unit there. Also, they want me to teach classes to the new recruits. If my leg heals, I may again be deployed overseas. I am not going to goldbrick this wound, whatever will be...will be."

Jack rose to his feet with support of his crutches. He shook Father O'Malley hand and said "Thanks".

"Come on, I'll walk you out." When they reached Judy and Theresa who were waiting at the entrance, Father O'Malley put his arm around Judy and kissed her on the forehead. Theresa hugged him around the chest and he gently brushed back her hair.

Judy, using both hands, placed Jack's hat on his head. She cocked it to the side and glared directly into her husband's eyes and said. "There is something special about a man in a uniform."

Father O'Malley watched them as they walked toward the street. He thought to himself, "True happiness only happens during moments in time and this was one of those moments. Thanks God."

****

On May 9, 1945, Jack Ryan was still ambulatory. The crutches were no longer necessary and he was able to get about with the use of a cane. This is the day that the war on the European front was over. The allies of World War II formally accepted the unconditional surrender of Nazi Germany. It was bitter sweet news to Jack. The war with Japan was still raging and his fellow Marines were dying every day. Over the next several months, his wound completely healed. There was no limp. The doctors cleared him for duty without any restrictions. He was now eligible to return to the Pacific for a combat assignment. Jack took it in stride. Like he told Father O'Malley, "Whatever will be...will be." But before Jack received transfer orders, the war in Japan came to an abrupt halt. On August 15, 1945, Emperor Hirohito, dressed in formal attire with a black top hat, signed the conditions of surrender aboard the USS Missouri anchored in Tokyo Bay. World War II was officially over. Celebrations were rampant not only in the United States but throughout the free world. The carnage had ended.

Jack finished out his enlistment. He returned to New Dublin and found employment at the plant. All was good in the Kelly household.

Chapter 15

Romance Blossoms (Circa 1946)

Sister Celeste had her class reading silently a chapter from Rudyard Kipling's *The Jungle Book*. Afterwards, they would have a discussion on the contents of the chapter. Sister Celeste could see Theresa passing notes to Johnny and Sam. She tried to ignore it but Theresa was persistent. Sister Celeste got up from her desk and walked straight to Theresa. She took the note and read it. She looked at Sam and asked, "Do you want to go to the Rialto tonight and see an Abbott and Costello movie?"

Sam answered out loud, "Yes."

Sister Celeste asked a second question. "Do you want to meet at the theater at six o'clock?"

Again Sam answered, "Yes."

Sister Celeste asked Johnny the same questions and he too answered, "Yes." She then turned to Theresa. "Don't you think this could have waited until after dismissal?"

Theresa responded sheepishly, "Yes, Sister."

Sister Celeste continued. "The three of you had better hurry and finish the reading assignment because you three are going to be the first ones I call on."

After class Sam teased Theresa by mimicking Sister Celeste. "Don't you think this could have waited until after dismissal?"

Theresa failed to see the humor. She hauled off and hit Sam on the shoulder.

"Boy that hurt," Sam said as he grimaced in pain.

Theresa responded, "Now that's funny." She glanced over to Johnny. "Do you have any amusing comments that you want to make?"

Johnny was no fool. He simply answered, "Nope."

Theresa and Johnny were standing in front of the box office when Sam came riding up on his bicycle. They bought their tickets and the first stop was the concession stand. Each got a soda and a bag of popcorn. They found three seats about mid way down the aisle. The theater was almost at capacity. The opening credits began. The title of the movie was *The Time of Their Lives.* Sam leaned over and asked Theresa as to what the movie was about.

She answered, "I think it's about two ghosts who were wrongly accused of being traitors during the revolutionary war."

"Hopefully it won't be too in depth so that you will be able to understand the plot."

"Ha Ha," Theresa responded caustically. "Now Shhhhhhhh!"

Sam ate all his popcorn. He asked the others if they wanted anything from the concession stand. They both shook their heads no. When Sam returned to his seat, Johnny and Theresa were holding hands. This did not sit well with Sam. It ruined the rest of the movie. Afterward, they went to the drug store to get a hamburger. Sam was silent. He was not his usual self. Theresa noticed this. She asked him, "Is there something wrong?"

Sam answered, "No."

Theresa was insistent. She knew Sam well enough to recognize when something wasn't right."

Sam reluctantly began to explain. "I saw you and Johnny holding hands. I don't care if both of you want to be boyfriend and girlfriend but if that happens, you two will want to be together and the three of us will no longer be friends."

Theresa wrapped her arms around the shoulders of Johnny and Sam. She kissed both of them on the cheek. "We will always be friends...no matter what!" She then made a fist. Johnny and Sam did the same thing and place their fists on top of Theresa's. They recited together, "Friends forever."

Johnny told Sam. "If what you say should happen, I will dump Theresa as a girlfriend and you and I can hang out together."

Theresa was not pleased. She hit Johnny squarely on the shoulder.

Johnny grabbed his arm. It hurt. "Girl, you have got to stop hitting us. You do it only because you know that we won't hit you back."

Sam spoke directly to Johnny. "What we need to do is find a girl who can hit back for us. What about Beatrice in the twelfth grade? She helps her father in the fields. She is the only girl I know who can work a plow behind a stubborn mule. She is one tough cookie."

Theresa's womanhood was in question. "I like Beatrice. She is a nice girl but if had to, I could easily whip her butt."

It was if it had been choreographed. Johnny said with a smirk on his face. "Look who just walked through the door." It was Beatrice. "Sam let's go tell Beatrice what Theresa said."

Johnny and Sam both got up from their seats. Theresa grabbed both of them by the shirts and pulled them back down. "Sit down and shut up."

"Do you promise not to hit us any more?" asked Johnny.

Theresa did not answer. She was caught in an awkward position. She was mulling over her options.

Sam pressed her, "Do you promise?"

Theresa was hesitant but she answered. "Yes, I promise not to hit both of you any more...except under extraordinary circumstances."

Johnny asked Sam, "What do you think?

"I think that's the best we're going to get."

As the rest of the year progressed, Theresa was insistent that Sam double date with her and Johnny. Sam was a good-looking young man. He was quite popular with the girls at school although there was no particular girl that he wanted to be his girlfriend. So he played the field. He double dated several times and his friendship with Theresa and Johnny never wavered. Beatrice had a Halloween hayride at her family farm. Sam invited Jeanie Tucker. Of all the girls he had dated, he liked her the best. Beatrice and her boyfriend sat in the seat. She handled the reins on the mule. The wagon bed was full of hay. It was cold. Everyone brought blankets. They all cuddled up with their dates. This was the night of Sam's first kiss...and his second...and his third.

Chapter 16

Sam's Requests a Family Meeting (Circa 1947)

Father O'Malley telephoned his brother Jimmy.

Bishop O'Malley picked up the receiver, "Hello."

"Jimmy this is Billy. Are you busy?"

"I'm never too busy for my baby brother."

"Sam wants a family meeting. He wants the three of us together. I don't know why. He won't even give us a clue."

"Do you think he has some terminal disease?"

"We think alike. I asked Dr. Swartz if he has been treating Sam for any illnesses and he said no. So, that rules that out. Pop and I have narrowed it down to three possibilities. Maybe he wants to get married but I see him at school every day. The girls think he is 'cute' but I have never seen him with one particular girl on a regular basis so that possibility is remote. Pop thinks that he may be interested in enlisting in the military. I think that he may want some advice on what college to attend because he graduates in the spring."

"I agree with you. I don't believe it is life threatening but whatever it is, it's important to Sam. All of you can come over this Thursday evening. I can get us some baseball tickets. There is a twilight game. We can make this a real family affair."

"I like that idea. I haven't been to a game in years. It'll be fun."

Jimmy and Billy terminated their conversation. Father O'Malley decided to stretch his legs and walked down to visit with Pop at the grocery store. It was a beautiful day. Even though it was late summer there was a touch of fall in the air. Father O'Malley strolled down the sidewalk greeting each and every pedestrian that he past. He opened the screen door for Mrs. O'Rourke who was leaving with a bag full of groceries. "Good morning, Father." He responded with a smile, "Top of the morning to you."

"For a cranky old man, you sure are in a jolly good mood this morning," said Pop.

"Of course I am. It is the day that the Lord has made."

"Did you get bored at saving souls today and decided to come down here and harass me."

"Harassment was one of my best subjects in school. I love to practice what I learned on you and Sean. It makes my day." Billy continued, "I just got off the phone with our big brother and we are going to have this family meeting at his Rectory on Thursday evening. Afterwards, we are going to a baseball game. How does that sound to you?"

"It sounds good to me. The baseball game is a good touch too."

"The baseball game can be cancelled if what Sam has to say is something serious but I don't think that is going to be the case."

"I don't either. He has been tight lipped. We won't know until he decides to tell us, but I have to admit, my curiosity is peaked."

Billy visited for awhile longer. He bought the last of Mrs. Shanahan's pies. It was a peach pie; his favorite. The screen door slammed shut as he left. He wondered what Sean was doing this morning. He stuck his head inside the hardware store. Sean motioned for him to come inside.

"Top of the morning, my friend."

Sean responded, "Oh no. Whenever you say 'my friend' it usually costs me money."

"You are so defensive. I am your Pastor and I just dropped by to check on a member of my flock."

"I know that you are a Priest but why am I skeptical of your visit. You don't normally drop by this early in the morning. You are up to something."

"Pop was leery too when I showed up at the grocery store. You two have some deep seeded emotional problems. Both of you want to subconsciously blame me as the source of all your problems."

Sean headed for the cash register. "OK I give up," he said as he hit the 'no sale' key and the cash drawer popped open. "How much do you want? Five dollars, ten dollars, twenty dollars…"

"Sean, you have hurt my feelings. My pie and I are going to leave now." He said as he headed for the front door.

Sean smiled as he watched him leave. This was typical Billy.

Billy walked back toward the Rectory with the pie in his left hand. There was an extraordinary step in his stride. Maybe it was the weather. All those he passed were greeted with a hand shake and/or with some form of pleasantry.

Later, when school was out for the day, Sam strutted into the store. As he walked pass Pop toward the storage room he asked, "Business good today?"

"It has been rather steady."

Sam took his apron off the nail. It is the same apron that Pop had given him about six years ago. Since Sam was now six feet tall, the apron actually fit properly. "What's up with Uncle Billy? He saw me in the hall and came up and gave me a big hug. He said he loved me."

"It is Uncle Billy being Uncle Billy. He was in one of his extra good moods today. He is such a good hearted person and he just loves people. That's exactly the way a parish priest should be." Pop continued, "He came by here this morning to let me know that we are going to Jefferson City the day after tomorrow so we can all meet with Uncle Jimmy. We are going to take in a ball game after that."

"That will work for me."

****

It was Thursday afternoon. Sam arrived at the grocery store at his usual time. He grabbed his apron and started sweeping the floor.

Pop said to Sam, "We'll leave in about an hour."

"Good. That will give me enough time to finish sweeping and get cleaned up a bit."

The hour quickly passed. Pop asked, "Are you ready?"

"Yep."

Pop put his "closed" sign on the front door. He and Sam walked down the street to the Rectory. Uncle Billy was at his desk when the two arrived. "Give me a second and I'll be ready to go."

Sam grabbed up the cars keys lying on the desk. He looked at Uncle Billy. "I'll drive. You make me nervous when you're driving."

"Ah, the youth of today...they have no respect for their elders," responded Uncle Billy.

The trip to Jefferson City was not without conversation. They discussed every thing from world events to frivolous folly. However, Pop and Uncle Billy did try to pry information from Sam in regard to the soon to be family meeting but to no avail.

Sam was enjoying the effect the family meeting was having. "You O'Malley brothers are like three old gossiping women. I bet you guys have been burning up the telephone lines in trying to find out what this meeting is all about. I will give you one hint. I do not have a serious disease. I am sure that has been one of your possible scenarios."

Uncle Billy looked at his brother. "The boy is good. He knows us pretty well."

Sam pulled the sedan into the Rectory parking lot. They all went inside and met with Uncle Jimmy. He led them to the parlor that was nicely decorated with fine furniture. It was the room where the Bishop met with local dignitaries and church officials. However, this was for show. Uncle Jimmy did not like the glitz and glamour. He preferred the more simple furnishings he had in the sitting room next to his bedroom. They all made themselves comfortable on the sofa and the high back chairs.

Pop spoke up. "Jimmy, we at least got out of Sam that he is not going to die anytime soon."

Uncle Jimmy responded positively. "Well, that's a good thing." He continued, "Sam you are making three old men crazy. Please tell us the reason for this meeting."

"I love you guys. I could have gone to any of you three to discuss this matter but I felt that if I did, I would possibly offend the other two. We are family, not a typical traditional family, but still a family. I have decided that when I graduate from high school I want to go to the seminary. The O'Malley brothers are the best role models any young man can have. You guys are outgoing. You have a deep love for your fellow man and at the same time, you preach the gospel not just in words but it action…"

The O'Malley brothers were busting with pride. They had a done a good job in rearing Samuel Jenkins.

"…but I have a real problem…I still like girls."

This brought laughter from all the O'Malley brothers.

Sam somewhat irritated said, "This is not funny. I am serious."

Uncle Billy chimed in, "We know you're serious. We're not laughing at you. We're laughing with you. Contrary to popular belief, in our younger days, we liked girls too. In fact, your Uncle Jimmy was a real lady's man. He had to beat the women off with a stick. I dated throughout high school and college until the time I decided to go to the seminary. Pop dated Sarah for years before he got married. He decided that being a Priest was not his calling. Marriage is no less of a sacrament than holy orders. It is a difficult decision to make but obviously you have given this much thought. You still have at least six years of college before you have to make that final decision. By that time you will know for sure if the Lord is calling you to the priesthood."

Uncle Jimmy added, "Sam, if this is what you want, I will get you enrolled in St. Joseph's. It's a good college. Uncle Billy and I both went there. It is only about 100 miles from here. When Billy and I went there, it took us three days to get there by horse and carriage. Now it only takes two hours. You can come home on long weekends and holidays."

"Yes sir, this is exactly what I want. St. Joseph's is my school of choice. It is a family tradition."

Pop stated, "Do you know what this means? We need to get you a new car."

"You don't have to worry about that," said Sam. I have enough money saved up to buy a good used car."

"Now where did you get that kind of money?" asked Pop.

"You have been paying me seventy five cents a day and two dollars on Saturday since I was twelve years old. This doesn't include all the money I have made on tips delivering groceries. I don't spend that much money and I have saved the rest."

Uncle Billy piped in, "I am impressed. Not only is he going to be a man of the cloth but he is also frugal. A characteristic that is useful when he becomes a parish priest."

Uncle Jimmy said with authority, "You are going to take that money and use it for school. You will always have incidentals to buy. That money will come in handy. I believe that we O'Malley brothers can muster together enough cash to buy you a new car. You need transportation that is dependable."

Sam answered in a humorous manner, "If you are going to be that generous then I want a brand new Cadillac."

"There is no harm in wanting but a basic Ford or Chevrolet will suit you just fine."

Sam answered. "There is no harm in trying either."

They all laughed. They all stood up. Sam hugged each one individually. Sam was right. This is not a traditional family but it is a family with a lot of love for each other.

Uncle Jimmy checked his coat pocket. He had the tickets. They all rode to the ballpark in Billy's car. Sam was the chauffeur. They strolled to the entrance. Uncle Jimmy handed the tickets to the gentleman who was manning the turn stiles. He tore the tickets in half and gave the stubs back and said "Bishop...hope you enjoy the ball game." He responded with a thank you. They walked up the long ramp to the lower deck. There was an usher there who examined the tickets and directed the Bishop and his party to box seats situated just above the dugout of the home team.

Uncle Billy told his brother, "These are great seats."

"You know how Sean is our friend and your benefactor. Well, Charles Stuart, the owner of this franchise is my friend and benefactor."

"That's good to know. I thought you might have gone back to selling indulgences."

"Billy, you do have a strange sense of humor. However, I did tell him that there is a special place in heaven for him."

"That line doesn't work on Sean anymore."

It was the bottom of the fifth inning. Sam had already inhaled three hot dogs and two root beers. The O'Malley brothers consumed mass quantities of roasted peanuts along with several Cokes each. There was a crack of the bat. A foul ball was blazing toward the box seats. Uncle Jimmy jumped to his feet and stretched as far as he could. He snagged the ball with one hand. It was a stinger. The batter saw the fantastic catch. He tipped his hat to the Bishop. Uncle Jimmy acknowledged it by giving him a wave back. As soon as the pain subsided, he took an ink pen from his pocket and signed the ball "Uncle Jimmy" and dated it "8/28/47". He handed the ball and pen to his brothers and they too signed it. Sam also penned his name. Uncle Billy gave the ball to Sam as a memento.

Sam responded, "This will go on the shelf next to my B-17 model."

Sam had one more hot dog before the game was over. He was a growing boy. The home team won. It was a good time for all. Sam dropped off Uncle Jimmy at the Rectory and headed back toward New Dublin. Uncle Billy and Pop were sound asleep before they even got out of town.

Chapter 17

Graduation Day (Circa 1948)

Commencement ceremonies were being held in St. Patrick's social hall. The hall was full. Seated on the stage were Father O'Malley and Sister Monica. The graduates were seated in the front two rows dressed in their black robes and mortar board hats with tassels; behind them sat the nuns.

After Father O'Malley gave an opening prayer, Sister Monica rose from her seat and moved to the podium. "I welcome all of you to this evening's event as we honor the graduating class of 1948." She looked at the twenty two graduating students sitting before her. She became a little emotional which is out of character for Sister Monica. "I know how a mother must feel when her children grow up and decide to leave home. It has to be a difficult moment. I reminisce as I look at all of you. I have seen you grow from children to young adults and now you must move on in your life. I love each and every one of you and I will miss seeing you every day. Hopefully, I will at least get to see you in church on Sundays."

Most of the nuns got teary eyed as Sister Monica spoke. They too were emotionally attached to the students that they have taught over the last twelve years.

Sister Monica continued, "At this time I would like to introduce to you the valedictorian for the graduating class, Miss Theresa Kelly."

Sister Monica returned to her seat as Theresa climbed the steps of the stage and moved to the podium. The audience clapped.

Theresa began, "I want to thank my fellow classmates for voting for me to be the valedictorian. It is an honor and a privilege to speak before you this evening. First, I want to thank Father O'Malley, Sister Monica and all the nuns for your untiring and dedicated service in giving us a good education."

Theresa had previously told her classmates that when she finished making her opening statement, they were to give them a standing ovation. They did as instructed right on cue. This was well received.

Theresa continued, "I also want to acknowledge Bishop O'Malley who is in attendance. He informed me earlier that he was not here in his official capacity but only as Sam's Uncle Jimmy." Theresa's speech was directed only to her classmates. "I wrote a speech. It was a good speech. I had every word memorized. It lasted exactly twenty minutes. I read over it again this morning and it was good but mushy and I knew you didn't want to hear mushy. So I tore it up. I was told that my address should be inspirational. I have grown up with all of you. I know what each of you plan to do after graduation and it is all good. Half of you are going to work on your family farms. The math that you have learned here at St. Patrick's will be beneficial when you're trying to figure out how many bushels an acre of land will yield. Sally and Betty have already enrolled in nursing school. Isaac, following his father's footsteps, is headed for medical school. Some of you have accepted employment at the plant. Some of us have been accepted at college. Johnny is headed for Notre Dame and I have been accepted at St. Mary's College, which is literally across the street from Notre Dame. He will be pursuing a business degree. I am going to get my teaching degree. I am hopeful that I will be able to teach here at St. Patrick's. Maybe some day I will be teaching your children. Sam, the pride of our class, is going to the seminary. We don't need to be inspired…we are inspired. But we do have an obligation. We must give back to New Dublin. This has to be one of the greatest towns in this country. We don't have all of the attractions that the big cities have but can any of you say that we didn't have a good time in growing up here. I bet all of us have seen every Roy Rogers and Gene Autry movies ever made. Remember all those good times when we went swimming down at the river. Let's not forget about the Friday and Saturday nights hanging out at the drug store. It may not sound like much fun to those city folks but it sure was a lot of fun to us. We have roots here and the bigger those roots grow, the better the town. There are five things that make New Dublin what it is: God, Country, Family, Friendship, and Community. We need to insure those attributes are not forgotten. We have that obligation to the three generations preceding us and to the generations to follow. I look forward to going away for school. It will be a journey that I will never forget but I will be back. Most of us will stay here too. Some of you may have to move away for reasons that you have little control over but New Dublin will always be in your memories. If the situation in life that took you away changes, you will be back too. He doesn't know this yet but in the far distance future, I am going to marry Mr. Johnny Jernigan and Father Samuel Jenkins will be the one that marries us. When it comes time to have children, Dr. Isaac Swartz assisted by Nurse Sally Foley and Nurse Betty Moran will be the ones overseeing the delivery. God is good and God has blessed the Class of 1948."

Sam took his elbow and poked Johnny in the side. Johnny was silent and stared straight forward with a blank look on his face. Sam said, "You have to admit, the girl does have spunk."

Sister Monica moved to the podium. "I don't know about the rest of you but I am inspired. By the way Theresa, you get that teaching degree and I will find you a class here at St. Patrick's." The audience applauded again. Sister Monica looked down at the graduates, "When I call your name please come forward and Father O'Malley will give you your diploma." One by one Sister Monica called a graduate forward. They rose and walked across the stage and shook Father O'Malley's hand as he presented them with their diploma. Sister Monica called "Theresa Kelley".

The hall erupted again with applause. Theresa was everyone's favorite. She bounced to her feet and ran up the stairs to the stage. She was smiling from ear to ear. Half way across the stage she stopped and did a curtsy. She then pulled up her robe exposing her basketball shoes and blue jeans. She began to do a quick Irish jig. The audience went wild. She headed for Father O'Malley who had his hand extended. She ignored it. She gave Father O'Malley a big hug and kissed him on the cheek. She grabbed her diploma and skipped off the stage with her diploma held high above her head.

After the last graduate received his diploma, friends and family gathered around a nearby table where the nuns were cutting up a large rectangular cake with "Class of 1948" written across the top. Each person was served a piece of cake and a cold soda. All the girls in the graduating class rushed toward Theresa. They wanted to know all the scuttlebutt about her and Johnny. Theresa told them, "I knew when we were twelve years old that I was going to marry Johnny someday. That feeling hasn't changed. It's destiny."

All the guys gathered around Johnny. They all wanted to know the scuttlebutt about him and Theresa. Johnny didn't say anything. He still had that blank look on his face. Sam spoke up, "Guys we need to leave him alone. Can't you see that he is in shock?" Everyone laughed except Johnny.

Sam caught up with Pop, Uncle Billy, and Uncle Jimmy who were making pigs of themselves in regard to the cake. Pop with his mouth full said "Congratulations!" Uncle Billy and Uncle Jimmy followed suit. Uncle Billy continued with, "Sam, you have made the O'Malley brothers proud." Sam acknowledged the compliment and continued, "If you guys don't mind we are all going over to the drug store." Uncle Jimmy said, "No problem. You go and have a good time." Uncle Jimmy pulled a five dollar bill out and gave it to Sam, "Buy everyone a malt on me." Sam took the five dollar bill and waved it in the air and called out to his fellow classmates. "Come on and let's go. The good Bishop is buying."

The Class of 1948 piled into the drug store. They grabbed up some tables and pulled them all together. Johnny and Sam sat down beside each other. Theresa took a chair and scooted in between the two. She wrapped her arms around Johnny's neck and kissed him on the cheek. He spoke for the first time. He was somewhat perturbed. "You got our lives all figured out." Theresa responded with confidence. "That's right big boy. There is no sense in fighting the powers above. You don't have to worry. We aren't getting married anytime soon. We have to wait until Father Sam here becomes a priest." Theresa was in a loving mood this evening. She wrapped her arms around Sam and kissed him too on the cheek. She then extended her fist. Sam and Johnny did the same. In unison they said, "Friends forever."

Chapter 18

Johnny Joins the Air Force (Circa 1949 - 1954)

It was Johnny and Theresa's senior year at college. Graduation was less than a month away. This will complete another chapter in their young lives. Four years in school has been fun but they were ready for school to be over with. No more 'all-nighters'. No more part time jobs. The thought was pleasing to the both of them.

Johnny was sitting outside Theresa's classroom waiting for dismissal. She came out and kissed him on the cheek, "Are you hungry?"

"I'm starving to death. Let's go to the cafeteria."

They found an empty table and put their books down in the chairs. Each of them grabbed a tray and their eating utensils and began to move down the serving line. Johnny paid the cashier and they proceeded back to their table. The cafeteria was always crowded and it was never quiet.

Johnny was serious when he said, "Theresa you know I love you and I would do anything that you asked me to do..." Johnny paused as he tried to gather his thoughts before he spoke.

Theresa was concerned. This was not typical Johnny. "Spit it out. What are you trying to say?"

"I talked with the Air Force recruiter here on campus. He said that after I finish Officer Candidate's School, I will be commissioned a 2nd Lieutenant. He guaranteed me that I will be accepted in flight school. I want to fly jet planes. I don't know how long this Korean War will last but I feel obligated to go. It's my duty."

Theresa was speechless. She gently grasped Johnny's hands and stare directly into his eyes. She composed herself. "Johnny, I love you with all my heart and soul. Your father and my father both served in World War II but I am scared that you might meet the same fate as Sam's father. I cannot imagine my life without you. But I will never tell you don't go because if every mother, wife or girlfriend had their way, no one would go to war. If it were not for brave men like you and our fathers, we would be speaking German today. I support you in whatever you decide to do."

"I have given this much thought and it something that I feel I must do. Why don't we go ahead and get married before I have to report for duty."

Theresa said emphatically and without hesitation, "NO! We don't get married until Sam becomes a priest."

Johnny didn't argue. "I don't even know why I asked."

Johnny and Theresa put their trays away. They walked from St. Mary's College over to the admin building at Notre Dame where the Air Force Recruiter maintained an office. They entered and were greeted by Tech Sergeant Reynolds. "Hello, Johnny. Come in and sit down." Johnny had been by the recruiting office on numerous occasions and he and Airman Reynolds had developed a friendly relationship.

"This is my fiancé, Theresa Kelly."

Airman Reynolds rose from his seat behind his desk. He extended his hand, "Nice to meet you."

"The feeling is mutual."

Johnny said, "I'm here today to sign the papers."

"Excellent. I can honestly say that this is not a spur of the moment decision on your part. You and I have discussed every aspect of your enlistment." Airman Reynolds pulled a form from his desk and handed it to Johnny. "Fill this out and sign it. I will do the rest."

Johnny did as instructed. When he got to the bottom of the form that required his signature, he looked at Theresa, "This is your decision too."

Theresa was silent. She laid her hand atop his and together they signed the form.

Airman Reynolds shook Johnny's hand, "Welcome to the United States Air Force. You will report for duty two weeks after graduation."

The month passed quickly. It was graduation day. Johnny's parents and Theresa's parents made the long trip together to South Bend, Indiana. Sam drove straight from the seminary. The hall was filled with graduates dressed in black caps and gowns. Spectators occupied every seat available. One by one each graduate was called forward to receive his diploma. John M. Jenkins, Jr. responded to his name and walked across the stage and proudly accepted his diploma. Slowly, each graduate received his diploma.

It was time for Theresa but at a different location. Graduation exercises at St. Mary's College were more congenial. The class of 1952 was much smaller than that of Notre Dame. Anyone who knew Theresa was not sure as to what she would do when she became the center of attention. She surprised all of them. She was very lady-like. However, she did contemplate doing the Irish jig as she had done at her high school graduation but this was not New Dublin. This graduating class was different from high school. Even though she knew everyone in her class, she didn't want to do anything that would embarrass her parents. Without fanfare, Theresa accepted her diploma and returned to her seat. Theresa's mother breathed a sigh of relief.

The next morning, Johnny's parents and Theresa's parents headed out back to New Dublin. Sam stayed and helped Johnny and Theresa load their personal belongings. There was no wasted space in the car. The car was packed to the hilt. The three of them shared the front seat. They departed South Bend later that afternoon. They took the long way home and did the tourist thing. They wanted to enjoy each other's company especially in view of the fact that Johnny would be reporting for duty in two weeks.

After a week on the road, Sam arrived back in New Dublin. Theresa was hanging out the window waving at everyone she knew. The first stop was Theresa's house where Johnny and Sam unloaded all of her belongings. She was greeted at the door by her mother who was happy to see her and that she had a safe trip. Her father was at work at the plant. The next stop was Johnny's house. Both of his parents were home. They, like Theresa's mother, were glad that they were safely back. Mrs. Jenkins offered Sam a piece of cake but he declined. It has been several months since he was last home and he knew that Pop was awaiting his arrival.

Sam, carrying his suitcase, swung open the screen door to the store. He looked around but he didn't see Pop. "How does a man get service around here?"

Pop was stooped over restocking the lower shelves. He stood. His face lit up. "Sam!" As he walked toward Sam, he was steadily wiping his hands on his apron. He gave Sam a big hug. "It's good to see you."

Sam responded, "I missed you too." Sam put his suitcase down at the foot of the stairs. He grabbed a soda from the cooler and hopped up on the counter. Pop sat on the stool by the cash register. They began to update each other as to what had been happening in their lives. Pop said that he was cooking a special dinner this Sunday and both of Sam's uncles agreed to be there. Pop also suggested that Sam invite Theresa and Johnny to join them. Sam liked that idea.

For the rest of the week, Theresa, Johnny, and Sam hung out together. They reunited with many of their friends. Many of which they had not been seen in years. Some had married and had small children. Two of their classmates had enlisted in the Army and were serving in Korea. Isaac was home from med school on summer break.

Saturday evening they took in a movie at the Rialto. It was the *African Queen* starring Humphrey Bogart and Katharine Hepburn. It was enjoyed by all three. Theresa said that parts of the movie reminded her of their raft trip down the Cherokee River. Johnny and Sam agreed but Sam added at least we didn't have the leeches. After the movie, they went to the drug store for hamburgers. They felt old in their youth. The place was full of high school students. The situation worsened when some of the kids recognized them and came over to say hello. The problem was they were addressed as Mr. Jenkins, Ms. Kelly and Mr. Jernigan.

St. Patrick's church bells rang as parishioners arrived for Sunday Mass. Theresa and her parents found an empty pew and sat down. Shortly they were joined by Johnny and his parents. Theresa and Johnny sat side by side. Pop sat in his unofficial reserved seat; the front pew next to the center aisle. Sam was in the sacristy donning his cassock and surplice. He was one of the morning altar servers.

The congregation stood as the procession began. After the entrance hymn was finished, Father O'Malley gave his opening blessing. He added, "As most of you are aware, Johnny Jernigan has joined the Air Force and will be reporting for duty this week." The congregation applauded. New Dublin was notorious for support of their favorite sons in the military. Father O'Malley continued, "Kevin Carey and Pat Collins are currently serving in Korea. This Mass is being offered for the well being of these three young men as they serve our country."

After Mass was over, Father O'Malley and Sam stood together and greeted everyone as they left the church. Johnny was inundated with well wishers. He was humbled by the World War II vets who shook his hand and voiced words of encouragement.

Pop spoke with Theresa and Johnny. "You two are coming for lunch today?"

Theresa answered, "Yes sir. I am already hungry."

"Good! We have plenty of food."

Later, Bishop O'Malley parked his car in front of the grocery store. He was the first to arrive. He entered the upstairs apartment. "This place sure smells good."

Sam looked around from the kitchen sink. "Uncle Jimmy, it's good to see you."

"It has been awhile. How are you doing with your studies?"

"I am not the best in the class but I am definitely not an embarrassment to the O'Malley brothers."

"You could never embarrass me. Now your Uncle Billy is a different story. He was a total embarrassment to our mother."

Pop piped in, "I agree with that."

Sam said, "You two are terrible...bad mouthing your brother when he's not here to defend himself."

Sam began setting the table. He put an extra leaf in the table to accommodate the extra guests. The others arrived. Theresa and

Johnny just sat back and watched. They didn't know that they were going to get entertainment with lunch. The O'Malley brothers were constantly joking with each other and ironically Sam was just as bad as the others. The meal was prepared and they all set down. It was a feast. Uncle Billy made the sign of the cross and began the blessing, "Bless us O Lord..." When he finished, he added "...and Lord please forgive the two gentlemen at this table who have been making slanderous statements about their dear brother. Amen."

When Uncle Jimmy raised his head, he looked straight at Sam and smiled, "Tattletale."

Sam shrugged his shoulders and grinned back. Everyone laughed including Johnny and Theresa even though they didn't fully understand the inside joke. When lunch was ended, Pop brought out one of Mrs. Shanahan's peach pies that he had heating in the oven. He cut slices and passed them around. No one ever turns down a slice of Mrs. Shanahan's peach pie. Compliments were paid to the chef. They were well deserved.

As they were all sitting at the table making conversation, Father O'Malley reached in his coat pocket and pulled out a St. Christopher medal. "Johnny, this is for you."

"Sorry, Father, but you are a little late." Johnny pulled out his own St. Christopher medal. "My future father-in-law beat you to it."

Sam and the O'Malley brothers laid eyes on the St. Christopher's medal with the bullet still embedded in it. As if on cue, the four of them made the sign of the cross. To them, this was a true artifact of a miracle granted.

Father O'Malley responded, "Johnny, you wear that medal as a badge of honor. Theresa's dad is a bona fide American hero."

"I agree. You know he still credits you with saving his life."

Sarcastically he answered, "You need to document that. The Vatican may some day need that information when they consider me for sainthood."

Theresa and Johnny were not sure if Father O'Malley was serious so out of politeness they did not respond but Sam, Pop and Uncle Jimmy roared with laughter.

"Contrary to the beliefs of my family here, I, the future 'St. Billy', will be praying to St. Christopher to intercede on your behalf. That medal has proven results. Just keep it close to your heart and you will be safe."

Johnny responded, "Thank you, Father. I will always remember that."

Johnny and Theresa complimented Pop for the excellent meal and they left. Sam had something on his mind that he wanted to discuss in a family meeting. Since everyone was present, this was the appropriate time and place. "Pop, I need your permission to join the military."

Pop was taken aback. This was something that he did not foresee. Sam has never indicated any desire about serving in the armed forces. He calmly answered Sam. "First of all, I can't give you permission. You are a grown man and a decision of such importance is solely up to you. But I can give you my advice. I suggest that you stay in school and finish your education. Johnny is leaving for the Air Force and two of your high school buddies are already in Korea and you feel that you need to do your patriotic duty. This is admirable but being a Priest is also admirable."

Uncle Jimmy continued the conversation. "I agree with Pop. Finish your education and get ordained. If at that time, you still feel that you want to make the military a career, then I guarantee to you that I will get you in the Chaplain corps."

Uncle Billy added his feelings on the situation. "The three of us almost never agree on anything but in this case, I concur with Jimmy and Pop. In two years the war may be over and you might change your mind."

Sam acquiesced. He knew that Pop and his Uncles were right.

****

It was Wednesday morning. Sam picked up Theresa and they traveled to Johnny's house. He was waiting on the porch along with his parents. The three of them walked to the car. Johnny's mother was crying. Seeing this, Theresa did everything possible to refrain from shedding any tears. Johnny's father was not a hugger. He shook Johnny's hand and patted him on the shoulder. "I love you son. Be careful." Johnny's mother hugged him and then kissed him on the cheek. "Write me often." Johnny threw his small suitcase in the back and then climbed into the front seat with Theresa and Sam. They drove away. The drive to Jefferson City was abnormally quiet. Sam pulled up in front of the induction center. He shook Johnny's hand and told him good luck. He stayed in the car while Johnny and Theresa stood outside saying their good-byes. Johnny turned just before going inside and waved. As Sam eased out into traffic, Theresa buried her face in her hands and began to sob. Sam was perplexed. He had never seen this side of Theresa. He tried to console her but his words were of little comfort.

Finally, Theresa regained her composure. "I'm sorry Sam. I've tried to be brave but seeing him for the last time, it just overcame me."

"This is not the last time you will see Johnny. He will be home again before deploying overseas and after that, he will be home safe and sound."

"You're right but that is not exactly what I meant. Johnny and I have never been apart for any extended period of time since we met in first grade. I felt the same way when you went to the seminary and Johnny and I went to Indiana. Now, Johnny is gone and you will be going back to school. I will be all alone. I know that I am being selfish but it hurts."

"You definitely won't be alone. When you take over the third grade class at St. Patrick's this fall you will have twenty five kids to keep you company."

"With God's help, I will survive."

****

Johnny stood before an Airman sitting behind a desk. He didn't look up. "Name?"

"John M. Jernigan, Jr., Sir."

The Airman stared at Johnny and went into a tirade. "Don't ever say 'sir' to me. Do you see any bars on my collar? It is obvious that we have enlisted another dumb recruit. The Air Force is going to pot. I can't understand why they can't find men of substance. Take your bag and go into the other room. Get out of my sight."

Johnny did as ordered but he did not say anything. He wasn't sure as how to address the Airman. This was Johnny's first taste of military life. Little did he know at the time, this was mild in comparison as to what he would endure during basic training and Officer Candidate's School. Johnny managed to survive the mental and physical abuse by keeping his mouth shut and doing as he was told. He felt pride and honor when the 2nd Lieutenant bar was pinned on his collar. The next step in his military transition was flight school. He was excited. He along with other prospective pilots boarded a C-47 and were flown to their next duty station. As they made final approach, Johnny peered out the window and saw a variety of aircraft parked on the tarmac. His eyes focused on the F-86 Sabre Jet. This was his plane of choice. It made all the prop-driven aircraft obsolete. It was the future of American aviation and he wanted to be a small part of that future. But first he had to learn how to fly. Today was the first time he had ever been airborne. The next few months involved more classroom work than stick time. But as time progressed the inverse happened. More stick time. The instructors were impressed with Johnny's ability. He was far and away the best in the class. One instructor commented that Johnny "...did not fly a plane...he finessed it." The class was eventually divided up so that each student pilot could be assign to a specific aircraft. Johnny got the one he wanted...the Sabre Jet. After hours in a flight simulator, Johnny made his solo flight. It was exhilarating. He was amazed at the power and agility. He put the plane through its paces. The response was fantastic. It was the melding of man and machine.

It was two days before Christmas. The flight school was shut down for the holidays. Johnny packed a small travel bag and went to flight operations. He was looking for a "hop" close to home. He checked the board and there was an aircraft that was heading for the east coast. He tracked down the pilots. They introduced themselves as Captain Morris and Lt. Stuart. They agreed to have him tag along. Captain Morris asked Johnny as to his destination and Johnny informed him that he was going to a town called New Dublin...about fifty miles north of Jefferson City. The pilot was apologetic. If there was an airport there, they would drop him off.

Johnny laughed. "The plane you are flying was built at New Dublin. As a kid, I remember these planes taking off and landing all day long. In fact, my father may have helped to build this particular plane."

The pilot answered, "If that's the case, you'll be home for Christmas." Captain Morris further questioned Johnny. "Are you a pilot too?"

"I am a student pilot training on the Sabre."

"You lucky dog...that's one fine aircraft."

"You're right but there is one draw back. You can guess where my next duty station will be."

"We're in the Reserves. We expect that our squadron will be activated after the first of the year. We may be seeing you over there. Make yourself comfortable. It will be about a three hour flight."

Captain Morris reached New Dublin. He circled the airfield to observe the windsock. The winds were calm. Inside the building, the senior John Jernigan, told everyone to quiet down as he listened. He recognized the sound of the engines. "That's one of ours!" The entire production line shut down and they all moved outside. The aircraft came in and touched down. It turned and taxied back toward the hangar. Captain Morris swung the tail around and brought the engines back to an idle. Johnny went up to the cabin and thanked both pilots.

Captain Morris said, "I see you have a welcoming committee."

"Yea, they're out here looking at one of their babies. See that gentleman with the red ball cap. That is my father." Johnny offered his farewell, "Merry Christmas."

Both pilots responded, "Merry Christmas."

Johnny opened the back hatch door and hopped outside much to the surprise of all those present especially his father. Johnny walked to the front of the aircraft and saluted the Captain. He returned the salute and powered up the engines. He rolled down the runway and was airborne.

Johnny's father was the first to greet him. "It's good to see you son. I knew that you would be coming home but I didn't know that you would be getting the VIP treatment."

"Dad, it's one of the perks of being in the Air Force."

"You can ride to the house with me. It's almost quitting time, Your Mama will be ecstatic when we come through the front door. Theresa has been impatient all week wondering when you were coming home. Sam is also back from the seminary. This is going to be a great Christmas."

Mr. Nelson, the owner of the company, had joined Johnny and his father. He shook Johnny's hand and said "Welcome Home." He turned to Mr. Jernigan and told him, "Take the rest of the day off. Your wife will kill us both if she finds out that Johnny was been here for several hours before he got home."

"Thanks, Boss. Have a Merry Christmas."

"Merry Christmas."

Johnny and his father made an effort to head for the car but it was difficult because everyone wanted to say hello to Johnny especially his high school buddies. He didn't want to be rude so he took his time and spoke to all of them.

Mr. Jernigan parked into the driveway and walked to the front door and announced, "Honey, I'm home."

Mrs. Jernigan yelled back from the kitchen. "You're early. Dinner is not ready yet."

"Forget about dinner. I have a present for you."

"A present?" Mrs. Jernigan questioned as she came from the kitchen. She screamed, "Johnny!" as she ran and hugged her son. "How did you get here?"

"A couple of new found Air Force friends flew me to the plant."

"You can't beat that." Theresa raced through her mind. "I've got to call Theresa." She dialed her number and Theresa answered. "Theresa, this is Mrs. Jernigan, there is someone here who wants to see you."

Theresa didn't say another word. The phone went dead. She went flying out of the house. She did not stroll the two blocks to Johnny's house. It was a flat out run. Johnny and his parents stepped out onto the front porch. It was not long until Theresa was seen sprinting down the street. Her hair tied in a pony tail swished with every stride she made. She flew into Johnny's awaiting arms. He picked her up. She kissed him on the lips...again, again, again...

"Slow down girl. I got to be able to breath."

Theresa gave him one more passionate kiss before Johnny put her down. Theresa thought of Sam. "I've got to call Sam." She went inside and dialed Pop's Grocery and Sam answered. She asked, "Where are you?"

"I am here. Where are you?"

"I am here at Johnny's house with my cutie pie."

"I'm on my way." Sam shortly arrived. He was happy to see his old friend.

Johnny could not have planned a better homecoming. He thought that he needed to leave more often.

The Christmas holidays came and went far too quickly. It was time for Johnny to leave again. He was returning to his base via commercial airline. It was too risky in trying to get a "hop" and he could not afford being late in reporting for duty. Sam, along with Theresa, drove Johnny to the airport in Jefferson City. The good-bye at the airport was extremely difficult for Theresa. She was well aware that this may be the last good-bye because Johnny would not be coming home before being transferred overseas.

****

Johnny climbed in the cockpit of his Sabre. Today started a new phase of training...Aerial Combat Tactics. It was a simulation of dog fights which, without a doubt, would occur in flights over North Korea. Johnny was intent on learning as much as he could absorb. It could mean life or death. Again, he excelled. He even developed several maneuvers that even impressed the instructors. The next two months was practice, practice and more practice. Johnny felt comfortable that he could carry out his bombing missions and defend himself in the event he encountered any MIG's (Russian built fighter aircraft) but he was also pragmatic. Training was one thing. Actual aerial combat was another.

Johnny received his silver bar as a 1st Lieutenant upon graduation. It was a matter of days when he and five other pilots boarded a military transport aircraft filled with soldiers, Marines and airmen. They "island-hopped" across the Pacific until they touched down in South Korea. He and his fellow pilots were all assigned to different squadrons. Tech Sergeant Jones was waiting for Johnny to disembark from the aircraft. He escorted Johnny to another plane sitting on the tarmac. Johnny and the Tech Sergeant Jones climbed aboard the U6A Beaver, a single engine, high wing airplane. Johnny introduced himself to the pilot and the co-pilot. The pilot cranked the radial engine and taxied out for take-off. It was a quick flight. As they were landing, Johnny noted all the Sabre Jets uniformly parked adjacent to the runway. It was an impressive sight.

Johnny followed Tech Sergeant Jones to headquarters. The Tech Sergeant instructed Lieutenant Jernigan to take a seat while he went inside to see the squadron commander.

He handed the sealed envelope to Lt. Colonel Mathis. "Sir, here is the paperwork for the FNG. He is sitting in the outer office."

"Thanks Bob. Let him cool his heels while I look through his records. Then send him in."

"Yes sir." Tech Sergeant Jones returned to his desk. After about ten minutes he stood and told Johnny, "Colonel Mathis will see you now."

Johnny entered the office. He stood in front of Colonel Mathis' desk at attention and gave a sharp salute. Colonel Mathis made a gesture with his right hand. Johnny used his imagination and interpreted it as a return salute.

"Stand at ease Lieutenant and have a seat."

"Your former squadron commander is a personal friend of mine. He always sends me the best of the class. He wrote a short note to me. *Lt. Jernigan is the best I have ever taught. He may be able to teach an old man like you new tricks.* Knowing the source, that is one hell of a compliment."

Johnny answered modestly. "Thank you, Sir."

"We have a morning briefing at 5:00 A.M. You will be flying tomorrow. Do you think that you are ready?"

"I'll let you know when we get back."

"Good answer." Colonel Mathis continued, "Bob will show you around and get you settled in."

"I assume 'Bob' is Tech Sergeant Jones. He doesn't talk much."

"Bob is all military. He believes that it is inappropriate for an enlisted man to fraternize with an officer. I personally believe that he has an inherit mistrust of officers. I have tried to break him but with no luck. I will see you in the morning."

"Thanks Sir. Should I salute you again?"

"No. I am not into all that pomp and circumstance. If you do your best and obey my orders then I am a happy man."

Johnny entered the outer office. "Come on Bob, you are going to be my tour guide."

"Sir, I prefer you address me as Tech Sergeant Jones."

"I sure will Bob." Johnny continued, "I want you to show me where I will be bedding down. I want to get rid of this duffle bag."

"Yes sir."

Tech Sergeant Jones also familiarized Johnny with the flight line, mess hall and the location of the briefing room. He introduced Johnny to many of the other pilots. During the tour, Johnny tried to engage Bob in conversation but to no avail. He was always respectful but he only answered the questions with no extra commentary. Maybe Lt. Colonel Mathis was right. Bob couldn't be broken.

"Sir, is there anything else I can do for you?"

Johnny answered, "No, Tech Sergeant Jones. Oh by the way, where are you from?"

"Jefferson City."

"I can't believe it but I am from New Dublin. We're neighbors."

Something happened. Tech Sergeant Jones lit up. "Yes sir. I have been to New Dublin many times. My parents would load up me and my sisters in the car and we would go to the St.

Patrick Day festival. In fact, my parents still go every year even though all of us kids are grown."

"I went to elementary and high school at St. Patrick's. You and I are about the same age. I bet we crossed paths. I was one of the altar boys leading the parade."

"It's a small world, sir."

"Yes it is, Tech Sergeant Jones."

"Sir, since we have a common history, you can call me Bob just as long as no one else is around."

Johnny agreed. It wasn't much but it was a start.

Bob continued, "Colonel Mathis and I run this squadron. If you need anything, come see me. I'll take care of you."

"I will keep that in mind. Thanks,"

"You're welcome, Sir."

Johnny proceeded to the mess hall and got an early supper. He returned to the barracks and sat down on the bed in his small private cubicle. He wrote a letter to Theresa. Actually it was two letters; one for her eyes only and the other one she could share with Johnny's parents and Sam. Johnny was tired from the long flight from the States. He turned in for the night. He wanted to be fresh for tomorrow morning.

It was 5:00 A.M. All the pilots had taken their seats on the benches behind the long wooden tables. The chatter ceased as Colonel Mathis entered the room. He proceeded to the podium. "Good morning, Gentlemen. In case you haven't met the FNG, his name is Lt. John Jernigan. He will be flying with the escort team today. Colonel Mathis took his pointer and circled an area on the map. "This is where the Army is engaged in an intense battle. We are on stand-by until they call for air support. I fully suspect that we will be making two or three sorties today. You escort guys need to be especially alert. We have intelligence where the Russians are providing more pilots for the MIG's. They are better trained than the North Koreans. In addition, they have been showing up more frequently at battle sites because they know that we will probably be making bombing runs. Tech Sergeant Jones has some forms for you guys to fill out. Good luck gentlemen.

Johnny finished filling out his form and he took it to Tech Sergeant Jones. Johnny in a low voice asked Bob, "What is a FNG?"

Bob laughed. "It is exactly what you are...a 'F..king New Guy'."

Captain Carlson came and introduced himself to Johnny. He was the flight leader for the escort team. He explained to Johnny what he could expect today. He also gave a brief synopsis of the flight procedures for the mission. They walked together out to the flight line and Captain Carlson pointed out the Sabre that was now assigned to him. Johnny went to the aircraft and inspected the interior and exterior. He met the crew chief.

"Sir, I am Staff Sergeant Cooper. The guys around here call me "Coop". I am in charge of this bird. She is a good aircraft. I've never had any major problems. I am constantly performing maintenance to keep her in tip-top shape. When it comes time for take off, you keep your eyes on me. I will get you safely out onto the runway. After that, you're on your own." Coop saw all the other pilots running for their aircraft. Coop told Johnny. "Sir, let me help you get strapped in...it's show time."

Johnny was excited. He wasn't afraid but then again it was early in the day.

Coop moved around to the left front of the aircraft. He raised his right hand in the air and rotated his hand in a circle. This was the signal to start the engine. Johnny flipped the starter switch and the engine began to whine. Coop pulled the chocks from the wheels. He watched as the other aircraft in the row pulled out. It was Johnny's turn. Coop motioned with both arms to move forward. He gave the hand signal to make a right turn. He then snapped to attention and saluted. Johnny returned the gesture.

The first sortie went without incident. The bombs were dropped and the flight returned to base. The second sortie was the same as the first. However, the third sortie was what war was all about...kill or be killed. The Captain came over the radio. "We have company." Johnny looked around and there they were...four MIG's. One locked in on Johnny. He began to take evasive action. Through a series of strategic moves, Johnny was in position to fire on the MIG. He squeezed the trigger on the fifty caliber machine gun. His first burst made contact with the MIG. It started smoking. The plane was out of control. The pilot ejected. Johnny moved in on another MIG. He wasn't as successful as his first encounter. The dog fight was short lived. The MIG's broke off the engagement. Captain Carlson radioed, "Let 'em go."

The Captain then directed his conversation to Johnny. "Where did you learn those moves?"

"Flight school."

"They never taught me anything like that."

Little did the Captain know but Johnny was modest in his answer. In reality, Johnny developed those maneuvers on his own.

Over the next months it was mission after mission, sortie after sortie. Encounters with the MIG's seemed to be on a weekly basis but the dog fight of all dog fights was June 7, 1953; a date that Johnny would never forget. The squadron's mission was to destroy a military camp deep inside of North Korea. The first leg was successful. Since the five aircraft dropped their ordinance, they were available to engage the enemy if need be. Half way home was uneventful but out of nowhere there were MIG's everywhere. They out numbered the Sabres two to one. Johnny was exceptional this day. He shot down two MIG's. He was now considered an Ace, an honor bestowed on a pilot who shoots down five or more enemy aircraft. This was the least of Johnny's concerns. He had a MIG on his tail. Unknown to him there were actually two MIG's working in tandem. The second MIG anticipated Johnny's evasive moves and when Johnny broke hard right, the second MIG was waiting. Johnny was a sitting duck. It was a direct hit and he was going down. He took his right hand and grasped his St. Christopher medal and used his left hand to pull the handle for ejection. He was propelled clear of the aircraft. Captain Carlson witnessed the whole event and saw Johnny's parachute deploy. He broke off to give Johnny air cover. He didn't want Johnny being shot while he drifted to terra firma.

Most pilots fantasized different scenarios as to what they would do if they were shot down. Johnny was no different. One of his scenarios was that if he was close to a waterway, he would build a raft much like he did as a kid. He looked out over the countryside and he could see the Imjin River. This was his passage to freedom. He was going down in an isolated area. He was fortunate to land in a small clearing. He gathered up his parachute as Captain Carlson buzzed him. Johnny waved at him to let him know that he was not hurt. Johnny took his survival knife and cut all the cord from the parachute. He would need it later. He buried the parachute under a bunch of loose brush. The prospect of being rescued was slim at best. He was on his own. He had to get out of the area as quickly as possible because he knew the North Koreans would be searching for him. A prisoner of war camp was not an option. He set a course of just south of due west which would eventually intersect with the Imjin River. Johnny ran hard and fast without resting until he reached the riverbank. He slipped down to the shore line. He took a bag from his survival kit and filled it with water. He moved back up on shore out of sight. Two water purification tablets were dropped in the bag. He followed the instructions on the bottle and waited until he thought the water was safe to drink. He downed the whole bag. The tablets may kill the bacteria but it didn't enhance the taste. Regardless, he had to drink the water. Becoming dehydrated could be a death sentence. He walked the edge of the bank until he found two suitable logs. He camouflaged himself in the underbrush. While he waited for nightfall, a North Korean patrol boat cruised by and later passed again heading back upstream. Johnny knew that they were looking for him. The sound of the engine faded out in the distance. It was twilight. Johnny felt safe enough to venture out in the open. There was still enough light to see what he needed to do. He took the white cord and sloshed it around in the mud until it was black. He tied the two logs together. He took a long piece of cord and tied it to his wrist. This was a precautionary measure in the event he fell off the log or if he had to go into the water to secrete himself. This way he was always tethered to the raft. Johnny pushed the logs out into the river and climbed aboard. It was the beginning of the monsoon season and the rising water increased the speed of the flowing water. Johnny paddled toward the middle where the current would be the strongest. He wasn't sure as to his exact location. He figured that he was anywhere from 50 to 75 miles behind enemy lines. If the current was running better than 3 miles an hour, he could possibly reach safety in two long nights.

After several hours of drifting, he heard voices coming from upstream. He paddled to the shore line and grabbed onto an overhanging limb. It was a sampan lit up with several lanterns. Johnny let it pass and then eased back out into the current. There was no moon which was a plus. As he floated farther south, he could see the glow of lights in the pitch black sky. It was a village. Johnny made the decision to find a place to secure the raft for the rest of the night. He wanted to pass this population center under the cover of darkness. Johnny climbed up on the bank and laid down in a heavy thicket. He occasionally dozed off, only to be awakened by boat traffic. It was a long day but finally the sun began to set in the west. It was time. Johnny was underway again. The glow of the night lights became brighter and brighter. It was not a village but a military outpost. He could see a spot light sporadically sweeping across the waterway. Johnny rolled off the raft into the cold water and pulled the raft near the far bank. On one sweep the spot light stopped as it shined directly on the raft. After a pause, the sweep continued. Apparently the operator thought that the makeshift raft was no more than river debris. As Johnny floated past the outpost, he could see armed soldiers on guard duty. They were definitely North Korean. Once Johnny was outside the scope of the spot light, he climbed back on the raft. He was shivering uncontrollably. He was fearful that hypothermia was setting in. After another miserable eight hours, the sun began to peek through the tree line. If his calculations were correct, Johnny should be well within friendly territory. But he wasn't sure. He tied off the raft and started moving inland. He marked his trail in the event he was wrong and he had to make his way back to the raft. Johnny knew that there was a road that ran parallel to the river. He found that road and hid in the cover of the tall grass. There was a lot of foot traffic and wooden carts being pulled by horses or water buffaloes. The problem was that North Korean peasants looked the same as South Korean peasants. Therefore it was still impossible to know if he had reached freedom. Johnny perked up. He could hear the sound of an engine. It steadily grew stronger. He cautiously rose above the grass. Johnny thought to himself, "Thank the Lord for the U. S. Army." It was a Jeep. Johnny leaped to his feet and ran out into the middle of the road. He began to wave his arms. The Jeep, occupied by two enlisted men, stopped. Johnny, shivering and teeth chattering, did his best to explain as to who he was and why he was there. The young soldier said, "Hop in Sir. I need to get you to the MASH unit south of here." Johnny silently thanked God and St. Christopher.

The Doctor immediately attended to Johnny. The first order of business was to get him out of his wet flight suit. He was wrapped in a blanket. Because of Johnny's youthful age and his excellent physical condition, the doctor felt confident that the hypothermia was not life threatening. However, he wanted Johnny to hang around over night for observation. This was fine with him. He was tired. All he wanted to do was sleep and that he did. He slept all the way through until the next morning. He awoke early. He began to get dressed in his dry flight suit and boots.

Chief Warrant Officer Hancock stood at the end of the bed. "Good morning. How do you feel?"

"I feel good." Johnny paused as he thought, "No, that's not right. I feel *damn* good. I am alive and I am not a prisoner of war. Life couldn't be any better." Johnny paused again as he corrected himself once more, "Life could be better if I had some food in my belly."

"Finish getting dressed and I'll walk you over to the mess tent."

CWO Hancock explained to Johnny that he was the pilot for the OH-13 helicopter. "If you don't mind stepping down to a *real man's aircraft*, I will fly you back to your unit."

"I would like that. I have never flown in a chopper before."

CWO Hancock sat the OH-13 down on the tarmac. Johnny shook his hand and yelled over the noise of the engine and rotor blades. "Thanks". Johnny had a new appreciation for the helicopter. It was actually more difficult to fly than the Sabre. The pilot had to coordinate both hands and feet at the same time, especially when it was hovering.

The sound of the helicopter was unfamiliar to the pilots of the Sabre squadron. Curiosity brought them out of the stand-by lounge. It was a pleasant surprise to see Johnny step out. They all stood and watched CWO Hancock come to a hover, rotate the tail and take off. Guys being guys began to make jokes. "It must be nice to be able to take several days off to go on a river cruise." Another "I want to know who is going to pay for the plane you crashed." Johnny took it all in stride because he knew it was all in jest. Through their insistence, they all returned inside the lounge and Johnny gave them a blow-by-blow account of the last three days. He summed up by telling everyone that he had to go and check in with the boss.

As he departed the lounge, Coop stopped him. Johnny said, "Coop, I am sorry about your baby."

"Don't be, Sir. She was good to the both of us. She died an honorable death." Coop continued, "Me and the boys over in maintenance are working on your new plane. I'm waiting for parts to come in from the States. It may be a week but I'll have you up and flying again."

"That's good news."

Johnny entered the outer office. Bob was truly glad to see him. He shook hands with him, "Sir, I am happy to see that you're still in one piece."

"Those are my sentiments too."

Bob stuck his head inside inner office. "Sir, are you busy? I have someone here who wants to speak with you."

Colonel Mathis motioned for Bob to enter. The Colonel glanced up. He was just as bad as the rest of the pilots. "What some guys will do to get out of completing a mission." He rose from his desk and shook Johnny's hand. "Good to have you home, Son."

"Thank you, Sir." Johnny had to repeat the entire story from beginning to end. The Colonel and Bob hung onto every word. Johnny also informed the Colonel about being double-teamed and how the second MIG snookered him. This was of major interest to him and he made a note to remind himself to bring this matter up at the next briefing. Colonel Mathis came around to the front of his desk and asked Johnny to stand. He pulled out a small envelope from his shirt pocket that contained a set of Captain's bars. He pinned them on Johnny's dirty and tattered flight suit.

Johnny was not anticipating a promotion. He humbly said, "Thank you, Sir."

"Don't thank me. It was Bob's idea. I am totally clueless as to how he got Brigade to sign off on this and get the paperwork here in lightning speed. To be honest with you, I really don't want to know. There is no sense in both of us going to jail."

Johnny laughed and looked at Bob, "Thank you Tech..."

Bob raised his hand to cut Johnny off from speaking any further. "You can call me Bob. We're among friends."

****

The rumors were flying that there may be a breakthrough with the peace talks at Panmunjom. The rumors seemed to have validity. Without the exception of a few skirmishes, military combat operations began to grind to a halt. No one wanted to be the last man killed. The rumors came to fruition. A peace treaty was signed on July 27, 1953. The Korean War was officially over. The fact that the war was over didn't mean the tour of duty was over. The squadron remained in tact for the next six months just in the event that the North Koreans decided to break the treaty. It was Johnny's first Christmas away from home. In late January, the word came down from Brigade that the squadron was being disbanded. Johnny received his orders. He was being assigned to an Air Force Base that was a three hour drive from New Dublin.

Johnny used some of his accumulated leave time before reporting to his next duty station. His homecoming was more exuberant than before. This time he was coming home as a war hero...an Air Force Ace. An honor bestowed on very few combat aviators. Theresa immediately set a wedding date that coincided with Sam's ordination.

The plant had retooled their operation after World War II. They were no longer manufacturing large military aircraft. The plant did have a few military contracts building single engine observation airplanes but their new business model was primarily catered toward the flying public. Planes were steadily rolling off the assembly line on a daily basis. Sales were better than originally anticipated. There was definitely a market for the small passenger plane.

Johnny wanted to be home on the weekends. The only way he could accomplish this is to fly. He could cut the travel time to a little more than an hour. He set up an appointment with Phillip Nelson, the owner of the aircraft plant. Mr. Nelson was amenable to selling Johnny a brand new airplane. He even agreed to finance the cost. Mr. Nelson was a man of impeccable character but he did have an ulterior motive. He saw Johnny as his replacement as General Manager. He had a college degree in business and he was an extraordinary pilot. Two qualities that Mr. Nelson felt were imperative for the future of his thriving company. Mr. Nelson could do a nation-wide search for the perfect candidate but it was doubtful that anyone could be better qualified than Johnny. Besides, Johnny's father was a long time employee and through that association, he saw Johnny grow from a boy into a fine young man. Mr. Nelson remained silent in regard to his intention inasmuch as it would be moot until Johnny finished his commitment to the U. S. Air Force.

Chapter 19

Wedding and Ordination (Circa 1954)

Today was the day that had been widely anticipated by all of New Dublin. It was the day that Theresa and Johnny would exchange wedding vows. However, there was a problem...they needed a priest. Not just any priest, it had to be Father Sam Jenkins, and the wedding would not take place until Sam was ordained. Johnny was home on leave. He was wearing his dress blues. He and Theresa along with their families occupied the front pew. Sam and Pop were seated in the front pew across the aisle.

After the opening blessing and the reading of the scriptures, Bishop O'Malley moved to the front of the sanctuary and summoned "Samuel Jenkins."

Sam, dress in a white cassock with his deacon sash draped diagonally across his chest, responded, "Present". He stepped forward to the sanctuary and stood in front of Bishop O'Malley. The Bishop then asked for testimony from a church official who in this case was Father O'Malley. Father O'Malley informed the Bishop that Sam was prepared and had been approved for ordination. The Bishop did not dispute the testimony and asked Sam if he was willing to accept Christ and his Church as a faithful Priest. Sam answered him, "Yes." Bishop O'Malley then grasped Sam's hand whereby Sam declared his obedience to the Church and his superiors.

Bishop O'Malley then knelt down at the altar and prayed silently for Sam. The congregation also joined in with their prayers. Sam then went to the foot of the altar and prostrated himself. Father O'Malley sang the *Litany of Saints*, a Gregorian chant which is a beautiful hymn especially when performed by an experienced vocalist. Father O'Malley did a masterful rendition. Afterwards, Sam knelt before the Bishop. Bishop O'Malley laid his hands upon Sam's head and prayed silently to invoke the Holy Ghost. Father O'Malley and the other Priests took turns in doing the same.

Bishop O'Malley, Father O'Malley and Pop assisted Sam in donning his new priestly vestments. They doted over every aspect making sure that everything was properly in place. Uncle Jimmy, Uncle Billy and Pop each took their turns in hugging Sam and congratulating him. It was more an act of love versus a religious ritual.

Bishop O'Malley finished the ordination by anointing Sam's hands with oil and then wrapping his hands in linen cloth. It was followed by the presentation of gifts.

Bishop O'Malley then led Sam down to the front of the Sanctuary. He then announced to the congregation. "Friends, visitors and parishioners, I present to you, your new Associate Pastor of St. Patrick Parish, Father Samuel Jenkins." Sam did a double take when the Bishop said this. He was not expecting to be assigned to St. Patrick's. Bishop O'Malley put his hand on Sam's shoulder and just smiled.

It is tradition that the first blessing of the newly ordained Priest be that of the Bishop. Tradition was broken whereby Father Sam blessed all three of the O'Malley brothers together as one as they knelt before him.

The conclusion of the Mass was suspended. Theresa and her parents hurriedly left the church. Theresa needed to change into her wedding gown. Bishop O'Malley and Father O'Malley sat down in the front pew with their brother. The other Priests also found seats in nearby pews.

Father Sam approached the pulpit. "I want to thank all of you for your prayers and words of encouragement. They are very much appreciated. I don't know if you noticed the shock on my face when Bishop O'Malley said that I was being appointed as the Associate Pastor of St. Patrick's. There is a lot more to this story. For months now, I have been told that I was going to be the new Pastor of a non-existent Parish on the other end of the Diocese. I was going to be responsible for the building of a new church much like Father O'Malley did here at St. Patrick's. Uncle Jimmy, Uncle Billy and Pop all offered their services and assistance in seeing that the project came to fruition. I didn't question the Bishop's decision...I just accepted it. Now I realize that I was the victim of one of their practical jokes. All of you can't see them but Bishop O'Malley along with his two sinister brothers are sitting here with big grins on their faces. They are real pleased with themselves. I have to give credit where credit is due. They did fool me. I fell for it hook, line, and sinker." Sam looked down at the Bishop and with heartfelt said, "Uncle Jimmy thank you for keeping me here at St. Patrick's. This is where I want to be and more importantly, I believe that this is where God wants me to be." The entire congregation gave Sam a long standing ovation. They were in agreement.

Father Sam continued, "I have been instructed by Theresa to talk for at least fifteen minutes to give her enough time to get ready. So forgive me if I start rambling. The first best day of my life was when I was thirteen. Johnny, Theresa, and I played hooky from school and went fishing. We had the best time...but we got caught. We had to pay the price. Johnny and I had our first encounter with Father O'Malley's paddle. Theresa met the wrath of Sister Monica who was fondly known at that time as 'Sister Witch with a switch'. The next best day of my life, which actually was three days long, was when I, along with Theresa and

Johnny rode our homemade raft down the Cherokee River to Jefferson City. It was a trip that I will never forget. But again, we got in trouble but it was worth it. The next best day of my life is today and the only way I can get in trouble is from Theresa if I don't keep talking. If you notice that the common denominator of the three best days in my life is that they all include Johnny and Theresa. We took an oath as kids that we would be friends forever and that holds true to this very day."

"Let me tell you an anecdote from our river trip. It is somewhat appropriate today. Theresa was floating in an inner tube that we had tied off to the raft. Johnny and I started yelling 'snake'. Theresa is one tough cookie but she is definitely afraid of snakes. She pulled herself back to the raft at lightning speed and climbed aboard. When she realized that we were kidding, she was not a happy camper. She hauled off and hit Johnny on the arm. She tried to hit me but I kept moving around on the raft until she gave up. She was mad. She banished Johnny and me to the front of the raft. As we were sitting there, I remember Johnny saying, 'I pity the man who marries Theresa.' Little did we know at the time that Johnny was going to be that man. Sam looked down at Johnny and joked, "Johnny you still have time to back out."

Sam said with a serious tone as he continued to speak to Johnny, "I believe that your marriage is a gift from heaven and I wish you and Theresa the very best." Johnny responded with a thank you.

As most of you are aware, I was orphaned at the age of twelve. I think of my parents every day. I wish they could be here today because they would have been so proud of their little Sammy. I know that they are here in spirit. However, I am grateful that I have my second family here..." Sam used his hand to motion to the O'Malley brothers sitting in the front pew. "...these three gentlemen could not love me any more than my own parents. Sam fondly continued, "...and the feeling is mutual." The response from the O'Malley brothers was reminiscent of Sam's first Christmas with the O'Malley family. The three of them suspiciously cleared their throats at the same time.

Father Sam glanced at his watch. "The time is almost here." Theresa's mother came down the center aisle and took her seat. Theresa and her dad were standing at the entrance. Theresa was dressed in a wedding gown that her grandmother had personally sewn for her own wedding. Theresa's mother wore it at her wedding. Jack Kelly, Theresa's dad, the rough and tough war hero, looked petrified. He was dressed in a coat and tie. He was definitely out of his comfort zone. Father Sam motioned to the organist to begin the *Wedding March*. As they began their 'march' down the aisle, Jack was stiff and peered straight ahead, whereas Theresa, with her outgoing personality, was beaming from ear to ear. The tomboy of yesteryear had blossomed into an attractive young woman. She waved at everyone at they proceeded toward the altar. Johnny took her hand and together that stepped up to where Father Sam was standing. There were no bridesmaids or groomsmen. This was Theresa's desire. She only wanted Johnny and Sam present when she made her wedding vows.

Father Sam began. "Theresa and Johnny, have you come here freely and without reservation to give yourselves to each other in marriage?"

Theresa and Johnny answered together, "Yes."

"Will you honor each other as man and wife for the rest of your lives?"

"Yes."

"Will you accept children lovingly from God, and bring them up according to the laws of Christ and his Church?"

"Yes"

"Since it is your intention to enter into marriage, join your right hands, and declare your consent before God and his Church."

"I, Johnny, take you, Theresa, to be my wife. I promise to be true to you in good times and in bad, in sickness and in health. I will love you and honor you all the days of my life."

"I, Theresa, take you, Johnny, to be my husband. I promise to be true to you in good times and in bad, in sickness and in health. I will love you and honor you all the days of my life."

Father Sam continued, "Theresa and Johnny, you have freely affirmed before God, your intentions of receiving the Sacrament of Matrimony. May almighty God bless this union for all the days of your lives. What God has joined, men must not divide." Father Sam then blessed the rings.

Johnny said as he placed the ring on Theresa's finger, "Theresa, take this ring as a sign of my love and fidelity, in the name of the Father, the Son and the Holy Ghost."

Theresa gazing into Johnny's eyes said, "Johnny, take this ring as a sign of my love and fidelity, in the name of the Father, the Son and the Holy Ghost."

Father Sam in conclusion declared, "I pronounce you man and wife. Johnny you may kiss..." Before Father Sam could complete his declaration, Theresa's joyous exuberance was not inhibited. She passionately kissed Johnny. She turned and hugged Sam and kissed him on the cheek. She turned back toward the congregation, lifted her wedding gown, and began to do an Irish jig. It did not surprise anyone.

Bishop O'Malley along with the other Priests returned to the Sanctuary. He gave his final blessing and the procession from the church began. They gathered in the front. Johnny's mother handed Johnny's cap to Theresa. She placed it on his head and cocked it to the side and said, "There is something special about a man in a uniform."

Theresa, Johnny, and Sam went to the entrance of the school gymnasium where the reception was being held. A reception line formed that curled all the way back to the front of the church. They greeted each and every person as they entered the gymnasium. There was food galore. It was a festive occasion. The band began to play. Theresa grabbed Johnny by the hand and led him to the middle of the room. It was their first dance. Theresa was graceful. Johnny lacked any semblance of dancing skills. It didn't matter. Love conquered all, even Theresa's sore toes. Afterwards, Theresa danced with her father. He was still out of his comfort zone. Johnny danced with his mother who suffered the same fate as Theresa.

Sam was seated with the O'Malley brothers. He asked, "Why don't you guys sing us a song."

"I don't think we can do that. We haven't practiced," responded Uncle Jimmy.

"I have heard you sing *Danny Boy* many times. You don't need a rehearsal."

"Maybe another day," replied Uncle Billy.

Sam was persistent. He wasn't going to take "no" for an answer. Reluctantly, the three agreed.

Sam stepped up on the stage. He asked the band to take a short break. He took the microphone and said, "Ladies and gentlemen, can I have your attention please?" It took several requests before the room went silent. "I have a surprise for all of you. We are fortunate to have a new musical group here today. This is their world-wide debut. Let's give a warm welcome for the O'MALLEY BROTHERS."

The O'Malley brothers took the stage and began to sing *a capella*. Sam was right. They didn't need a rehearsal. Their harmony was perfect. Everyone remained silent while they sang. When they finished, the sounds of "encore" filled the room. Bishop O'Malley agreed only if they were accompanied by all those present. It was a sentimental moment. *Danny Boy* was considered the unofficial Irish national anthem. Everyone knew the words by heart. It evoked emotions that only a true Irishman could feel. Afterwards, and by special request, the O'Malley brothers sang several more Irish ballads.

Sam took the stage again. "Let's give the O'Malley brothers another round of applause. They did a fantastic job." After the applause subsided, Sam continued, "Please gather around the table in the back. Theresa and Johnny are about to cut the cake."

Theresa and Johnny held the knife together and cut the cake. Johnny took the piece and delicately fed it to Theresa. Theresa picked up her piece of cake. Everyone anticipated that she was going to smash it in Johnny's face but quite the contrary. She was very lady-like. They also shared a glass of champagne. Sam raised his glass and toasted the happy couple. The class of 1948 was busy during this time. They painted the back window of Johnny's car with "Just Married." Tin cans were tied to the bumper. The guests began to meander outside. They lined both sides of the sidewalk that led to the street. Theresa and Johnny changed in more suitable clothes for traveling. They ran from the gymnasium as rice showered down on them. They drove away with Theresa hanging out the window waving good-by. The tin cans clanked behind them. It was not a long drive. Johnny parked at the plant. He had already conducted a pre-flight inspection on his airplane and topped off the fuel tank. They stowed their luggage in the back seat. Theresa climbed into the pilot's seat. She was now an accomplished pilot in her own right. Johnny had taught her well. She taxied out onto the runway and took off. She made a low buzz over the Church and tipped her wings. Everyone on the ground waved. Theresa set a course of 180 degrees...dew south to the Florida Gulf coast. It was another great day in New Dublin.

Chapter 20

Birth of the Triplets (Circa 1955)

Theresa entered the clinic and stepped up to the reception desk. Sally greeted her. "Good morning, Theresa. Are you here for a check-up?"

"Yes."

"Come with me. I will take you to the examination room." As they walked, Sally asked, "Are you feeling ok?"

"I'm fine."

"...any morning sickness?"

"No."

"Consider yourself fortunate. When I was pregnant, I started each day hugging the toilet. It was miserable."

"I am six months along. Do you think I will start now?"

"I wouldn't think so."

Theresa changed into a gown and lay down on the examination bed. Betty entered and exchanged pleasantries with Theresa.

She helped Theresa to adjust the pillows while Sally took her temperature and blood pressure. Afterwards, Sally took her stethoscope and started moving it around on Theresa's extra large belly. When she finished, she handed the stethoscope to Betty and made eye contact. This was unusual. Normally either one would listen for the baby's heartbeat but not both. Betty handed the stethoscope back to Sally and said, "Let me go and inform Isaac that his patient is ready."

Sally responded, "I think that is a good idea."

Isaac came into the room, "Good morning, Theresa."

"Good morning."

Isaac immediately took his stethoscope and listened for the heartbeat. Sally and Betty were locked in on Isaac's facial expressions. With a quick glance, he confirmed the same as what they had heard. "Betty, will you go and get my dad?"

Theresa was concerned, "Is there something wrong?"

Sally comforted her and assured her that everything was fine. There was something a little out of the ordinary.

Betty returned with Dr. Swartz. He said, "Good morning, Theresa."

Theresa responded, "I don't know if it is a good morning or not. I am worried that something may be wrong."

"Don't worry. There is nothing wrong. Give me a second and I will tell you what I found." Dr. Swartz was in agreement with the others. He looked down at Theresa and said, "All of us hear three strong heartbeats."

Theresa surprised, place her hands on her face and exclaimed, *"OH MY GOD. I AM HAVING A LITTER!"*

They all smiled and offered Theresa congratulations. Theresa was in shock. It would take time to digest the fact that she was having triplets.

Dr. Swartz reassured Theresa. "You are a young, healthy woman. I do not see any reason why you don't carry to term."

Theresa's students immediately came to mind. "I have almost two more months of school before the summer break. Can I keep teaching up until then?"

"Medically, I don't see a problem. It may be uncomfortable but the decision is strictly up to you."

"I am already uncomfortable and I waddle a lot."

"Expect to be more uncomfortable and expect to waddle a lot more. You are going to get bigger. You need to see Isaac every two weeks. Also, you, Betty or Sally should talk to each other every day. We need to monitor your progress. If anything out of the ordinary should occur, you let us know immediately."

"Yes sir."

****

Theresa made it through the rest of the school year. Dr. Swartz was right. She did get bigger but it was no longer a waddle. It was a strain in every step she made. If fact, she got a cane to help her keep her balance. All she wanted to do was to spend the rest of her pregnancy in bed or in her soft leather recliner. Johnny did as much as he could to cater to Theresa. However, he was gone all week and only came home on the weekends. Theresa's mother and mother-in-law were godsends. They took turns in spending the night during the week. They also cooked meals and did everything around the house that Theresa would normally do. Besides, they were excited about being grandmothers which will come in handy when it came time to take care of three babies.

Through all the inconvenience and hardships, Theresa suffered to three days of her due date. Fortunately it was Saturday and Johnny was home. He was asleep on the couch. He was there by choice and not because Theresa had banished him from the bedroom. Theresa tossed and turned all night long and she needed the entire bed to roll over. It was in the early hours of Sunday morning. Theresa yelled, "Johnny!"

Johnny was instantly on his feet and went to her bedside. She said, "It's time."

Johnny, an Air Force Ace and a man who used his wit and cunning to evade capture by the North Koreans was not a good expectant father. He was a befuddled mess. "OK, let's go."

"Calm down Johnny. First, go call Isaac and tell him to meet us at the clinic. After you do that, call Sam."

Johnny quickly returned. "I can't find the phone number."

"Look in the address book next to the phone."

"Oh, ok."

"That's done. Now let's go."

"...not yet, Johnny. You need to get out of your pajamas and put on some clothes."

"Oh yea, I forgot." Johnny did as he was told. "I'm ready. Let's go."

"We're almost there. Get my robe and help me out of bed." Theresa rolled out of bed with Johnny's help. He assisted her in putting on her robe.

"Do you need your cane?"

"No. You can help me walk."

Johnny was not thinking straight. "OK, let's go."

"You need to get my bag."

With bag in hand, Johnny used his other hand to steady Theresa as they moved toward the door. She asked, "Do you have the car keys?"

"Oh, no. We might need those to get the car started." Johnny got the keys. He placed his hand under Theresa's arm. "Now we're ready to go. We need to hurry."

"What did you do with my bag?"

"I put it down when I got the keys."

Finally they made it out of the house and into the car. Dr. Swartz, Isaac, Sally and Betty were at the clinic awaiting their arrival. When they pulled up to the entrance, they took over. Johnny was instructed to go to the waiting room. Johnny made several quick phone calls to his parents and his in-laws. Sam was already there. He offered little morale support. He was more befuddled than Johnny. They paced the waiting room. When the soon-to-be grandparents arrived, they brought a sense of calm to the waiting room. However, it did not stop the pacing.

Inside the delivery room, the medical staff were actively preparing for the birth of the triplets. They had mentally and physically prepared for this moment over the last three months. They even purchased some large blank baggage tags and an ink pad. On each tag was printed, 1, 2 or 3. As each child was born, a foot print would be imprinted on the back of each tag along with the time of birth. Then the tag was to be loosely tied to the child's ankle. This was to insure that no mix up would occur as to the order of birth. An extra copy was to be placed in the medical file.

The contractions were coming on a more frequent basis. It would not be long now. Theresa was totally dilated. Dr. Swartz instructed Theresa, "Push". The process began. The first born arrived. "Theresa, it's a boy. He looks healthy. He has all his fingers and toes."

Theresa tried to muster a smile but the pain was unbearable. She was having second thoughts about having a natural child birth.

The next one arrived. Dr. Swartz repeated himself. "Theresa, it's a boy. He too is healthy. He has all his fingers and toes." Dr. Swartz continued, "You're doing just fine. Keep pushing." The third one was more stubborn than the others but finally he made his initial appearance in the world. "Congratulations Theresa. You are the mother of three healthy boys."

Theresa was now able to smile. "Thank you Dr. Swartz."

"How are you doing?"

"I am still in pain but nothing like before."

The babies were cleaned up and placed in Theresa's arms. Her smile was contagious. She had three beautiful boys. It was not long before Betty and Sally took the triplets and put them in nearby basinets and then pushed them into the adjacent nursery. Theresa needed to rest. There would be plenty of time to bond later. Isaac went and informed Johnny that he was the father of three boys. He and the others could see the triplets through the window of the nursery.

Theresa was moved from the operating table to a bed. She asked Sally, "Can you do me a favor and ask Johnny and Sam to come in?"

Johnny and Sam entered the room and went to both sides of the bed. Each of them grasped one of Theresa's hands. She asked Johnny, "Have you seen them yet?"

"Yes, they are three good looking boys."

Sam asked, "How are you feeling?"

"I'm fine but I am extremely tired." Theresa continued, "I wish one of them could have been a little girl."

Johnny, trying to be compassionate said, "We can always try again."

This was not what Theresa wanted to hear, at least not at this point in time. "Are you crazy? It is your fault that I have gone through this living hell for the past nine months. You will *never ever* touch me again. You and Sam will have at least one thing in common...both of you will be celibate for the rest of your lives."

Sam looked at Johnny and shrugged his shoulders as if to say, "You poor guy."

Johnny tried to mitigate the situation. "You're right honey. The main thing is for you to get back on your feet." Johnny leaned down and kissed Theresa on the lips, "I love you."

Sam kissed her on the forehead and repeated, "I love you."

Theresa responded, "I love both of you too. Now you guys get out of here. I need to sleep."

When Johnny and Sam left the room, Sam was conciliatory to Johnny. "Theresa was just emotional. I don't believe she meant what she said."

"I say this to Sam my friend and not Sam the Priest but I hope you are right."

****

Theresa did not have a difficult time in naming her new borns. They were named after the men in her life. The first born was named John M. Jernigan, III after her husband and father-in-law. Jack K. Jernigan was the second born and he was named after her father. Samuel J. Jernigan was named in honor of her best friend, Sam. Theresa was pleased with her selections.

Chapter 21

Sister Monica Retires (Circa 1956)

Sister Monica took her cane and tapped on Father O'Malley's opened door.

"Come in and sit down, Sister."

Sister Monica, bent over with scoliosis, made her way to the chair in front of Father O'Malley's desk. Age had taken a toll on her body but mentally she was still sharp as a tack. "Father, I think it's time for me to retire."

"You can go one more year."

"That's what I have been saying for the last five years. No, the time is now."

"Are you going to stay at the convent?"

"No, it wouldn't be fair to the others. Don't forget they are getting elderly too. I plan on going back to the Motherhouse. We have a good nursing care facility there." Sister Monica continued, "We don't have any replacements to send you. There's none at the nunnery."

Father laughed, "You made a funny."

"I keep them in stitches over at the convent."

"Obviously, you have given this much thought. Who do you have in mind for principal?"

"I have discussed this with my fellow Sisters. None of them want to take on the responsibility. We have come to a consensus agreement that Mrs. Jernigan is the perfect candidate."

"She is young and lacks experience but I think that she will do an excellent job. I would be hesitant to promote her if the faculty was leaving too. They don't need any guidance and they can help her in becoming a good administrator. You and Theresa are alike in many ways."

"I take that as a compliment. Mrs. Jernigan is a fine young woman."

"That's only because you took the switch to her many years ago."

Sister Monica laughed. "Now you made a funny."

"I keep them in stitches over at the Leprechaun." Father questioned, "Have you discussed this with Theresa?"

"No. I thought that you should do that."

"To the contrary, Sister. It will mean so much more if you talk to her. She has a tremendous amount of respect for you."

It was settled. Sister Monica slowly arose from the chair. She used the edge of the desk for stabilization. She relied heavily on her cane as she left Father O'Malley's office.

****

A reception was held in the gymnasium. It was amazing as to the number of people Sister Monica had met over her thirty eight year career as Principal of St. Patrick School. From all outward appearances, most of them were present. A soft high back chair was placed on a small platform so that Sister Monica could sit and greet her well wishers face to face. She was inundated with cards and gifts. She extended her hand to each individual as they passed through the reception line. Sister Monica was somewhat of a phenomenon. Her elderly age did not prevent her from recalling everyone's name. Why not? They were all a part of her extended family.

It was Theresa's turn. She was humbled. "Sister Monica, I am going to miss you so much. I have my doubts as to whether or not I will be able to fill your shoes."

Sister Monica made another funny. She glanced down at Theresa's pumps. "You're right. Your feet are much bigger than mine." Sister Monica continued with words of encouragement. "You will do just fine. Don't be timid in asking one of my fellow sisters for advice. They want you to succeed too." Sister Monica had a request for Theresa. "Will you do a few steps of the Irish jig for me?"

With a strong Irish brogue, Theresa responded, "I would be honored, My Lady." Theresa moved back and pulled her skirt up to her knees. She danced and when she was finished, she bowed. All those close by clapped. Theresa leaned forward and hugged Sister Monica and kissed her on the cheek. Theresa whispered in her ear, "I love you."

Sister Monica, teary eyed, answered, "I love you too."

****

Theresa assumed the position of principal in September. Her inhibitions dissipated in a short period of time. It was mainly due to the support she received from the nuns. The curriculum of the school never changed. There was no reason. Nothing was broken. However, Theresa soon realized that being an administrator was more difficult than she had anticipated.

****

Meanwhile, Johnny petitioned his superiors to transfer to the active Reserves to finish out his commitment to the U.S. Air Force. His request was approved. His reserve unit was located at the same air force base. Therefore, he would still make that flight in his own personal aircraft only once a month versus once a week. This allowed him to seek employment in the private sector. His first job application would be at the plant in New Dublin. Unbeknownst to Johnny, there was already a job waiting for him.

On the Friday evening after he received his new orders, he touched down on the runway at the plant. Phillip Nelson was standing there awaiting his arrival. Johnny shut down the engine and secured the aircraft.

Phillip Nelson went up and greeted Johnny. "I hear that you are transferring over to the Reserves and you're looking for a job."

"The news travels fast in New Dublin."

Mr. Nelson smiled. "I have an informant embedded in the company organization."

"I am glad that I never shared any top secrets with my father." Johnny continued. "Yes I am looking a job and I was coming to see you."

"You never knew this but there has been a job opening for you for the last several years. I was waiting for you to get out of the Air Force. It came sooner than I expected. I want to make you Vice President of Operations and in a few years I will promote you to General Manager.

This conversation took Johnny totally by surprise. "Now Mr. Nelson if I understood you correctly, you want me to take over the complete operation of this company."

"You understood me correctly. I am getting older and I plan to move up to Chairman of the Board which is primarily a do-nothing job. My senior staff members are nearing retirement. The future of this company is to have young blood at the helm."

"I know that the jet engine is the future of aviation. I don't see why a business class jet aircraft can't be built that can cruise at 500 MPH that can compete with the commercial airlines that are switching over from prop engines."

"That is exactly why I believe that you are the best candidate to fill the General Manager position. You have the experience as a jet pilot and you have the vision as to where to lead this company."

"Mr. Nelson I am overwhelmed. I was coming to see you for a job making enough money so that I could stay in New Dublin. I never expected an executive position."

"If it makes you feel humble. I need a test pilot on a part time basis. We check out the airworthiness of every plane prior to the customer taking possession. It will get you of the office maybe ten hours a week."

"I have no problem with that." Johnny continued, "Thank you very much Mr. Nelson. This news is going to make Theresa a very happy lady."

Chapter 22

The O'Malley Brothers Retire (Circa 1957 – 1958)

The next big boon to come to New Dublin was in the form of a four lane concrete highway. On June 29, 1956, President Dwight D. Eisenhower signed into law the Federal-Aid Highway Act. This created the new interstate highway system. The plans showed the interstate to originate in Jefferson City and would skirt the edge of New Dublin. What had taken over an hour in travel time from Jefferson City to New Dublin had been reduced by about thirty minutes. New Dublin was now an attractive suburb of Jefferson City. In anticipation of future commercial prosperity, entrepreneurs began to build new businesses. This was progress. But progress had consequences and Pop was a victim of those consequences. A new grocery store was constructed. Literally overnight, Pop's business declined dramatically. It was difficult to compete with the lower prices that a large chain could provide. Pop still had his loyal customers but it wasn't enough to keep the doors open. The situation only prompted Pop in doing what he had thought about for sometime...retire. He discussed retirement with his brothers and they too had been contemplating the same thing. It was decided.

Shannon Dorsey and her new husband, Daniel, entered Pop's Grocery carrying five pies. "Good Morning, Pop."

Pop responded in kind. "You are just as punctual as your mother."

"I am like my mother in many ways. We are both creatures of habit." Shannon changed the subject. "I brought my husband with me because we have a question for you. You told me several weeks ago that you were considering in going out of business. Daniel and I would like to know if you are interested in selling this building."

"As a matter of fact, I am. I have been interested in the vacant white house across the street from the church but I needed to sell this store first. This may be perfect timing."

"Daniel and I want to do what you and your wife did...live upstairs and have a business downstairs. We want to open a bakery called, "Mrs. Shanahan's Pies and Pastries."

"I am not a person who would give you false hope but I believe that would be an excellent business decision. Even though my sales are slow, your pies sell out every day. You have mastered your mother's recipes."

"Thank you. We have plenty more recipes that are just as good. I inherited Mama's house and I have a buyer for it. She also had a modest life insurance policy. So I shouldn't have any problems in buying your store. Do you have a price in mind?"

"No, I don't. I will get with Mr. Ryan who owns the white house. He is familiar with property values in New Dublin. He will be able to tell me what this building is worth. I will offer it to you at a fair price. I have lived here almost forty years and there are a lot of sentimental attachments but to see you move in here would make it a lot less painful."

"That is very nice of you. We will talk again as soon as you have more information."

After Shannon and Daniel departed, Pop called Sean and set up a late afternoon appointment to look at the white house. Jimmy was driving up to New Dublin after he finished a pre-scheduled meeting.

Sean was standing on the porch as he watched Sam and the O'Malley brothers stroll over from the Rectory. They greeted each other. Sean unlocked the door and led them inside. He was not giving his normal sales pitch. These were his friends. If they liked it, so be it. If they didn't like it, so be it. Sean explained that it had a large kitchen, dining room, living room, three bedrooms and one bath."

Billy was the first to speak up. "I see a problem already. There is no way I am going to live with my two brothers and only have one bathroom." Pop and Jimmy laughed but they were in total agreement.

Sean suggested that two of the bedrooms were large enough in which each could accommodate a bathroom. The O'Malley brothers possessed mechanical skills and constructing two bathrooms would be a simple home improvement project. Pop was impressed with the kitchen, especially in view of the fact that he would be the resident cook. There was enough room to put his kitchen table in the middle of the room where most meals would be served.

Sean took everyone outside on the porch. It expanded the entire front of the house. Sean recently had the house painted so outside maintenance would be at a minimum. The wood frame house had very little front yard because it sat close to the sidewalk. This was satisfactory with the O'Malley brothers. They could sit on the front porch and speak to their friends as they walked passed the house. Sean led them down the driveway that led to a two car garage in the back. Jimmy began formulating ways to transform the garage into a workshop.

Of course, Billy had objections. "If you turn this into a workshop, where am I going to park my car?"

Jimmy snarled back. "How long have you had your car?"

"About six years."

"During those six years, how many times have you put it in a garage?"

"Zero."

"Exactly. You can park your car next to mine right here in the driveway."

"You have always gotten your way, even as kids."

"That is because I am the oldest."

Sam was amused as he watched the two exchange barbs. This was a sign of things to come. Harmless sibling rivalry was going to re-emerge with the three O'Malley brothers living under the same roof. It was going to be an annoyance in view of the fact that Sam would most likely be the referee in settling any disputes.

Sean asked, "What do you guys think?"

With the exception of the bathroom situation, all were in agreement that the house was perfect. Pop told Sean about the fact that Mrs. Shanahan's daughter was interested in buying his building and he asked Sean if he could come up with a fair market value and handle all the paperwork on the house and the store. After Pop shook hands with Sean, the deal was done.

Over the next several weeks, Jimmy started making arrangements. He had to find a replacement. He had a priest in mind. It was a second cousin on his father's side, Monsignor Joseph O'Farrell. He was an ideal candidate. He had an outgoing personality. He was liked and respected by the other Priests in the Diocese. Approval from Rome should not be a problem. There was another side to Jimmy's decision to recommend Monsignor O'Farrell. They had an agreement that Sam could stay at St. Patrick's as long as he so desired. Jimmy assumed the title of Bishop Emeritus and assigned himself and his brother Billy as Associate Pastors of St. Patrick Parish. He promoted Sam to Pastor. This didn't mean that Jimmy and Billy were going into total retirement. They would still be instrumental in assisting Sam in the day to day operations of the Parish.

The O'Malley brothers set some days aside to build the two new bathrooms. On one of these days, Sam walked over while the three of them were totally engaged on the project.

Sam was wearing his cassock and biretta. Uncle Billy said, "Obviously you aren't dressed for work."

"That's because someone has to administer to the souls of this Parish and I am here checking on three lost souls."

"That's funny but we have some jokes that we know you will like," replied Uncle Jimmy.

They began telling bathroom jokes. The fact that they even knew these crude jokes was amazing in itself, especially in view of the fact that two of the three were Catholic Priests. Sam thought that none of the jokes were particularly humorous. Maybe it was a generational thing but Sam had to laugh. Not at the jokes themselves but watching the three of them with uncontrollable laughter every time one of the others would tell a joke. It was heartwarming for Sam to see how the three O'Malley brothers enjoyed each others' company.

Another week passed. The bathrooms were finished and it was moving day. Sam had lined up ten high school boys to do the heavy lifting. The Rectory was first. All of Billy's personal belongings were packed up and moved across the street to the white house. Next was Sam's bedroom. The boys dismantled the entire room and carried it piece by piece to the Rectory. Sam gathered up his three most prized possessions: The pictures of his Mom and Dad, his B-17 Model airplane and the baseball signed by him and the O'Malley brothers. When he got to the Rectory, he placed the model airplane and the baseball in a prominent place on the shelf directly behind his desk. He put the pictures of his Mom and Dad on the nightstand beside his bed. He spoke silently to them, "Mom...Dad. Today is the beginning of a new chapter in my life and I believe that this will be the best chapter. Don't worry about me. The O'Malley brothers are still taking good care of your son. Love you both."

The rest of the apartment was moved to the white house. Jimmy's belongings arrived by a moving company. His woodworking equipment was situated in the garage at his direction. He knew where he wanted every piece. When the movers finished with the garage, Jimmy was pleased. He had a first class workshop. The movers then unloaded the dining room table and china cabinet that Jimmy had personally built years ago. They were two of his better pieces. Pop's furniture was used to fill in the vacant spaces in the living room. The kitchen table that Jimmy had built when he was in the seminary was the same small table that he and Sam had shared many a meal. It was the center piece in the kitchen. The dining room table would only be used on special occasions. The O'Malley brothers "Special Chairs" were set down in the living room. Each of them looked as if they should be sent to the junk yard. The O'Malley brothers described their chairs as being "broken in" and as long as they lived in the house, the chairs would stay.

Theresa and several of the nuns had been hanging curtains for most of the week. They finished on moving day with the curtains that they made themselves and those they had ordered through the Sears and Roebuck Catalog.

It had been a long and hard day for Sam and the O'Malley brothers. Sam suggested a pint of beer and a corned beef sandwich at the Leprechaun. This met with unanimous approval.

The next morning, the O'Malley brothers pulled four kitchen chairs out onto the front porch. They were joined by Sam as they drank their freshly brewed coffee.

Tommy, the paperboy, was pedaling his bicycle down the sidewalk. Billy went to the sidewalk to meet him. "How much is a paper?"

"Ten cents, Father."

"Here's a quarter. You keep the rest."

Tommy liked the tip. "Gee thanks, Father."

"Can you start delivering us a paper every morning?"

"Yes sir."

Billy returned to the front porch and split up the different sections of the newspaper.

Jimmy spoke up. "The first thing on the agenda is to build us four nice rocking chairs. I have a feeling that we are going to be spending at lot of time on this porch."

The next morning the four of them were sitting on the kitchen chairs. They kept peering down the street looking for Tommy.

Pop was the first to see him. "Here he comes."

Billy held up his arms and Tommy was right on target. "Good throw Tommy."

"Thanks Father." Tommy yelled back as he didn't miss a beat and continued on his route.

It has been two weeks since the O'Malley brothers officially went into "retirement". Jimmy had finished the four rocking chairs and Pop and Billy painted them white. Sam figured that it was about time for the O'Malley brothers to come out of retirement. After everyone had finished reading the morning paper, Sam called the informal meeting to order. "Gentlemen, the 10:30 A. M. Mass is overflowing and we need to add a second Mass on Sunday at 8:00 A. M."

Jimmy interjected, "That's an excellent idea. I can be the celebrant and Billy can be the concelebrant."

Billy was not in agreement with Jimmy's plan. "I will be the celebrant and you can be the concelebrant. I was the pastor who founded this church."

"...but I am the Bishop Emeritus and I should be the celebrant."

Sam could see that he was losing control. "Children, children, stop your fussing or I will send both of you to your room." Sam continued, "I have a schedule here and the three of us will rotate each week. If two of us are scheduled at the same Mass then the first name on the schedule is the celebrant. Do either of you have a problem with that?"

Jimmy responded, "Who made you the boss?"

"Uncle Jimmy, you did. One of the last edicts you issued when you were Bishop was assigning me as the Pastor of St. Patrick Parish. You also assigned yourself and Uncle Billy as Associate Pastors. If I understand the appropriate pecking order, the Pastor is the boss over the Associate Pastors."

Billy said, "I am going to appeal to the Bishop."

"You can forget about that. Bishop O'Farrell knows the O'Malley brothers very well. In this case, blood is not thicker than water. He told me if either of you gave me a hard time, then let him know. He would take care of you both."

Pop wasn't saying a word but he was enjoying this tête-à-tête.

Jimmy looked at Billy and smiled. "This young whippersnapper has covered all the bases. I guess we will have to do what he says."

"You're right but that doesn't mean that I have to like it."

"I am not through yet. School starts next month and Theresa has made up a schedule for you guys to teach religion classes. This means you too, Pop. You know as much about the Catechism as we do. I think you will make a great teacher."

Pop was please with the thought of teaching religion.

Billy asked, "Are we through now? I want another cup of coffee."

"I am just getting started, Uncle Billy. I have bought you a brand new top of the line power lawn mower. You are to keep the grass cut here at the house and at the Church. I have set aside a small budget so that you can purchase flowers and other supplies that you may need. Sam turned to Uncle Jimmy. "I need some more cabinets in the sacristy and when you finish that, I have a few more projects for you. And Pop, you have the most important job of all. You are responsible for keeping the four of us fed." Sam then addressed the three of them. "All of you have heard the saying, *idle hands are the devil's workshop.* The three of you are full of the devil anyway and I figure if I can keep you guys busy then it won't get any worse."

Billy with his quick wit replied. "I apologize for the devil being in the three of us. We can't help it. It's in our genes. We inherited it from our distant cousin, Lucifer O'Malley."

They all laughed. Pop, Jimmy, and Billy were glad to be able to help Sam in anyway possible. Besides, retirement was boring.

****

One morning, the four had finished reading the newspaper and drinking their coffee, Pop asked Sam, "We are going down to the

Hardware store. Sean has started carrying television sets. We thought we might buy one. He is getting good reception on his sets. I don't know if they have boosted the signal out of Jefferson City or if these new outside antennas are better quality. At least there is no snow. Do you want to tag along with us?"

Sam answered, "Now I know where you guys have been going every afternoon. You all have been going over to Mr. Ryan's to watch the *Howdy Doody Show*."

None of the three O'Malley brothers laughed. Pop and Jimmy knew that Sam's slighted remark would demand a response from Billy.

Billy was on cue. He was joking but he made it sound as if he was scolding Sam. "Young man I have you to know that the O'Malley brothers enjoy watching the *Howdy Doody Show*. We like Buffalo Bob and Clarabell. My favorite is Phineas T. Bluster. I find it appalling that you ridicule us." Billy turned to his brothers, "Now I know who Howdy Doody reminds me of...it's Sam here. Look at those chubby little cheeks." Uncle Billy moved forward into Sam's face and pointed to several spots. "Look he even has freckles. Sam is a dead ringer. And on top of all that, all of us have seen how Theresa pulls his strings."

Sam sat there. He took his fist and lightly beat his forehead. He mumbled to himself, "I know better. I know better."

Pop replied, "Sam when are you ever going to learn. Jimmy and I both knew the moment that you said what you said that Billy was not going to let you slide."

Sam was reconsidering his earlier remark. He replied to Pop. "I was kidding when I said you guys watch the *Howdy Doody Show* but how does Uncle Billy know all the characters?"

Uncle Jimmy jumped in. "Let it go, Sam. Let it go. You know that you will never win."

Uncle Billy smiling reached over and patted Sam on the knee. "Come go with us. This is your television too."

****

There was excitement in all of New Dublin. *Mrs. Shanahan's Pies and Pastries* was having an open house on Saturday. It has been months since anyone had tasted her culinary delights. Sam rounded up the O'Malley brothers and they ambled their way down the sidewalk greeting everyone they passed. There was a steady stream of customers coming and going from the bakery. Shannon was excited when she saw Sam and the O'Malley brothers. She wanted their approval in regard to the renovations. They were impressed. There was no resemblance of Pop's Grocery. It was bright and colorful. The aroma was overwhelming. Shannon motioned the four over to the outer wall to show them a photograph.

She said, "I found this picture in one of the closets upstairs. I had it blown up and framed. I hope that you don't mind."

It was a photograph of Pop and a young Sam wearing their aprons standing near the cash register. It brought back fond memories.

Sam responded, "Shannon that is a nice touch. Both Pop and I appreciate you giving us such a place of honor in your new store."

Shannon was still anxious. "Please don't leave. I have several gifts for you." She left and then returned carrying a framed picture with a white cake box on top. "I had an extra copy of the photograph made up for you." Pop graciously accepted it. Shannon then opened up the cake box. "This is a freshly baked *Mrs. Shanahan's Peach Pie*. All of you enjoy."

When Sam and the O'Malley brothers returned to the house, Pop immediately put the pie in the oven to heat it up. He then grabbed a hammer and a nail from the kitchen drawer. He went into the living room and hung the picture. It was reminiscent of a good time in his life...a memory that he never wanted to forget. He took the original photograph that Shannon had taped to the glass and put it in the family album.

The others had filled glasses of milk. Pop pulled the hot pie from the oven and sliced it up. The four of them did exactly as Shannon had told them....they enjoyed.

****

It was the beginning of Advent...the start of the Christmas season. When Sam reached adulthood, Sam and the O'Malley brothers agreed not to buy each other presents. The "give" in the phrase, *"It is better to give than to receive"* was more of a hassle than a pleasure. However, they did maintain two family traditions; a day set aside to decorate the Christmas tree and a family feast on Christmas day.

Today was the day for decorating the Christmas tree. The O'Malley brothers got all the boxes of decorations down from the attic. They were sitting on the living room floor sorting through everything when Sam came in. Pop said, "I am glad you're here. Maybe you can help me untangle these lights. Someone in this room just threw them in the box last year."

Billy glanced at Jimmy as if it was Jimmy fault. "Billy, don't look at me like that. You know full well that it wasn't me. It wasn't Pop or Sam either. So that only leaves one person."

"Oh yes. I seem to remember something about that. That was the day I had an epileptic seizure."

Pop was disgusted with Billy's paltry explanation. "That is the most ridiculous thing I have ever heard. You have never suffered from epilepsy."

"I did too. It only lasted one day. I healed myself. You guys need to document that. It may be helpful in my canonization."

Jimmy felt compelled to respond. "I can see it now…St. Billy O'Malley…the patron saint of idiots."

"You may think it's funny but I am here to tell you that all the idiots of the world need someone like me looking out for them."

Pop couldn't restrain himself. "You're right Billy. It takes one to know one." Pop then motioned to Sam, "Plug 'em in." The string of lights lit up. Only a few bulbs needed to be replaced. "Outstanding. Now let's go and get a tree."

The four of them walked across the street to where the Boy Scouts were selling Christmas trees. In retrospect, Uncle Billy wished that he had simply admitted his guilt for the tangled lights. Pop and Jimmy were relentless. Every comment they made had a reference to sainthood and/or idiots. Sam stayed out of the playful fracas. He preferred to remain neutral. The O'Malley brothers examined every tree on the lot. They finally settled in on one particular tree but fifteen minutes of debate ensued as to the pros and cons of the near flawless tree.

Pop said to Jimmy, "Any idiot can see that this is the perfect tree."

Jimmy answered, "It's too bad that there is no idiot around here to help us. Oh wait a minute…Billy is the village idiot…let's ask him."

Sam had to intervene. He didn't want to spend the entire evening in a Christmas tree lot. "This one is fine."

Billy said, "If Sam is happy then I am happy."

The discussion shifted as to who was going to pay for the tree. It was decided that they were going to draw lots. While the O'Malley brothers searched around for suitable lots, Sam slipped off and paid the young Scout. When he returned, who was going to pay, still had not been decided.

Sam said, "If you three are finished with all your foolishness, do you think you can carry the tree back to the house?"

Pop responded, "We need to pay for the tree."

"I took care of it."

All the way back to the house the O'Malley brothers blamed each other for Sam having to pay for the tree.

The tree was set up in the living room with the one bad spot positioned against the wall. Slowly but surely the tree was decorated. Sam, as always, had the honor of plugging in the lights. The living room lit up. Sam and the O'Malley brothers stood side by side and admired their handy work.

Sam was the first to speak. "This is the most beautiful Christmas tree that I've ever seen."

Billy responded, "That is what you said last year and the year before that."

"I know but we keep getting better."

There was a long pause. Pop said, "Sam, you're right. This is the best Christmas tree ever."

****

It was late afternoon. Sam arrived for dinner. Uncle Billy was sitting alone on the porch working the crossword puzzle. Sam said, "I would think that you would be brushing up on your pagan rituals. Tomorrow is the winter solstice."

Uncle Billy, without hesitation, created an almost plausible scenario. "Sam, Sam, Sam, you are so young and naive. All adult males of Irish descent look forward to December 21st of every year. This dates back to pre Stonehenge. As you are aware, Ireland and England were seldom in agreement but the Irish did adopt one of their heathen festivals. We gather at a local pub. At exactly 6:00 P.M., we raise our pints of beer and pay homage to the great pagan god Brewmeister. You are cordially invited to join us."

Sam responded sarcastically. "I will take your invitation under consideration. I always enjoy our little conversations. I learn so much from you in regard to Irish lore."

"Any time, Sam...any time."

"What's for dinner?"

"Pop is pan frying some chicken."

"Mmmm...one of my favorites.

****

It did not take long before the front porch became the morning meeting place. Sean and Albert became regulars. Jimmy built two more rocking chairs. Pop bought a bigger coffee pot. The highlight of every morning was waiting for Tommy. They would all peer down the street until he came into sight. "Here he comes" would be the signal to get ready. Sam and the O'Malley brothers would take turns and they always caught the paper. This morning was different. Albert expressed the desire to be the catcher. He stood on the porch at he top of the front steps. He held his arms up ready for the pitch. As usual, Tommy was on target however, the paper went right through Albert's hands and slapped him in the face.

"Sorry, Mr. Swartz."

"No problem Tommy. It was my fault."

Albert demanded, "I want a 'do over'."

"You had better practice today," answered Billy.

The next morning was the same. "Here he comes!" Albert got into position. Tommy made the pitch. Albert bobbled it several times but was able to catch it.

"You're getting better Mr. Swartz."

"Thanks Tommy."

Albert wasn't satisfied. It was his competitive spirit. He wanted one more chance. The next morning came. The ribbing from his fellow coffee drinkers was brutal. Albert secretly hid his nervousness. Jimmy was the first to see him. "Here he comes." Albert was ready. Tommy made his throw. It was a bad pitch...high and outside. Albert reached out with one hand and snagged it perfectly.

"That was a fantastic catch Mr. Swartz."

"Thank you Tommy. You have made my day." Albert turned to the naysayers and did a victory dance in front of all of them.

****

It was late February. Everyone had finished reading the morning paper. Impulsively, Pop said, "We need to do something for St. Patrick's day."

Sean replied, "What do you have in mind?"

"Nothing really. Maybe we can sell food."

Billy added, "You can make Irish stew and Sean can make his corned beef and cabbage."

Albert voiced his approval. "Sam, what do you think?"

"I am agreeable to anything you guys want to do just as long it makes money for the school. St. Patrick's day is always hectic for me so you need to count me out."

Jimmy said, "Pop every now and then you come up with a good idea. I say let's do it."

The wheels of motion began. The menu was established. A booth would be constructed at the edge of the sidewalk. It would have a roof in the event of rain. The front would be painted green, white and orange; the colors of the flag for the Republic of Ireland. Albert knew a very creative seamstress who was a member of his congregation. He would commission her to make green top hats and green vests. Sean said that he would contact Shannon to purchase some heavy duty pie plates. These will be used as serving dishes. Jimmy agreed to build two picnic tables to place in the yard while the others committed to constructing the booth. By the time the last cup of coffee was finished, the master plan was completed. Over the next two weeks, Jimmy, Billy, Pop, Albert, and Sean utilized every bit of their spare time to implement the master plan. The day before the festival everything was in place with the exception of food preparation. Pop and Sean had all their ingredients and they would start cooking early the next morning.

Everyone gathered as usual for their morning ritual. Tommy was on time and on target. After the paper was read, Sam, Jimmy, and Billy prepared for the morning Mass. Sean, Albert, and Pop had donned their green vests and top hats which were respectfully removed upon entering the church. When Mass was over, the congregation gathered in the street. The parade began lead by Sam, Jimmy, and Billy. They marched throughout New Dublin and ended back at the Church. Sean, Albert, and Pop rushed back to the booth. They were shortly joined by Jimmy and Billy who readily put on their green hats and vests. The five of them were busy in making their final preparations. They were ready. All they needed now were customers but it was still too early for lunch. They stood out on the sidewalk talking with all the passer-bys. Sam and Theresa were making their rounds by visiting with all the volunteers, thanking each of them for their time and talents. They strolled up to Father O'Malley.

Theresa said in reference to his colorful Irish attire. "Now, don't you look adorable."

Father O'Malley responded as if he was offended. "Babies are adorable. I prefer that you refer to me as fashionably handsome."

Theresa said as she reached over and fondly pinched him on the cheek.

"You're right. You are fashionably handsome but at the same time you are adorable."

"Where is your husband?"

"He's at home taking care of the triplets. They will be here later and when you see them, 'adorable' will come to mind."

Father O'Malley said, "Excuse me. We have our first patrons." It started slow with this elderly couple. The five of them doted over them and gave them extraordinary service but this was quickly abandoned. A line was forming. They began filling orders at a frantic pace. Compliments were flowing. The ultimate compliments were from those patrons who came back for seconds.

Later, Johnny walked up with the triplets. Father O'Malley greeted them. He now understood what Theresa meant earlier. The triplets were adorable. They were dressed head to toe in leprechaun outfits.

Johnny said, "Boys say hello to your Great Uncle Billy." They extended their hands and Great Uncle Billy, bent over at the waist and shook each of their hands.

Great Uncle Billy invited Johnny to get some good Irish stew.

Johnny responded. "I have to wait for Theresa and Sam."

"You're in luck. Here they come now."

Sam told Theresa and Johnny to eat a nice meal in peace. He would take the boys across the street and buy them a hot dog. Without debate, Theresa and Johnny agreed.

After they all had their fill, Theresa, Johnny, Sam, and the triplets met up again. They were all holding hands as they strolled down the street to continue their good-will ambassador duties.

The O'Malley brothers stood there watching them with love and affection. Pop spoke. "You know, Jimmy...God is good."

"You're right."

Billy added. "You're both right. God is good but God is going to be mad if we don't get back to work."

Chapter 23

New Dublin Becomes a City (Circa 1959)

By 1959, New Dublin had gone through a major transformation. Thanks to the completion of the interstate highway, it was now a bedroom community of Jefferson City. The expanding population increased the need for city services. There was no police department. All law enforcement needs were provided by the Sheriff's Office but they had hundreds of square miles to patrol and New Dublin was only a small piece of their jurisdiction. The volunteer fire department did an excellent job but their response time was not optimum. By the time an alarm was received and the volunteers left work and got to the fire station and then traveled to the scene, valuable time was lost. Garbage collection was a disaster. There was no consistency in service. A petition was initiated to incorporate New Dublin into a municipality. It was widely supported. When the referendum finally made it to the ballot, it easily passed along with a bond issue. It was official. New Dublin was now a city. The first thing on the agenda was to elect a mayor and council. A popular grass root movement began to convince Sean Ryan to run for mayor. He was the most logical candidate because he had been instrumental in the growth of the community. However, he was reluctant because of his age. He was seventy but a young seventy. Eventually he agreed to only one term. He was unopposed. Pop was approached as being a councilman but he adamantly refused. He enjoyed teaching religion which had developed into a full time job. He was of the opinion that young blood was needed to fill the councilmen's positions.

A temporary city hall was established in one of Sean's storefront buildings on Main St. Sean assigned each councilman to oversee the various departments: Fire, Police, Sanitation and Parks/Recreation. They immediately began to fill all the positions with qualified employees. Bids were sent out to acquire all the necessary equipment to support the different departments. Sean hired an architect to draw up building plans for a facility that would house all the departments of the city government.

Sean, in a true gesture of altruism, donated about two hundred acres of land that bordered the Cherokee River. The city received one hundred acres with the stipulations that the waterfront be improved with sidewalks, benches and lighting so that the citizens would be able to enjoy the riverfront day or night. In addition, the city could never utilize the land for anything other than a public park. The other one hundred acres which adjoined church property was donated to St. Patrick Parish with the only stipulation that the riverfront be developed in coordination with the city's plan.

The land donation could not have come at a better time. Both the elementary and high schools were busting at the seams. Overcrowding was becoming a major problem but there was not enough property available for expansion. Father Sam saw this as a gift from God. In tradition of his Uncle Billy, he set out to build a new high school and football stadium. The Parish was blessed with a surplus of funds but not enough money to complete the entire project. But with aggressive fund raising and some outside financing, Father Sam felt confident that he could accomplish the aggressive project.

Father Sam formed a committee in which he was the chairman. He also asked Theresa and the O'Malley brothers to be members. They all agreed. Theresa's knowledge as to how the school was to be designed was essential. Her responsibility was to work with the architect. It was requested from Uncle Jimmy to contact the Bank of New Dublin and/or his friends in the Jefferson City financial community to obtain the funds necessary to complete the project. Pop was put in charge of the local building fund. Uncle Billy, with his past experience in the building of the church, convent and two schools, was the ideal candidate to oversee the day to day construction process.

During their first meeting, Theresa suggested that the current high school be converted into a middle school. Everyone was in agreement. Father Sam put his friendship aside. He had the utmost respect for Theresa's ability as an administrator. He told her that she was to be the principal of all three schools and that she should begin a personnel search for three assistant principals. He also informed her that she should create a physical education department. He wanted to have a solid athletic program that included football and baseball. An architect was employed and was working on some general concepts.

At the next meeting, Uncle Jimmy advised that financing was not going to be a problem. Pop presented his building fund financial statement. He was proud to say that they had their first one hundred dollars. He also told the committee how difficult it was to pry it out of Uncle Billy's pocket.

Six months of untiring efforts by the mayor and the city council finally paid off. The new government center was completed. Father Sam's committee was also successful. The school and the stadium were finished. New Dublin always held their war heroes and their distinguished citizens in high esteem. The new government center was named in honor of Robert Kelty, the Medal of Honor recipient from World War II. The City Council proclaimed the new sports complex as Sean Ryan Park. St. Patrick High School's stadium was fondly named the O'Malley Stadium. However, the first football season was a dismal failure. The best game of the year was when St. Patrick's lost by fourteen points. But optimism was abound. The team's best seasons were yet to come.

Chapter 24

The Plant is For Sale (Circa 1962)

Johnny Jernigan called a company-wide meeting. He and the owner, Phillip Nelson climbed the stairs to the walkway that towered above the assembly line. Below were all the employees who were all anxious. A meeting of this kind had never occurred before.

Johnny began. "Mr. Nelson has decided to retire. This is a good thing. He deserves to live out his life playing with his grandchildren. But in order for him to retire, he must sell the company. This could also be a good thing but I am worried that the new owner may not be as good of a boss as Mr. Nelson has been over the years. Mr. Nelson feels as I do...we are all family. There are three serious offers on the table for the purchase of this company. Mr. Nelson prefers to sell the company to all of us. He wants five million dollars. This is substantially less than what is being offered by these other companies. It is more than a fair price. I know this to be a fact. I have given this some thought. We can issue five million shares of stock and sell each share for one dollar. I have already gone to the Bank of Dublin and they will loan the company two and a half million dollars to purchase half of the outstanding shares. This stock will be available for us to purchase as our personal funds become available. A payroll deduction from our paychecks each week may be one way to go. But first, we must sell the remaining shares. Theresa and I have decided that buying stock is a good investment. We have agreed to take all of our money out of savings to purchase as many shares as possible. Those of you who know my wife know that she has good judgment. If she says this is a good investment then it is a good investment. The problem is this. At last count we have two hundred eighteen employees. That means that each of us will have to come up with about nine thousand dollars each. That's a very tall order. Some of you will have to dig up some of that cash that you have buried in the backyard. But seriously, we all have to make a commitment to invest every dollar we can spare and then ask our friends and family to invest whatever they can afford. I believe that we can do this but I can't take the chance unless we are all in this together. I want to take a voice vote."

Mr. Jernigan stated out loud. "All those in favor of buying the company say *Aye*." *Aye* was sounded loudly by all present.

"All those in favor of not buying the company say *Nay.*" The room was silent. It was unanimous.

Johnny continued, "This is encouraging. If God is willing, we can do this, but if by chance, we fail, all is not lost. We aren't going to lose our jobs. The new owners will need us as much as we need them. But it is the future that I worry about. After several years are they going to sell out to another company? Are they going to be good business managers? I am convinced that this industry has a solid client base. I rather see the profits come to us versus some big wig in New York City. Now I understand that some of you are unable to financially invest in the company. That doesn't mean that you can't support the cause. You can still talk up the investment. As your finances improve, you will still have the opportunity to buy stock. Go home tonight and discuss this with your spouse. Your immediate family has to be committed too."

Johnny took the stairs that led down from the walkway. His destination was the Graphic Arts Department. Along the way he was greeted by many of the employees who were enthusiastic about the purchase of the company. Johnny took time to speak to each one that had approached him. He was a hands-on manager and he knew every employee by their first name. Finally he made it to the supervisor, "Walter, I need you to make me a sign that has a big thermometer on it. At the top of the sign print in big letters "Company Purchase Plan". Underneath that put "Goal $ 5,000,000.00." Below that show the thermometer. Show increments of $ 500,000.00 from zero to $ 5,000,000.00 going up the thermometer. You can paint in the first $ 2,500,000.00 with red paint because we already have a guarantee of that money. Update the thermometer every day showing how much money we got in. Do you have the concept?"

"Yes sir."

"Good. Work your magic."

Over the next two weeks stocks were being sold on a steady basis. Walter filled in the thermometer up to $ 3,750,000. The following week was disastrous. Sales trickled to zero. Only three weeks were left to fulfill their goal. The future looked bleak. Johnny had heard from many of the employees that the Bank of New Dublin was denying all loan applications from plant employees because the proceeds from such loans would be use to purchase shares. The reason was strictly financial. The bank had already extended credit to the company and adding on the liability of loans to the employees would put the bank in a precarious position by exceeding their loss ratio limit. If by chance the plant had a downturn in plane sales and profits became non-existent then the bank would ultimately have to declare bankruptcy. This was too much of a risk for the bank. Johnny was hard pressed to come up with a solution whereby more money would flow into the coffers. He had an idea...a far fetched idea...but an idea. He went to see Sam. Johnny explained the situation and the purpose of the meeting. He wanted Sam's opinion as to whether or not it would be advisable to approach Uncle Jimmy to intercede on behalf of the plant employees with some of the bankers in Jefferson City. Sam was a strong advocate of the buy out plan. He was also agreeable to speaking with his Uncle for assistance. The two of them walked over to the house. Uncle Jimmy readily offered his support. Within thirty minutes he had good news. Uncle Jimmy had spoken to a personal friend who is the president of the largest bank in Jefferson City. He was sending a loan officer to the plant tomorrow to take applications from all employees who were seeking loans. Johnny went from a state of despair to elation. He now had hope. Johnny returned to the plant where he distributed a memo informing all the employees of the status of the company buy out program.

The next morning the loan office arrived just as Uncle Jimmy had said. He was greeted with enthusiasm by all those who were seeking loans. It was productive too. Every day, Walter painted more red into the thermometer. It rose to $ 4,500,000.00. It was close but not close enough. There was a half million dollar shortage. Everyone was maxed out. There was no more money and the deadline was nearing. Johnny's short lived hope turned back to despair. He had reconciled himself to the fact that the buy out was not going to happen.

The phone rang. Johnny answered, "Hello."

"Johnny, this is Bishop O'Malley. How are you doing this morning?"

"Not too well Bishop. We fell short of our goal."

"...by how much?"

"...to be exact...four hundred and ninety eight thousand, three hundred and thirty two dollars."

"Don't give up yet. I have one more ace up my sleeve. Stay by the phone. I will call you back shortly."

Johnny sat at his desk contemplating the series of events that brought the buy out to fruition. It would have never have come this far without the help of Bishop O'Malley. He was convinced that if the employees are able to meet its goal, it would be providence. How else could you explain it?"

Johnny grabbed the phone on the first ring. "Hello."

"I am happy to tell you...you have the money. As we speak, a courier is on his way to your office. Your benefactor is Arthur Morton. He is the owner of the First National Bank of Jefferson City. It was his bank that made all the loans to your employees. He is impressed with the fact that so many people were willing to risk everything they own to buy a piece of the company. The check you are receiving is from Arthur's personal account. That is how confident he is about the future of your company."

"Bishop, I can't thank you enough. Had you not come through, it is doubtful that we would have made our goal."

"You're welcome, Johnny. I based a lot of my support on you. I have watched you, Theresa, and Sam grow up. You are a person of character. But you now have a tremendous burden on your shoulders. You must be successful. The lives of many hard working individuals rest with the decisions you make. The best analogy I can give is that you are like the shepherd and the company employees are your flock. You must protect them from all perils. "Besides," Bishop O'Malley said jokingly, "Pop bought five thousand shares on behalf of the O'Malley family and St. Patrick Parish invested twenty five hundred dollars. So I have a personal interest in your success. You must not fail."

Johnny returned the comment humorously, "Does this mean excommunication?"

"Definitely, however, I will waive the burning at the stake."

"That's a relief. But seriously Bishop the responsibility is daunting. I am confident that I can do it, although, a few prayers might be helpful.

"You got 'em."

Chapter 25

Death of the O'Malley Brothers (Circa 1965)

All three of the O'Malley brothers had been in good physical shape up until the previous six months. Jimmy was the first to show signs of deteriorating health problems. It wasn't long before Billy and Pop were having basically the same symptoms. Their conditions steadily worsened to the point that they were hospitalized. Dr. Swartz made accommodations for the three of them to be in one room. Johnny, Theresa, and Father Sam had been taking turns in staying in the room. On the morning of the fifth day, Dr. Swartz came to the door and motion for Father Sam to come into the hallway.

Compassionately, Isaac said, "Sam, the prognosis is not good. Their bodies are shutting down. Your prayers should be for their souls and not for their recovery. It won't be long now."

"Isaac, are we talking days?"

"Maybe days...maybe hours."

"...which one?"

"...all three of them."

"...all three?"

"This is not an uncommon occurrence. Usually we see this in spouses who have been married for sixty to seventy years. I have not found any record of three brothers who have literally died at the same time but then again I don't think there are too many brothers who have been devoted to each other as Bishop O'Malley, Father O'Malley and Pop. They may be lucid from time to time so you should use those opportunities to say your good byes." Isaac and Sam had been friends since they were kids and out of that friendship Isaac hugged Sam, "I am sorry for your loss."

"Thanks, Isaac."

Sam returned to the room and sat down. He buried his face in his hands. Optimism turned to realism. Death was imminent. Thoughts of his Mom and Dad got intermingled with his concerns for Pop and his two uncles. As hard as tried not to, Sam cried.

Pop could see Sam and in a weak voice said, "Sam, don't be sad. We are going to a better place."

Sam arose from the chair. He kissed Pop on the forehead. "I love you so much."

"I love you too Sam. You have been the greatest blessing that God has bestowed on me. Remember ashes to ashes, dust to dust. None of us are immune from the inevitable." Pop then asked a favor of Sam, "Please push our beds together."

Sam did as requested. Pop reached out and grabbed the hands of his brothers. They both aroused. Sam expressed his love to each of his uncles. He held Uncle Jimmy's hand whereby all four were united. Sam said a heartfelt prayer. All responded with "Amen". Even on his death bed, Uncle Billy was able to joke one last time. "Don't worry Sam we are going to get past those pearly gates without a problem. St. Peter will be there to meet us. He is one of our distant cousins. It is a little known fact but his given name is Peter O'Malley. Also, I want you to keep working on my canonization." This brought smiles to all four of them. The O'Malley brothers drifted back to sleep.

There was a tap at the door. It was Theresa and Johnny. Sam motioned for them to come in. Theresa sat down on the arm of the chair and hugged Sam. She asked, "How are they doing?"

"Not good. Isaac says it could be a matter of hours or days."

Johnny responded, "I'm so sorry, Sam."

Theresa added, "I can't help but believe that this is a gift from God to the O'Malley brothers for their life long service to Him. Can you imagine how depressing it would be for the others if there were two O'Malley brothers and then one?"

Sam responded, "You're right. There is no other explanation. It is divine intervention."

****

It was the day of the funeral. The entire city was shut down. The Church was full with standing room only. Outside were hundreds of mourners. Speakers were set up so everyone could hear the Mass and the eulogy. Bishop O'Farrell was the celebrant of the funeral Mass. Father Sam, along with all the other Priests in the diocese, was concelebrants.

Father Sam rose and moved to the pulpit. "As Christians, today should be a glorious day. It is a day that Lawrence "Pop" O'Malley, Father William O'Malley and Bishop James O'Malley will meet Jesus Christ face to face. Pop told me just before he died. He said, "Sam, don't be sad. We are going to a better place." I know in my heart that he was right but I am a mere mortal. Maybe it is selfishness on my part. I can't help but to be sad because they will never again be a part of my life. If you feel the same way, let not your heart be troubled. We can't resist it...we are human."

"I was an orphan at twelve years old. My father was a pilot on a B-17. He was shot down and killed in World War II. My mother died from a freak accident at the plant. Before she died, Pop and Uncle Billy promised my mother that they along with their brother Jimmy would raise me and that I would never go to an orphanage. This was paramount to my mother because she and my father were both raised in an orphanage. From that day forward, I was a member of the O'Malley family. I cannot begin to describe the love that the O'Malley brothers had for each other and when I came along they poured that love upon me. No one could ever ask for a better adoptive father than Pop. He was always there for me. He helped me with my homework. He made sure that I had clean clothes. His forte was cooking. We always ate well. This didn't mean that we had gourmet meals every night. The man could make a mean peanut butter and jelly sandwich. When I needed discipline, he was firm and forthright but he never raised his voice in anger. But that was a different story about Uncle Billy. He was notorious for using the 'paddle'. I only had one encounter with the 'paddle' when Johnny, Theresa, and I were caught playing hooky from school. Father O'Malley's bark was worse than his bite. The anticipation of being paddled was worse than the paddling itself. He had true love for life and his fellow man. When I became a Priest, Sister Monica...bless her soul...told me a story about the first day she and her fellow sisters meet Father O'Malley. It was right here in front of the church. He told them 'We have all dedicated our lives to Jesus Christ but that doesn't mean we can't have fun and be religious at the same time. A good laugh and a smile can sometimes work miracles.' That sums up Uncle Billy's life. In fact, he was joking with me with the last words he spoke. If you weren't aware of it...and I didn't...but St. Peter was a distant cousin of the O'Malley brothers. He was also concerned about his Canonization. Pop and Uncle Jimmy use to tell him that he was going to be the patron saint of idiots. So all of you idiots out there need to pray for his possible sainthood." Everyone smiled.

"Every time I come to this pulpit, I am reminded of Uncle Jimmy. He built this pulpit nearly fifty years ago. To me, it is a work of art. The intricate carvings were meticulously done by a true craftsman. He was a man of many talents. After I became a member of the O'Malley family, Uncle Jimmy would come to New Dublin whenever time permitted. He was busy in Jefferson City doing those things that Bishops normally do. However, he never missed what became one of our family traditions. During the Christmas season, we would set one evening aside to decorate the tree. We would take turns in putting on the ornaments. I have always had the honor of being the one who plugged in the lights. Afterwards, the four of us would stand side by side and admire our work. It was also a consensus opinion that it was the best Christmas tree ever. Now if you think this only occurred when I was a young boy, I am here to tell you the contrary. I am talking about this last Christmas. Affectionately, I believe that these three men, even though they were in their late seventies, were kids at heart."

Father Sam continued, "I want you to raise your hand if Pop ever gave you a free piece of candy or an Eskimo Pie when you were kids. This includes those of you outside." Hands went up especially among many of the older parishioners. "Please keep your hands up."

Father Sam went down a list of requests. "I want all of you that were married by Father O'Malley, please raise your hands."

"All of you, who were baptized by Father O'Malley, please raise your hands."

"Please raise your hands if you received the Sacrament of Confirmation from Bishop O'Malley and finally, raise your hands if you were ordained by Bishop O'Malley."

With the exception of a few, the entire congregation inside and outside of the church had their hands in the air. This included several of the Priests sitting near the altar.

"I want each of you to look around. It is amazing how these three men have touched so many of our lives. I know that I will miss Pop, Uncle Billy and Uncle Jimmy but all of you will miss them too."

Father O'Malley continued with the congregation, "Many of you requested to speak today but it would just be redundant because all of us would basically say the same thing. In view of the outpouring of O'Malley brothers' stories, I feel that it would be appropriate if each of you would write down your relationship with one or all of the O'Malley brothers...and how that relationship affected your life. It can be an amusing antidote; A religious experience or how they changed the course of your life. I will compile all of your essays into a book. I will make sure that each of you in the Parish will receive a copy. I believe that this will be the best way to honor these three men and at the same time, preserve their memory."

Father O'Malley summed up. "May almighty God bless the souls of Lawrence "Pop" O'Malley, William O'Malley and James O'Malley."

Bishop O'Farrell gave his final blessing. The altar boys led the way. Bishop O'Farrell and the other Priests were behind them. The pall bearers, carrying the three caskets, were next in line. Theresa, holding the hands of Johnny and Sam, followed. It was reminiscent of Sam's mothers' funeral twenty two years earlier. The pall bearers placed the caskets in three separate weathered horse drawn wagons. A symbolic reminder of the O'Malley youth days growing up in New Dublin. The procession began down Main Street to the cemetery. The only sounds were the steel strapped wooden wagon wheels meshing on the concrete roadway along with the clanking of the steel horseshoes.

The procession entered the cemetery. The wagons stopped at the foot of the final resting place. The pallbearers removed the caskets and in unison moved toward the three grave sites. They carefully skirted the openings and gingerly placed the caskets into their respective cradles. The pallbearers removed their boutonnieres and placed them on top of the caskets.

Bishop O'Farrell removed his miter and spoke to the crowd not as the Bishop but as a family member. "My Grandmother was the sister of Connor O'Malley. As many of you are aware, he died a hero in the Spanish American War. There were no other siblings. I am sad to say that the O'Malley family name will also be buried here today but the family tradition will long live within all of us Irish descendents of New Dublin. As a kid I was proud to say that I was related to the O'Malley brothers. They were my inspiration and role models. It is because of them that I decided to become a priest."

Bishop O'Farrell turned to Sam and spoke to him directly. "My Grandmother told me on more than one occasion that it was providence that you came to live with Pop. He along with his brothers could not have loved you more than if you were of their own flesh and blood. Sam, please accept my heartfelt condolences." Bishop O'Farrell put back on his miter and said, "Let us pray..."

****

Sam sat on the edge of his bed and looked at the photographs of his Mom and Dad. "I miss you so much. This house feels empty without the O'Malley brothers. It gets lonely at night. The silence is deafening. It used to be filled with laughter and love. But this is life and things change. Theresa, Johnny, and the boys will always be there for me. They are my family. It may look bleak today but tomorrow there is hope and optimism. So, there is no need for you to worry about your little boy. I love you both."

Chapter 26

Sam Gets into Trouble (Circa 1966)

The fifth grade class rose as Father Sam entered. "Good morning Father," was said in unison.

Father Sam motioned for everyone to be seated and returned their greeting, "Good morning". He laid several books on the desk.

One of the students asked, "Before we start, will you tell us another O'Malley story?"

"I will if you don't tell Mrs. Jernigan. She gets mad at me. When we were kids about your age, she used to beat me up."

Barry asked, "How can that be? You are much bigger and stronger than she is."

"It was always a one sided fight. She could hit me all she wanted but I couldn't her back. Boys don't hit girls."

Father Sam thumbed through his book titled *O'Malley Stories*. He came to one of his personal favorites. "This is a good one. It's short. This one was submitted by the daughter of Sean Ryan. I need to give you a bit of history so that you can better understand the story. Mr. Ryan was a very wealthy man. He was also very generous. The park is named after him. He donated substantial sums of money that helped build this church and school. He had a friend named Albert Swartz. You may know his grandson, Dr. Swartz. You have probably gone to see him when you were sick. The O'Malley brothers, Mr. Ryan and

Mr. Swartz were all buddies. They were always hanging out together. Back in those days there were no places to buy hamburgers or go to the store to get groceries. You grew your own food or you went hunting. The young boys favored squirrel hunting. This story involves a green snake. They are harmless. I used to play with them when I was younger. Now Mrs. Jernigan is really, really, really afraid of snakes even if it is a green snake. I teased her one time with one. Afterwards, was one of the times she beat me up.

Father Sam began reading. *My father told me this story several times as I was growing up. My father, Albert Swartz and the O'Malley brothers were all childhood friends. One day they went squirrel hunting. They had two .22 caliber rifles and they took turns using the rifles. They had been hunting all morning down by the river. They decided to rest for awhile. Jimmy O'Malley feel asleep while the others laid there talking. My father saw a green snake crawl up Jimmy's pants' leg. He quietly alerted the others. All of a sudden, Jimmy jumped to his feet, kicked off his shoes and threw off his pants. He got mad because the others were laughing at him. He started chasing after them. He was barefoot and in his underwear. He chased them all over the woods but he never caught any of them. He then realized that he could not remember where he left his clothes. He searched high and low but was unable to find them. When he got home, his mother was not happy. She gave him another pair of pants and told him not to come back until he found his other pants and shoes. It was well after dark when he got home carrying the extra pair of pants and wearing his shoes. His two other brothers were on the porch making fun of him. Again, he started chasing them all over the yard until their mother put a stop to all of their shenanigans.*

The entire class laughed. They liked the story. Mrs. Jernigan was walking the hallway and she heard the laughter. She could never recall when religion class was funny. She entered the room and went to the desk. She told the class to get out their religion books.

One of students raised his hand. Mrs. Jernigan acknowledged him, "Yes, Donny."

"Is it true that you used to beat up Father Sam?"

Father Sam was standing behind Mrs. Jernigan. He started shadow boxing. All the kids laughed again. Mrs. Jernigan turned to look at Father Sam. She gave him the "evil eye". Irritated, she turned back and answered Donny. "Yes I did and I am about to do it again."

Susie raised her hand and asked, "Mrs. Jernigan, are you afraid of snakes?"

Father Sam made his arm in the fashion of a cobra. He acted as if he was striking Mrs. Jernigan on the neck. Again, all the children laughed.

Mrs. Jernigan was steaming. She turned and gave Father Sam the "double evil eye". This was definitely a sign that Mrs. Jernigan was not happy. It was also a sign for Father Sam not to tread any further. To do so, could be hazardous to his health. She poked him in the chest. It was not a love tap. It was hard enough to knock Father Sam back a step. She then pointed to the religion book and said, "Understand?" Father Sam fully comprehended her symbolism. She was upset when she left the classroom but before the door fully closed, there was more laughter. Mrs. Jernigan shook her head in frustration but kept walking. She loved Sam with all her heart and soul but there were times she could wring his neck...and this was one of those times. She mumbled a plea, "Jesus, Mary and Joseph please help me make it through this school year."

****

The following Sunday after Mass, Father Sam was outside greeting the parishioners as they departed. The triplets came up and gave their Uncle Sam a big hug and then raced off to play in the yard. Theresa purposely avoided Sam as she left. Johnny came up to Sam and said, "You are in big trouble."

Sam questioned, "How long does this last?"

"If you're lucky...maybe two weeks."

"I can't let it go that long." Sam walked down the front steps to where Theresa was standing. He grasped both of her hands and kissed her on the cheek. "I'm sorry."

Theresa did not respond. She ignored him.

"I am going to embarrass you in front of everyone here by getting down on my knees and begging your forgiveness."

"That's not going to embarrass me. I like that idea."

Sam realized that he spoke before any forethought. "Do you really want me to do that?"

"Oh, Yes."

Sam was obedient. He got down on his knees and folded his hands. "Theresa, please forgive me."

Theresa switched roles. She cracked a smile. Not that noticeable. It was more like a Mona Lisa smile. "You're offenses are forgiven, my son. Your penance is five 'Hail Marys and five 'Our Fathers' and promise that you will not offend me again."

"Yes ma'am."

Theresa turned to Johnny. "This is a lesson that you can learn from Sam."

"What do you mean, I shouldn't offend you or that I should get on my knees and beg your forgiveness?"

"Both!" She then walked away. She may have forgiven Sam but he was still on her "bad boy" list.

Johnny helped Sam to his feet. "You look pathetic."

"It's called humility."

"Call it what you want but it is still pathetic. You have made my life just a little bit tougher."

Sam said, "I am sorry about that but there is one thing that I am thankful for."

"What's that?"

"You're married to Theresa and not me."

An impatient Theresa and the triplets were standing at the end of the sidewalk. Johnny patted his friend on the shoulder. "I've got to go or else I *will* be in trouble."

Chapter 27

The Triplets Play Hooky (Circa 1967)

Sister Louise stepped inside the principal's office. "Are the boys sick today?"

"No. Why do you ask?"

"They were not in class this morning."

Mrs. Jernigan's ire was rising by the second. She responded politely, "Those boys are going to be the death of me." She pointed to her hair. "Look Here. Do you see the gray? The triplets put them there. Thank you Sister. I will take care of it."

Mrs. Jernigan had a strong suspicion as to where they were...down at the river fishing. She marched down to the river. She was boiling by the time she found the boys at her favorite fishing hole from years ago. The boys were startled but not surprised to see their mother. She was mad and they knew it was best not to say anything.

"I can't deal with you three this morning. You better be thankful that your father is out of town on business. I want you to go see your Uncle Sam. Tell him I said to *handle it*."

"Young Johnny asked, "What do you mean by *handle it*?"

"Just tell Uncle Sam. He will know what it means. Now get!" The boys started walking casually toward the Rectory. A leisurely stroll was not Theresa's intention. "When I said *get*, I meant *get!*" The boys understood completely. They took off running.

They appeared at the Rectory door. They were out of breath. When Uncle Sam saw them he said, "This must be my lucky day. It's my favorite nephews. Come on in boys and sit down."

Jacky blurted out, "Mama sent us here and said for you to *handle it*."

"That's not a good sign. You boys must be in trouble."

Young Sam replied, "You've got that right! I don't think I have ever seen Mama this mad. We decided to go fishing instead of going to class."

Uncle Sam answered as he pointed to each of the triplets, "That was dumb, dumb, and dumb!"

Jacky said, "We have heard stories how you, Mama, and Daddy played hooky and went fishing. We figured if you did it, we could too."

"I understand what you are saying but our mother was not the principal of the school. So it was dumb."

Johnny said, "I tried to tell them that we were going to get caught but they wouldn't listen."

"If that was the case, then why did you go along?"

"We have a pact...the Three Musketeers' Pact...'All for one...one for all'. I was overruled by Sammy and Jacky. If we get caught, we get caught together,"

"That's admirable. I like that pact. You boys should always look out for each other. But it was still dumb."

Uncle Sam got up from his seat and took the paddle off the wall. It had been out of commission for years. Sam used it as a wall decoration and a memorial to his Uncle Billy.

Jacky became concerned. "I know my mother pretty good and I don't think that was what she meant by *handle it*."

"I have known your mother a lot longer than you have. I assure you, this is exactly what she meant. There is a story that Father O'Malley used this paddle and spanked one boy so hard that he couldn't sit down for three days." Fear came over the triplets. Uncle Sam instructed the boys to stand up and lean forward with their hands on the front of the desk. Uncle Sam slipped around the desk and moved the chairs out of the way. The triplets were grimacing. Uncle Sam took the paddle and slapped the seat of the chair making a loud 'pow'. All three jumped. Uncle Sam proceeded down the line and gave each boy five licks. They were so light that the boys barely felt them.

Uncle Sam instructed the boys, "Now take a seat."

Sammy was somewhat confused. "Is that it?"

"Yes, that's it."

"You're the greatest Uncle Sam."

"Don't get too excited. I am not through with you three. But first, if your mother asks, you tell her that I gave each of you five licks with the O'Malley paddle. She may also ask if it hurt. If she does, you say, 'No ma'am. We took it like men.' This way we aren't lying. Do you guys understand?"

"Yes sir."

Uncle Sam reached into his desk and pulled out three sheets of paper and three pencils. He handed them to the triplets. "I want each of you to write a note to your mother. Make sure the entire page is filled. You write whatever you think is appropriate but it must contain something that says you are sorry and that you love your mother. Now split up. I don't want you copying each others paper."

It took the boys about thirty minutes before they finished. Uncle Sam read each one. He did everything possible to refrain from laughing. The best line was from Jacky. *"...You keep telling me that I am full of the devil. That is the reason why I can't be good all the time..."*

Uncle Sam asked, "Did you get your fishing poles from under the house?"

"Yes sir."

"They're still down at the river."

"Did you guys catch any fish?"

Young Johnny proudly answered, "Yes sir...three big bream and one small bass."

Uncle Sam thought to himself that that was plenty for dinner tonight. "We need to go and get the fishing poles and the fish. It's a sin to waste food."

Afterwards they returned to the house. Uncle Sam gave the boys orders. "Get the lawnmower, the rake and the hedge clippers. I want this yard cleaned. When you finish, get the pail and soap from under the kitchen sink and wash my car. Do you understand?"

All three answered, "Yes sir."

While the boys were busy in the yard, Uncle Sam cleaned the fish. He cut out eight nice fillets. He wrapped them up in tin foil and placed them in the refrigerator. He would cook them later. Uncle Sam returned to the Rectory. He had Father Sam work to do.

The dismissal bell rang. Uncle Sam stepped outside and he could see the boys finishing up on washing his car. He grabbed up the masterpieces written by the boys and headed across the street. "Let's put everything away. Your mother should be ready to go home."

The four of them entered the principal's office. The triplets gave their mother a group hug and handed her the notes. She inquired, "What kind of punishment did you get?"

Jacky answered, "We had to clean Uncle Sam's yard."

Young Johnny continued, "We washed Uncle Sam's car."

Sammy finished, "Uncle Sam gave us five licks with the O'Malley paddle."

Theresa responded, "Oh my goodness! Did it hurt?"

"No ma'am. We took it like men."

Theresa did not know how to respond, "I guess that's good."

Uncle Sam secretly gave the boys a thumbs-up.

"You boys go out and wait for me by the car."

Theresa sat down and began reading the notes. Tears of joy began to flow along with an occasional burst of laughter.

Sam said, "Theresa before you get into bed tonight, get down on you knees and thank God for blessing you with three fine boys. They are no worse than we were at their age and we turned out ok. There is still hope for the boys."

"I know but there is a difference. I am a mother now." Theresa stood up and kissed Sam on the cheek, "Thank you."

"You don't need to thank me. I should be thanking you. I got my grass cut, my car washed and I have fresh fish for dinner tonight."

Chapter 28

Father Capodanno (Circa 1968)

Marine Corps Sergeant Joseph Flynn, dressed in civilian clothes, appeared at the Rectory door. Joe was one of Father Sam's favorites. He had attended both the elementary and high schools at St. Patrick's. Father Sam glanced up and said, "What a pleasant surprise." He stood and walked toward Joe. They shook hands. As he motioned to the chair, he added, "Sit down and make yourself comfortable."

Joe sat down. "It's good to see you Father."

"The same here. Have you healed up?"

"I am as good as new. The only evidence that I was ever wounded is the nasty scar."

"That's good to hear."

"I am fortunate...an inch to the right and I wouldn't be here today. You will be happy to know that I am still wearing the St. Christopher medal that you gave me."

"That is a tradition here at St. Patrick's that was started by a young Father O'Malley. It dates back to World War I. St. Christopher was interceding on your behalf."

"I firmly believe that."

"I spoke to your parents at church last Sunday. They said that you were coming home on leave."

"Yes, I will be here for a week and then I have to report back to duty. My enlistment will be up in several months."

"Are you going to re-enlist?"

"Yes, but not as a Non Commissioned Officer (NCO) but as a Catholic chaplain."

"That's fantastic. I always thought that some day you might consider the priesthood."

"But Father there are a lot of things that have to come together to make it a reality. I want to transfer to the Active Reserves and go to the Seminary at the same time. In order to do that, I have to find a Seminary close to my weekend duty station but first I have to find out where that duty station will be. Also, I need to find out if the Diocese will allow me to do that."

"Joe, I don't know the answer but when there is a will...there is a way. I will do what ever is necessary to make it happen."

"Thanks." Joe wanted to be courteous. "Father, do you have any appointments or commitments? I want to tell you the story as to why I want to become a chaplain. It may take a while."

"For you, you have my undivided attention."

Joe began. "Have you heard of Father Vincent Capodanno?"

"No."

"I spent some time at the library doing some research. He was born in 1929 at Staten Island, New York. His parents were both Italian immigrants and Vincent was the youngest of ten children. He was named after his father. In 1958, he was ordained as a Maryknoll Priest...and Father you know as well as I do that the Maryknolls are cut from a different mold. He served as a missionary in Taiwan and Hong Kong. When the Viet Nam war broke out, he knew that this was where he wanted to be. He requested through his Bishop to be reassigned to the U. S. Navy Chaplain Corps. This was approved and he was sworn in as a Lieutenant in late 1965. His goal from the outset was to be a Chaplain with the U. S. Marine Corps and he never wavered."

"When I was doing my research I also came across another Maryknoll priest named Father William T. Cummings. He had a mission in the Philippines when World War II broke out. He went to the U. S. Army command in Manila in an effort to join the Army as a chaplain. His request was granted. He was severely wounded when he was ministering to the patients at a hospital that came under extensive bombardment. Before he was completely healed and against doctor's orders, he went to the front line to be with the young men to meet their spiritual needs. Unfortunately, he was captured and had to endure the Bataan Death March. He died as a prisoner of war aboard a ship that was taking him and other soldiers to a concentration camp in Japan. I bring this up because I am impressed with the dedication of military chaplains but also the fact that Father Cummings was accredited with coining the phrase, "There are no atheists in foxholes." I have heard this saying many, many times but I never knew where it had originated."

Father Sam interjected. "I have heard that phrase myself and like you, I never knew where it came from. But it is so true."

"You're right. It is true." Joe continued, "Father Capodanno arrived in country during Holy Week of 1966. He was assigned to the 7th Marines headquartered at Chu Lai. He was the only Catholic Priest for the entire regiment. Officially the 1st Battalion was his home base but he managed to serve the other two battalions. He was constantly on the move especially if the battalion was involved in a combat operation. It was not uncommon for him to assist the wounded and to administer the Last Rites. All this while under enemy fire. His goal in life was to be with his fellow grunts when they needed him the most. A grunt is an infantryman who is on the front line fighting the enemy and the elements. He is a soldier who stinks from the lack of bathing, who sleeps in the rain and is constantly fighting the mosquitoes. Father Capodanno may have been a Catholic priest but he was also a grunt. He shared the discomforts the same as the rest of us. He was a Marine. His comrades in combat affectionately referred to him as the Grunt Padre."

"After eight months in the field, Father Capodanno was transferred to the field hospital. He was well aware of the importance of attending to the wounded and the dying but he personally longed to be in the thick of the action. When time permitted, he would catch a chopper out to the field and spend several days with the troops saying Mass and administering the sacraments. Father Capodanno was becoming a "short-timer". That was lingo for a Marine who was nearing the end of his tour in Vietnam. Father Capodanno made a request to extend his tour by six months. This was rare for a chaplain to make such a request and it was even more rare for the request to be approved. However, his second tour was authorized. Those that extended their tours were afforded the opportunity of returning home on leave. When Father Capodanno arrived back in country, he did not go back to his old unit. He was assigned to the 5th Marines. That was also my regiment. I was in Company M of the 3rd Battalion."

"It was September 4, 1967, a day that will be forever etched in my memory. The day before, I had attended Mass. Father Capodanno greeted us all after church. He was a personable and likeable individual. He always had a kind word. Company D of our sister Battalion was on a search and destroy mission. This was the beginning of Operation Swift at the village of Dong Son. Search and destroy is where you sweep through a village to root out the enemy at which time you destroy them. This is a common military practice. Most of the time you don't meet any resistance but if you do, it is usually results in a minimal firefight. But this day was different. When Company D neared Dong Son they met an overwhelming force. Unbeknownst to Company D, they had stumbled upon an estimated 2500 regulars of the North Vietnamese Army (NVA) hunkered down in the area. Apparently they had been there awhile because they were well entrenched in and around the village. The NVA were better trained and astute in military tactics. Whereas the Viet Cong (VC) were masters of guerilla warfare; they would hit, inflict their damage, and run to fight another day. On this early Monday morning, Company D had met a formable foe with the NVA who outnumbered them by a wide margin. Company B was called up to reinforce Company D. The fighting continued to be intense. Company K and M were ordered to be transported by helicopter from the base camp to the aid station that had been set up near Dong Son but the landing zone (LZ) was extremely *hot* and the flight had to divert to another LZ miles away. We had to *hoof it* over hilly terrain and through rice paddies. Intelligence reports that we were receiving revealed that my company and Kilo Company were about to encounter the NVA near the village of Chau Lam which was still about a mile away from Delta Company. We took more of an offensive posture. My company was flanking Kilo Company. As my platoon topped a hill and started down the other side, we came under enemy fire. We were literally face to face with the NVA. I was wounded in the left shoulder. I had no feeling in my left arm. All I could do was lay there. I couldn't move or shoot back. To do so, would expose my position and the machine gun fire was deadly accurate. I had some cover behind a small fallen tree. I learned of the numerous acts of heroism by Father Capodanno after the fact. The command post had been set up on the other side of the hill out of direct fire. Our radio operator contacted the Company Commander and informed him of the dire situation. When Father Capodanno heard this, he left the relatively safe position and proceeded over and down the hill to the radio operator's location. The two of them crawled back, dragging the radio with them. They had to take cover several times before making it back to safety. Father Capodanno then again headed back down the hill and began to aid the wounded and perform the last rites to the dying. As I was lying there, Father Capodanno appeared out of nowhere. He flopped down beside me. He told me to keep the faith and that help was on the way. We said the Lord's Prayer together as he bandaged my wound. I thought that he was going to stay with me because of the intense enemy fire but the next thing I knew, he was up and gone. How he stayed alive as long as he did was a miracle in itself. This was the last time I saw him. He earned three Purple Hearts in a matter of hours. He was shot in the hand but he kept going. A mortar round exploded near him and his right arm was mangled but he kept going. Later in the day he went to the aid of our corpsman that had been shot. Father Capodanno was hit with machine gun fire as he tried to shield the corpsman. But tragically, both died from their wounds. When they recovered Father Capodanno's body, he had twenty seven bullets holes in the back. What he did that day was not only heroic but it was God's work. The man should be considered for sainthood. It is my understanding that Father Capodanno is being recommended for the Medal of Honor."

"I laid there. I kept my M-16 in my right hand with my finger on the trigger. I took my two 'frag' grenades and put them where I could easily get to them. I fully expected that the NVA would try to overrun our position but luckily for me, this didn't happen. When night fell, I was able to inch my way back to the other side of the knoll. When I found out about Father Capodanno's death, I regretted that I didn't force him to stay with me. But in retrospect, I don't think that would have happened even if I had the use of both arms. He was a man on a mission."

Joe finished. "...and Father that is why I want to become a Catholic Chaplain."

Father Sam responded. "After hearing the passion in your voice in telling the story, I am ready to go and enlist myself."

Joe laughed. "Father, you have your own breed of "grunts" right here in New Dublin. They need you just as much as the Marines needed Father Capodanno."

"Joe, you talk with your superiors and I will talk with the Bishop. I am sure that we can work out all of the details."

Chapter 29

Tech Sergeant Jones Retires (Circa 1969)

Bob Jones entered the employment office and questioned the receptionist. "Do you have any job openings?"

"Yes sir. We have six positions available." She handed him an application. "Fill this out and you can meet with our Personnel Manager."

Mr. Jones finished. The receptionist escorted him into Mr. O'Brien's office.

Mr. O'Brien glanced down at the name on the application. "Sit down Mr. Jones while I look through your paperwork." Mr. O'Brien commented. "I see one of your references as being John Jernigan."

"Yes sir. He and I served together in Korea. I knew that he was from New Dublin and I had heard that he was working here. I haven't seen him in years."

"Would you like to see him?"

"I sure would. That would be great."

Mr. O'Brien was briefly gone. He returned with Johnny. Johnny was the first to speak. "...if it's not Tech Sergeant Jones!"

"...actually it's Chief Master Sergeant Jones." Bob extended his hand, "It's good to see you Johnny."

Johnny sat down in Mr. O'Brien's chair. He propped his feet up on the desk, leaned back and clasped his hands behind his head. "Bring me up to speed on your life since Korea."

"I stayed with Lt. Col. Mathis. He was promoted to a full bird Colonel. We were transferred to Lackland AFB in Texas. I liked Texas. Colonel Mathis retired about ten years ago. He was replaced by Colonel Tucker. I was worried about breaking in a new boss but he turned out to be a good guy. We both got transferred to Tan Son Nhut AFB in Saigon. We were then transferred to Tinker AFB in Oklahoma City. That was another good duty station but word came down that I and Colonel Tucker were scheduled for another tour of duty in Vietnam. Colonel Tucker had thirty years of service and I had twenty years. We both decided to retire. Two wars were enough for me. My wife wanted to get back home so we moved back to Jefferson City. This is the first place I have tried to get a job." Mr. O'Brien was standing at the back of the office. Bob leaned forward and spoke to Johnny in a lower voice so as not to be overheard. "I would appreciate if you could pull some strings and help me get a job. I need a weekly paycheck."

Johnny replied in a normal voice, "Me and the boss are real tight. He does everything I tell him to do. He is one of the finest men on the face of this earth." Johnny glanced up to Mr. O'Brien. "Don't you agree, Tim?"

"He is a nice fellow but I question the fact that he is the finest man on the face of the earth."

"I am going to tell him what you said."

"I don't care. He doesn't scare me. I would tell him the same thing straight to his face."

At Johnny's request, Tim went down the list of the various openings. Johnny thought that none of them fit Bob's expertise. "I think we need to make Bob an aide to the boss. He needs a fancy title...how about...Executive Assistant. What do you think, Tim?"

"...sounds fancy to me."

Johnny spoke again to Bob. "This job may entail you picking up the boss' laundry, handling paperwork, running interference..."

"You mean what I have been doing for the past twenty years."

"...exactly!"

"Tim will help you get settled in. I have a meeting to attend. We have plenty of time to talk later."

Johnny left the office. Bob said to Tim, "This boss sounds like a decent fellow."

"You should know. You have been talking to him for the last ten minutes."

Bob smiled. "I can see that I am going to like it around here."

"If you don't, then there is something wrong with you."

Chapter 29
The Triplets Take a Vacation (Circa 1973)

Young Johnny pulled into the parking lot of *Shorty's Burgers and Fries,* a local drive-in restaurant. It was a hang-out for St. Patrick High School students. Johnny backed the Volkswagen bus in between two cars. The bus was a gift for their seventeenth birthday. Theresa wrote a daily schedule as to which triplet had the control of the bus on a particular day. This system worked well but the triplets were always swapping days, especially on the weekends when one of them had a date. However, it came at a cost. One Saturday was worth two week days. The triplets will never be called *neat freaks*. Food wrappers and athletic gear were strewed throughout the interior. The foul smell of unclean sweaty clothes never bothered the triplets or any of their dates. However, Theresa refused to ride in the bus. She swore that it was contaminated with typhoid.

The triplets walked up and placed their orders. They were greeted by many of their fellow students. The Jernigan triplets had reached iconic status because of their play on the football field. The triplets took all of the attention in stride. They were not arrogant and were friendly with everyone. They got their burger baskets and headed back to the bus. Sammy slid back the door and the three of them sat down in the open doorway.

Jacky said, "We have been out of school for three weeks. I am bored. Let's do something different."

Johnny responded, "What do you want to do?"

"I don't know. What do you want to do?

"I don't know."

Sammy jumped into the conversation. "I've always wanted to go to Key West."

Johnny replied, "Key West is a long way from here. It has to be at least 800 miles. Besides, Mom and Dad will never approve."

Sammy said, "We don't ask. It is a lot easier to get forgiveness than it is to get permission."

Jacky stated, "Dad would be all for it but he does whatever Mom tells him."

Sammy said, "So you're saying that Dad is a wimp."

"Yes. Our father and Uncle Sam are both wimps when it comes to Mom."

Johnny was still reluctant. He pondered the consequences out loud. "Is a trip to Key West worth the never ending grief we are going to get from Mom?" Johnny paused and then answered his own question. "Yea, it's worth it."

Sammy asked, "How long do we plan to be gone?"

Jacky answered, "Probably a week."

"Mom will be insane by the time we get back."

Jacky began figuring how as to how much money was needed. "It'll cost about $ 40.00 round trip for gas; food will be about $ 100.00. We can save some money if we eat bologna sandwiches. We won't starve."

Johnny asked, "What about motels?"

Jacky answered, "We'll sleep in the bus."

Johnny responded adamantly, "I don't think so. Sleeping in the bus for two nights is okay but after that, we need to get a motel room. We'll need a shower and a good night's sleep. You guys will be stinking by the end of three days."

Sammy responded, "What makes you think that you won't be ripe?"

"I will but I don't mind smelling myself."

Jacky said to Johnny. "You make a good point. Let's figure $ 75.00 for motels. Throw in some extra spending money and we can make this trip on $ 250.00." Jacky pulled out his billfold and he had $ 24.00. Johnny had $ 22.00 and Sammy had $ 18.00. Jacky continued, "Tomorrow is our birthday. Our grandparents and Uncle Sam usually give us cash. That should come to about $ 150.00 but we are still going to be short."

Sammy hesitantly revealed, "I have about 60 bucks hidden in our bedroom."

Johnny asked, "Where did you get 60 bucks?"

"I'm not like you two. I save some of my money."

Jacky did some quick math. "We have enough money if somebody doesn't decide to give us a gift instead of cash."

The triplets finalized their travel plans.

****

The next morning when they got up, their parents had already left for work. Johnny said to his two brothers, "Happy birthday." They responded with "Happy birthday to you too." Johnny continued, "Let's get some breakfast. Then we need to get started. We have a lot of things to do."

The triplets cleaned the bus and removed the rear seat. They packed their camping gear. Afterwards, they went to a gas station, filled the tank and purchased maps. They returned to the house and studied the maps. It was decided that they would follow the coastline as much as possible. There was no more to do until it was time to leave which would be tonight after their parents went to bed. The boys sacked out on the large wrap around couch because they wouldn't get much sleep tonight. They were awakened when Theresa came home. She greeted them with "Happy birthday." "Thanks Mom" was their response.

Theresa said, "I am cooking your favorite meal...pot roast."

Johnny answered, "That sounds good to me."

For the triplets, it seemed like forever until dinner was ready. They were hungry. The entire family was there including the triplets' maternal and paternal grandparents and Uncle Sam. Uncle Sam said the blessing. When dinner was finished, the women cleaned the table. Shortly thereafter, they emerged from the kitchen with cake, ice cream, and singing *Happy Birthday*. The men joined in. The triplets blew out the candles together. Theresa handed wrapped gifts to her three sons. It was exactly what they needed...shorts and t-shirts. The triplets were relieved when they received birthday cards from their grandparents and Uncle Sam. The boys opened the envelopes and read the cards out of courtesy but their main concern was how much money they contained. It was more than they expected. The trip was a definite "go".

It was close to midnight when Theresa and Johnny turned in for the night. Sammy said to his brothers, "I thought they would never go to bed."

Jacky added, "Let's give them about an hour to make sure they are sound asleep."

It was time. The triplets quietly slipped into their bedroom and gathered up their clothes. They got the ice chest from the storage closet and raided the refrigerator. They took the left over roast beef, mayonnaise, and all the sodas that the ice chest would hold. Jacky grabbed some silverware and a carving knife. Johnny got what was left of the birthday cake along with a loaf of bread. Sammy left a note on the kitchen table. They eased out the front door to the bus. The triplets pushed the bus out of the driveway and down the street. They jumped in and cranked the bus. Jacky yelled, "Key West here we come."

Theresa was the first to rise. She made a pot of coffee and then noticed the note on the table. She let out a blood curdling scream. Johnny was immediately on his feet and rushed to the kitchen. "What's wrong?"

"My boys are gone!" Theresa handed the note to Johnny, "Read this."

"Good for them."

"What do you mean…good for them? These are our sons. They could be robbed or have an accident." Theresa demanded, "Go and get the airplane ready. We'll see if we can find them."

"They have probably been gone for hours. Besides, it would be like looking for a needle in a haystack."

"Then let's call the police. They can issue an 'all points bulletin' so that they can be stopped and sent back home."

"The police can't do anything. The triplets are eighteen years old…"

"…but they're still in high school."

"That doesn't matter. They are now adults."

"So what you're saying is that we do nothing."

"Exactly. We have raised three smart boys. I am sure they have given this trip much thought."

Theresa wasn't pleased with Johnny. "With or without you, I am going to do something."

She stormed out of the kitchen. Johnny could hear her crying in the bedroom. He thought it was best to let her be. It was not long before she reappeared. "There is nothing we can do?"

"No. They will be fine."

"Can I worry the whole time that they are gone?"

"Yes. That's what mothers are supposed to do."

****

It was getting late in the afternoon when they reached Myrtle Beach, South Carolina. As always, they were hungry even though they had been eating roast beef sandwiches since before daybreak. Pizza was the food of choice.

Johnny said, "We need to call home."

Sammy responded, "I'm not talking to Mom. Let's call Uncle Sam and have him pass on a message."

The triplets were in agreement. They found a pay phone at a convenience store. The problem was that none of them knew how to make a collect call. They followed the instructions in the front of the telephone book.

The operator made the connection. "I have a collect call from Jacky Jernigan for Father Sam Jenkins. Will you accept the charges?"

"Yes"

"Uncle Sam this is your favorite nephew, Jacky."

"Where are you and your brothers?"

"Right now we're in Myrtle Beach, South Carolina. We're heading for Key West."

"So that's where you're going. In your note, you didn't say."

"That was done on purpose to keep Mom from trying to track us down. Don't tell her where we are going. She would fly down and be at the city limits waiting for us to arrive. Just say that we are going to Florida."

"Why don't you call her yourself?"

"Uncle Sam that is a dumb question. You of all people know full well why we don't call Mom."

Uncle Sam thought a second. "You're right. That was a dumb question." He continued, "Your Dad and I don't feel the same way as your mother. You boys have a good time. Be safe."

"We will. We'll call again tomorrow."

The triplets found a place on an isolated beach to spend the night. As the sun went down, they built a small fire. There was no noise except for the waves breaking on the shore. It was dark too. No lights could be seen in any direction. They laid out their sleeping bags and settled in for the night.

****

The triplets were awake when dawn came. It was beautiful. They had an unobstructed view as the sun rose above the horizon. The bright red ball reflected over the calm ocean. Johnny got the camera and took a picture. It was one of those moments that was worthy of remembrance.

They piled into the bus and their first stop was a diner where they got a good southern breakfast. It was not long before they were on the road again heading south toward Savannah, Georgia. As they neared the entrance to Ft. Stewart, there was a sign that said "Pick-Up Station Ahead. Give a Soldier a Ride". The triplets slowed down and stopped. A young soldier walked up to the passenger window. Johnny asked, "Where are you heading?"

"I'm going to a small town called Okeechobee." Johnny pulled out his Florida map and the soldier pointed to the city. "If you're going that far, you can drop me off in Ft. Pierce."

"We're going to Key West and you're welcomed to ride along but we are not on a schedule. It may be tomorrow or the next day before we get to Ft. Pierce. Also, we have been spending the night in the bus."

"I have plenty of time and I've slept in worse places."

"I take that to mean yes. Throw your gear in the back and climb in."

The soldier introduced himself. "My name is Henry Turner but everyone calls me Hank"

"My name is Johnny and this is my brother Sammy and my other brother Jacky."

"I would have never guessed that." Hank said with a sense of humor.

Jacky spoke up. "We're triplets and all the babes consider me to be the best looking." Both Johnny and Sammy gagged at that remark.

Sammy asked, "What do you do in the Army?"

"I'm a crew chief on a plane that you've never heard of…the O-1 Bird Dog."

"We're familiar with the Bird Dog. The three of us are pilots."

Hank didn't say anything but he questioned the fact that these three guys were actually pilots.

Jacky who was seated beside Hank started laughing. He spoke to his brothers. "You should see the look on Hank's face. He doesn't believe that we can fly an airplane." Jacky continued by talking directly to Hank. "We are familiar with the Bird Dog. Our father's company manufactures the Bobcat, a plane similar to the Bird Dog. His company also makes the Exec-Jet, a business class jet engine aircraft. We are pilots, my mother is a pilot, and my father flew the Sabre jet in Korea. He taught all of us to fly." Jacky turned back to his brothers. "I still don't think that we have convinced him." He said to Johnny, "There is an old company brochure in the glove box." Johnny handed it to Hank.

Hank glanced through the crumpled and stained brochure. "I guess you guys aren't handing me a bunch of bull."

"I tried to tell you that." Jacky changed the subject and asked Hank if he had been to Vietnam.

"I did a year tour of duty. I didn't see any combat. Only a few mortar attacks. Occasionally I had to go out in the field when a plane had a problem. What irritates me is that I was old enough to go to a war zone but I am not old enough to buy a beer here at home."

"How old are you?"

"I'm twenty."

"We turned eighteen several days ago."

Hank asked, "What do you guys do?"

"We are seniors in high school. We play football."

"Are you any good?"

"We were state champs last year."

"Not bad."

Sammy inquired, "Are your parents excited about you coming home?"

"No. The reason why I joined the Army was to get away from home. I'm going to see several buddies of mine. They're letting me crash at their apartment."

Sammy didn't ask any more questions about Hank's family life. "We got to stop and get gas. You can change out of that uniform."

Hank returned to the bus dressed in shorts, t-shirt, and sandals. He now fit in with the Jernigan brothers except for his military style haircut. Hank paid for the gas. There was one more stop to be made at the grocery store before they started looking for a place to spend the night. They also took the time to call home.

They found a remote beach. Hank did his best to keep a straight face. "We need to be careful. I saw on the local news where there had been reports of alligator attacks at the beach. Gators like to feed at night." The triplets were concerned. They had anticipated potential dangers on the trip but being eaten by a gator wasn't one of them.

It was an hour past sunset. The fire gave light to the dark beach. They roasted hot dogs; each eating three apiece. As they sat there, a rustling sound in a nearby thicket was heard by all. Hank screamed, "Gator! Run!" The Jernigan brothers, at lightning speed, were on their feet fumbling and stumbling all over each other as they fought their way into the bus. They slammed the door shut. Hank never moved. He stayed by the fire, laughing so hard that it made his stomach hurt.

Moments later, Sammy cracked open the sliding door, "Is it safe?"

Hank, still laughing, said, "Yes ladies, it is safe."

Slowly the triplets stepped out from the bus. Sammy asked, "Did you make up that story about the alligator attacks?"

"Yes. Everybody knows…except for you guys…that gators don't like salt water."

"Well, what was that noise we heard?"

"It was probably a possum or a raccoon. You have to watch out for them. They will come up during the middle of the night and chew on your fingers." Hank had second thoughts. The triplets were gullible. If he didn't tell them the truth, they would stay awake all night. "I'm joking. There are no critters out here that will hurt you but we do have to make sure that we don't leave any food out because the possums and raccoons will definitely go after that."

****

The next morning with all their fingers intact, the Jernigan brothers and Hank continued southward. Hank said, "We need to stop in Daytona Beach. You can cruise up and down the beach. Plus there are plenty of girls in skimpy bathing suits."

Hank was right. It was like one continuous parade. There were a lot of convertibles filled with girls and they were friendly too. Sammy pulled the bus off to the side. They started tossing around the football. It wasn't long before four *hot* girls strolled up. It was no big deal for the triplets. They were used to it but Hank was amazed that that such good-looking girls could be that forward. After small talk and some heavy flirting, the girls continued down the beach. Hank grabbed the camera and snapped a picture of the bikini clad young women as they walked away. He then whistled at them and they turned around and waved as Hank took another picture. Hank told the triplets, "These are my pictures. You've got to make me a copy. I can tell some tall stories when I get back to the barracks."

As Sammy drove south on Dixie Highway, he noticed all the billboards about Disney World. He said to his brothers, "If we have enough money left, I want to go there on our way back." Jacky and Johnny thought it was a good idea.

The closer they got to Ft. Pierce, the less talkative Hank became. He had something on his mind. Finally he spoke up. "I've had a lot of fun hanging out with you guys. But the more I think about it, the less I want to go anywhere near my home. Okeechobee is a small town and I may see some people that I don't want to see. If ya'll don't mind, I would like to tag along with you guys. I will share the expenses and you'll have enough money to go to Disney World. You can drop me off where you picked me up."

The Jernigan brothers didn't have to talk it over with each other. They already knew the answer. Hank was their new best friend but it was payback time for the story about the alligator attacks. They thought of every excuse imaginable as to why they shouldn't let him tag along. Finally Sammy brought it to an end. "We like you and Key West won't be the same if you're not there."

Hank's face lit up. "Thanks guys. You had me worried. The way you were talking, I thought you were going to just slow down in Ft. Pierce and throw me out."

The boys found a small motel on the beach. They were able to find a room with two queen size beds. They would bunk together. After they checked into their room, Johnny suggested that they flip a coin to see who would get the first shower. He pulled out a quarter and flipped it in front of Sammy. Johnny called as the coin was in the air, "Heads I win…tails you lose."

Sammy lost and said to Johnny, "You are the luckiest person I know. You always win."

Hank could not believe what he just saw. He spoke to Sammy and Jacky, "You're not going to fall for the oldest trick in the book?"

Jacky asked, "What do you mean?"

"There is no way you can win. Johnny has been scamming you."

Sammy thought about it and said, "You're right. I don't know how we didn't catch it earlier. This has been going for about a year." He turned to Johnny and ordered with contempt, "You will go last."

Johnny, with a devious smile, said, "It was fun while it lasted."

Jacky followed, "Let's do 'rock, paper, scissors' like we used to before our brother became a low-life cheater." Hank was the winner and Sammy was second.

After everyone had a shower, they were sitting on the edge of the beds. It was time to call home.

"Uncle Sam, this is your favorite nephew, Sammy. We're just checking in to let you know that we are okay."

"Where are you now?"

"We're in a motel near Port St. Lucie." Johnny asked, "What about Mom?"

"She is about to drive me crazy. She calls every five minutes to see if I had heard from you boys. I'll call her as soon as I hang up with you. Also, say hello to your brothers."

"I will. They and Hank are right here with me."

"Who is Hank?"

"Hank is in the Army. We met him up in Ft. Stewart, Georgia. He is riding along with us. His is a good guy."

"Remember, tomorrow is Sunday."

"Don't worry. We will go to church in the morning."

Johnny ended the telephone call. Hank had overheard the conversation and said, "Your Uncle Sam must be a religious fanatic."

The triplets laughed. Johnny said, "You might say that…he is a Catholic priest."

Hank was embarrassed. "I'm sorry. I didn't mean anything by it."

"We know that. He would think that it was funny too."

Hank continued, "I was baptized as a Catholic. We seldom went to church. If we did, it was usually at Easter or Christmas."

"Good. You will go with us tomorrow."

****

Hank made a suggestion. "It might be better to take the interstate versus driving down Dixie Highway. There is nothing but city after city…stoplight after stoplight…from here down to Miami. It'll take forever."

Johnny was the driver. "You know the area better than I do."

They traveled I-95 until it ended in South Miami where it merged into Dixie Highway. It was not long before they passed a sign that read, "Welcome to the Florida Keys". Hank said, "I have never been this far south. From here on out, this is new scenery to me." A campground was found in Key Largo where they would spend the night. The nightly call was made to Uncle Sam. Everything was still the same at home. The four of them walked down the street to a local restaurant that claimed to have the best hamburgers in the Keys. The Jernigan brothers and Hank would be the judge of that.

After they finished, Johnny admitted, "That was the best hamburger I have ever eaten in the Florida Keys."

Sammy added, "I agree, but than again, these are the only burgers we have eaten in the Florida Keys. The ultimate hamburger could be waiting for us just down the road."

****

Midway of their journey was only hours away. The Keys were beautiful with crystal clear water and sandy white beaches. The Gulf of Mexico was on the right and the Atlantic Ocean was on the left.

Hank said, "We're coming up on the Seven Mile Bridge. I have several friends who come down here on a regular basis. You can fish from the catwalk that runs along the side of the bridge."

There were plenty of fishermen. Hank said, "Look there. That man's rod is bent over. He's bringing in a fish." Sammy slowed to a stop. The man lifted the fish over the rail. It was a large red snapper. Hank continued, "I wish I had a rod and reel. I would love to be out there fishing."

As they neared the city limits of Key West, Sammy said, "We will soon find out if Uncle Sam ratted on us." They were on the lookout for their mother. Sammy glanced into the rear view mirror. "There is car coming up fast behind us."

Johnny turned around and looked. "I don't think it's Mom unless she recently grew a beard."

Jacky added, "It could still be her. She may be wearing a disguise."

The boys breathed a sigh of relief when the car passed without slowing down.

Hank was totally confused. "What are you guys doing?"

Sammy explained, "Our Uncle Sam is the only person who knew where we were going. If he felt obligated to tell our mother…"

Johnny injected, "…or she beat it out of him…"

Sammy continued, "…then she would have flown the plane down, rented a car and be sitting right here when we came into town. That is why we are on the lookout. Since we haven't seen her yet probably means that she is not here."

Hank said, "Your mother must be a terror."

Jacky answered, "No, just the opposite. She is a fantastic mom but when it comes to us, she is protective and strict. It will not be a happy homecoming. She will be mad for awhile but she will get over it."

Sammy found a parking space. They walked down Duval St. and gazed inside the windows of the various shops. Jacky commented, "This is not what I expected. Key West is no more than a typical small town. Based on the number of bars I see, this place is paradise for the man who likes to consume mass quantities of beer." After several hours, the triplets and Hank had seen everything they wanted to see.

Johnny stated, "When we crossed the Seven Mile Bridge, there were a bunch of campers at the foot of the bridge. Let's go back there and spend the night."

They walked out onto the catwalk and watched the fishermen catching fish. They returned to the bus and pooled there money. They had plenty to cover the cost of going to Disney World. It would be a long day of driving to make it in one day. Hank knew of a spot near West Palm Beach where they could spend the next night.

****

Hank and the Jernigan brothers checked into the Contemporary Resort. Each of them took a much needed shower and changed into clean clothes. Then it was off to the Magic Kingdom. They boarded the monorail that literally stopped at their front door. As they entered the park, they were greeted by Snow White. She agreed to take a picture of Hank and the triplets as they posed in front of the Cinderella Castle. They began riding the rides and visiting the exhibits. They took a break in the late afternoon to call Uncle Sam.

"Uncle Sam, this is your favorite nephew, Johnny."

"I have been expecting your call. Where are you boys today?"

"We're hanging out with Goofy here at Disney World. This place is amazing."

"So you're having a good time."

"Yes sir. We just dread facing Mom. It's not going to be pretty."

"I have felt you mother's wrath on more than one occasion. I'm glad that I am not in your shoes."

Sarcastically Johnny responded, "Thank you for your words of encouragement."

"You're welcome. That is what I am here for."

"We plan to leave here tomorrow morning and drive straight through. You can tell Mom that her little boys will be home around six o'clock."

"Be careful."

"We will."

Hank and the triplets left the park just before closing time and returned to their room.

****

It was the last leg of their journey. They were headed for Ft. Stewart, Georgia. Sammy had a thought. He asked Hank, "When do you have to report back to duty?"

"…a week from this Monday."

"How would you like to go home with us?"

Hank enthusiastically answered, "Sure. It will be better than hanging around the barracks."

Johnny said, "That is a fantastic idea. With Hank around, Mom will mellow out."

Jacky added, "Hank you may want to think about it. It's a given that we won't have the bus. We'll have to walk everywhere and there is no telling what she has planned for us."

Sammy said to his brothers, "Let's make him the fourth musketeer."

Hank questioned, "What?"

Sammy explained, "We have the Three Musketeers' Pact...all for one...one for all. Whenever the four of us are together, it will be the Four Musketeer Pact. That also means that our punishment is your punishment."

Jacky saw a problem. "If we have to vote, it could be a tie."

Johnny had the solution. "In that case, we use 'rock, paper, scissors' to eliminate one person. We then vote again."

Jacky said, "That will work for me."

Sammy asked in an aristocratic voice, "Hank, do you accept the anointment as the fourth musketeer?"

"Yes I do, my lord."

The four of them bumped their fists to seal the pact.

Hank was silent but he was honored to be accepted by the Jernigan brothers. Little did the triplets know but this gesture was the highlight of the best week in his life.

****

Sammy pulled in the driveway. The four of them put on their Mickey Mouse hats. "Let's get this over with." They entered the front door. Their father got up to greet them as he yelled, "Theresa come here. The Mickey Mouse Club is here."

Theresa came into the living room and hugged her three sons.

Johnny said, "Mom…Dad, this is Hank." Hank shook hands with both of them.

Theresa said, "Hank please excuse us for a few minutes. You can have a seat on the couch." She motioned the triplets to follow her into the kitchen. Theresa had a difficult time in refraining from laughing as she looked at her three tall and muscular sons wearing big mouse ears. Theresa held out her opened hand. Sammy knew exactly what that meant as he gave the bus keys to her. "I have been worried sick since you boys have been gone. Why didn't you tell me where you were going?"

Johnny answered the question with a question. "Would you have let us go?"

Theresa did not respond.

"Of course, you wouldn't. So we thought that it would be easier to get forgiveness than it would be to get permission."

Theresa changed the subject because she knew that those were her exact words from years ago. "Starting tomorrow morning, I want this house painted and the yard spotless. When you finish, you will do the same thing at your Uncle Sam's house. After that, I have some landscaping work that needs to be done at the school. Do you understand?"

The triplets answered at the same time. "Yes ma'am."

"Now, who is Hank?"

Sammy said, "He is an escaped convict we picked up in Georgia. He swears that he was framed for the murder of his girlfriend and we believe him." Both Johnny and Jacky snickered.

Theresa wasn't amused. "Give me a straight answer or I will think of some more jobs for you boys to do."

Sammy told his mother about Hank and he finished with the fact that Hank had a terrible childhood.

Theresa, with compassion, said, "That poor boy."

They all returned to the living room. Theresa said to Hank, "I guess you have been hearing from my sons as to how terrible I am."

"No ma'am. They kept saying how mad you would be when they got home but they never said that you were terrible. They also never said how pretty you are."

"Thank you, Hank."

The triplets and Hank headed back to the bedroom.

Theresa turned to her husband. She held her chin up high and said with arrogance, "Hank thinks I'm pretty." She asked, "Do you think that I am pretty?"

He knew that this was a loaded question, "Hank is just finding out what I've known since we were kids."

"Good answer."

Johnny silently breathed a sigh of relief.

As soon as the bedroom door was closed, the triplets began to praise Hank. Johnny began, "I can't believe you said what you said. It was perfect…pure genius."

Hank responded, "You guys are 'chick magnets'. I have to work hard to get a date. I learned a long time ago that there is no woman on the face of this earth who doesn't like to hear that she is pretty." Hank was curious. "What was the verdict?"

Sammy said, "She took the bus and gave us thirty days of hard labor."

Jacky said to Hank, "You keep it up with the compliments and we'll be driving again by Saturday night."

****

Theresa's mother instinct came out in regard to Hank. She doted over him like a new found puppy. Hank didn't complain. He liked the attention.

Late Saturday afternoon, Hank and the triplets were lounging around in the living room watching a baseball game. Theresa came in dangling the bus keys. She laid them on the coffee table and said to her sons, "This doesn't mean that I condone what you did but it is not fair for Hank to suffer too. You boys go out and have a good time tonight."

After Theresa left the room, Jacky jumped up from the couch and gloated to his brothers and Hank. "I told you that we would be driving by Saturday night." He went over and rubbed Hank on his head. "It's all because of prince charming here."

****

It was midweek. Theresa, Johnny, and Hank were in the living room watching the evening news. The triplets were in the bedroom. Johnny asked, "When is your enlistment up?"

"February of next year."

"Are you going to re-enlist?"

"No sir."

"I can use a good man with your experience. If you want a job, there will be one waiting for you when you get out of the service."

"Thank you sir. I definitely want it."

"Also, I have an Exec-Jet scheduled to come off the assembly line tomorrow. After I test fly it, we can use it to fly you down to Savannah after lunch on Sunday."

"That's great. I hate riding the Greyhound."

Theresa added, "I want you to consider this house your home. You are welcomed at any time. She asked, "Do you think that you will be able to come home for Labor Day."

"Yes ma'am. I should have one or two days of leave built up by then."

"Good. Somebody will fly down and pick you up." Theresa added, "When you get back to Ft. Stewart, I expect at least one phone call from you every week."

"Yes ma'am."

****

After Mass on Sunday, Theresa hugged Sam and asked, "Are you coming over for lunch?"

"I wouldn't miss it. You have been cooking some fantastic meals since Hank has been here."

"I just want him to feel at home. Tomorrow I go back to fish sticks. After we eat, we are going to fly Hank down to Savannah. Do you want to come along?"

"Sure. That sounds like fun."

Everyone sat down at the dining room table. Uncle Sam leaned over and spoke in a lower voice to Hank. "I like it when you are here. We eat a lot better. This meal is for your benefit. It has been years since I've seen a spread like this."

Hank whispered back, "I can see that it's the little things in life that make you happy."

"You're right and a good home cooked meal is one of them."

Theresa performed the pre-flight check. She was flying first seat. Everyone buckled up. In a matter of minutes, they were airborne. As he sat in the plush leather seat, Hank looked around the cabin at the triplets, their parents and Uncle Sam. It was the first time that he felt a true sense of family.

Chapter 30

High School Football (Circa 1973)

The telephone rang in the St. Patrick High School Physical Education Department. Coach Parker answered, "Hello".

"This is Danny Dugan. I am the head coach for the Notre Dame football team. May I speak with Coach Parker?"

"This is Coach Parker. It is a pleasure to speak with you."

"Thank you. Did you recently send me a letter about three of your players?"

"Yes sir. You are referring to the Jernigan triplets."

"I receive many letters every day regarding potential players; many of which are bogus. I just wasn't sure about this one."

"No sir, this is for real. If you want to win another National Championship, I would get down here and talk to these boys. You won't have a hard time in recruiting them because Notre Dame is their first choice. Their father is an alumnus. But if you don't recruit all three of them together, they will go to choice number two and that is the University of Alabama. Bama has already had recruiters in the stands watching these boys play."

"Are the triplets as good as you say?"

"Yes, but you need to come and see for yourself. We have two games left but I expect to be in the playoffs. We were state champs last year. I expect a repeat this year. I hate to see them leave. My program will suffer."

"Tell me about the quarterback."

"That would be Johnny. Sammy and Jacky are the tight ends. But all three could play quarterback. All three could play tight end. All three could play wide receiver. All three could play line backer. These boys are natural athletes but the configuration of Johnny as quarterback with Sammy and Jacky as the tight ends is what they prefer. They are constantly practicing their timing and it is flawless. Because they are such a threat to the defense that they are often doubled team. This allows our running backs to be more productive. They are not identical but they possess the same characteristics. Each is 6' 2" tall, 210 lbs and fast. They are smart, clean cut, good looking young men but they are always getting in trouble with the Principal. But then again, their mother is the Principal. They will not only be an asset to the team but they will be an asset to Notre Dame. I promise you they will be the darlings of the national sports media."

"You have peaked my interest. Do you have a game this Friday night?"

"Yes, we will be playing at O'Malley stadium here at St. Patrick's."

"I am personally going to be there. I will be flying by corporate jet. Is Jefferson City the closest airport?"

"If the corporate jet you are flying is the Exec-Jet, it was built right here in New Dublin. They have an airstrip. The triplets' father is the General Manager. In addition, their Uncle is their spiritual advisor. He is the Pastor at St. Patrick's. They come from a good family."

The two coaches finished their conversation. Coach Parker called Johnny Jernigan at the plant and informed him of the fact that Coach Dugan would be in town on Friday night. Johnny assigned Bob with the task of coordinating Coach Dugan's visit.

It was game night. Johnny and Theresa sat in their regular spot in the bleachers. Bob and Coach Dugan were already seated on the bench behind them. Bob introduced everyone. Father Sam was on the field leading the team in a prayer. Afterwards, he went up to the press box where he gave the invocation and led the crowd in singing the National Anthem. His voice was no where near the quality of the O'Malley brothers but what he lacked in talent he made up in passion. His rendition was not a solo performance. He was accompanied loud and clear by everyone in the stands. Father Sam then made his way to his seat. He shook hands with Coach Dugan and sat down next to Theresa.

Coach Dugan commented, "Father, I have been coaching for a long time. I have never seen such crowd participation in singing the National Anthem."

Father Sam responded, "There is a story behind that. Years ago I had a difficult time in finding someone every week to sing the National Anthem before our home games. So I decided to do it myself. I told everyone in the stands that I had a lousy voice but I would sing if everyone joined in. I sang the National Anthem to the best of my ability but I heard very few voices singing along. I sang it the second time and it got a little bit better. I told the crowd that the game would not start until everyone sang. The third time was a charm. It has now become a weekly tradition. In fact, several other high schools in the area are doing the same thing."

"I find it impressive."

"You are going to be more impressed when you see my nephews play. The team they are playing has lost only one game this year so this should be a good match up."

Coach Dugan questioned, "Will the boys be nervous knowing that I am in the stands?"

Theresa answered, "To the contrary. They actually play better when they are under pressure."

The game, as expected, was close but St. Patrick's was victorious by a touchdown. Coach Dugan commented that it was one of the best high school games he had ever seen. He also knew that he needed to get the Jernigan boys to commit to Notre Dame. They were good...real good.

After the game, they all made their way down to the field. Bob did his best to keep the Notre Dame fans from crowding around Coach Dugan. Coach Dugan met Coach Parker and the triplets. He congratulated all of them on a well played game.

Coach Dugan addressed the triplets. "I understand you boys want to play football for Notre Dame."

Young Johnny was the spokesman for the three. "Yes sir. Our Dad graduated there and our Mom graduated from St. Mary's College. Notre Dame is our first choice as long as the three of us are on the team."

"That will be no problem but I can't guarantee that you will get much playing time your first year. As you boys know, we have a good team. Most of my starters are juniors and they have one more year of eligibility. I am not about to fix something that isn't broken. You boys can understand that."

"Yes sir. In fact, that is exactly what we expected."

"We will be back in touch with your parents and work out all the details."

A local sports reporter was present. He snapped a picture of Coach Dugan shaking hands with the Jernigan boys. He also managed to get a brief interview with Coach Dugan. When they were through, Coach Dugan graciously bid his farewell to all of the Jernigan family and Father Sam. Bob drove him back to the plant where the corporate jet was awaiting. Bob watched the jet lift off heading back to South Bend, Indiana.

The next morning, Johnny and Theresa were at the breakfast table drinking coffee and reading the newspaper. Theresa became excited when she saw the front page of the sports section. There was a large photograph of her three sons along with Coach Dugan. The headline read, *The Jernigan Triplets Recruited by Notre Dame.* This story was picked up by all of the major wire services. This was the beginning of the end of anonymity for the Jernigan boys.

Chapter 31

Notre Dame Football (Circa 1974 – 1978)

Father Sam had high priority church business that required the approval of the Bishop. He telephoned Bishop O'Farrell. When he answered, Father Sam identified himself. They exchanged cordial greetings.

Father Sam began, "Before I get to my main point, I know that we have a shortage of Priests in the Diocese. The two gentlemen who are studying to become Deacons will be extremely helpful to me in teaching religion classes and assisting me in clerical duties. I don't mind celebrating the Saturday evening Mass and the two Masses on Sunday morning. I am not complaining but I have a scheduling problem. I know that you are a die hard Notre Dame football fan so I am sure you will understand my dilemma. You know Johnny and Theresa Jernigan and that their sons are playing for Notre Dame this year. The three of us plan on being at every game. We are going to use the corporate jet so we will be able to see the game and get back in the same day. The conflict is that I won't be able to attend the games and also celebrate the Saturday evening Mass. I have about twenty parishioners who attend this Mass. The rest of the Parishioners are old school. They prefer to go to church on Sunday. To get to my point, I would like to know if you have anyone available to celebrate the Saturday evening Mass. If that's not a possibility, how do you feel if I suspend it.

Bishop O'Farrell responded, "To answer your first question, there are no extra Priests to fill in for you. In regards to your second question, you are the Pastor and you can schedule your Masses anyway you feel is appropriate for your Parish. The only problem I foresee is that you get to the game and then you can't get back home."

"I have already thought about that. We will know the weather conditions before we leave. If there is any indication that there will be inclement weather then I won't go. If I have a wedding set for Saturday, I won't go. If by remote chance we have mechanical problems, Father Daniels at St. Mary's and Father McDonald at St. Ann's have agreed to cover my Sunday Masses."

"It sounds as if you have all your bases covered. I will give you my blessing under one condition. I can come along from time to time."

"You're welcomed to travel with us every week. There is enough room on the plane. You can bring a guest with you. I just need to know in advance, so that I can get you tickets for the game."

"I appreciate the offer but if I do decide to go, it will be once in awhile. I am like you. Scheduling a weekly trip is difficult but I will definitely make it at least one time. I am excited about the Jernigan boys. If they can perform as well as they did in high school, Notre Dame can expect to be in the top ten for the next four years."

Father Sam tried to be realistic. "Don't be too excited this year. I have a feeling that the triplets will be warming the bench. The quarterback is a senior this year and he is fantastic and they have two good tight ends but they too are seniors. So it is doubtful that the coach will replace any of the current team. Next year is a different story. The Jernigan boys will put New Dublin on the map."

"I am truly envious of you. You all have a good time. Please pass on my best regards to the Jernigan family."

"I will and thanks for you support, Bishop."

Two weeks passed. It was game day at South Bend, Indiana. Johnny, Theresa, Sam, and Hank climbed aboard the corporate jet. They were full of pleasant anticipation about their inaugural trip.

Johnny told Sam, "Hop in the second seat. It's time you learn how to fly this plane."

Sam was not that confident. "I don't believe that that is a good idea."

"If I can teach Theresa, I can teach you."

Theresa yelled from the back of the plane, "I heard that."

Johnny had filed a flight plan via the telephone with the control tower at Jefferson City. He went through a pre-flight checklist. He gave Sam a brief description of all the controls. The engines began to whine. Johnny added power and the jet moved forward. He told Sam to loosely hold onto the yolk so that he could get the feel. They stopped at the end of the runway. Johnny powered up with the brakes applied. Johnny scanned the skies to make sure that there was no other aircraft in the area. He doubled checked by radio with Jefferson City air traffic control. He was cleared for take off. The jet leaped forward and steadily gained speed. Johnny pulled back on the yolk. They were airborne. Next stop...South Bend.

The flight was less than two hours. Johnny touched down at the local General Aviation airport. Bob did his job well. The ground crew was standing by awaiting their arrival. They would refuel the aircraft and perform an overall service check. As they deplaned, Johnny anticipated a cab to take them to the stadium. He didn't see any. A man in a black uniform approached the plane. "Are you Mr. Jernigan?"

Johnny answered in the affirmative.

"Please follow me. Your limousine is ready."

This is not what Johnny had expected, but it was a nice touch. Theresa, Johnny, Sam, and Hank were simple people with humble backgrounds but the four of them did enjoy the pomp and circumstance. The chauffeur parked in front of the entrance. He opened the back door. He told Johnny that when the game was over he would be parked here to take them back to the airport. Johnny explained that it would be a delay in departure because he had to first say hello to his sons after they leave the locker room.

Theresa, Johnny, Sam, and Hank found their seats. They were right on the fifty yard line, high enough to give them a good view of the entire field. As the kick off time neared, the Fighting Irish came roaring onto the field. They scanned the team until they locked in on the triplets. The boys were toward the back of the line. When they got to the sidelines, they searched the stands until they found their biggest fans. All of them exchanged waves.

As predicted, the Jernigan boys never played a single down but Notre Dame was victorious. The chauffeur was where he said he would be. He drove them back to the airport. Johnny tried to pay him and give him a tip but the chauffeur refused both. He said that Mr. Jones had taken care of all the expenses. Johnny thought to himself that he had made the right decision when he hired Bob.

It was a safe flight back even though Sam took the controls under Johnny's watchful eye. He made some wide turns and varied the altitude. Sam liked it. He was hooked and looked forward to his next lesson. Johnny gave him a textbook and other literature on the theory of flight.

Over the next six weeks, Sam read everything that Johnny had given him along with every book that the library had on the shelves. Today was a big day. Johnny was going to let Sam taxi the jet and handle the take-off. Sam performed perfectly. He was a good student. Johnny was hesitant to allow Sam to land the plane. That would be for another day. The chauffeur greeted Johnny and his small entourage which included Bishop O'Farrell. It was the seventh game of the season. The Jernigan boys were still warming the bench. At the end of the first half, Notre Dame was behind by two touchdowns. Their undefeated season was in jeopardy. Notre Dame received the kick off to start the second half. They steadily moved the football down the field. Apparently the half time adjustments were working but then disaster struck. The quarterback was sacked. The crowd went silent. He was injured...a serious injury. He grabbed his right leg and there was no doubt that he was in pain. The coach told young Johnny to warm up. The team trainer summoned the stretcher. It was a broken leg which would sideline him for the rest of the year. The crowd applauded as the quarterback was carried off the field on a stretcher. Young Johnny trotted onto the field. His debut left a lot to be desired. His first pass was behind the receiver. His second throw was high and almost intercepted. The field goal unit came in and was successful. Notre Dame was now down by eleven points.

Notre Dame kicked off. The defense limited the other team to a field goal. Notre Dame was now back to a fourteen point deficit. Young Johnny was again disappointing. It was three plays and out. Young Johnny and his two brothers approached Coach Dugan and pled their case. Young Johnny explained that he has not practiced with any of the receivers and the timing was not there whereas he and his brothers have played together for the last five years. Coach Dugan contemplated the change. What convinced him was when young Johnny told him with confidence, "We can still win this game."

It was the beginning of the fourth quarter. The score was the same. Theresa, Johnny, Sam, Hank, and Bishop O'Farrell were on their feet when the three Jernigan boys huddled up. The next four plays were passes to either Jacky or Sammy. Each reception resulted in a first down. The defense was in disarray. They over compensated and paid too much attention to the tight ends. The next play young Johnny pitched out to the running back. He hit the line untouched and continued unabated to the end zone. The crowd went wild.

The other team did not score on their next possession but they did take valuable time off the clock. There was a little more than five minutes left to play. The ball was on the thirty five yard line. Young Johnny mixed up the plays from runs to passes. They were moving the ball. Young Johnny took the snap and dropped back to pass. The defense was blitzing. Young Johnny was being chased around the backfield. Jacky saw his brother in trouble and broke for the open field. Young Johnny planted his right foot and threw a perfect spiral. Jacky caught it in full stride and scored. The extra point was good. The score was tied. Theresa was going berserk. She was telling everyone around her that those were her three sons.

Notre Dame's defense held but it cost them all three of their time outs. There was less than two minutes left on the clock. Young Johnny went to work. He was surgical. It was one pass after another to either Jacky or Sammy. After each completion, they managed to get out of bounds. They were now well within field goal range. Eighteen seconds to go. Young Johnny threw a safe pass to the corner of the end zone. Sammy caught it but the referee ruled him out of bounds. The kicker then trotted onto the field. The line was set and the ball was snapped. The kick was up and away. It split the uprights. Notre Dame was now in the lead but there were still three ticks remaining. Enough for one more play.

The kick off was caught by the fastest player on the opposing team. He broke several tackles. The crowd was unbelievably quiet. After a short scare, he was tackled at the fifty yard line. The crowd then erupted. The game was over. Notre Dame won.

This was only a glimpse of things to come. The Jernigan triplets became household names. The rest of this season and the following three years Notre Dame got Bowl invitations; one of which resulted in the national championship. Sam became an accomplished pilot. Hank's new girlfriend also became a regular on the weekly trips. Bishop O'Farrell attended more games than he had originally intended. Upon graduation, the triplets were considered first round draft picks for the National Football League but they implemented the *Three Musketeers' Pact.* Either they went to the same team or they wouldn't play at all. They just sat back and waited, and sure enough, it came to pass.

Chapter 32

Father Sam Meets Matt (Circa 1980)

Father Sam was seated at his desk when he heard a knock on the wall next to the open door. There stood a young man dressed in his school uniform. Father Sam motioned for him to come inside.

As the young man moved toward the desk he said, "I first spoke with the Principal and she said that she couldn't help me and that I needed to talk to the *Big Cheese*. Father, are you the *Big Cheese*?"

"If Mrs. Jernigan thinks I am the *Big Cheese*, then I am the *Big Cheese*."

The young man extended his hand with confidence, "My name is Matthew Taylor. My friends call me Matt."

Father Sam rose from his chair and shook young Matt's hand. "My name is Samuel and my adult friends call me Sam but you can call me Father Sam." He sat back down in his high back chair. "You're new here. I haven't seen you before."

"Yes sir. My mother and I just moved here. We live in the 'New Barracks' apartment complex. My mother got a job at the aircraft plant."

"Ah, *Rosie the Riveter*." Father Sam said knowing full well that that term was almost two generations out of date.

"No Father. She is a secretary and her name is Alice."

"Alice was my mother's name. It's such a pretty name."

"Yes Father, it is a pretty name."

Curious, Father Sam inquired, "What can I do for you today, Matt?"

"My mother is always telling me that I am the man of the house. I just turned twelve years old and I think it is time for me to go to work to help pay the bills."

"You do, huh?"

"Yes sir. I have been looking around the school and the church and I think you need some help in sweeping the floors and cutting the grass."

"You do, huh?"

"Yes sir. I have a good eye for these things."

"You do, huh?"

"Yes sir."

"Well Matt I tell you what I can do for you. When you get out of school at three o'clock you can sweep the halls and the classrooms at the school. You can only work until five o'clock because everyone has gone home by that time. On Saturdays you come here to the Rectory at eight o'clock. You can sweep out the Church, cut the grass or do any chores that I need to get done. You won't work past noon. Does that meet with your approval?"

Matt responded with positive affirmation. "Oh yes sir!"

"Matt, may I ask you about your father?"

"Yes sir. My father was a helicopter pilot and he was killed in Vietnam. He was a hero. My father was awarded the Distinguished Flying Cross. I don't remember my father. I was only one year old when he died."

"I am sorry to hear that. I know how you feel. My father was also a pilot and he was killed in World War II. He too was a hero."

"It's like we are connected."

"Yes Matt, I think we are connected." Father Sam didn't want to dwell on the past. He continued with Matt, "When you leave here, I want you to go straight to the Principal's office and see Mrs. Jernigan. I want you to tell her exactly the following, 'The *Big Cheese* has spoken and I am to start tomorrow sweeping the floors.' Can you remember that?"

"Yes sir." Matt repeated it, "The *Big Cheese* has spoken and I am to start tomorrow sweeping the floors."

"Perfect!"

Father Sam got up and walked around to the front of the desk and shook Matt's hand to confirm the employment arrangements. Matt then turned and headed for the door. Father Sam shouted, "Matt, stop! Don't you want to know what you are getting paid?"

Pay was an afterthought to Matt. "Yes sir."

"I will pay you three dollars a day during the week and six dollars on Saturday. Is that okay?"

"Yes sir." Matt then turned and disappeared through the doorway.

Father Sam knelt down on one knee, made the sign of the cross and silently prayed to God. "Dear heavenly Father I have been having doubts as to if you were going to send me a replacement. I met young Matthew today and you have made an excellent choice. Amen."

Chapter 33

Epilogue (Circa 1980)

It has been a long journey for the Irish Immigrants who arrived in America in 1880. They began the transformation of New Dublin from a small farming community in 1886 to a thriving suburban city of 1980.

In 1907, the management of the Jefferson City Paddle Boat Co. was baffled. Benjamin T. Putnam had done an excellent job for over eight years. Literally overnight, the New Dublin operations began to have major problems. Customer complaints were at an all time high. Company reports were atrocious. Drastic measures had to be taken to correct the situation. The owner (Mr. Putnam's brother-in-law) was in an awkward position. He couldn't fire Benjamin T. Putnam because he wanted to keep peace in his family. He didn't want Mr. Putnam back in Jefferson City so he transferred him farther away to Springfield. He was assigned an office and given the title of *Manager of Corporate Fundamentals.* Benjamin T. Putnam was impressed with his new position but he never fully understood as to what he was supposed to do. Little did he know, that was the whole purpose. Benjamin T. Putnam had reached the pinnacle of his career. He had a position of prominence that allowed him to have uninterrupted afternoon naps. He was happy. His sister was happy and his brother-in-law was happy. All turned out well for Benjamin T. Putnam.

Michael Ryan, who survived the sinking of the RMS Titanic, had a variety of jobs while working for his cousin Sean. The job he enjoyed the most was being the bartender for the Leprechaun Pub and Grill. He worked there for almost thirty years. In 1965, he died at home surrounded by his family.

The former Captain Stephen Stewart, who had the unfortunate job of notifying the next of kin of the death of their loved one, settled in New Dublin after World War II. He opened his own accounting office. He didn't return to New Dublin with the purpose of courting the widow Ann Kelty. But romance seemed to blossom even with the most unintended intentions. Ann refused to accept a date with Stephen until she spoke with her mother-in-law. Ann didn't want to defile her deceased husband's memory. Ann's mother-in-law was compassionate. She gave Ann her blessing under one condition. That she would always be able to refer to Ann as her daughter-in-law. Ann readily agreed. These two had a very strong bond. Ann and Stephen eventually married. They had a son and a daughter. They have five grandchildren and one on the way. Ann and Stephen currently are aboard a cruise ship in the Caribbean celebrating their 33rd wedding anniversary.

The Swartz clinic is now the Rabbi Albert Swartz Memorial Hospital. Dr. Jacob Swartz is enjoying retirement. He is still active in city affairs. His son Dr. Isaac Swartz is the hospital's chief administrator. Betty Moran Stone is the head of nursing and Sally Foley Lockett went back to school and obtained her medical degree. She has her own practice specializing in pediatrics. Several additions were added to the Synagogue to support the ever growing Jewish community. There was a movement within the congregation to build their own school. This was overwhelmingly defeated. The rationale was that if St. Patrick school was good enough for Dr. Jacob Swartz and Dr. Isaac Swartz, it was good enough for their children.

Staff Sergeant "Coop" Cooper, Johnny's crew chief in Korea did not re-enlist in the Air Force. He found employment as a jet engine mechanic with Eastern Airlines in Miami, Florida. He found the climate much more suitable than the cold Korean winters.

Shannon Dorsey and her husband David were successful entrepreneurs. They have three additional locations of *Mrs. Shanahan's Pies and Pastries* in Jefferson City. New stores are under construction in nearby cities. Copies of the photograph of Pop and Sam are prominently displayed at every location.

Tommy, the paper boy, was a standout baseball player at St. Patrick High School. He got a four year athletic scholarship at Independence University. He was a good baseball player but not good enough for the major leagues. He graduated with a Bachelors Degree in Political Science. He was the youngest person ever elected to the City Council. He is now the full time Mayor of the City of New Dublin. Politics flows through his veins. The rumor around town is that he is preparing to make a run for Governor. It is well within the realm of possibility that he will be successful.

New Dublin holds the honor of being the richest city per capita in the state. It is not a result of the affluent moving to New Dublin but it is due to the fact that many of the employees who bought stock in the aircraft plant years ago were now millionaires.

Joseph Flynn became a Priest. He is currently a Navy Chaplin assigned to the Marine Corps. He has modeled his life as much as possible to the memory of Father Vincent Capodanno. Fortunately for him and all the other active duty personnel, there have been no major armed conflicts since Vietnam.

Hank Turner is still employed at the aircraft plant. He is now the floor manager overseeing the Bobcat assembly line. Hank married a local girl and Father Sam performed the ceremony. After several years of marriage, Hank became the father of a beautiful girl. He and his wife proudly named her Theresa. Whenever the Jernigan brothers are home during the off season, the Four Musketeers' Pact is in effect. Hank often wondered what his life would have been like had he not had the chance meeting with Johnny, Sammy, and Jacky. He knew one thing. It could not have been better.

Bob Jones resigned with the blessing of Johnny. Bob became a sports agent and his first three clients were the Jernigan triplets. It did not take long before Bob was representing some of the highest paid athletes. It was the perfect job. He knew how to cater to his clients and at the same time, he was feared by the team owners when he was seated on the other side of the negotiation table.

St. Patrick Day festivities is now a major production. Theresa could no longer handle this responsibility along with the duties of being the principal. She hired a full time employee to oversee all operations in coordinating the parade, vendors and volunteers. New Dublin is literally transformed overnight when over fifty thousand visitors descend on the city. The money derived is used to keep the tuition to a minimum. No student is ever turned away for financial reasons.

Made in the USA
Lexington, KY
23 November 2013